TH

Nora Sakavic

ALL FOR THE GAME

-

The Foxhole Court
The Raven King
The King's Men
The Sunshine Court
The Golden Raven

CHAPTER ONE
Jean

Friday morning practice started with a brief team meeting. As each Trojan arrived, one of the coaches was on hand to redirect them to the huddle rooms. "Whichever one has seats" was the only directive they received, but for the most part the players segregated themselves by offense and defense out of habit.

Unsurprisingly, striker Ananya Deshmukh had eschewed the status quo to sit with Cody Winter and her fiancé Patrick Toppings, both of whom were backliners. Movement in the doorway had her looking up to check the newest arrivals, and her jaw dropped when she saw Jean Moreau's battered face.

"Good lord," she said, too loudly, and all eyes swung his way.

Catalina Alvarez briefly pressed a shoulder against his arm, but Jean didn't care if they looked. He'd been a bruised and bloodied mess most of his career with the Ravens. His former teammates were quick to mock him and quicker to take advantage of his weakened state on the court, but they knew better than to ask questions. Most of them assumed his injuries were due to the master's displeasure, especially since the perfect Court was called away daily for private sessions. Whether or not they truly believed it or simply refused to think critically of their beloved captain, Jean would never know.

"We left you alone for twelve hours," Pat said. "Did you get hit by a car or something?"

A stupid question deserved a stupid answer, so Jean said, "Yes."

"We're going to talk about it, I'm sure," Jeremy Knox

1

said. He'd preceded Jean into the room, but now he was half-turned to study Jean's distant expression. He said nothing else, but Jean saw the question in his searching look. Jean didn't waste his breath responding but stepped toward him and sent one last glance around the room. Lucas Johnson and his friends were yet to make an appearance, but as far as Jean could tell the rest of the defense line was accounted for.

The room was arranged as five rows of five seats each, with a table at the front for Coach Jimenez to use as needed. Sophomores William Foster and Jesus Rivera were in the first row with the over-eager freshmen, though they were now all turned to unabashedly stare at Jean. Cody's lot had claimed the second row, and fifth-year Shawn Anderson was in the fourth with Shane Reed. Those two had nothing to say yet, but their stares were heavy and unwavering. Jean's injuries only benefited one of them, the man whose spot he planned on taking this season, so Jean didn't waste his time returning their searching looks.

Jeremy led Jean and Cat down the third row so he could take a seat behind Ananya. Cat gave Cody's shaved hair an affectionate scritch when she ended up behind them, but Cody was too busy staring at Jean to greet her. The three had just gotten settled when Laila Dermott arrived. She'd detoured by the lockers alone to put their lunch away, but now she took the chair on Cat's other side and said, "Lucas is here."

It was a split-second warning before Lucas finally stepped through the doorway, and the entire mood in the room shifted. Shane was on his feet immediately with an alarmed, "Jesus Christ, Lucas."

The hours since Grayson's visit had been unkind to them both: reddened skin and faint shadows had bloomed into technicolored bruises that covered too much of their faces. Both of Lucas's eyes were blackened, courtesy of his broken nose, and Jean had long scratches down his face from cruel fingernails. Lucas hadn't bothered to cover anything up, and Jean had only slowed long enough this morning to tape new gauze over the teeth marks left on his throat and wrist.

"This has to stop," Shane said, looking between them. "You're teammates, for god's sake."

"Shane," Jeremy started, but Lucas beat him to the punch:

"We didn't do this," Lucas said as he led Travis Jordan and Haoyu Liu onto the fourth row. Because Shane and Shawn had gotten there first, it forced Lucas into the open seat behind Jean. Jean didn't feel like turning far enough to keep an eye on him, so he folded his arms across his chest and faced the front of the room. Lucas stopped behind him but didn't sit until he corrected himself with a quieter, "He didn't. I did."

"What's that supposed to mean?" Shane asked. "Jeremy? Jean?"

Jeremy was still turned enough to see the door, so he just said, "Coach."

Eduardo Jimenez entered the room with Jackie Lisinski only a few steps behind him. Since neither James Rhemann nor Michael White showed up, Jean assumed they were handling the other room. Lisinski's face was a thundercloud, but Jimenez's expression was harder to read. The defensive line coach did a quick headcount before slapping a folder against his palm.

"Good morning," he said. "Couple quick announcements and then we'll get you back on track. First things first: Lucas and Jean will be on no-touch jerseys until further notice and will not be participating in scrimmages today."

Cat's hand on his knee was meant to be reassuring, but Jean only felt the warning in it. He had a half-second to hope the coaches didn't see his reaction to the news, but of course they had. Jimenez met Jean's guarded stare and said only, "We will evaluate your progress daily and upgrade you when it is safe to do so. This is nonnegotiable."

Jean couldn't argue, so he bit the inside of his cheek to bleeding and thought, *No*. He'd spent all week with that jersey as an unwelcome noose around his neck. Today should have been his last day suffering its restrictions. Instead they'd pushed him three steps back and off the court completely.

"If you do not have this number saved to your phone, please add it at this time," Lisinski said as she turned and scribbled on the whiteboard. She underlined the phone number twice, capped her marker, and rapped her fingernails on the board as she surveyed the room. "This is the line for campus security. We will have an escort while we are at Lyon, and you will notice their increased presence in the area when you are dismissed for lunch."

Jimenez flipped open his folder at last and pulled out a full-page color photograph of Grayson Johnson's face. The head-on shot and dark background made Jean think they'd taken it from the Ravens' promotional site. Even in a picture Grayson radiated malevolence, and Jean averted his gaze from the man's piercing stare.

"If you see this man anywhere on campus, you are to report to campus security first and any of us second," Jimenez said. "I don't care if he's asking you for directions, I don't care if you just see him tying his shoe on a corner. You even think it's him, you dial it in. Do you understand?"

"Wait," Ananya said, leaning forward to stare hard at the photograph. Uncertainty slowed her down, but Jean could hear her figuring it out as she struggled with her memory: "I know that face. That's a Raven. That's—oh," she said, turning to stare at Lucas. The brothers were a few years apart, and Grayson carried more weight and rage than Lucas ever would, but the similarities were still too glaring to be ignored. "That's your brother, isn't it? Gray?"

"Grayson," Lucas agreed, sounding defeated. "He came up to Los Angeles yesterday looking for Jean. Said he just wanted to talk, but—" He swallowed so hard Jean heard it. Somehow Lucas had the common sense to boil Grayson's violence down to the weakest truth: "He tried to kill Jean."

"Both of you, looks like," Shawn said.

"He didn't care about me. He was just mad that I got in the way, but I couldn't do anything to stop him. If Coach L hadn't shown up, he…" Lucas trailed off.

Jean wasn't interested in revisiting this conversation so soon, but the quiet horror in Lucas's voice had him picking at his bandages. "Of course you couldn't handle him," he said, with enough annoyance to earn a pained look from Jeremy. "The only one who could ever take Grayson in a fight was—"

The answer snagged in his throat unexpectedly, sharpened to something unrecognizable in the wake of yesterday's attack. He'd cut his tongue to shreds if he forced it out, but it echoed in his ears louder than his own heartbeat. *Zane.*

Zane Reacher, who'd promised to protect him from Grayson's violence and who'd fought tooth and nail for years to ensure he would always be better when it mattered most. Zane, who'd wanted so badly to be perfect Court that Jean couldn't help but trust him, who could've easily thrown Grayson out of their room at any point once he knew Jean got the message but who'd only rolled over and told them to keep it down.

For a moment Jean was months away from here, on his knees in desperate supplication. He heard his voice cracking in the air as he begged Riko to finally number Zane; he felt his bloodied fingers slide against Riko's

5

wrist. More than anything he remembered the look in Riko's eyes: the cold amusement at Jean's unsolicited debasement withering into deadly malice the moment Riko realized Jean was more afraid of their sudden alliance than he was Riko's potential retribution. He should have beaten Jean for forgetting who his King was. Instead, he'd made Jean watch as he turned Zane and Grayson against each other.

His stomach roiled; his mouth burned as he forced back a rush of acid. Jean carved lines into his forearm to find his center. Jeremy caught his wrist to stop him, and Jean forced his gaze to the far wall. The pale paint with its bright designs was a blinding difference from the Nest and a keen reminder he was as far from West Virginia as he could go. Riko was dead, Zane had graduated, and Grayson would have to leave California tomorrow for the Ravens' summer practices.

The new silence in the locker room was uncomfortable, but Jimenez finally said, "If any of you see him, do not under any circumstance approach him. Understood? Any questions? All right. Thank you, I'll turn you over to Lisinski. Coach?"

"Let's get moving," Lisinski said, clapping her hands. "I want everyone dressed and ready to run in five."

The other meeting had gotten out before them, as it hadn't been derailed by sidebar conversation. Prying stares followed Lucas and Jean as the defensemen headed for their lockers. The raucous morning chatter that echoed off these walls all week was gone today, replaced by a heavy and morose silence that sat like a too-familiar weight against Jean's bones.

The warmup lap around campus was eerily quiet, and Lisinski split them into the usual groups once they arrived at Lyon. She would rotate between them as needed, checking progress here and pushing harder there, and Jean was not at all surprised when she started with Xavier's small team. That she checked on the freshmen first was a see-through pretense. It didn't take her long to make it to his side.

Lisinski watched with a heavy-lidded stare as Jean went through his shoulder presses, studying the smoothness of the motion. Jean felt the twinge in his wrist almost immediately, but he was familiar enough with pain to know this discomfort was all surface level. He kept his expression calm and his gaze averted from his coach, and eventually she moved on. Jean waited until she'd crossed the room to the seniors before digging a thumb into the aching heat in his wrist.

It was just a split-second of weakness, but it was more than enough to summon Xavier to his side. "Here."

Jean took the proffered bottle, but a glance at the label made him tense. "Who let you have this?"

Xavier didn't immediately answer, and he made no move to take the bottle back when Jean thrust it toward him. Lisinski's back was mostly to them, but if she turned even a little, she'd have a clear line of sight on them. There'd be hell to pay if she realized Xavier was carrying medication, and Jean was not about to take a beating for something that wasn't his problem. Since Xavier refused to take it from him, Jean leaned over and set it out of sight behind the machine. He went back to his set, but Xavier didn't leave.

"Friend," Xavier said at last, "it's just ibuprofen."

"I can read," Jean said.

Xavier was unmoved by his irritation. "And you know what it is?" He put both hands up at the mean look Jean sent him. It was not the calming gesture he probably hoped it was, maybe because Xavier looked halfway to helpless laughter. "I've never seen anyone react like that before. Is it a controlled substance in West Virginia or something?"

He said it with easy humor, but Jean thought about the

7

clipboard hanging on Josiah Smalls' office door at Evermore. Anyone who wanted medication outside of being immediately treated for an injury had to put in a written request, and Josiah would approve it if he was feeling charitable. Ibuprofen was always his go-to, as useless as it generally was. Jean knew he had stronger pills in stock, but for the most part those were saved for Riko himself. Not cost effective to coddle the rest of the team, Jean assumed, since the Ravens were endlessly injured. Certainly not worth it to waste that medicine on Jean.

Unbidden he thought of the pills Abby Winfield gave him in South Carolina. The name had been far too long and complicated to retain, but Jean remembered the easy way it sank through him to send him under. Jean wouldn't think about how freely Abby dispensed it to someone who wasn't even technically her problem and who'd never once thanked her for her trouble.

There was a warning twinge in his chest, warning him not to follow this road back to the Ravens. *Why* was too deadly a question to ask, especially when it came to Edgar Allan.

"I was joking," Xavier said when the silence stretched too long. He wasn't smiling anymore, and Jean knew better than to meet his searching stare. After a beat Xavier put the bottle away, motioned to him, and turned away. "Watch this. Emma, Mads," he called, and the freshmen immediately paused their chatter to face him. "You girls have ibuprofen on you?"

"Left it in my locker, sorry," Emma Swift said, but Madeline Hill was already rummaging through the coin purse she'd brought with her from the stadium. The bottle she withdrew was slimmer than the one Xavier owned, but even with three machines between them Jean could see the matching color scheme. She tossed it over, and Xavier made a show of skimming the label.

8

"Thanks," he said as he returned it. "Couldn't remember if it was four or six hours."

"Oh, sure," Mads said as she put it away again.

Xavier cocked an eyebrow at Jean, a silent but unmistakable *See?* that did nothing to quell the churning in Jean's stomach. Xavier gave a jerk of his chin. "Walk with me a sec," he said, and Jean didn't have the right to refuse him. They attracted a couple curious looks as they crossed the room, but they made it to the water fountains across the room uncontested. Xavier took a quick drink before holding the medicine out again.

"Here," he said. "You keep this one. I'll pick up another tonight."

Jean couldn't stop himself, and even he heard the edge in his, "Just like that." It was too late to take it back, and the keen look on Xavier's face said the other man wasn't going to let it slide. "You'll just go and replace it like it's nothing."

"It *is* nothing. It's an over-the-counter drug. Got it from the grocery store for a couple bucks. Why would anyone think twice about me having some on hand?" A rhetorical question, apparently, because Xavier didn't wait before saying, "Making me a little uncomfortable that you're so riled up about this, if I'm being honest. What on earth did they give you when you sprained your LCL?"

Jean picked at his bandages. His gaze went unbidden to his bare forearms, but the telltale bruises and rashes of ragged restraints were long gone. All that was left were the angry lines he'd put there this morning. If it was any other teammate, Jean would simply ignore the question until he was left alone, but Xavier was his vice-captain. He considered lying instead, but the only answer to come to mind was the very medicine Xavier was so dismissive of. The truth was a hideous thing to put into words, but maybe some ugliness would finally get Xavier out of his business.

9

"Nothing," he finally said.

Xavier's face went dangerously blank. "Come again?"

"It wasn't their problem," Jean said.

Between one heartbeat and the next he was back in Riko's shadowed room, so much blood in his throat he could barely breathe. He reached unbidden for his head, looking for the spots where his hair was still uneven. Even now most of that night was a horrific haze he refused to dwell on. He didn't remember Riko stopping; he didn't remember Riko storming out of there and leaving Jean a crumpled mess in his wake. Maybe Riko realized he was going to kill Jean if he didn't retreat, or maybe he'd simply seen the time and known he was due on the court for practice. It didn't matter which. It didn't. It couldn't.

The urge to smack the medicine out of Xavier's hand was sudden and violent, and Jean dug his nails into his scratched arm to stop himself. He dragged himself out of dark memories and said, "I convalesced in South Carolina. My treatment was the Foxes' responsibility. You would have to ask their nurse what she prescribed if it matters that much to you."

"I don't care about the Foxes. You were injured in West Virginia. You can't tell me you went from Edgar Allan to Palmetto State without any treatment or care. *Jean*," Xavier tried, a hint of desperation sneaking into his voice when Jean stared past him toward the far wall. "Tell me I'm misunderstanding you."

"I still have sets to do," Jean said instead. "Are we done?"

"No, we're not," Xavier said, disbelieving. "Where is your rage?"

He'd asked as much on Monday, going so far as to call Jean unexpectedly docile. Jean curled his lip a little in displeasure and demanded, "What reason do I have to be angry? I am Jean Moreau; I am perfect Court. Ravens understand the cost of being the best, and we are not

10

afraid to pay it."

"*We*," Xavier said, gesturing sharply between them, "are Trojans. Don't you ever 'we' the Ravens again, you hear me? They do not deserve you."

"Neither does a team who can't win first."

Xavier's jaw worked with everything else he wanted to say. "Listen," he said at last. Jean turned toward the other man, but it took Xavier another moment before he spoke. "You don't want me in your business, I get it, but hear me when I say this: if you're hurting, we're hurting. If you won't let us help you, we need to know you are taking care of yourself. Okay?"

They weren't the right words, but it was close enough to *your failure is our failure* that Jean hesitated. "Yes."

"If you won't take this from me, at least get something from the nurses when we get back to the stadium." Xavier gave him a last chance to take the bottle before pocketing it for good. "We're so close to having you on the line at full strength. Don't let a little recklessness put you back on the sidelines."

"I am not reckless," Jean said.

"I'm going to trust you. Don't make me regret it."

Xavier left Jean to his own devices for the remainder of the workout, but Jean didn't miss the way his smile didn't sit quite right as he chatted with the Trojans' enthusiastic freshmen. So long as Xavier stayed out of his way, Jean was willing to return the favor, but getting the conversation and his wretched memories out of his head again was impossible.

Threaded through Xavier's dismayed *"Where is your rage?"* was Jeremy's quieter *"You're not angry about what really matters"* from this past May. How easily they spoke of outrage, this team that refused to fight. How hypocritical, how exhausting. What did these easygoing children know about anger?

Equally irritating was how hard it was to focus this

11

morning. He'd spent years burying the worst Evermore had thrown at him, chaining down anything he could and forcibly moving past what he couldn't. He'd been teammates with Grayson for too many years to be this rattled a day later. But even as he tipped in and out of bloody memories, he knew there was no easy way past this. If he stopped thinking about Grayson, he'd have to think about yesterday's other visitors, and that was a road Jean refused to go down. It was too much to bear; the grief and horror would surely break him in half.

At long last they were done with the morning workout. The Trojans jogged back to the stadium for quick rinse-off showers before Lisinski dismissed them for lunch. As usual, Jean finished first and went to wait on the bench near Jeremy's locker. That turned out to be a mistake, as most of the offense line had been with the dealers in a different meeting room this morning. Only their youngest had seen Jean at the gym. The remaining five were getting a close-up of Jean for the first time today.

Derek Thompson, who'd ridiculously introduced himself as "Big D" on Monday to the freshmen, was the first to arrive. He worked a brush over his tight curls as he contemplated Jean and finally offered a, "You don't look so hot," as Derrick Allen joined them. Derek nudged his partner to get his attention but directed his words toward Jean. "True you're out of scrimmages this afternoon?"

"Yes," Jean said.

"Good news for you, since you still haven't figured out how to handle him," Derrick said with unrepentant cheer. "He's gonna kick your ass next week, just watch."

Jean expected bravado, but Derek only said, "Yeah, probably. Would be better if it happened today." Derrick seemed equally surprised by the honesty, but Derek jabbed his brush in Jean's direction before setting it in his locker. "Look at him, tense enough to make me uptight by proxy."

"Nice SAT word," Ashton Cox said as he wandered past them to get dressed.

"Getting too smart for this crew, right?" Derek tapped a finger to his temple. "I'm just saying, throwing someone through the court wall would probably fix him. It'd be good practice for White Ridge, too."

"You just want to fight someone your size," Derrick said, as if he wasn't nearly six feet himself. "If you get Coach L to sign off on it, I call next."

"And me," Nabil Mahmoud said as he arrived, then asked, "What are we calling for?"

"Derek wants Jean to go feral," Derrick said.

Jeremy made it over in time to hear that comment, and it was enough to stop him at the end of the row. "I'd rather we don't go down that road," he said, looking from one teammate to the next. "Jean agreed to play the game our way this season. Asking him to bring Raven violence to summer practices when he'll be held to a different standard in August is unfair."

"Not trying to set him back, cap," Derek said, "but he's got the same look my brother gets before he does something stupid."

"I am not stupid," Jean said.

"No, I didn't—" Derek faltered and asked Jeremy, "How good is his English, again?"

"Better than your French," Jean said, with enough of an edge Derek put his hands up in self-defense. "Good enough to tell you your failures in our scrimmages this week are on your weaknesses and not my strengths. You've wasted so much time giving ground as a Trojan you don't remember how to hold it. It should be no surprise your opponents can run you over like an unwanted dog."

"Whoa, whoa. Why're we hurting dogs?" Timothy Eitzen asked as he appeared at Jeremy's elbow, and Jean

13

gave up on the entire line as a lost cause.

He pushed past all of them on the way to the backliners' row again, but the sight of so many teammates gathered there wearied him. Ridiculous that a locker room so big and bright could feel more suffocating today than the Nest, but Jean turned and kept going. He stalked from one huddle room to the next, steering clear of the coaches' hall and ending up near the nurses' offices. He pressed his thumb to his wrist, looking for an ache that had faded before they'd even made it back from Lyon.

During the summer the Trojans' three nurses alternated who was on duty: one remained at the stadium while the other two filled shifts at the campus health center. Today Ashley Young was on-site. Jean hadn't realized the room had a radio, but Young was bobbing her fork in time to the beat as she flipped through files one-handed. The realization he was interrupting her lunch had him taking a step back out of sight, but she must have seen movement in her peripheral vision.

"Come on in," she called, and Jean braced as he moved back into the doorway.

She finished skimming her page before looking up, and realization startled her into a moment of stillness. "Oh," she said as she pushed her lunch aside and flicked the radio off. "Jean, I'm glad you stopped by. Come next door with me."

They moved to the same room Rhemann had put Jean in yesterday, and Young took quick stock of his stained face and jaw. She had the authority to simply rip his bandages off, but Young only pressed careful fingertips to the tape and asked, "Do you mind?"

"You are my nurse," Jean said.

She peeled it free in one steady move and dropped the gauze into the nearby bin. She looked her fill while Jean contemplated the same photograph he'd studied yesterday. The antiseptic didn't sting nearly as much today, and

14

Young waited until she'd covered his injuries up again before trying to catch his eye. Jean feigned not to notice, but it didn't stop her from asking,

"Do you want to talk about it?"

"There is nothing to talk about."

"No?" Young's fingers dropped unerringly to the violent scratch marks on his arm. "This is not a solution, Jean. I don't want to see this from you again."

She gave him a moment to defend himself before setting to work on his wrist. Jean let her test his range, silently hoping her vote in his favor would override the coaches' decision to sideline him, but the dull ache from this morning's weight routine was quick to make an appearance. Young's expression was grim as she traced the line of scabs. Grayson had bitten him with every intention of breaking bones, and he'd gotten dangerously close to the delicate veins in Jean's wrist.

"You were very lucky," she said, like she'd read his thoughts. She wrapped his wrist with easy efficiency and dug a brace out of the nearby cabinet. Jean balked at the sight of it, but she slid it over his hand and into place even as he tried to pull away. She pressed the Velcro straps into place, said, "Test it?" and made a few quick adjustments as he slowly flexed and clenched his fingers. "Good. Do you have anything for the inflammation?"

"Xavier told me to ask you," Jean said.

She accepted that with an easy nod and rummaged through a drawer. "We'll start with this," she said as she pressed a packet of two pills into his palm. "Check back with me before you leave for the day. If it's not helping, I'll send you home with something stronger to take this weekend. Anything else we need to address?" She waited for his refusal before stepping out of his way. "Go eat, then. I'll see you this afternoon."

He hadn't been gone for more than ten minutes, but the locker room had cleared out for lunch in his absence.

Only his friends and Xavier remained, waiting on the strikers' row with the lunchbox by Cat's feet. Xaiver's agitated tone carried even if his words didn't, and when he followed Jeremy's gaze to Jean, he went quiet and still.

When Jean reached them, Xavier offered a polite, "Good work this morning," before setting off toward the door.

Jean waited for him to leave. "He is angry with me."

"No," Jeremy said, and when Jean wasn't convinced, emphasized, "No, I promise he's not. He's just concerned. You told him Edgar Allan wouldn't treat your LCL?"

"He asked," Jean said.

"Oh, he is *so* mad at them," Cat said. She scooped up the lunchbox and got to her feet. "Come on! It's too nice a day to eat inside. Let's have a picnic."

Up the street and across from the football stadium was a museum with a grassy lawn. A group of kids had claimed most of the available space and were running wild while their parents watched. Backpacks and bottled drinks were scattered along the curb where a half-dozen teenagers were skateboarding in the street. Despite the chaos there was plenty of room for the four of them, and Cat passed out lunches after they were settled.

They were only a few bites in when Jeremy's phone made a sound Jean hadn't yet heard. Cat hooted and planted herself against Jeremy's shoulder.

"Bishop?" Cat asked.

Jeremy's correction was distracted as he considered his texts. "Sheldon."

Laila was sprawled spreadeagled on the grass on Cat's other side, but she poked her sunglasses up to her forehead so she could squint at Jeremy in obvious disapproval. "Last I heard, he told you to lose his number. Why didn't you?" Jeremy's smile was so slow and satisfied Jean had to look away. Laila huffed and slid her sunglasses back into place. "Never mind, I don't actually want the answer to that."

"Oh!" Cat slapped her fist into her palm. "Isn't he the one with the huge—"

Laila swiped at her. "*Cat.*"

Cat rolled her eyes but obediently changed what she'd been saying. "Should we skedaddle?"

"Skedaddle," Jean echoed.

Cat turned on him, eyes bright with mirth. "Oh, please say that again."

Jean scowled, and Laila took pity on him. "Leave."

"Get the hell out of dodge," Cat agreed, which was a less helpful response. She shifted out of Jeremy's space and waved a curious gnat away from her half-eaten lunch. "You never told us what your second language is. German? Spanish? Uhhh. Italian?" She scrunched up her face in thought but gave up only moments later. "Give me a hint, I don't know anything about the European education system."

"Irrelevant. I was homeschooled."

"Explains the dire lack of socialization skills," Cat said.

"I had youth Exy," he said, which was and wasn't true.

The Exy court at Campagne Pastré was about ten minutes from his home in Sainte-Anne, an easy enough drive for his mother to make once she vetted the families of the other kids on the team. He'd been forbidden to mingle with his teammates outside of practices and games, and he'd known better than to talk to them about anything but Exy. His mother drove the point home early by killing off his first captain and her entire family. A boating accident, he thought—the memory was vague, but the lesson had stuck.

His only other contact with the outside world was the Japanese tutor his mother hired on his eighth birthday. She came by the house every evening to work with him, and although he'd known there was an ulterior motive he'd

17

been unable to separate the language from the sport he loved playing. He was thirteen before she was allowed to start him on English. Jean had resented those extra lessons until he was sold off to the Nest a year later. Communicating with Kevin and his new masters had been easy; learning English via the Ravens had been a nightmare and a half.

"Avoiding the question," Cat said. "Again."

"The first was never answered." Jean looked toward Jeremy.

"Huh? Oh, no. He won't be in town until Sunday." Jeremy had his phone halfway to his pocket when it started ringing. He spared a glance for the caller ID before putting it to his ear with an upbeat, "Hey, Coach. Yeah, Jean's with me. We're just up—" Jeremy went so silent and still even Laila sat up to stare at him, but Jeremy didn't seem to notice. He listened for a minute, then gestured frantically to his friends to pack it up. "Yeah, yes, we're on our way back right now. Do you know—okay. Okay."

Laila turned this way and that, looking for the lunchbox they'd set aside, and froze to stare. "Fuck," she said, too loudly. "Jeremy, we have a problem."

Jean half-turned to follow her gaze, but the only new addition to the area was a pair of police cars with their lights on. The teenagers who'd been playing in the street retreated to the lawn at their approach, yelling at each other to move faster and clinging to their boards. Instead of passing, the cars pulled up to the curb. Four officers got out only a few moments later, but they didn't even spare the tense teens a second look on their way toward the Trojans.

"Jean," Jeremy said, with unexpected urgency. Jean obediently turned back toward him, but Jeremy was looking past him at the police. The shuttered look on Jeremy's face made him a stranger, but Jeremy pressed on

18

even as he got to his feet and dusted off his shorts. "It's Grayson."

Jean sucked in a slow breath through clenched teeth. "He's here?"

"No," Jeremy said. "He's dead."

CHAPTER TWO
Jeremy

There was a limit to how many ways Jeremy could answer the same few questions.

Yes, he'd heard of Grayson Johnson. He knew there was bad blood between Grayson and Jean, but did no one at the LAPD pay attention to NCAA Exy? The Edgar Allan Ravens had been fighting with Jean since he transferred off their lineup mid-championships this past spring. No, Jeremy hadn't known Grayson was coming to town yesterday, and no, he hadn't even seen him when he turned up at the Gold Court. Jeremy missed both the fight and Grayson's flight and only saw the awful aftermath. Yes, he'd been home all night with Cat and Laila.

"But Moreau left," the cop said, for the fourth or fifth time.

"He came back around midnight," Jeremy said yet again.

His phone gave a discordant chime. It was the sixth message from home in the last fifteen minutes, and he was in no more hurry to answer this one than he had been the first. Laila's stare was a heavy, knowing weight on the back of his head, but Jeremy refused to return it. He kept his gaze on the doorway like looking would make it easier to hear what was being said down the hall. Now and then the familiar rumble of Coach Rhemann's voice carried as he intervened in the conversation, but he wasn't who Jeremy desperately wanted to hear.

The cop rapped his pen against his notebook and asked, "Am I boring you, *Knox*?"

Jeremy was saved from answering when his phone went off again, this time with an actual phone call. The eerie, wailing tone was one reserved for his family. He hesitated, weighed the consequences of sending it to voicemail, and reached for his phone. The bold WILSHIRE flashing on the screen did nothing to help his mood, but Jeremy turned the phone so the cop could see. The cop huffed a little but collected his notebook and left the room at last. Jeremy waited for him to disappear through the doorway before answering on speaker.

"Hey, I'm driving," he lied. The cop had had him pull a chair up to White's desk at the front of the room, but now Jeremy turned so he could finally see Cat and Laila. They'd claimed seats in the front row and were watching him intently. "Can you make it quick?"

"Your mother has been trying to reach you," his stepfather said, with a tone Jeremy had wearied of years ago. Across from him, Laila gave the phone a look that should have melted its circuits. "Stop avoiding her; you're making her worry."

And who told her there was something to worry about? Jeremy wanted to ask, but he knew how that argument would end. Warren Wilshire had two brothers in the LAPD, a detective and a deputy chief, and a recumbent father in Congress. Jeremy would never be a Wilshire, had refused the name every time his mother suggested taking it, but people knew who to call if Jeremy's name popped up anywhere. He'd tested it his junior year in high school, collecting speeding tickets just to watch Warren get them quietly removed, and had been made to sorely regret that little rebellion.

Idly he wondered who the police had called first when their system popped up a potential connection between Grayson and the USC Trojans: Warren or Coach Rhemann.

"It's been a bit hectic here, as I'm sure Milton already told you," Jeremy said. He'd seen his step-uncle only in passing when they first arrived back at the stadium, as

21

Milton was part of the crew currently bullying Jean in the next huddle room. "I'll call her when I can."

"That chance has passed," Warren said. "You're coming home for dinner so we can discuss this."

Jeremy smiled to keep his tone light when he said, "I can't promise that. The police might have more questions for us, and as team captain I need to be where my teammates can reach me. Leaving campus would be a mistake."

"Captain," Warren echoed. He'd forgotten; Jeremy could hear it in his voice.

That was Cat's last straw. She cupped a hand over her mouth and said, "Welcome to Jackie's, can I take your order?"

"Who was that?" Warren demanded.

Jeremy aimed a cheery "One sec, please!" off to the side before moving his phone closer to his face. "I told you I was driving. Laila and I are grabbing lunch to take back to the stadium for everyone. I need to let you go, okay? I'll call Mom as soon as I have a minute." Warren immediately started arguing, but Jeremy said, "Hi, yeah, we'll have—" and hung up.

He set his phone down on the desk with more force than intended and looked toward the doorway again. He wanted the police out of his stadium. He wanted Jean away from their pointed, barbed questions. What more could they possibly want to know? How unkind could they be after what Jean suffered yesterday?

Last night Grayson slammed Jean into the unyielding walls of the Gold Court and bit his throat to bleeding. Less than twenty-four hours later he was dead. The police had given up very few details, including where he'd been found and how he'd died. All Jeremy could parse from their repeated, antagonistic questions was he'd passed away in the middle of the night. Hopefully they'd been more gracious with Lucas, who'd been taken to the station

22

with Coach Jimenez, but Jeremy had little faith in their humanity.

Thoughts of Lucas made Jeremy's heart ache. "I should talk to Lucas."

"You absolutely will not," Laila warned him. "Leave him to Cody or Xavier."

"They don't—" Jeremy started, but a sudden ruckus down the hall distracted him.

Jeremy got up so fast he sent his chair flying. From the doorway he watched Rhemann escort the police down the hall toward the exit. Jeremy didn't see Jean with them, though there was a chance he was ahead of the group. Jeremy hurried to the next huddle room with Cat and Laila on his heels. The vise around his heart eased a bit when he saw Jean sitting alone in the front row, and he took a seat at Jean's side. Cat stole the chair on his other side, leaving Laila to plant herself in front of him.

"Hey," Jeremy said quietly. "How are you?"

Jean said nothing but fidgeted with the bandages on his throat. Jeremy wondered how long he'd been at it, that the edges were so frayed already. Maybe the police had demanded he bare his injuries to corroborate his story. Jeremy remembered what they looked like fresh, with spit and blood glistening on torn skin. He thought about Jean standing fully dressed in the locker room showers yesterday, the haunted look on Jean's face last night when Neil Josten finally dropped him off again, and his quiet *"If I asked you to kill me, would you?"* that kept Jeremy up most of the night.

Rhemann stepped into the doorway and looked from one Trojan to another. "Let's go. I'm taking you all home."

Jean tensed, but Jeremy refused to believe he was surprised. It was enough that he stood without argument, and the four trailed Rhemann out of the stadium. Jeremy waited until they were on the road before asking, "Do you need me to call anyone?"

"We've got it covered," Rhemann assured him.

The rest of the short ride to Laila's house was silent. Rhemann pulled up behind Jeremy's car and put his hazards on. He turned in his chair to consider the three packed into his backseat and said to Jean, "Lean on them as much as you need today. Lean on me if you are willing. If any of you need anything this weekend, reach out to any of us, any time of day. Understood?" He waited for Jean's tense nod before glancing over at Jeremy. "Stay a moment."

Cat and Laila got the back doors open, and Cat held hers so Jean could slide out after her. Jeremy watched out the passenger window as they went up the stairs to the front door. He thought about Jean tugging the chain last night, rattled and worn. He wouldn't have to lock the door today. How horrible of Jeremy, to feel such relief at that thought.

Jeremy waited until they were inside before asking Rhemann, "Is Jean a suspect?"

"Perhaps the most obvious one, if not for the rock-solid alibi. Do you know where he was last night?"

Jeremy gave a helpless shrug. "Neil Josten showed up on our doorstep and whisked him away somewhere."

After last year's chaos, Jeremy didn't have to elaborate on who Neil was. He doubted there was a single person in NCAA Exy who didn't recognize the name. The Foxes' vice-captain was apparently born Nathaniel Wesninski and had confirmed connections to two different crime families. The investigation into the late Nathan Wesninski was an ongoing fiasco that was nine-tenths rumors still, but it was sure to be a spectacular mess when it finally got off the ground.

"Ah, a target by association, then," Rhemann mused. Jeremy frowned, not understanding, but Rhemann took a minute to think things through. At last USC's head coach sighed and said, "Listen. If he brings it up with you, let me know. Not the details," he amended, with a hand up like he could ward off Jeremy's words. "They're not my business, and I don't want to know. All I need is reassurance we're not sailing into a storm here. Understood?"

"No," Jeremy admitted. "What's going on, Coach?"

"If I knew, you'd know," Rhemann said.

He obviously knew more than he was willing to admit, but Jeremy didn't push it. He had a hand on the doorknob when his phone started ringing, this time with a tune he almost never heard. Jeremy cracked his knuckles against the door in his hurry to dig it out of his pocket. It would be rude to answer with Rhemann right here, so he silenced the ringer with distracted apologies. Rhemann's gaze was knowing when Jeremy looked up again; he'd been Jeremy's coach long enough to know all of Jeremy's raucous alerts forwards and backwards.

"I'll let you take that," Rhemann said, motioning permission to leave. "I'll check in after I've talked to Lucas and the school board."

"Thank you, Coach." Jeremy clambered out of the car as fast as he could go. He had his phone at his ear even before he pushed the door closed behind him, as he wasn't sure how many rings he'd missed. "Yes, I'm here, hello."

For a half-second he thought he was too late, and then the familiar rumble of his father's voice said, "Jeremy. Heard you're in a bit of a scrap again."

"Yes, sir." Jeremy sat on the front steps and waved as Rhemann pulled away. "I'm guessing Mom called you."

Even with nearly six thousand miles between them, Jeremy heard his father's distinctive, disgruntled huff. "A half-dozen times or so. Mathilda never was one to respect time zones. Do you know what time it is here?"

Every time his father moved, Jeremy learned to calculate the hours between them, so he said, "Yes, sir, I

25

do."

He clapped a hand over his free ear and strained to hear: not his father's voice, but for any hints of where he was. He thought he heard voices and music, but considering the predawn hour it was likely commercials or a radio. Jeremy ached with the need to ask: *where are you, who are you with, are you happy?* but knew from experience what his chances of getting a straightforward answer were.

The moment passed as soon as Trent Knox said, "You want to tell me why she's blowing up my phone, then?"

Jeremy spied a loose thread on the hem of his shorts and tugged at it. "Yesterday one of our rivals came by the stadium to pick a fight, and last night he turned up dead. The police need to do their song and dance to make sure none of us had anything to do with it."

"Did you?"

That hurt enough to startle a quiet, "That's unfair," out of him, but Trent didn't waste his time apologizing. The growing silence made Jeremy think he was still waiting for a real answer. Jeremy wanted to refuse him, but without a voice in his ear all he had were his thoughts. "No, sir. We were all at home or otherwise accounted for. Mom's just trying to micromanage the aftermath. You know what she's like."

It was less his mother's fault than Warren's, but mentioning his stepfather felt a low blow. Mathilda had always known that deployments were part and parcel of Trent's career in the Air Force, just as Trent knew she would never sacrifice her career or family home to relocate with him around the globe. Maybe they'd always known it would end in heartache, her raising his kids with another man and him missing all five—four—high school graduations. Jeremy had never asked; some fights weren't worth getting into.

"That's her duty as your mother," Trent said. "Man up

26

and stop avoiding her. I don't need her calling me."

"Yes, sir," Jeremy said. "I'll call her as soon as the police have wrapped things up here."

"See that you do," Trent said.

There wasn't a goodbye; there rarely was. His father had said his piece, and the conversation was over. Jeremy lowered his phone and watched the flashing numbers indicating the call time. Not the shortest call they'd had over the years, but not the longest, either. In high school he'd kept track of each call in a notebook: what day his father called, what drove him to bridge the gap between them, and how long they'd spoken before his father decided enough was enough. In four years, Jeremy had only filled a few lines. They were strangers; they always would be. The only thread left holding them together was the name Jeremy kept.

He passed his phone back and forth between his hands, then got to his feet and headed toward his car. He heard the front door open behind him but didn't bother to look back. He knew it'd be Laila, just like he knew she'd stop him when she realized what he was doing. He got in on the passenger side anyway and tugged open the glove compartment. Right on time, Laila reached in and pushed it shut.

"No," she said. "You're not allowed to stink up my house."

"Jean?" he asked.

"Cat is keeping an eye on him."

Jeremy scrolled through his phone in search of his mother's number. Despite Warren's and Trent's insistence she was trying to reach him, he was immediately directed to her voicemail. It wouldn't be the first time she rejected his calls in a fit of pique. He sighed as he tapped out a message to the family butler instead: "Mom home?"

It took William Hunter only a minute to check her schedule and get back with him: "She has surgery

27

scheduled this afternoon. I have set out an appropriate outfit for tonight in your room."

He'd just missed her, then. "Thank you."

Laila waited until he'd set his phone on his thigh before giving his hand a short squeeze. Jeremy was afraid to return it, sure he'd crush her hand, so he settled for a quick kiss on her knuckles. She smiled, and though it didn't reach her eyes he was comforted.

"Let's go," she said. "Jean needs you more than they do."

He let her haul him out of his seat and slowed only to lock the car behind him. The living room was empty when they stepped inside, but Jeremy followed the heady aroma of fresh coffee to the kitchen. There were only three stools at the island, and while he'd half-expected Cat and Laila to bracket Jean between them, they'd given him a spot on the end. Laila reclaimed her spot while Jeremy poured himself a drink. Jeremy leaned against the short side of the island nearest Jean and studied the other man's face.

He wasn't sure what he was looking for. Grief? Lingering trauma? Triumph? Jean just looked exhausted. The scabs running down his face looked stark in the overhead light, and Jeremy's gaze snagged again on the cut that went right to the corner of Jean's eye. He cast about for something to say. Condolences for the latest tragedy to wrack the Raven line was the obvious route, considering how hard the last few had hit Jean, but Jeremy couldn't form the words.

"We should be at practice," Jean said, right on cue.

"We should not," Jeremy said. "It'd be in poor taste, don't you think? Lucas will be back in San Diego by dinner, and you need time to process what's happened. No one will be able to focus after they hear the news, so it's best to just call it and start fresh again next week."

Jean frowned his disapproval, but Laila chimed in with, "Where is your head, Jean? You've lost another

28

Raven."

Cat opened her mouth on what was sure to be a strident protest, but Laila gave her arm a warning squeeze. They stared each other down for a few tense seconds, Cat's indignant anger against Laila's unyielding calm. Laila won, as she usually did, and Cat frowned but held her tongue. At Jeremy's side Jean seemed oblivious to the silent argument, staring into the distance as he weighed Laila's words.

"He's really gone, isn't he?" Jean said, so low Jeremy might have imagined it.

Jeremy studied the shadows in his eyes and the tug at the corner of his mouth. Jean cradled his throat in his palm and tapped an agitated rhythm on the bandage. For a moment he looked lost; for a moment he looked unbearably young. It made Jeremy ache to see Jean like this, but then the tension seeped out of him. His mouth twitched again, but Jean dug his fingernails into his lower lip to stop the smile from forming.

The self-censure was regrettable, but then Jean said, "Pop. How easily these monsters die in the end."

The ease with which he called Grayson a monster put a hopeful twinge in Jeremy's chest. Jean's relationship with the Ravens was a complicated mess of love and hate, torn through by his refusal to face the horror of what they'd done to him at Edgar Allan. The few times he'd slipped up—*Not Grayson, please; I didn't ask*—he'd retreated as quickly as he could behind dismissals and evasion. That Jean felt safe enough now to look so unabashedly relieved was enough to warm Jeremy all the way through.

Cat was encouraged by his response enough to say, "Good riddance, too."

"Yes," Jean agreed.

Laila allowed them a few moments of triumph, but she'd put the pieces together as easily as Jeremy had. "If

29

Warren's doing preemptive damage control, the police suspect foul play. We know you're not capable of something like this, but the Ravens have done a number on your reputation this summer. Public opinion is an unforgiving monster when it gets going. We need a plan to get them off your back."

Jeremy looked from Laila to Jean. "Coach said Jean has a good alibi."

"They already confirmed it," Jean said. "They cannot hold this against me."

"You were with Neil." Jeremy hoped Jean would elaborate on his own, but the other man only sipped at his coffee. "You said he wouldn't have come here if he had a choice. What was he even doing here?"

Cat had no patience for tact: "What did he do to you?" When Jean only frowned at her, she smoothed his hair out of his face and said, "You were in rough shape when he brought you home, and he has a bit of a reputation. You can't blame us for being worried about you or for not trusting him."

"You do not have to trust him," Jean said. "I do."

It wasn't the answer Jeremy was expecting. Maybe Jean didn't expect it either, judging by his small frown as he turned his attention back to his coffee. Jeremy swallowed his reservations and doubts and said, "After everything he said about the Ravens last year, I wasn't expecting the two of you to be friends. If he's still in town you should invite him over for dinner."

Jean didn't even hesitate. "That ill-bred child is not my friend."

"One day you'll make sense," Laila mused. Jeremy's phone gave an ugly chime before Jean could respond, and Laila sent an annoyed look Jeremy's way. "Doesn't he have anything better to do today? Why isn't he at work?"

"This is his week—" Jeremy forgot what he was saying when he saw the name attached to his newest message. The dread that settled on him was heavy enough to be a second skin. "It's Joshua."

"Don't," Laila warned him. "Jeremy, do *not*."

Joshua had spent the last four years pretending Jeremy didn't exist, looking past him and through him at every holiday and mandatory family event. That he would reach out to Jeremy today of all days wasn't a coincidence.

"Babe, I'm begging you—" Laila reached across the island, but Jeremy moved his hand out of the way before she could snatch his phone from him.

Jeremy tapped into the short message, read it in silence, and dropped his phone into his mug of coffee a heartbeat later. Cat's stool fell with a loud clatter as she ran to grab the rice, and Laila nearly took Jeremy's fingers off as she pulled his mug out of his grip. He was distantly aware of Jean's heavy, unwavering stare, but Jeremy watched as Laila fished his phone out and quickly took it apart. Cat was back in moments, pouring rice into a square Tupperware so quickly she spilled it everywhere.

"Here, here," she said, and Laila shoved the pieces of Jeremy's phone as deep as she could. Cat dumped the rest of the bag in for good measure and patted the mound down. She started to put it on the island before glancing at Jeremy and thinking twice. He watched her carry it over to the counter because it was easier than facing Laila as she approached him. She pressed a lingering kiss to his temple, and Jeremy wound her long brown curls around his fingers in return.

"Think that'll work?" Jeremy asked.

"I hope it doesn't."

Jeremy sighed as he let go of her. "I had to know."

She said nothing, and the silence that settled in the kitchen was tense. Cat could only stand it for so long before she drummed her fingernails on the counter in an agitated beat. "I didn't get to finish lunch, and I'm starving. I'm going to make us something to eat."

31

Jeremy wasn't at all hungry, but he said, "Sounds good."

Jean held his hand out toward Cat in silent demand. She looked poised to refuse his help, then set him up to dice some peppers while she got to work on an onion. When she left to dig a frying pan out of the cabinets, Laila straightened and gave Jeremy's shoulder a push. He obediently took Cat's abandoned middle stool, and Laila settled at his side. Jeremy folded his hands together on the island and willed his heartrate down from its frenetic pace. For a few minutes no one spoke, and the kitchen slowly filled with the smell of peppers and grease.

"Sorry," he said. "Can someone text Coach and tell him I'll be out of a phone for a bit?"

"William and the floozies, too," Laila suggested as she set her phone in front of her. She tapped out a couple rapid-fire messages, then leaned forward to look past Jeremy at Jean. "Are we adding you to the group chat, or are you not ready to be that sociable yet?"

"I would also destroy my phone if it went off as incessantly as yours do," Jean said.

Laila rolled her eyes and got back to work. "Sometimes a simple 'no' is enough."

"A single word is seldom rude enough to make a point."

"I'm giving your number to Cody," Laila decided.

Jean said nothing, and Jeremy idly wondered if he sensed a losing argument or honestly saw no reason to protest. The two had spent a good part of dinner chatting last weekend, and Cody had swung past Jean as often as they could during practices without stepping on Xavier's toes. Fondness was a gentle heat against the icy pit in his chest, and finally Jeremy could breathe without feeling like he'd tear his lungs.

He looked toward Jean. "Do you want to talk about Neil?"

Jean curled his lip. "Do you want to talk about Joshua?"

"French, then," Jeremy said. Jean frowned at him, not following the abrupt jump in topics. Jeremy smiled like Jean's easy challenge hadn't kicked him in the chest and said, "The first time we met, you hit me when I asked if you would teach me. But you didn't seem to care that Neil could speak it last night."

"I was not allowed to speak French at the Nest," Jean said, in a tone that said Jeremy was being unforgivably obtuse on purpose. "When they found out I taught Kevin anyway, they were—furious." By the way Jean's gaze flicked away from Jeremy at that, Jeremy sensed it was a massive understatement. Equally intriguing was the news Kevin could speak it, but Jeremy set that insight aside for later since Jean was still speaking. "They would capitalize on it later when it suited their needs, but they never forgave me for that disobedience."

Jeremy ticked through his options and Jean's possible reaction before asking, "So it's not the knowing, but the teaching. Meaning I could learn it somewhere else and that's fine, right? I don't think I can squeeze another class in my schedule this semester without cutting something else out, but I bet I can find a course on CD or something. I'm going to be doing a lot of driving back and forth this fall from campus to home."

"Too much driving," Laila muttered under her breath, but Jeremy feigned not to hear.

Jean drummed his fingernails on the side of his mug. "There is no reason to learn. My English is passable."

"Your English is fantastic," Jeremy said. "It's not about that. It's your native language, and none of us here can share it with you. That's reason enough for me to learn." Jeremy allowed him a few moments to think it over before pressing on with, "If you don't want me to study it, I won't. Just tell me now if it would bother you."

Jean studied him, maybe waiting for a better reason or judging Jeremy's sincerity, and finally said, "Do as you like."

Jeremy smiled victory, but it was quick to fade. "Speaking of Kevin, I think someone ought to tell him what's going on. I don't know if he should find out via the news that one of his former teammates died in Los Angeles."

"He will not care," Jean said. When Jeremy frowned at him, Jean gave a dismissive wave of his knife and pushed his scattered pepper chunks into a pile on his cutting board. "The Ravens were a means to an end, and he was always undeniably their superior. He will not waste his time pretending to mourn dead weight; he will be as silent about this one as he was the rest."

It seemed a callous assessment of Kevin's character at first glance, but Jeremy had heard too many of Kevin's private opinions over the years to dismiss it out of hand. Whether Kevin's refusal to meet the press about the Ravens this summer was due to apathy or grief was a mystery for another day; when he came to town for the joint interview in August Jeremy could ask him outright and get a proper answer face to face.

"It's not just Grayson," Jeremy said, trying and failing to catch Jean's eye. "You were hurt yesterday. Kevin will want to know."

"He will not care," Jean said again.

Jeremy was flabbergasted. "He is your friend."

"He is not."

It was such a fierce refusal Jeremy lost his train of thought. He sent Laila a wild look, but she was only studying Jean with a too-sharp stare. Jeremy turned back on Jean and tried, "He's the one who recommended you to us. He's done what he could this summer to help make this transition easier for all of us. And you really think he wouldn't want to know you're safe? You give him too

34

little credit."

"You give him too much. You know nothing about us."

"You were both abused at the Nest," Laila said, and Jean went still. "You know who broke his hand, and he knows who broke your ribs. But neither of you will confront Edgar Allan and put the blame where it belongs. He could have said something this spring when they were spreading such horrific rumors about you. Why didn't he?"

"I don't know which is more offensive: that you think he could have changed anything or that you think any of us wanted him to." Jean slammed his knife down on the cutting board when Laila looked like she might protest. "They would have destroyed him if he dared speak out against them, and I would have helped them do it. Ravens do not turn against the Nest."

"You say that, but you're angry he couldn't protect you."

"He was not my partner. It was not his job to protect me, and I didn't want him to. I just wanted him to die."

Jeremy's heart skipped a beat. "You don't mean that."

Jean dug cruel fingers into his bandages. "I was glad when he lost his hand. Exy is all he has and all he loves; I knew it would destroy him to lose it. A month in the Nest without it, maybe two, and he would have no recourse but to kill himself. I was only alive because he made me promise to survive. If he died, who could hold me to that? I would have slashed the tires on his car before I let him escape us, and he knows it."

The silence following that unsettling confession was deep enough to drown in, and then Cat pushed her pan to a cold burner so she could join them at the island. She held her empty hand out palm-up and said nothing. Jean looked from her face to her hand, puzzling it out, then tried to pass the knife over. Cat wrapped her fingers around his wrist and waited for him to look up again before speaking.

"I'm glad you're alive," she said. "I'm so happy you're here with us, and I hope you're happy, too. I hope you tell us when you're not so we can help you. You're our friend, and we love you."

Jean's flinch was full body. "Don't say that to me."

Cat lifted her chin in defiance. "Why shouldn't I? It's the truth."

"It can't be. I am just—"

Whatever Jean meant to say got caught in his throat, and Jeremy watched as the light went out of him. It was the same look he'd come home with last night: the hollow stare of a man fast running out of something to hold onto. Jean wrenched out of Cat's grip with a force that almost pulled her up onto the island. The knife was dropped halfway to the door as he stormed out, and Jeremy was off his stool even before Laila said his name.

He caught up to Jean in their bedroom. Jean was sitting cross-legged in the middle of his bed, one hand clenched around his ankle and the other knotted in his shirt over his heart. He didn't look up at Jeremy's entrance. Jeremy climbed onto the bed as carefully as he could, waiting for a rejection that didn't come, and settled down back-to-back with him. Jean was tense as a board but didn't move away.

"Can I stay?" Jeremy asked. "I won't say anything else if you don't want me to."

Jean's voice was rough as gravel. "You are my partner. I will not tell you to leave."

Jeremy wondered how Jean could still put stock in a system that had let him down so horrifically, but it would be cruel to mention Riko now and Jeremy had seen Jean skirt Zane's name enough to know the man was an equally touchy topic. One day he would ask, maybe. There were bigger problems right now, none of which had easy solutions. The one Jeremy fell back on wasn't the one he meant to start with, but with Joshua's text eating at his thoughts it was what slipped out.

"I didn't like it either, the first time she said it to me," he admitted. Jean didn't respond, but Jeremy felt his head turn and knew he was listening. "Felt like I'd been waiting forever, so it wasn't at all fair to come from her first. Isn't that ridiculous?"

"Most things about you are," Jean pointed out.

Jeremy laughed. "Yeah, you're probably right. But Jean? I'm glad you're here, too. Our lives are better with you in them."

"Mine would be better if you would stop talking."

He sounded tired, not annoyed, so Jeremy chose not to take it personally. He closed his eyes and let himself relax, testing the easy way Jean took his weight without protest. He wasn't sure what time it was or how long he had until he needed to start home, but Jeremy was in no rush to sort it out. This was enough, for now: the heat of Jean's back against his and the silence that cradled them both as Jean tended his inscrutable thoughts.

CHAPTER THREE
Jeremy

For one delirious moment Jeremy thought he'd make it out of the room first. It was always a toss-up, since the longstanding seating arrangement at the table put the Wilshire-Knox kids in age order. Joshua's chair was basically decoration, so Annalise was the only real obstacle. Most days she was in a hurry to vacate his side and the drama his presence inevitably started, but today she was distracted answering some texts. Jeremy was able to get up before her, and he made it all the way to the dining room door before his mother stopped him with a brusque,

"Jeremy."

It was as effective as an anchor, snapping him to a halt two steps from freedom.

Jeremy turned to face her, but Mathilda was already distracted helping Warren with his cufflinks. Warren was off for drinks with some of his colleagues tonight. Jeremy wished they'd gone for dinner instead and saved him some of tonight's stress, but luck was running a bit scarce these days.

Annalise impatiently motioned Jeremy out of her way as she caught up with him. Warren was right behind her and gave no sign he noticed his stepson off to the side. Bryson remained seated at the table. Mathilda turned a cool gaze toward him as the others left.

"Did you need something else?"

"I'm finishing my tea," Bryson said, but made no move to sip it.

Lingering for the sake of eavesdropping, and they both knew it, but Jeremy couldn't call him out on it and

Mathilda wouldn't waste her time doing it for him. She accepted Bryson's lie in silence and turned a shrewd look on Jeremy.

"Your LSAT guides are still wrapped," she said.

Sealed, yes, and tucked away in the bottom drawer of his desk. That she'd been digging around in his room was not as surprising as he wished it was. The years spent rebuilding her trust were all for nothing; one call from the police and she would always assume the worst from him.

He hesitated too long; her tone was stern when she said, "Explain yourself."

"It's too early to worry," Jeremy reassured her. "I still have time."

"The earlier you apply, the better your chances," Mathilda said. "You should have taken the test this spring; barring that, you should have signed up for a summer slot. Admissions will open soon, and you are nowhere near ready. This isn't the sort of test you can just roll out of bed for. You do understand that, don't you?"

Bryson tipped his cup toward Jeremy. "I told you, didn't I? He's planning on failing so he can embarrass us again."

Mathilda pursed her lips in disapproval. "Jeremy."

"I'm not," Jeremy argued. "I won't. The summer just got away from me because I've been helping Jean adjust to Los Angeles." It took a moment too long for recognition to set in, no matter that Jean's assault was what had forced this meeting. Jeremy couldn't keep the impatience out of his, "Jean Moreau, the transfer student who was attacked on campus yesterday."

"The newest Trojan faggot," Bryson said. "Have you slept with this one yet?"

Jeremy rounded on him to demand, "Why? Is Warren shopping for another Beemer?"

Mathilda's voice was like a whip: "Jeremy Alan."

Looking away from Bryson's cold sneer took

39

everything Jeremy had. "He's out of line."

"Bryson, stop antagonizing your brother," Mathilda said. "Go on, now."

Bryson drained his tea, pushed the empty glass aside for someone else to deal with, and left the room with a last sly smirk for Jeremy. Jeremy wished the dining room had a door he could slam in Bryson's wake. He had to settle for crossing his arms over his chest so hard his ribs ached. When he turned on his mother again there was no sympathy or warmth in her eyes, only disappointment. One day he'd stop looking for more than that.

She said nothing for a few moments before reluctantly asking, "Did you?"

"No." When she looked unconvinced, he said again, "*No*. He's not even my type."

A complete lie, but the truth was a complicated mess she couldn't handle. She was so discomfited by the reminder that Jeremy had a type that she didn't bother to push it. Jeremy looked away as she struggled to find an emotional landing point somewhere between regret and disgust.

"I wish you would work things out with that girl. The mixed one you're always visiting, whatever her name is. A diplomat's daughter would be a good match for you."

"It's never going to happen."

"Would it really be so terrible to try? She's pretty enough, all things considered."

Jeremy knew exactly what she meant by *all things considered* and it was enough to make his stomach roil. "Jesus, Mom. Can we please not do this today?"

Mathilda was relentless. "The war is taking a toll on public opinion. We need to make a statement: we have no quarrel with our Muslim neighbors here at home, just with the terrorists threatening our safety and sovereignty overseas."

"She's not even practicing," Jeremy said.

"Even better."

The relief in her smile irked him into saying, "Nabil's Muslim. What about him?"

He regretted the cheek immediately; the revolted look she gave him had him fixing his stare on the floor. Mathilda didn't waste her breath acknowledging his comment, but she did need a minute to get her temper under control. When she trusted herself to speak, she picked up right where she'd left off:

"Welcoming her into the family could be a good look for your grandfather, if his team can sort out how to safely spin it. He's losing ground with younger voters. They have more opinions than common sense."

"He is *not* my—"

"Enough," Mathilda warned him. "We've been over this a hundred times."

Jeremy dug his nails into the starchy sleeves of the shirt William had set out for him. Silence stretched between them, terrible and brittle enough to cut. Jeremy cast about for anything that would get him out of here and settled on the easiest lie: "I'll think about it."

"Good. That's all I'm asking."

She didn't understand what she was asking, or she didn't care. Jeremy didn't want to know which. He tried to drag the conversation back on track with a peace offering: "I'll bring the guidebooks back to campus with me."

"Don't bother. We ordered you a second set so you can keep one at either end. William knows where they are; see him before you head out." At his weak nod, she finally crossed the room toward him. Gentle fingers smoothed his hair out of his face, and she hummed thoughtfully as she studied him. "It's growing on me, but you'll need to touch it up soon. I'll tell Leslie to expect the charge."

"Thank you."

"Go on," she said, letting go of him. "That's all for now."

41

He should have gone looking for the butler, but Jeremy made a beeline for the stairs instead. It was unsurprising to find Bryson waiting at the top for him. With him square in the middle of the landing, Jeremy had no choice but to stop two steps down and stare up at him. Bryson considered Jeremy with a heavy-lidded stare of lofty arrogance, his hands tucked deep in the pockets of his gray slacks.

"Personally, I'm glad you're going to fail the test," Bryson said. "It'd be disturbingly out of character if you finally got something right."

"Let me by," Jeremy said. "I need to get back to campus."

Bryson's smile was slow and oily. "I said, I'm glad you're going to fail. The first few times you sit for it, anyway." When Jeremy opened his mouth to argue, Bryson neatly spoke over him: "Tit for tat. You do this for me, and I'll make sure Mom doesn't find anything unexpected in your room the next time she goes on a scavenger hunt. What do you think?"

"That's an empty threat. There's nothing to find."

"I wouldn't be so sure. I bet I can find just about anything in there if I look hard enough."

It took only a moment for Jeremy to understand. "Don't you dare."

"Please," Bryson prompted him.

"I'll tell her it's yours," Jeremy warned him.

The sudden weight of Bryson's hand on the back of his neck jarred him to stillness, and Jeremy stared up into his brother's face. Bryson's expression was deceptively calm, but Bryson never touched him unless he was ready to put Jeremy back in his place.

"Blaming me didn't save you last time, but sure, let's try the same old trick again."

It was enough to knock Jeremy's heart into his spine. "I never blamed you."

"But you took me down with you anyway." Bryson held on a moment more to make sure Jeremy had nothing else to say, then clucked his tongue in disapproval and withdrew. "We'll make the best of it, one way or another. Tell you what: I'll even reinstate your friends and family discount. You'll need it to fall back on when you've ruined your life beyond repair."

Jeremy didn't need to get changed that badly; he could pick up his clothes the next time he came home. He retreated a step, fighting to ignore the victorious smirk that cut his brother's face in two, and turned to go. His escape route was blocked by William, who was halfway up the stairs with a package in his hand. Jeremy froze, wondering how much William had heard. Bryson took advantage of his hesitation to elbow him into the railing and start down the stairs.

"I'll have my travel arrangements soon, I expect?" Bryson said.

William turned sideways to allow Bryson by. "I've set the envelope on the mail drop."

Jeremy didn't stick around to hear Bryson's response but made a beeline for his room. He left the door open since William would be by in just a moment and set to work on his buttoned shirt with unsteady hands. He threw his shirt in the general direction of his hamper and was yanking his belt free when William rapped on his doorframe.

"Yeah." Jeremy heard the rough edge in his voice and swallowed hard.

"Your books," William said, entering to set them on his nightstand. He collected Jeremy's shirt from the floor, briefly studied it to see if it could be salvaged after only an hour's use, then draped it over his arm to wait. As soon as Jeremy stepped out of his pants, William took those too and carried them away.

"Bryson will be in Edmonton for the next week," he

said as he gathered Jeremy's shoes.

It was a promise of temporary peace, but Jeremy couldn't be comforted. He didn't trust himself to answer but set to work tearing open the package at last. He already knew what William had brought him, but the sight of the LSAT guides turned his stomach inside out. He was distantly aware of William moving up alongside him again, but he didn't look until he saw a flash of blue in his peripheral vision. William was holding up one of his old phones.

William waited for him to take it before saying, "Miss Dermott said your phone was temporarily out of service. I was able to find this one, but I haven't reassigned your line to it yet. She thought yours might be salvageable."

"I dropped it in my coffee," Jeremy admitted as William backed out of his space. Jeremy chucked his LSAT guides on his bed and inspected the phone. William must have charged it over dinner, because the screen came to life as soon as he tapped the buttons. Jeremy felt his heart creep toward his throat, a warning not to dwell on it, but he couldn't stop himself from saying, "Joshua texted me."

He felt the weight of William's calm stare pressing into him, but Jeremy couldn't look up from his phone to return it. William gave him a minute to see if anything else was forthcoming, then said, "I do not imagine he was kind."

Jeremy set the phone down on his nightstand so he wouldn't throw it. "I don't deserve kindness from him. I just want—" *Forgiveness* was too much to ask for, and *reconciliation* wasn't far behind it. Jeremy had thought he'd settle for Joshua's hatred, at least, because that meant Joshua would be thinking about him enough to have an opinion, but this morning's message had nearly sliced the soul out of him. He finished with a lame, "I don't know."

"If you don't know what you need, how can he ever

provide it?" William asked.

"Had my therapy session for the month, thank you."

William's expression was calm, but there was a careful rebuke in his, "Week."

The correction made Jeremy wince, and he glanced toward his open door. He knew William would never willingly betray his trust, but he'd still put the man in an uncomfortable position by telling him the truth last year. Jeremy listened for any sign they might have been overheard, but strain as he might he only heard silence.

Jeremy finally tugged on the white tee and bright gold shorts he'd arrived in. The outfit had earned a rather scathing appraisal from Warren, but it was better to be scorned and comfortable than to wear an ironed shirt and starch-stiff pants for longer than was necessary. He stuffed his old phone into one pocket and scooped up the unwanted guides.

He felt restless and out of sorts, worn raw beneath his family's antagonism and expectations. He knew what would solve it—knew a few things, really—but he wasn't sure he could pull it off. He started for the door, trusting William to follow him out.

Over his shoulder he said, "I'm going to go for a run and clear my head before I deal with crosstown traffic. If anyone wonders why my car's still out front when I'm supposed to be gone…"

"I will explain if they ask," William said when he trailed off.

"Oh." Jeremy hesitated halfway down the stairs. "I'm going to start studying French. Any idea who's got the best program these days?"

"I will look into it," William promised.

"What would I do without you?" Jeremy asked.

"What would any of you do?"

William's usual response for once lacked its prim humor, but Jeremy knew that dour mood wasn't really directed at him. Jeremy took the remaining stairs two at a time and scooped up his keys on his way out the door. He detoured by his car long enough to toss the phone and books into the passenger seat, then set off on a slow jog up the street. It was all for show, as he'd seen everything he needed to on the drive in, but it was necessary to pull this off.

Two streets up and one over was Leonard Foster's house. On Friday evenings Tessa Foster hosted a candlelit "coffee and crime" book club on her front lawn. She'd been setting up when Jeremy first entered the neighborhood, but Jeremy had been less interested in her than he was the familiar black car at the head of her driveway.

Jeremy made a meandering lap of the neighborhood, scanning manicured lawns and sprawling decks for prying eyes. Jeremy wasn't supposed to be within fifty feet of the Foster house, and anyone who mattered knew that. Warren was as generous to his friends as he was hateful to his least-liked stepson.

Satisfied by the shuttered windows and empty lawns, Jeremy made his way back to Leo's place. Most of the backyard was framed by tastefully trimmed trees, and Jeremy knew from experience which part of the fence had the fewest flowering vines twisted around it. Shimmying up and over with so little room to work with was uncomfortable enough to put a small tweak in his knee, but Jeremy made it into the yard with no one the wiser.

From there it was a practiced climb: up the patio steps to the lower deck and an almost-too-far jump to the second-floor balcony. Luckily the metal railing there was hooked and swirled, giving him plenty of places to grip as he dragged himself up. The trickiest section was going from the second floor to the third, as there was no direct path up. Jeremy had to get over to the private balcony outside the master bedroom before making his way up to the one outside of Leo's, and he crossed his fingers for luck before making the jump.

At last he was where he needed to be. The sliding door to Leo's bedroom was unlocked, as usual, and the yellow curtains were drawn tight. Jeremy eased the door open a few inches and put his ear to the crack to listen. A minute dragged by without any discernible sound, and Jeremy risked poking the curtain open an inch. Leo was propped up on an obscene amount of pillows in bed, headphones jammed tight against his skull as he flipped through a magazine. The bedroom door across the room was open, but when Jeremy saw no movement in the hall, he tugged the curtain further open.

It took a couple waves to get Leo's attention, and the other man jumped so hard he dislodged his headphones. Leo gaped at him for a minute, then threw himself out of bed and ran to close his bedroom door. He was smart enough to be quiet about it, and Jeremy let himself in as soon as Leo turned the lock.

"Jesus, Knox, a little warning?" Leo asked. "What if Mom saw you?"

"She's nose-deep in some sordid story with her friends," Jeremy said. "Want me to leave?"

"Fuck no." Leo was already peeling his shirt over his head, and Jeremy laughed as he followed suit.

A long run would've been the safer bet, but losing himself in Leo's hungry kisses and familiar embrace was infinitely more satisfying. Summer was boring when Jeremy's usual hookups were all out of town. He'd found a couple new faces at coffee shops and bars this May when going back and forth from home to Laila's, but he'd spent June utterly distracted by Jean. He'd missed this. Leo too, if he was honest, but there was as much bitterness wrapped up in Leo as there was nostalgia.

Leo waited until after they'd worn each other out before pressing a cheshire-cat grin to Jeremy's temple.

47

"Not that I'm complaining, but what's the occasion?"

"I can't visit an old friend?" Jeremy ducked in for a last, lingering kiss and was rewarded with a nip at his lower lip.

Leo's heavy-lidded gaze tracked him as Jeremy rolled off the bed. Jeremy could almost hear the gears working as Leo thought, and he knew it wouldn't take long for the other man to draw the right conclusions. They'd gone to the same high school, after all. They'd been teammates for four years and clumsily unsubtle lovers for most of one. Then Warren offered Leo a car if he climbed out of Jeremy's bed, and Leo needed only two hours to choose his side.

Whenever he was home for school break, he parked the BMW where Warren was sure to see it. Jeremy had considered keying it beyond repair for a while there, and for two years the sight of it was enough to make him ill. Last year he'd run into Leo by chance at the beach, and Leo had taken him up the coast to desecrate the backseat. After that the car was a little less of an eyesore, but there was still a chasm between them neither man could fix.

"Bryson's in town," Leo decided. "When is that cocksucker going to move out for good? Annie did."

"Annalise," Jeremy corrected him, never mind his sister wasn't around to take offense to the nickname. Jeremy pushed around Leo's jeans with his foot, looking for his other sock, and finally found it near the baseboard. "Glass houses, anyway. We're still living at home."

Leo sat up just to immediately slump back against the headboard. He scratched idly at his bare chest and watched with keen interest as Jeremy tugged on his clothes. "We're in undergrad," he said only after Jeremy's ass disappeared into boxers and too-bright shorts. "How's he ever gonna get picked up by a firm in Manhattan if he's back here so often? I can call around, maybe, see if I can namedrop him to the right people. Not that a Wilshire needs my help getting placed, I mean."

"He is not a Wilshire."

Leo was unmoved by the flat tone but beckoned Jeremy back to him. Jeremy waited until he'd yanked his shirt on before letting Leo pull him in. "Ah, there you are," Leo said, tracing the hard line of Jeremy's mouth with his thumb. His grip on Jeremy's wrist went bruising when Jeremy tried to pull free, and he kissed Jeremy to take the sting off his words: "Denial didn't save you then and won't save you now. He made his choice, and you made yours, *Knox*."

"Let me out."

"What's the rush?" Leo let go and put another pillow behind his head. "Let's chat a bit. You've been holding out on me."

"I've stayed too long as it is." Jeremy crossed the room and motioned at the curtain. "Come on."

"Love him and leave him," Leo mocked him.

Jeremy leveled a cool look at him. "You made that choice for both of us."

"And I'd do it again," Leo said, without an ounce of guilt or shame. He was at least smart enough to get up, knowing his words were likely to send Jeremy out onto the balcony unattended. He gave a half-assed attempt to find his briefs before moseying over to Jeremy in the nude. Jeremy stepped out of view as Leo tugged the curtains wide open, but Leo didn't bother to slide the door open yet. "Don't be stingy. You've got a Raven on your lineup. How'd you pull that off?"

"Luck," Jeremy said.

Leo waited, but Jeremy gazed back in silence. Leo gave an exaggerated shrug and said, "It's about time the Trojans gave up the gag, honestly. It'll be good to see them get dirty this year. Good for you, too. You tried it their way for four years, and what did it ever get you except failure right at the finish line?"

"Our way." Jeremy tilted his head away from Leo's kiss. "Signing Jean doesn't mean we're changing how we do things. I wouldn't want us to."

"You can't be serious."

"I believe in us," Jeremy insisted. "We can win without sacrificing who we want to be."

Leo's smile was too amused to be pitying. "You couldn't even beat the Foxes when it mattered most."

Jeremy regretted the loss, but not the choice his team had made that night. Trying to explain himself to Leo would only start a fight, so Jeremy gazed back at him in silence until Leo turned away at last. The other man tugged the door open and stepped out onto the balcony. He made a show of stretching and yawning, his head on a slow swivel as he checked the neighbors' windows for any witnesses.

Leo motioned an okay when he was done, and Jeremy stepped out alongside him. Leo propped his elbow on the railing and said, "Mind the roses when you drop. Mom'll kill me if you fuck 'em up."

"Yeah, yeah."

Jeremy hoisted himself up on the railing. Getting down from the third floor was marginally easier than getting up. The fall from three to two was the iffiest, a half-second longer than Jeremy always expected it to be, but he managed to not hit the patio set outside the sunroom when he landed. Dropping to the garden was easier, a hand-over-hand shimmy down and a push off the railing so he wouldn't land in the bushes. Leo would be back inside by now, so Jeremy snapped a white rose off its stem and booked it for the far side of the yard.

It was a short jog back to his house. Jeremy checked his pocket for his keys as he reached the looping driveway out front. The rose was tucked into his cup holder for safekeeping, and Jeremy glanced toward the front of his house as he turned the key in the ignition and pulled away.

Tumbling with Leo this close to home was risky, but it had been the right move. The inevitable ache from a family meeting now sat no heavier than a bruise on his heart, easily ignored beneath the memory of Leo's eager hands.

Jeremy drummed his fingers on the steering wheel in an uneven beat before cutting the radio on to drown out his thoughts. He couldn't carry a tune to save his life, but he belted out whatever lyrics he knew with all the enthusiasm he could muster. It was enough to settle him, and by the time he reached Laila's house he had put dinner completely behind him. He parked at the base of her driveway, neatly blocking her car in, and brought his things inside with him.

The TV was on, but from here he couldn't tell what was playing. He toed out of his shoes and went in search of his friends, only to hesitate in the living room doorway when he realized the girls had fallen asleep there. Cat was slouched against the back of the couch while Laila used her thigh as a pillow. Jeremy dug up the remote to mute the TV. Neither stirred at the abrupt silence. He wondered if he ought to wake them, as it was too early to be in bed, but there was plenty of time this weekend to fix their schedules.

Jeremy found Jean in the kitchen. The gray-eyed backliner was perusing one of Cat's tattered cookbooks, and the relaxed line of his shoulders was reassuring. Jeremy studied his calm expression and tried not to think about Leo's unkind assessment. Jean put a finger to the page to mark his spot and looked up, and Jeremy smiled apologies for interrupting him.

"Any idea how long they've been out?" he asked.

Jean glanced toward the clock and said, "An hour at most."

Jeremy set his things aside and went in search of a makeshift vase for his rose. He collected a clean glass

51

from the cabinet, filled it halfway with water, and dropped the flower in. There was room on the windowsill for it, so he set it between a picture of Barkbark von Barkenstein and an empty terracotta pot. He framed the view between his fingers as he took a few steps back.

Satisfied with the setup, Jeremy turned back to Jean for his opinion. Jean didn't notice, as he was staring at Jeremy's study guides with a look of palpable disdain. Jeremy forgot whatever he'd been going to say but quietly went to the island and turned the guides over. Jean slanted a cool look at him, but Jeremy only said, "Did anything happen while I was gone? Any updates or calls we need to deal with?"

He expected Jean to allow the change in subject. With one or two exceptions, Jean had avoided their personal business all summer long. Even this afternoon's fiasco with Jeremy's phone had gotten little more than a fleeting dig. This should have followed the pattern—except of course it wouldn't, because law school and an Exy career could not coexist. Jeremy should have taken that into account, but Jean's annoyed, "These aren't yours," caught him off guard.

"Yeah," Jeremy said. "I'm taking the exam this fall."

Jean gave him a minute to come up with something better, then said, "No."

"Family tradition," Jeremy said. He meant to leave it at that, but the look on Jean's face told him that wasn't good enough. Jeremy pushed the books in slow circles with his fingers. "That's why I'm studying English, you know? It's a decent starter degree for getting into law school."

It hadn't been his first choice by a long shot, but it was better than his mother's suggestions of political science or criminal justice. It had taken weeks to wear her down even after he brought home articles to justify his choice. He didn't dislike it as much as he'd thought he would, but it helped that he offset his classes with fun electives each semester. Equally helpful was watching his teammates in more ambitious degrees suffer through sleepless nights and lethal levels of caffeine at exam time.

"Your traditions are irrelevant," Jean said. "You are going to play after graduation."

"There's no harm in at least taking the test." A transparent lie, but one Jeremy couldn't afford to linger on right now. He pushed his books aside and leaned against the island with a bright smile. "You ever think about where you'll be signed? I imagine you'll get offers from just about everywhere."

Jean considered it for only a moment. "No."

"Really? No preference at all?" Jeremy waited a beat but was undeterred by Jean's reticence. "I used to think I wanted to stay here in California, but Oregon or Arizona might not be that bad. I'm not sure how well I'd do on a southern team, but I guess anywhere but New York or Texas would still work. Not that I'd turn them down if they were the only offers. Any port in a storm, and all that."

Jean made a derisive sound in the back of his throat. "You waste our time pretending to be modest. We both know your statistics and records. They will fight to the death for you, and Court will be waiting in the wings."

He'd heard such reassurances from his friends over the years, but they were his friends; filling in the holes his family carved out of him was something they'd always done because they loved and supported him. It was different, from Jean—not that Jeremy didn't consider Jean a friend, but that Jean said it with such impatience. Jean didn't know or care about the rest, the Wilshires or their expectations or the ugly manipulations happening behind the scenes. He saw only Jeremy Knox, captain of the USC Trojans, and he knew what Jeremy was worth on his own.

"There you are," Jean said.

53

It was jarring enough to shake the warmth out of him. Where Leo had said it with hungry satisfaction, Jean only sounded thoughtful.

"Jean?" he asked.

Jean turned a considering look on him. "You go away when you go home."

Jeremy studied him, but there was nothing curious or prying in his expression. He didn't want to get into it after the day they'd had, but he risked saying, "You never ask."

"Ravens do not have families." It wasn't the first time he'd said as much, but Jeremy was sure he'd been calmly dismissive before. The sharp edge biting at his words now was startling, and Jeremy couldn't miss the way Jean dug his fingernails into his bandaged wrist. "You are my captain and my partner. You are my teammate. Who you are outside of that is irrelevant."

"You are not a Raven," Jeremy said.

Jean nearly tore the bandage off as he dragged his grip loose. "Take me to the court."

"You've been sidelined," Jeremy reminded him, as gently as he could. "Would you settle for a run around campus?"

"Bad idea," Laila said as she joined them.

Rather than explain, she gave Jeremy her phone and smothered a jaw-cracking yawn behind one hand. A text from Xavier was open for him to read: the news was out that Grayson Johnson was dead. He'd apparently been found in his hotel room by housekeeping when he failed to check out on time, though Xavier said cause of death was still being withheld. All the article had said was he'd passed away sometime in the middle of the night.

Beneath that was the warning that had Laila urging caution, so Jeremy passed it on to Jean: "Coach says the press've been by the stadium looking for a statement. He turned them away, but Shane saw one or two of them near the dorms. Guess they didn't care for Coach's official

54

statement." He returned Laila's phone and grimaced an apology at Jean. "It's late enough in the day they should've given up, but I don't know if we want to risk it."

"They aren't here," Jean pointed out.

"Of course not." Cat wandered in and went straight to the fridge to look for her pitcher of pineapple juice. "As far as anyone knows, only three Trojans live off-campus during the school year." She twirled her finger to indicate Jeremy and Laila. "It's been established that Jeremy lives at home, and no one's going to blindly assume you live co-ed with me and Laila. The team knows to be vague and unhelpful if anyone asks where to find you."

"Remember that my uncle owns half of the houses right around here," Laila added. "Even if our neighbors have figured out who you are, they know better than to snitch. But once you're on campus you're fair game."

"I am not allowed to speak to the public," Jean said. "Their presence changes nothing."

"You're allowed to talk to people who aren't Trojans," Jeremy said in patient correction. "So long as you're careful with how you represent the team, I mean. But you don't have to talk to anyone you don't want to, at least not until your interview next month. We don't mind running interference for you wherever we can. I'll have to say something as team captain this weekend, but they can't make me bring you along."

"It might work in our favor in the long run." Cat went to Jean's side and gently pressed her cold glass to his bruised cheek. "The official story is still that you left the Ravens mid-championships because you sprained your LCL. That Edgar Allan let you go when you would've healed up for summer practices raised a few questions, but no one knows what you really went through or what the Ravens are capable of. This is the first real proof we have that they're nasty pieces of work both on and off the

55

court."

"It will backfire on us," Laila predicted. "Their loudest fans were happy to jump onto the hate train this spring. They don't care that Jean transferred for an injury; they care that Jean left when his team needed him. Riko killed himself when he lost to the Foxes, and two others followed his lead. Their more enthusiastic fans need someone to blame for this absolute disaster. They won't look at Jean's injuries and see what the Ravens are capable of. They'll think Grayson was justified in turning on him, and they'll pin his death on Jean no matter what."

Jeremy thought of how vile spring had gotten. "I'm inclined to agree with Laila. It's twice as likely to work against you until people have a chance to get to know you."

"I do not care what people think of me," Jean said. "Their opinion has no bearing on my performance."

Jeremy drummed his thumbs on his hips as he thought. At last he relented with, "It's not our reputation at stake, so we can't make the decision for you. If you want to see how it plays out, that's your call. We'll support you all the way either way and do what we can to put out the fires. Do you still want to go for a run?"

"Yes," Jean said without hesitation.

Jeremy glanced at the girls in silent invitation, but Cat answered with a pitying look. "Listen, love you both, but absolutely not." She put her hands up as if they were scales and weighed her options for him: "Go for a run or take advantage of an empty house. Easiest choice we've made all year, right babe?"

"Make it a very long run," Laila said. Jeremy saluted as he pushed away from the island and started for the door. He was nearly there when Laila somehow noticed the newest décor in her kitchen. He felt her stare boring holes in the back of his head as she demanded, "Why is there a Foster rose on my windowsill, Jeremy?"

Jeremy smiled over his shoulder but didn't slow. "You always said you liked them!"

He put on his shoes while Jean changed into something easier to run in. It didn't take long for Jean to catch up with him, and Jeremy grabbed his keys while Jean knotted his laces. Neither girl came to see them off, likely content to listen for the lock, and Jeremy led Jean down the stairs to the street.

"Rock paper scissors," he said, holding out his hand. Jean frowned but did as he was told, and Jeremy nodded satisfaction. "North it is! Want to see where the Dodgers play?"

"Summer team?" Jean asked as he fell in alongside Jeremy.

"Baseball," Jeremy corrected him. "I'll take you to a game one day."

Jean's lip curled in disdain. "There is no value in watching other sports."

"I'm telling Derrick you said that when the Kings' season starts."

"Now you are making teams up," Jean decided, and Jeremy could only laugh.

For the first time all day—all week, perhaps?—their luck finally held. Jeremy saw no one he recognized, no strangers jumped in their path at the sight of Jean's numbered face, and the only two police cars they spotted turned off before Jeremy and Jean passed them. For now, Jean was safe. The rest they would deal with one day at a time.

CHAPTER FOUR
Jean

The weekend was oddly peaceful, at least for Jean. On Saturday the press approached Lucas in San Diego with prying questions and eager demands, but his parents weren't beholden to USC's tedious rules. They reacted so poorly to the intrusion that the reporters had no choice but to retreat. Rhemann and Jeremy bought the Johnsons some peace by making a joint statement a few hours later. Laila advised Jean not to watch it, seeing how they would have to be achingly diplomatic about the whole thing, but Jean waved aside her concern as misplaced. He propped his shoulder against the living room doorframe and listened as Jeremy performed.

Jeremy was significantly better at this than Riko or Kevin ever were, perhaps because he had real pain to lean back on. Whatever Jeremy's honest opinion of Grayson, he truly regretted the effect it would have on the struggling Raven lineup and he ached for the men whose lives Grayson had upended. Anyone who listened to him speak would believe Jeremy was one invitation away from attending Grayson's funeral himself. This spring Jean had found his press face too annoying to stand. Today the act was almost calming, since Jeremy was acting as the first line of defense for Jean.

More important than Jeremy's statement was the way it forced the LAPD's hand. Once Jeremy expressed the Trojans' unwavering, unequivocal support of Jean as he supposedly grieved yet another teammate, the police had to officially declare Jean's innocence. They were less kind about it than Jeremy was, but Jean wasn't bothered by their attitudes. All that mattered was that none of them explained why they were so sure. Perhaps Special Agent Browning had put the fear of God into them when they called to confirm his alibi, or maybe they decided it was too far above their collective paygrade to deal with.

Saturday evening the police gave up and officially ruled Grayson's death a suicide. The case was closed, and Jean was safe—from them, anyway. Cat spent the remainder of the weekend tracking the response across half a dozen forums and news stations, though she withheld the finer details from Jean. He interpreted that the only way he could: general opinion was as unpleasant and bullheaded as Laila had worried it would be. There was nothing he could do about it, so Jean focused on what little he could control.

Renee was a steadying presence even from so far away. She knew how to interpret his curt response to her check-in and so spent the rest of the weekend sending scattered slice of life updates. It helped pull him out of his thoughts and away from all of this.

Monday morning Jeremy drove them to practice, never mind that the stadium was an easy walk and easier jog from Laila's house. Jean had forgotten that Lucas would be absent this week. The other backliner was laying his brother to rest in San Diego, trying to come to terms with both Grayson's violent reentry to and abrupt departure from his life. It annoyed Jean more that Lucas was missing drills than it did knowing he was mourning. He thought about Riko's death, of Renee trying to hold his jagged pieces together and Kevin sitting in the pews at Riko's funeral. Jean would only drive himself mad if he tried to understand the toxic mystery that was the human heart.

Without Lucas around to fawn over, the Trojans turned their considerable attention on Jean. They'd seen Jean's and Lucas's battered faces Friday morning, only to find out at lunch that Grayson was dead. With afternoon

59

practices canceled, Lucas whisked from campus to the police station to San Diego, and Jean locked away at Laila's house, the team had gone all weekend without any real answers or outlet for their confusion. It would make sense if they blamed him, no matter what the police had to say about it. Instead, they closed ranks.

It started off subtly enough: first with Xavier, who came by his locker to ensure Jean remembered his wrist brace. Then there was Jesus, reassuring him out of the blue that his face was looking much better today than it had Friday. Cody had a peach for him, though Jean was sure he hadn't told Cody he liked them. Cat's doing, most likely, as she'd spent half of the summer trying to figure out which fruits Jean would eat.

Produce had been strictly regulated at the Nest: a necessary addition for the sun-starved team, but too sugary to win the nurses' unanimous approval. Most of the staff wanted the Ravens to rely on supplements, but Hamrickson somehow got the master to approve a produce delivery once a week. Bananas and oranges were her go-to, but now and then she managed to bring in kiwis. Supposedly she showed up with papaya once, but Jean had been unconscious that day.

Jean turned the peach this way and that, savoring the feel of its soft fuzz against his fingertips. There was no time to eat it now, since they were only moments from heading to Lyon, but the locker room was cool enough to keep it safe in his absence. He set it down on his shelf and pushed his court shoes in front of it, hiding it from prying eyes and greedy hands. Cat tweaked his hair when she caught him at it but said nothing to draw attention to his prize.

Derrick fell in alongside him on the run to the stadium, which meant Derek wasn't long in appearing at his other side. Derrick wasted no time at all on a good morning but said, "Jeremy says you've never been to a hockey game. That right?"

"Please don't get him started on hockey," Derek said, like Jean had invited either of them.

"Don't listen to him, he's a killjoy," Derrick said. "He has fun as soon as he's bundled up enough. But just you wait, I'm gonna find us a weekend game and we'll make a day of it. You, me, Big D, Cherise—"

"What a colossal waste of time," Jean said.

Derrick continued like he hadn't heard. "—Shane, uhhh. Hey Shawn!"

Jean interrupted before Shawn could get involved. "You aren't going. Maybe if you hadn't allowed yourself to get so distracted by outside interests you would've fixed your stance years ago. Why are you allowing this behavior?" he demanded of Derek. "He is your partner. Why can't you corral him?"

"Hey, hey," Derrick said, even as Derek held up his hands in self-defense. "What's wrong with my stance?"

"Why are you always moving?"

"Oh, easy. I'm jamming to the tunes." Derrick smiled, like that was at all a legitimate response. Jean stared him down a minute, waiting for something more, before turning his attention back on the saner of the two. Derek only shrugged expansively and refused to elaborate. Derrick took the incredulous silence as some sort of permission and began air drumming with enthusiastic sound effects.

Jean could have—should have—left it at that, but a name finally sank through his annoyance. "Cherise is not a Trojan."

"Oh, she's Derek's cousin," Derrick said. "I'm going to marry her one day."

"Keep dreaming," Derek said. "She is never gonna marry a white boy."

"I'll change her mind yet." Derrick nudged Jean. "You've *got* to see the rack on—"

Derek swung half-heartedly at him, and Derrick took off toward the front of the line with a shout. Derek gave chase, hollering for Derrick to come back so they could "just talk". The breeze carried Derrick's boisterous cackle back to Jean, and Jean dug a thumb into his temple to ward off a burgeoning headache.

Lisinski let Jean try the weights both with and without his brace but said nothing about his chances of participating in drills that day. Jean nearly bit his tongue to bleeding to keep from asking her. Surely Jeremy could find out, using his authority as captain, but Jean wouldn't catch up with him until they were back at the stadium.

Jean didn't look for his peach until he finished his rinse-off shower. It was right where he'd left it, so he dressed for lunch and settled on the strikers' bench with it cupped between his hands. Ananya was often amongst the last back to the row, as the women generally chose to dress in the restroom. Somehow she still beat Jeremy to the lockers, and she smiled at the sight of the fruit cradled in Jean's hands.

"If you like peaches, you should try Cat's tarts," she said. "They're fantastic."

Jean closed his fingers protectively around his snack. "An unnecessary embellishment."

She nodded in the face of his rejection and went looking for Cody and Pat. Jeremy appeared almost as soon as she'd left, with Cat and Laila on his heels, and the four of them made their way up the street once more.

Cat dug into her lunch as she chatted about a new exhibit at the nearby museum. Laila was an easy enough sell on the idea; if Cat was that excited to see the exhibit, then of course Laila would be happy to take her. Jeremy seemed oblivious to the chatter going on overhead, as he was sprawled on his stomach with one of the LSAT guides he'd brought home Friday. Neither Cat nor Laila had seen fit to comment on their sudden appearance, an unexpected bit of self-control for such an opinionated pair.

"We could go Saturday," Cat said, then realization had her tilting toward Jean. "Oh, no, wait. My uncle's dealership is getting a shipment out of San Francisco this week, and his driver's gonna detour through Daly City to get the starter bike. You and I can go pick it up Friday after practice, okay? Saturday we'll have to get you a permit."

Jean still wasn't sure which way to swing on that decision, so he stalled with: "I don't know where Daly City is."

Cat contemplated the surrounding buildings before pointing over her right shoulder. "About six hours that direction. Most of my fam's in the bay area, actually! Have you ever been? Really?" She clasped her chest dramatically when he shook his head. "Well, it's a quick flight from here if you ever wanna pop up there for a weekend. I can find us some cheap tickets, I bet."

Jean wasn't sure what constituted as "cheap" but decided not to ask. He'd gone from his parents' tight grip to the Nest's suffocating control. He understood capitalism and economics in theory, thanks to tremendously boring business classes and conversations with the Ravens, but money was not something he was used to needing or having. That first visit to Fox Hills in May had been a rude awakening. Laila nearly had a meltdown when she realized how out of his depth he was, though she'd repeatedly reassured him it wasn't him she was so upset with. He hadn't really understood until he saw how quickly everything added up at the register.

Laila and Cat had shouldered most of his expenses since then, allowing him to chip in only for the occasional forgotten ingredient or the new sheets for his smaller bed. Leaning on them meant Jean wasn't getting any better at understanding how to manage cash, but he had no idea how to change the situation. He knew he'd get a salary

63

after graduation—twenty percent of one, anyway—but what was he supposed to do between now and then? He'd come to Los Angeles with only the four hundred dollars Coach Wymack slipped in his suitcase.

It was too big a problem with no real solution, so he said, "I don't like flying."

Laila turned her head his way. "Afraid of heights?"

"I don't like airports."

Cat didn't seem to know what to make of that. "Huh. Well, I'm always up for a road trip, but we'll need to plan for it a little better since it'll take longer. Heyyy, Cody!" She raised an arm in greeting, and Jean watched as Cody cut across the lawn toward them. "Taking a break from double trouble?"

"Ananya wanted to pop back to the dorms." Cody sank down between Cat and Jean and jerked their chin toward the museum. "You been yet? Saw the flyers announcing it finally opened."

"Soon, I hope," Cat said, enthused.

Cody glanced over at Jeremy, and Jean didn't miss the way their expression went cool as they saw what Jeremy was doing. It was more disapproval than Jean had seen from Cat or Laila, but even Cody didn't see fit to comment. Their willingness to let Jeremy entertain other career paths was annoying enough Jean had to reach out and flip the book shut. He whacked Jeremy in the face in the process, since Jeremy couldn't pull away in time, and answered Jeremy's bewildered look with a cool stare.

"Stop wasting your time," he said.

"I don't have a whole lot left," Jeremy said as he pushed himself up.

Despite the protest, he made no move to get back to his studying. Jean would take it as a victory if Jeremy's phone wasn't the greater distraction. They'd put it back together Saturday night, and it had spent most of the evening going off with one alert or another. Jean made a quiet note to silence it the next time Jeremy left it unattended. This quiet trill was the one Jean had heard on Friday. Jeremy checked his message and glanced across the street toward the football stadium.

When Cat nudged him with her foot, Jeremy only said, "Bishop."

"Oh, football's finally back?" Cody asked. "Slackers."

"You shouldn't associate with other teams," Jean said.

"We're all Trojans," was Jeremy's easy response. "We all represent the same school. For the most part they're good people. I think you'd like some of them if you gave them a chance."

"No," Jean said, and Jeremy only smiled like he found Jean's attitude endearing.

"He's a bit scarce on options here, isn't he?" Cat asked. "Meeting the floozies first might've skewed your perspective a bit, but truth is we're still outnumbered four to one on the team. Not a lot of boy kissers, for obvious reasons." She made a noise in her throat like she found the idea repulsive and laughed when Cody gave her a playful push. "Like you'd know, chickenshit. Or did you finally grow a spine?"

Unsurprisingly, Cody ignored the question. "Jeremy's been the token gay on the team for two years. Endangered species around here."

"Last one was Julian, and he was an asshole," Cat said, souring immediately. "He was so cruel to Xavier, and for what? I was so glad Coach transferred him out of here." She yanked up a few strands of grass and twisted them into knots between her fingers.

Laila gauged her dark mood in a glance and finished for her. "Most of our teammates accept us as we are because they like us too much to judge. A few are still working on it, as you've likely noticed," she said, and he assumed she meant Lucas and his rude mouth. "But being friends with us doesn't mean they're willing to be propositioned, so…" She gestured toward the football stadium. "Cast a wider net."

"Preference is a weak excuse," Jean said.

Most of the Ravens had identified as straight, but with so few women on the line and the team so isolated from everyone else, they'd made do with any man willing to tumble. Aside from Riko and Kevin, Jean knew only two other Ravens who'd refused to cross that line at the Nest. One, technically, since the other had that choice ripped away from him in January. Jean dug his nails into his bandaged wrist until the sting quieted his thoughts.

Cody sent him a curious glance before asking Jeremy, "Meeting up today?"

"Probably not the best day," Jeremy said. "With everything that's happening, I mean."

"Excellent day," Cody insisted, and pointed from him to Cat. "You go meet up with Bishop, and you take Laila to the museum. Leave Jean with us! Have you given him a tour of campus yet?"

"I showed him the highlights," Jeremy said.

"Before he had his schedule?" Cody asked. When Jeremy nodded, they motioned to Jean. "Then we'll take you on a proper tour and show you where your buildings are. Put a little order to the chaos and give you a better idea of what to expect. We'll even feed you something you don't have to cook."

"Oh, good luck," Laila said dryly, even as Cat said, "He's going to be a master chef one day, just you watch."

"I will never understand you," Cody said, with only fondness in their voice.

"Cody can't make anything more complicated than grits," Cat told Jean before jabbing an accusatory finger at Cody. "They're almost as useless as Jeremy is in the kitchen. Jeremy's got a private chef. What's your excuse?"

"Laziness," Cody admitted without hesitation or shame.

"Living off cereal and takeout is why you're so short," Cat decided.

Cody leaned toward Jean. "Don't listen to her. Mom is four-ten."

Jean stared. "You're lying."

"No, look, I got a picture of her here." Cody rocked to one side to dig their wallet out. The plastic flap that should have held their ID instead had a picture of Cody and Mrs. Winter. Jean wasn't sure what was more appalling: the thick neon green hair Cody sported in the photograph or how abysmally short their mother was. That Cody had gotten to five-five was a miracle of nature, even if it made them the third shortest on the team after Min Cai and Emma.

Jean cast a sidelong look at Cody's current hair, which was now buzzcut and fire engine red. "Do you even remember what color your hair is supposed to be?"

"Oh, blond," Cody said, and grinned over at Jeremy. "*Naturally* blond."

"Explains a lot, honestly," Cat said. Her watch beeped a warning, and she packed her dirty dishes into the lunchbox with a melodramatic sigh. "Lunch gets faster and faster every day, I swear. We ready?"

They headed back to the stadium as a straggling group. Cat and Cody went a mile a minute about an upcoming event, but Jean stopped listening when he realized they were talking about one of their online games. Jeremy was drumming an uneven beat on the back of his guidebook with his blunt fingernails. Halfway back to the stadium he thought to look over at Jean and ask,

"Are you up for it? Going with Cody, I mean."

"It is a more practical use of my time than a museum."

Cat interrupted herself to offer an indignant, "I heard that!"

"Jeremy is also terrible company," Laila said. "The last time we tried to bring him anywhere cultured he disappeared on us almost immediately. Said he was going to the bathroom and ended up dozing in the café near the gift shop. It took us almost an hour to realize he hadn't come back."

Jeremy answered her accusatory look with a toothy smile. "If you didn't even miss me, no harm no foul."

They were among the first back, and Coach Jimenez was lying in wait for them. He motioned Jean over and sent him along to the nurses' corridor for a quick check-up. Jeffrey Davis was on duty today, and Coach Rhemann was waiting with him. Jean tolerated Davis's poking and prodding in silence, hoping his pliant behavior would win Rhemann's favor. Rather than give a verdict, Davis just motioned and left the room. Jean looked from the closed door to the whistle hanging from Rhemann's neck.

"Your teammates are of the unanimous opinion we should put you in for drills today," Rhemann said. "Davis seems to think you're up for it physically, but I want to know where your head is." He folded his arms across his chest and rolled his stool closer to Jean. It was an attempt to catch his eye, but Jean skirted it easily. "Thompson was careless enough to admit he thought the violence would do you good, but I don't want you out there if you're going to hurt yourself or them."

"Yes, Coach."

"Can you play today as a Trojan?"

"Yes, Coach."

"You're allowed to think about it," Rhemann said wryly. "I would trust you more if you did."

"Yes, Coach."

Rhemann studied him. The longer they sat, the more certain Jean was he'd done something wrong. Or was Rhemann waiting for him to answer again? Jean weighed the potential consequences of speaking out of turn and decided silence was the better course of action. In the end Rhemann cracked first.

68

"When is your first session with Dr... Dobson?" he finished, a little uncertainly.

"First week of August, Coach," Jean said.

"And there it is," was the weary response. "Last Thursday you sat in this exact spot and said you were going to call her. As soon as you got home, you said." He waited a beat, but Jean sat silent and frozen. "There is only so much we can do for you here. I want to know you're getting the help you need."

Jean clawed for the only thing that might save him: "I had an unexpected guest, Coach."

Rhemann's face was inscrutable. "Neil Josten. Is he getting you into trouble?"

That malfunctioning cretin existed to cause trouble for everyone in a thousand-mile radius, but Jean only said, "No, Coach." When it was obvious that wasn't a reassuring enough answer, he added, "I had asked him to look into something for me, so he was sharing the results." An easy enough lie, since it was the foundation of what they'd told the FBI. Neil had told Browning he was in Los Angeles to hear what Stuart Hatford had found out about—

The hot weight of fingers around his wrist snatched him back from dangerous thoughts, and Jean was almost startled into looking Rhemann in the face. He hesitated when he realized he'd dug half-moon marks into the back of his hand. Slowly he relaxed his grip, and Rhemann released him shortly thereafter.

"And you think you're steady enough to be on the court," Rhemann said.

It wasn't quite a question, but Jean knew he was two seconds from being relegated to the bleachers all afternoon if he didn't work his way back into Rhemann's good graces. "This won't impact my performance, Coach," Jean said, lifting one hand to his temple. "I am perfect Court; I can always play. I will not fail you. Please let me prove it."

"Has it occurred to you that there is no perfect Court anymore?" Rhemann asked. "It was Moriyama's obsessive daydream, and he is unfortunately no longer with us. Day rejected his place in it, and Josten only had his number for a few months. You're the last man standing. I'm not questioning your skill or dedication," he added, putting a hand up like he honestly expected Jean to argue, "but you've got to start looking beyond that narrow dream. If there's no perfect Court, there's just you, and you have to take care of you. You've got to learn how sooner rather than later. Do you understand?"

"Yes, Coach."

"Look at me when you say it."

Jean dragged his stare up and knew immediately from the look on Rhemann's face that "Yes" was not the right answer. He amended it to an "I'm trying, Coach," and that was enough to take some of the stiffness out of Rhemann's expression.

"Here's the deal," Rhemann said, and waited to make sure Jean was listening. "I'm going to let you participate in drills and scrimmages this afternoon on the condition you pull yourself should anything start acting up. On top of that," he said before Jean could respond, "I want you to call Dr. Dobson and see if she can speak with you once a week until your regular schedule starts in August. I will follow up with you tomorrow to see what her response is."

Jean could see no quick way out of it. "Yes, Coach."

"All right." Rhemann rolled his chair out of Jean's space and said, "Go suit up."

Jean went for his locker like he thought Rhemann would change his mind. As soon as he lifted his helmet off its hook, Cody made a loud yipping sound. It was picked up by the rest of the defensemen in increasing volume, and Jean sent a nonplussed look at Cat when she joined in. She just grinned and knocked her helmet to his in

70

encouragement. Jean wrote the line off as a half-mad loss and focused on getting changed.

Jimenez and White took turns putting the Trojans through their paces: suicide runs, cone drills, and a half-dozen other exercises that put a good ache in their thighs and a steady prickle of sweat down their backs. After a week it was easier to remember where the Trojans tweaked theirs from standard—or where the Ravens had, Jean wasn't sure—and Jean was content to throw himself into everything the coaches put in front of him. Thinking about Exy was easy, and it was loud enough and big enough to drown out all the rest.

The first partner drill of the day was a basic one: a simple push and shove to practice getting past each other. All last week Jean had been working with Jeremy, but today Derrick came jogging over with a wild smile.

"Okay, okay, let's see it," he said. "Show me why my stance is bad."

"You should already know," Jean said as Derrick settled in front of him.

White hadn't blown his whistle yet, but Derrick was already moving, bobbing almost imperceptibly. It sent him rocking on his feet, a subtle heel to toe and side to side that Jean assumed made it easy for him to change direction on a whim. Besides being irritating, its fatal flaw was how predictable it was. Like Derrick had said earlier: he was bobbing to music only he could hear. He was slave to a beat, and Jean could count it out with little effort. As soon as White blew the whistle, Jean put his foot forward. He caught the underside of Derrick's foot right as he was shifting, and Derrick teetered off-balance immediately.

"Danger, Will Robinson," Derrick yelped as he stumbled.

There was no such person on the team, so Jean waited in silence for him to take his place again. Derrick almost immediately settled back into his rhythm, and Jean idly counted it as he waited for the whistle. The timing this second time let Derrick get a step on him, but Jean didn't try to follow; he didn't have to. He simply darted his foot out to the side and got his toes right into Derrick's arch again.

"Technically speaking, tripping isn't the Trojan way," Derrick said as he went back to the starting position. He was smiling, though, like this was the funniest thing he'd dealt with all day. "So this is smart and all but if you go around kicking our opponents Coach is gonna pull you off the line."

"This team's sole redeeming quality is its talent," Jean said, annoyed. "The thrill you take at being pushed around is nonsensical."

"When you figure it out, you'll understand."

"Speaking nonsense for the sake of hearing your own voice," Jean accused him.

Derrick gave an explosive huff and rolled his eyes, then launched into motion at the sound of White's whistle. Despite Derrick's warning, Jean was feeling meanspirited enough to kick his arch a third time in a row. The look Derrick sent him in response was almost pitying.

"Like, here's the thing, yeah?" Derrick said. "The Ravens are very good, no one's denying that. Insanely talented, wicked fast, just—" He made a whooshing noise that Jean assumed was supposed to convey his level of respect and envy. "But there's just so much hatred in their playstyle. If someone told them to win a match without getting a single card, they couldn't do it."

"Penalties and cards are part of the game," Jean said. "There is no benefit to treating them as if they're taboo."

"See, that's where you get lost." Derrick pointed his stick at Jean. "We're not out here like oooh, fighting's so childish, we could never stoop so low, oooh. It's like…" This time Jean's kick was hard enough he nearly fell, but Derrick only grimaced and settled back into place. "It's

72

not about being superior, it's about being better. Does that make sense?"

"No."

"The only way you can stop me is by kicking me and hurting me," Derrick said. "And maybe you'll always win in our matchups. But if it's dirty tricks and not talent you're falling back on, I'm still the better player in the end. Right? That's the thrill for us: finding a way to come out on top without resorting to violence and cheap shots. We don't need to hurt our opponents. We're faster and slicker and we move better on the court. When's the last time we lost more than one fall game?"

"I haven't studied your team's history that closely."

"Ah, no big, I don't know the answer either."

This time Derrick added an unexpected side-to-side weave where his beat should have been, and he shouldered past Jean with ease. He dropped to his knees and put his arms to the air as if celebrating a game-winning goal, head tipped back so he could howl victory at the court ceiling. Jean watched him for only a moment before planting a shoe to one shoulder and pushing him over.

"Take all the fun out of it, why don't you!" Derrick griped as he got to his feet.

"Exy is not supposed to be fun," Jean said.

Derrick stopped to stare at him. "The hell?" he managed after a minute. "Of course it is. Hey no," he said, catching at Jean's racquet when Jean started to turn away. "You're like—you're *Jean Moreau*. Perfect freaking Court. What do you mean it's not fun? You play like you do and what, it's all just a bothersome chore? I don't know if I should be impressed or terrified that we're so far beneath your notice."

"You are not," Jean said, because as frustrating as this team was Jean couldn't lie about their abilities. "The only reason I agreed to transfer here is because your team is good enough to be worth my time."

"But it has to be fun," Derrick said, clinging to the least important statement like a barnacle.

"Why?" Jean demanded. "Will you refuse to play if it is not?"

Derrick scrunched his face up as he thought. Across the court White blew the whistle to signal the end of this set of drills. Jean started to turn away, but Derrick refused to relinquish his stick. He followed when Jean tugged and finally offered up a response:

"Yeah, I would. I'm not saying every day is sunshine and kittens, but Exy's gotta be fun. When it stops being that and starts just being a tiresome thing I'm forced to do, then it's time for me to walk away.

"I mean, right now I don't have a choice," Derrick conceded. "On account of my scholarship and whatnot. But after I graduated? If I hadn't come back around to enjoying it again, I'd drop it like a hotcake and find something new to chase. Life's too short to be miserable all the time. You really going to stop playing when you leave here, then?"

That violent twist in Jean's chest might have been grief; it was just as likely to be acidic resentment. "I will never stop playing," he said, and wouldn't dwell on the *I can't* that echoed like a second heartbeat against his thoughts. "This is all I am."

"You said that at introductions last week," Derrick recalled as he finally let go of Jean's racquet. He studied Jean, expression uncharacteristically serious, and finally asked, "I thought it was just some cool catchphrase, but you really mean it, don't you?"

There was no point repeating himself, so Jean simply left. He caught up with Cat halfway to the starting point for their next drill, and she knocked her stick to his in greeting. Despite her smile, her eyes were intent as she studied his face.

"Looking kinda grim," she said. "Moreso than usual. Holding up all right?"

Dwelling on Derrick's hypothetical future was a waste of time, so Jean put his energy toward the more offensive part of their conversation: the assumption that Derrick was the better player. The Trojans were a phenomenal team and had been for almost the entirety of their existence, but Derrick couldn't hold a candle to Riko or Kevin. He wasn't even good enough to think himself Jeremy's equal. That he would declare himself more talented than Jean was repugnant enough to put Jean on edge. If they were at Evermore, Jean would put Derrick in the nurses' care for such arrogance. Here that wasn't an option.

"I'm going to destroy him," he said.

"Hyperbolically speaking, I hope," Cat said.

Jean only shrugged and left it to her to decide.

CHAPTER FIVE
Jean

For better or worse, Jean was not put against Derrick
again that day. Instead he rotated through Ananya, Nabil,
and Jeremy at scrimmages. That was satisfying enough to
push Derrick from mind for now, as Ananya and Jeremy
were the starting strikers for the Trojans' second-half lineup and Nabil was their dedicated sub. This was the talent
he deserved to square off against, even if Ananya was
selling herself short by using a light racquet.

Mindful that one bad foul would have him sidelined,
Jean wasted far too much energy keeping himself in check
that afternoon. Ignoring the nonstop openings his
opponents left him was insulting and did them no favors
in the long run, but Jean settled for simply ripping their
sticks out of their hands for now. As boring as it was, it
bought him time to analyze them. He studied how they
stood and tracked how they moved, how often they went
left or right from a standstill and how many steps they
took before passing the ball. These three had an obvious
synchrony from playing together for years, and there was
plenty of valuable insight to be gleaned from watching the
way they worked together.

Toward the end of the day Jean had finally seen
enough to start digging in. He waited until the teams were
resetting before pointing an accusatory finger at Nabil.
"You take too long to set up your shots." As far as Jean
could see, it was the only real reason Nabil was second-
string to Ananya. He had exceptional awareness of what
was happening on the court and could turn on a dime, but
he was so conscious of potential interference down the
line he didn't take enough risks. All players were slow

76

compared to the Ravens' style, but this was too extreme to tolerate. "Stop overthinking it."

"Thank you for the advice," Nabil said, "but I'd rather ensure a completed pass than risk interception."

"It is not just your burden," Jean said, and hooked his stick behind Nabil's to hold him in place. "Trade to the other team. When you want to score, simply call for the ball, and I will give it to you."

Nabil considered him a few moments, then nodded and tugged his racquet loose. He jogged to the half-court but flagged Derek down on the way. Jean watched the two exchange words before switching spots on the line. More than one Trojan half-turned to send a considering look Jean's way, but Jean turned his back on all of them as he went to his own designated spot.

He stretched as he walked, pushing until he felt a faint ache in his shoulders and elbows, and flexed his fingers as he slowed to a stop. It'd been months since he was on a Raven court, but Jean had spent five—seven—years mastering Raven drills. Muscle memory wouldn't fail him now; it couldn't.

The whistle sounded to start them off, and the teams pushed forward as one. Jean's team had scored last, so Min got them started with a serve up-court. For a respectable amount of time, they managed to keep the ball on that end of the court, and then Cody stole it and shot it down-court to Ananya. Derek and Jean went down the court in time, Derek trying to open an angle for her and Jean dogging him every step of the way. Ananya had to fire off a pass their direction before Cat could take the ball away from her, but the crack of Cat's heavy against Ananya's light had it landing short of where it needed to.

Jean was nearly to it when he heard Nabil call, "Jean!"

He had only a half-second to find Nabil, but a half-second was all he needed. Jean was turning before he even snagged the ball, needing the momentum for such a long

77

shot. The second it hit his net he whipped around and fired it off. It hit the wall with a satisfying thud: the perfect speed, the perfect angle. It went straight toward where Nabil and Pat were squaring off, and Nabil only had to get there first.

If Nabil was a Raven, that would have been enough. He would have trusted it to reach him and already calculated the force he needed on his own shot toward the goal. Nabil caught it, but he wasn't ready to throw it. He ran with it instead, and Jean swore viciously in French as Nabil wasted the flawless setup.

"Good lord," Derek said, scratching the side of his helmet with his racquet. "It always startles me when you guys do that."

"It would startle me more if you could actually follow through," Jean said, annoyed.

"He caught it," Derek protested, and then the flow of the game forced an abrupt end to the conversation.

It was another minute more before Nabil tried again. Derek heard the call as well, and this time he knew what was coming, but he still wasn't fast enough. Jean looked from himself to Nabil, and Nabil to the goal, and let the ball fly with everything he had. A second time in a row Nabil squandered it, and Jean had had enough of that. He cast his racquet aside and started that way, but Derek grabbed his elbow to haul him to a stop.

"Easy now," he tried. "Talk it through with me before you try and tear his head off. What's he doing wrong?"

"Tell me why he is refusing to take a shot," Jean demanded. "He calls for a pass from me, so I give him exactly what he needs to score. He shouldn't call for it if he can't handle it."

"He's being chased by Pat," Derek pointed out.

"Irrelevant," Jean insisted. "There shouldn't be a chase. All he needs to do is shoot."

Derek frowned, thinking that through. Across the court

Cat hollered a warning when she realized too late the two were distracted from the scrimmage. Derek turned, but Jean was already reaching out to snatch the ball from midair. He felt the impact knife down his forearm; all of the protection on Exy gloves was along the backs of a player's fingers and hands to guard against overeager stick checks. Jean pushed the ball into the shallow net on Derek's racquet so he could give his hand a vicious shake.

"Trade back with him," Jean said. "Call for it when you are ready. I will give it to you exactly how you need it. Don't carry. Don't think. Just throw."

"Just shout your name?" Derek asked, skeptical.

"I don't care what you say," Jean said.

A grievous mistake in hindsight, because a few minutes later Derek yelled "Oui señor!" at full volume.

Across the court Cat called a scandalized, "Hello?!"

Jean would unstring his racquet later, but for now all that mattered was the game. It took three steps to get past Nabil, two more to catch up to the ball, and Jean let it fly. Pat knew by now what it meant when his marked partner called out to Jean, but knowing would only save him if he was faster. This time he was. Derek caught the ball and immediately went to throw it, but Pat got his stick up under it to ruin the shot. Not an ideal outcome, but an acceptable one: at least Derek had tried to do as he was told.

In the last minute of scrimmage Derek tried again: "Oui oui!"

From here there was no good angle, but Jean had been called on and he had to make it work. He ricocheted it off the back wall, opening up the space he needed, and was ready on the rebound. He put everything he had into the pass. It hit the side wall, cracked against the far court wall over Shane's head, and went back to Derek. This time he was just fast enough to outrun Pat, but he hesitated for a critical second after he caught it. Fighting his instincts, perhaps, but all that mattered was that Derek snapped it at the goal before Pat reached him.

He didn't have the right motor control to pull it off; his entire career he'd had to put too much thought into his passes and shots. He couldn't score here, especially not against a Trojan goalkeeper, but it was enough that he tried.

Jean looked at Nabil as the coaches called an end to practice. "Do you understand?"

"No," Nabil admitted. "I don't think I like that. It's impressive, sure, but it seems very... sterile," he said after a moment's thought. "That's the kind of trick I can imagine falling back on in a panic, but I wouldn't want to play my entire game like that."

"You would win," Jean insisted.

"Yes, but would I enjoy it?"

"Presumably more than you would enjoy a loss, if you actually cared."

Nabil turned a look of calm rebuke on him. "I do care," he said, quiet but firm. "That's why I want to play it my way. If I have to be a Raven or a robot to take first place, then what is the point?"

It didn't make sense, but Jean was done arguing with these brick walls. He pushed Nabil aside to start for the court door, and Nabil didn't try to call him back.

Jean made it two steps off the court before Jimenez flagged him down and redirected him to the nurses' ward. Jean peeled out of his gloves so Davis could give his wrist a cursory check. Jean was beyond tired of these questions and this prodding; he'd said on Friday he was fine, and his answers hadn't changed. Their obsession with his injuries was grating, as it only drove home how readily they would take him off the court. But Jean couldn't argue with a nurse, especially with Coach Jimenez watching from the doorway.

At last Davis sat back. "Everything seems to be

healing well. He's all yours," Davis said over his shoulder. "Until you bang him up again, anyway."

Jimenez lifted his fingers from one bicep to motion Jean out of the room. "You're free to go, then. Good work today. Form looked good."

"Thank you, Coach."

The delay meant he was the last to the showers by several minutes. Unsurprisingly, Jeremy was still standing under the spray as he chatted with Sebastian and Preston. Jean wouldn't let his gaze linger, but he saw enough to put a hungry knot in his gut.

Luckily Xavier served as an easy distraction to find his footing. All last week Jean had been in and out before Xavier ever showed up, but today Jean had been delayed long enough for the vice-captain to beat him here. Jean might not have given him more than a passing thought, but Xavier was showering with black shorts on. Jean considered asking, decided he didn't care enough to endure a conversation, and found a showerhead as far away from the others as he could manage.

It bought him only thirty seconds of peace before Tanner appeared at his side. The freshman backliner was scrubbing furiously at his hair as he stared owl-eyed up at Jean. He didn't wait for Jean to acknowledge his uninvited presence before asking, "How did you learn to pass like that?"

"The obvious answer would be drills," Jean said.

"Well, yeah," Tanner allowed, "but I mean, I've been playing almost nine years now and I can't throw like that. What kind of drills are we talking about? Is there a book? A video? Can it be taught?"

Jean thought about Evermore's eight precision drills that took Raven freshmen anywhere from weeks to months to master. Perfecting them was the only way to earn game time at Edgar Allan, and the consequences for failing were brutal.

81

For a moment Jean was looking through Tanner at Ryan, a freshman who'd started alongside Jean. He'd had so much promise, but he never could get past the fifth drill. No amount of hazing from his teammates or beatings from the coaches could unlock what he needed. One day the master finally hit him a few too many times. The official cause of death was a hit and run, an unfortunate accident suffered when making laps around campus between classes. His partner had obediently confirmed the story to anyone who asked.

"Ummm... Is that a no?" Tanner asked.

Jean forcibly focused on the upturned face in front of him as he cranked the water off. "It can be taught. Whether it can be learned is another story."

"I can learn," Tanner was quick to say, but Jean was already turning away. "I promise!"

"Perhaps," Jean said noncommittally as he headed for the door.

"You really do shower like you're allergic to water," Xavier commented as Jean drew even with him again. "I'd heard you were insanely fast, but I thought it was an exaggeration."

"Military shower." That confident declaration was from Preston. "My sister's quick like that whenever she comes home."

"Oh, wow," Tanner said. "I didn't know you served."

Jean slowly turned to stare at him, sure he'd misheard. But Tanner looked genuinely interested, and Preston gave no sign he was aware of his idiocy. The least Jeremy could do was look ashamed by the braindead fools he was captaining, but his too-wide smile said he was seconds from bursting into helpless laughter. Jean scowled at him, and Jeremy only tipped his head into the spray to send water streaming down his face and throat.

The lashing they deserved would have to wait; Jean needed to get out of here. He settled for a sour, "A team of all talent and no intelligence," as he stepped through the doorway.

"Rude," Preston protested as Jean let the door slam behind him.

A half-dozen backliners were at the lockers when Jean arrived, in varying stages of undress. Cody's baggy t-shirt was sticking to them in places where they'd been careless drying off, and they only added to the mess when they tugged the hem up to swipe along their hairline. They smiled at Jean as he started unloading his clothes from his locker and snatched up a piece of paper to show off.

"Coach Rhemann was able to print off your schedule," they said. "Just let us know when you're ready to head out."

Jean wasted no time getting scrubbed dry and dressed, but Tanner still managed to catch up with him before he could leave. The backliner had remembered a towel but hadn't slowed to dry, and he left puddles on the floor where he planted himself in Jean's path. He lifted his chin in defiance and insisted, "I can learn. Just give me a chance."

His persistence was promising, but Jean motioned for him to step aside. "It would require additional court time. I don't have the authority to grant that."

Tanner didn't budge. "Coach Jimenez could. I'll ask him." That he thought it at all appropriate to bypass both his captain and vice-captain to directly ask a coach for a favor was borderline repulsive. Jean felt every muscle in his back tense at such a presumptuous statement. The look Cody sent him said his expression gave him away, but Tanner was too invested in his argument to notice how many lines he was crossing. "If he says yes, then it's a yes from you, right? That's your only hangup?"

Cody propped their elbow against Tanner's shoulder and asked, "What are you trying to bully out of him this late in the day?"

"I want him to teach me drills."

"Raven drills," Jean elaborated when Cody quirked a brow at him.

"Yeah, Raven drills," Tanner enthused. "I want to learn to pass like he does."

"Well, maybe get dressed before you break down Coach's door," Cody suggested as they lifted their arm. "But we've got plans tonight, so I'm stealing Jean. If you find time to ask before you leave today, just message me his response and I'll let Jean know. You do have my number, right?"

"Got it," Tanner promised, and bolted for his locker on the far end of the row.

Cody caught Jean's gaze, but Jean didn't need encouragement to follow. They reached the strikers' bench about the same time Ananya did. A touch of her hand was enough to draw Pat from his conversation with Derek and Derrick, and the four headed for the door with a chorus of goodbyes following them out.

Pat held the gate open for them and slipped his hand into Ananya's as soon as they were free. The other hand was offered to Cody. Cody didn't see it, or was good at pretending they didn't, and busied themselves with inspecting Jean's schedule. Pat huffed, equal parts exasperation and fondness, and set forth toward campus. Cody hung back a step, but Jean didn't miss the way they glanced after Pat and Ananya as soon as they thought it was safe to do so.

Cody noticed that he noticed and cleared their throat. "Okay, look," they said, turning Jean's sheet toward him as the pair followed Pat and Ananya. "You've got an easy schedule here: four of your classes are all in the same building, and the last isn't that far away. Good thing, since you've only got this ten-minute gap on either side of it. Only one class on Fridays, too. That's nice, it'll make it easier with our away games."

They'd just reached Lyon when Cody heard from Tanner. "Rhemann and Jimenez want you at the stadium tomorrow morning," they told Jean. "We'll be in the pool without you, so it's good timing. Sounds like they want to see these mysterious drills before they sign off on them."

Jean nodded understanding, so Cody tapped out a quick response and passed Jean's schedule over. "Okay, every morning this fall we'll meet here from six to seven-thirty. Let's start with the odd days: Monday, Wednesday, Friday. Where are you heading from here?"

And so they went: first from the fitness center to Hoffman Hall where he'd be taking business writing with Shane, then over to Watt where he and Jeremy had wheel throwing. Afterward it was right back to the first building, and Cody smiled triumph as they came to a stop in front of it. Jean considered it and was satisfied: it was an austere building of pale stone, tall enough to stand out from the rest and be an easy landmark.

"Tuesdays and Thursdays, you come here and stay here for your last two classes," Cody said. "How boring."

Ananya lifted her free hand to point past Hoffman. "That's the edge of campus," she said, glancing over at Jean to make sure he was paying attention. "You'll have easy access to the park and stadium, but you'll have to go down a bit to find a crosswalk. Not like it should matter too much. I think I remember you having an open period after your last class."

"Hour and ten across the board," Cody confirmed, leaning over to check Jean's schedule. Four days of the week Jean's classes would end at one-fifty, and the Trojans' afternoon practice ran from three until eight. Cody pointed to the statistics class Jean had scheduled after ceramics on Mondays and Wednesdays and said, "I'm in this one with you, so I'll make sure we find something to eat afterward. Coaches will give us snacks at break but waiting until eight-thirty or nine for a real dinner is miserable."

"I like late dinners," Pat said, almost apologetic.

"Weirdo," Cody grumbled. "But speaking of dinner, how about we eat before I die?"

"Do you like malai kofta?" Ananya asked. Jean wasn't sure if that was a place or food, but Ananya only nodded when he frowned confusion at her. "Then that's what we'll have. You'll like it, I'm sure of it."

"Maybe." Cody eyed Jean. "Laila implied you were a picky eater."

"Mindful," Jean corrected, a touch frostily.

"If you say so," Cody said.

"As if Laila can comment on anyone else's eating habits when she drinks that—what is that stuff called?" Pat looked from Cody to Ananya for help. "That weird tea with the chewy balls in it."

"It's not that bad," Ananya protested, as Cody said, "It's absolutely foul."

"Horrendous," Jean agreed, and Ananya sighed defeat.

They set off for the north end of campus. There was a crosswalk nearby, but at this time of day the neighboring traffic lights created just enough gap they could safely jog across Jefferson without it. The restaurant Ananya was aiming for wasn't much further. Only two tables were taken, but Ananya appeared pleased to find the place so dead.

"Summer really is better here," she said. "Soon as the school year starts it's going to be a madhouse."

There were tables down the center and booths along the wall. Ananya requested the latter and put a gentle hand to Pat's back. Jean noted the look they exchanged and assumed it was the reason Cody reached the booth first. Pat slid in beside them, and Ananya offered Jean a beatific smile as she took the spot across from Cody. Jean didn't care who he sat next to, but he glanced toward Cody anyway. Cody appeared relaxed as they tugged napkins off the stand, so Jean sat without argument.

"Our treat, for indulging our company," Ananya said. "Any allergies? No? We'll get a bit of everything, then."

Jean assumed she was exaggerating, but when the server came by to hand out glasses of water Ananya had a list of dishes to rattle off from memory. Jean understood very little of it, as only one or two names were in English, but Cody's and Pat's happy reactions to a few of the options said they were able to follow along. Jean wasn't reassured, but it was too early to be concerned.

The three flitted from one topic to another in quick, light-hearted conversation. They left space for him to join in, slipping in a question here and there when he'd been silent for too long, but Jean was content to stay out of it wherever possible.

Peace lasted until the first dishes arrived, and the sight of fried dough had Jean leaning back in his seat. The others were quick to snatch them up. Ananya broke hers open to show him the inside, as if somehow the peas and potato filling would make up for the disastrous outside.

"It's fried," he said.

"It's delicious," Cody said as they dug in. "If you don't want yours, can I have it?"

"Throw it away."

"Absolutely not."

They were interrupted by the arrival of more plates, and Jean watched with growing disapproval as unfamiliar dishes were laid out before him. There were chunks in bowls of sauce and cream, plates piled with rice and meat, and a small pile of bread slathered with an off-color spread. The smell of warm yeast and heavy spices settled over the table, and through it was the savory scents of meat and cheese.

Ananya rearranged the dishes with the ease of long practice, offering up names and spice levels as she put a new order to the madness. It wasn't until she was done that Jean realized she'd separated the chicken and lamb dishes from the vegetarian ones. Even the latter were unsettling: what vegetables Jean could see were half-buried in gravies and dark broths. Jean didn't know what to do with any of this, and he wasn't sure he could trust her to walk him through it after she'd started off with a fried pastry.

"What do you want to start with?" Ananya asked him.

"Nothing," Jean said. "None of this looks appropriate."

"Appropriate," Ananya echoed, offended. "In what way?"

Jean considered the simplest way to break it down and settled on Cat's interpretation. "Macronutrients," he said, and scowled as it came out more French than English. He tried again, sounding it out with painstaking care, and the blank look on Ananya's face faded into understanding. "Raven meals are provided by the staff to ensure we—they—receive exactly what is needed to excel at practice. Cat is teaching me to make meals that match these numbers. I can't account for this if I don't know what it is."

"You're thinking too much about it," Pat said. "It's just one meal."

"Your disrespect for nutrition is nothing to be proud of," Jean warned him.

"Give us some examples," Cody suggested as they set their bread aside. Jean obediently counted off breakfast, lunch, and dinner on his fingers. A mistake, perhaps: his teammates were left staring at him like he'd grown a second head. Cody was the first to find their voice. "Not every single day. Jean," they pressed when Jean only frowned at them, "tell me you had some variety."

Jean thought about it. "Sometimes they brought us fruit."

"Right," Ananya said, dragging it out. "Ummm. Okay.

88

Let me think." The pensive look on her face as she considered the spread before them did nothing to inspire confidence, but at length she said, "The biryani?" and Cody passed her a dish from the far corner. Ananya set it down near Jean's glass. "I confess I don't normally think about food in such strict terms, but this should be a close enough match."

Should be wasn't good enough. Jean made no move to serve any. "What is it?"

"Chicken biryani," she said.

He stared at her until she counted off ingredients on her fingertips. Everything she listed was known to him, save for the basmati rice, and Jean peered down at the dish. On a surface level, it sounded safe and acceptable, but without Cat's easy expertise to rely on Jean was floundering. There was the chance he was adding it up wrong, or that Ananya had carelessly left off an ingredient. Jean couldn't risk it. He moved the biryani out of reach.

"No," Ananya guessed, with obvious disappointment.

"It's just chicken and rice," Cody protested. "I've seen you eat that for lunch."

"I will eat later," Jean said. When Cody looked ready to argue, he added, "I am not hungry."

"Not to be rude, but I don't believe you," Pat said.

"What you believe is not my problem."

"Jean," Pat said, and tried, "Moreau," when Jean initially refused to look at him.

Jean turned a baleful stare on him, but Pat ignored the clear warning in it. His jaw had a stubborn set to it as he studied Jean's face. Jean wasn't sure what he was looking for, but he didn't have to wait long. Pat reached out and dumped a pile of deep-fried vegetables on Jean's plate. Jean shoved it away from him before anyone could think he intended to eat it, and Pat slammed the tongs down with a deafening clatter.

Ananya put out a hand toward Pat in warning. "Darling, we're in public."

Pat didn't look at her, but he was at least smart enough to keep his voice down. "That's not conscientiousness, Jean—that's fear. You're afraid to eat." There was more dismay than anger in his accusation, but Jean still felt his hackles rising. "What the fuck was Edgar Allan thinking? That's not normal or okay."

"You do not get to tell me what's normal," Jean shot back, savage enough that Ananya leaned away from him. "You don't know anything about me."

"No, but—"

Jean didn't want to hear it. He got off the bench and yanked out of Ananya's grip when she caught hold of him. "Phone," he said, and left without looking back.

He pushed the door open so hard its hinges made a threatening crack, and he retreated to the street corner to watch oncoming traffic. Home wasn't far from here, he knew: from this vantage point he could see the intersection at Jefferson and Vermont that he crossed everyday for practice. A short walk, a couple turns, and he'd be safe in familiar territory. It was almost cruel how close it was.

He hoped the creaking door behind him was from a different shop, but Cody stepped up beside him only moments later. They followed Jean's gaze and asked, "Heading home?"

"I can't," Jean said, and for once it galled him to admit it: "Ravens can't travel alone."

I am not a Raven was a jagged echo in his temples. Jean wanted to claw it out.

"I'll walk you home after dinner," Cody offered. "Come back in?"

"I need to make a call first," Jean said. "I promised Coach Rhemann"

Cody nodded and stepped back. "See you after, then."

90

Jean watched for the door to close behind them before looking down at the phone in his white-knuckled grip. The thought of dialing out set every nerve on edge, but Jean slowly scrolled to the number he'd saved under the name IGNORE. He tapped on the call button too lightly to trigger it, wondering if it would be easier to get away with a text, and finally pressed down. Perhaps she would be asleep, and he could at least tell Rhemann he'd tried.

"Hello, Jean," Betsy Dobson's voice said at his ear only one ring later. "I had hoped I would hear from you this week."

She'd seen the news, then. "My coach ordered me to call you," Jean said, and left the *this is not my choice* unspoken. "I will tell him you are too busy to speak this week. All you need to do is confirm it if he asks."

Jean heard the smile in her voice as she ignored that to ask, "Are you free now, or would sometime tomorrow be better?"

"No time will be better," Jean said. "I have nothing to say to you."

"I can do the talking until we are more comfortable with one another."

Jean hesitated as a stray memory nagged at him. "You said Kevin gave you permission to tell me whatever it is he said to you. Yes?"

"Yes, that's right," Dobson agreed. "If nothing else, I think he wants you to know how much I already know about where you've come from. It potentially creates a safe space for you to work within until you are ready to branch out into new territory."

Jean pressed his fingernails into his lower lip as he thought. At length he grudgingly said, "Later, then. I will listen only."

"Would this time tomorrow work?"

No, Jean thought, but only said "Yes" and hung up.

If she called back, he might chuck his phone into

traffic, but she only texted him a confirmation a few moments later: "Moreau – Dobson, July 3rd 7PM PDT". Jean almost deleted it before deciding he'd need it as evidence for Rhemann. He started to put his phone away, then muttered rudely in French and updated her contact information before Rhemann caught sight of it. With that odious task out of the way, he finally rejoined his teammates inside.

They made a few token attempts to include him in the conversation, but Jean stayed out of it whenever possible. Studying them was more interesting, as they were bound together by an obvious and easy affection. Cody and Pat packed leftovers into plastic containers while Ananya settled the bill, and the four of them filed out of the restaurant in a short line.

"See you in a bit," Cody said.

Ananya wound her arm through Pat's. "Good night, Jean."

She and Pat set off one way while Cody and Jean went the other. Every step Jean put between him and them made it a little easier to breathe. Maybe it was less their absence and more the destination, because when Laila's house finally came into view Jean felt settled. Cody stopped beside him at the base of the stairs and held up a takeout bag in offering.

"The biryani," Cody said, calm in the face of Jean's disapproval. "You said you trust Cat with your meals, so ask her to go over it with you. If you don't like what she has to say about it, feel free to toss it." Cody waited for Jean to take the bag before turning away, but they slowed to a stop and turned back only a few steps later. "If no one's home, is that going to be a problem for you?"

Jean glanced past them to where Jeremy's car was still gone. "I was alone at Palmetto State," he said, and grudgingly added, "Once."

Cody's expression turned serious. "I'll stay, then. I

heard how that ended."

"I don't remember," was out before he knew it was coming, a quiet confession he'd avoided when his friends carefully tried to address that disastrous day. Jean thought about frigid water and shattering glass. He dug the teeth of his key into his thumb and said, "Most of it is a blur even now."

"Maybe that's for the best."

"Maybe," Jean allowed, and unlocked the front door to let them both in.

Cody waited just inside the door while Jean made a lap in search of Cat and Laila. Every room was dark and empty, so Cody toed out of their shoes and locked the door behind them. They ended up in the kitchen so Jean could put his takeout away. Jean was almost hungry to the point of irritation by now, but he settled for tugging the water pitcher off its shelf. Cody nodded when he held it up, so Jean went to collect two glasses next.

"Thanks." Cody settled on a stool and pointed. "What's behind your fridge?"

Jean didn't have to look to know what Cody had spotted. "Their ridiculous cardboard dog. Jeremy keeps moving it into our room."

"Damn." Cody sounded admiring, but they weren't talking about the dog. "Is that how you say it? Jeremy." They sounded it out, trying to match Jean's accent. Jean wondered if he ought to be offended, but Cody saw the look on his face and hurried to say, "No, no, it's so good. Please don't ever change it. Jeremy," they tried again, slightly better this time. "I bet he hit his knees the first time you said it. I would've."

Jean refused to go down that road. "Drink your water."

Cody filled their glass. "Can I ask you something? You can lie if you want."

Jean took one look at their face and said, "You cannot."

93

The smile that tugged at Cody's mouth said Jean's prompt refusal was answer enough, but Cody was good enough to let it go with the subtlest of barbs: "Well, that still leaves us twenty-six other teammates to gossip about. Who should we start with?"

They predictably began with the defense line. Cody named a player, and the two of them compared insights and potential areas for improvement. Cody refused to touch the goalkeepers, laughingly saying they were too afraid to offend any of them. They'd just started on the dealers when Cat and Laila arrived home, and the girls followed the light to the kitchen. Cody skipped a greeting to throw Jean under the bus:

"Finally! Jean was going to starve to death if you took any longer."

Cat rocked to a stop halfway to them. "I thought you went out to eat. What happened?"

"Good luck," Cody offered Jean.

They had the gall to sound sympathetic. Jean glared at them, but Cody only hopped off their stool and gave Laila a quick hug goodbye. Unsurprisingly, Cat followed Cody to the front door to demand a better explanation. Laila remained behind, studying Jean with a serious look. If she wasn't going to say anything, neither was he. Jean focused on drinking his water until Cat came back. She went straight to the fridge, tugged his takeout off its shelf, and set the container in front of him.

"Walk me through it," Cat said.

Jean broke it down for her: the ingredients first, the best guess at numbers after. Some he knew by heart by now: the rice and chicken were easy, if basmati rice was anywhere close to the brown rice Cat preferred. The spices were negligible, and while he couldn't remember how yogurt worked out, he knew she could correct him. He added it up when he was done and waited for her to confirm it.

"You already know you're right," she said. "Why couldn't you trust your work?"

"I could have been wrong."

Cat searched his face. "By what? Five or six carbs? Two grams of fat? That's negligible in the grand scheme of things." When Jean didn't answer, she tore open his plastic sleeve of silverware and lightly bopped his nose with the fork. "Say you forgot to carry a one somewhere and ate too much. Would Cody have dragged you into the street? Would I? It's not a rhetorical question, Jean," she pressed when he didn't answer. "I need to know if you're scared of us."

"Of a team that can't fight?" he asked, offended.

Cat's smile was fleeting but satisfied. Jean knew he'd been had even before she agreed, "Of a team that won't fight. God, that's delicious," she added as she stole a bite of his dinner. She leaned across the table to plant a kiss to his forehead. "You know what you're doing. Trust yourself, okay? Now eat up before you wither away. If you genuinely don't like it, we'll make you something else."

Laila motioned over her shoulder. "Come find us if you need us. My show's about to start, so we'll be in the other room."

Jean pushed his food around its container for a few minutes after they'd left, his thoughts a muddled mess, and finally took a bite. He almost wished he hated it after the stress it had caused them all tonight, but even cold it was good enough to dig into.

He was nearly done when Cody texted him a simple, "Eat?"

"Ate," Jean confirmed. After a moment's debate he added, "It was good."

":)" was all Cody sent in answer, so Jean set his phone aside to finish eating.

CHAPTER SIX
Jeremy

Finding out the Ravens didn't recognize federal holidays was not how Jeremy thought he'd start his morning. He stared Jean down over his mug of coffee, willing the caffeine to hit his system a little faster so he could keep up with Jean's startled anger. Maybe someone should have reminded him that the team wouldn't have practice on Wednesday, but who would have guessed he needed the heads-up? Jean was French, but he'd been in the United States long enough to know about the 4th of July.

"It's a holiday," Jeremy said, for the third time.

"Every year?" Jean demanded.

"Like clockwork," Cat said as she cheerily pushed eggs around a pan. "Considering the role France played in the war, you should consider it your patriotic duty to spend today partying."

"Missing practice for something that happened two hundred years ago is irresponsible."

"You really are a ray of light sometimes," Laila said. She set her coffee aside and cradled her face in her hand to consider him. "If this doesn't count as a legitimate holiday at Edgar Allan, then what does? New Year's and Christmas, I assume, but what…"

Jeremy didn't like the way she trailed off, but he knocked back the rest of his coffee before looking between them. The stubborn set of Jean's jaw was answer enough, but Jean didn't hesitate to spell it out: "Ravens cannot recognize winter holidays when championships start in January. That time is critical."

"They have to have a day off," Laila insisted. "Don't

tell me they never stop."

For a moment Jeremy feared Jean's answer, but then Jean said, "The last day of each month and first four days after finals are enforced recovery periods."

Jeremy tested the weight of the coffee pot but didn't refill his mug yet. "When else?"

Jean looked over at him. "When else what?"

"Good lord," Cat said. "Effective immediately you are required to acknowledge every major holiday. When's your birthday?"

"November."

Cat waited, but nothing else was forthcoming. "Like all thirty days of it, or do you want to narrow it down some for me?"

Jean tipped his head as he thought, and Jeremy wished he'd find a trace of suspicion on Jean's face. Reticence due to distrust would be better than whatever this was. But Jean kept thinking, idly tapping a thumb to the island as he worked through it, and he came up emptyhanded. "November," he said again, and shrugged his unconcern. "It will be on my file somewhere, perhaps."

"You don't know your own birthday?" Jeremy asked.

Jean looked at him. "Why would I? It is irrelevant at Evermore."

"Not recognizing it and not knowing it at all are two very different problems," Jeremy said. Jean tried waving him off, so Jeremy tried, "Kevin knows his birthday, and he was at Evermore longer than you were."

Jean's stare was steady. "And?"

The challenge in that simple response made Jeremy hesitate. He conceded with a weary, "And he refuses to celebrate it. But you know why as well as I do, I assume." Jean didn't answer, but he did look away. Jeremy tried again: "Even if the Ravens didn't care for birthdays, you were at home until you were fourteen." When it was clear Jean was waiting for him to get to the point, Jeremy was forced to draw the only conclusion he could: "You mean they didn't do anything for it, either. Really? Your own family?"

"And I thought *your* parents were assholes," Cat commented, grimacing at Jeremy.

Laila didn't even hesitate. "They are."

"Thanks, guys," Jeremy said as he refilled his mug.

"Yeah, anytime." Cat sounded distracted as she scrolled through her phone. Jeremy was halfway back to the island with his drink when Cat dialed out, and he didn't miss the way Jean went tense at her cheery, "Heyyy, Coach. Are you busy? I was hoping you could look something up for us." She waved off Jean when he reached for her phone. "Did Edgar Allan tell you when Jean's birthday is? Yeah, we already tried that. Three guesses as to why I'm asking you."

Jean swore quietly and put space between them. Jeremy put out a hand, trying to beckon him over, but Jean wasn't getting anywhere near Cat until she hung up.

"Oh, shit, really? Awesome, thanks, you're the best." Cat set her phone aside, beaming with triumph. "Lisinski says it's on the ninth."

"You can't just call a coach," Jean insisted.

"I can and I did." Cat went to mark the calendar. "Why else would I have their numbers, if I wasn't allowed to use them? Look!" She tapped the square she'd written Jean's name on before counting ahead a few spaces. "You're three days before Cody. We could have a double birthday bash and go all out."

She started back toward July one month at a time and paused on August. Jeremy couldn't read her notes from the island, but he knew in a glance what was on the page already. August 27th was the first day of classes, and two weeks before that was Jean and Kevin's joint interview. Cat tapped the 11th, decided not to bring it up, and came back to July at last. The only thing she'd written on this month was a starred note at the bottom: a reminder that someone ought to check in with the Foxes on July 23rd.

"Coming up quick," Cat said, distracted by the same set of days. She ran her finger along the week and sent a grim look over her shoulder at Jeremy. "Has Kevin said anything about it yet?"

"No," Jeremy said, and admitted, "I haven't asked him. I'm not sure what to say."

"'Hope your teammate gets acquitted, XOXO'?" Cat suggested as she pushed away from the calendar. "Word online is Aaron waived his right to a jury, but I can't track those rumors back to a credible source yet. Risky business, trusting your verdict to a single man, but it's probably for the best considering the Foxes' reputation. Who could they trust to be fair?"

Laila sighed. "They really can't catch a break, can they?"

"Maybe this will be their year," Jeremy said.

Jean waved that aside. "Last year was their year."

"Sure," Laila said dryly. "Ignoring the fatal overdose, the kidnapping, the murder charges, the rampant campus vandalization, and—Andrew," she said, with an uncomfortable pause. "Great year for them otherwise."

"They won finals," Jean pointed out.

Laila looked to the ceiling for patience. "Oh, right. How could I have forgotten?"

"Seeing how you needlessly threw away your season against them, I would hope you remembered."

Jeremy set his coffee down and fixed Jean with a serious look. "Jean, look at me," he said, and waited until Jean obediently gave him his undivided attention. "It's important to me that you understand we didn't throw anything away.

"Never before in Class I history has a team done what the Foxes pulled off last year. And yeah, they were building on momentum from the year before, and Kevin made a major difference on the lineup, but that only explains so much. We wanted to understand that meteoric rise, so we needed to test ourselves against them at their level. We weren't sure we'd ever get the chance again. Who's to say they can pull it off two years in a row, right?"

"You gambled and you lost."

"The Ravens didn't, but so did they," Jeremy pointed out. Jean looked away: not in avoidance, but in thought. Jeremy gave him a few seconds to interject before continuing. "We can do what the Ravens can't, what they've never learned how: we can weather a loss and learn from every team we face. We're stronger for playing against the Foxes, and we're stronger for losing. It's what we needed, so we'll focus on that golden opportunity instead of the disappointing outcome. If Palmetto makes it that far again, I have every faith we can come out on top."

"If they do, Kevin's going to be your problem," Cat said to Jean. It was a bold assumption to make when Jean would start the year as a sub, but Jeremy couldn't imagine Rhemann making any other decision. "Can you handle him?"

Jean was honest enough to say, "Unknown, considering the Trojans' restrictions. First I have to destroy Allen."

"Derrick?" Jeremy asked, startled. "What did he do to you?"

"He thinks he's better than me," Jean said, with a sour look. He tapped another agitated beat on the side of his mug and said, "I don't face him enough on the court. I need to study more games to see how he plays outside of drills. No practice at all today?"

"No practice at all," Jeremy confirmed.

Jean said something that sounded rude and left the room. Cat sent an exasperated look after him where she was halfway through dishing up their breakfast, then

100

quirked a brow at Jeremy and asked, "When are you gonna tell him we're going to Santa Monica for the fireworks?"

"Maybe when we're putting him in the car," Jeremy suggested.

Laila smiled. "At least let him watch a match or two first. It'll calm him down."

"One can hope." Jeremy held out his hand for Jean's plate. "Do you need the TV, or can I plant him in front of it?"

"All yours," she said, so Jeremy went to pry Jean off his laptop.

This wasn't how he'd planned to spend his morning, but once Jeremy got a game going on the TV it was easy to settle in beside Jean on the couch. He'd picked a game at random, but by ten minutes in he remembered the match and was pleased with his choice.

More interesting than the game was how Jean interacted with it. He'd been silently avoidant with every movie they inflicted on him, but Jean was hooked on this from the start. He peppered the match with idle observations and rude commentary, and even tried to hush the commentators when they talked over him with an opposing opinion. It was more endearing than it should be, and Jeremy hid a smile against his long-empty mug whenever Jean got particularly rude.

When on-screen Jeremy missed a shot he really shouldn't have, Jean turned to stare at him. He looked so genuinely scandalized Jeremy couldn't help but laugh. "Sorry. He and I have history, so I was distracted by our conversation." More specifically, Ivan Faser had been listing everything he'd let Jeremy do to him if Jeremy came by his hotel room after the match. Jeremy attempted a solemn look and crossed his heart. "Won't happen again, scout's honor."

Past-Jeremy redeemed himself ten minutes later when

he managed to escape both defensemen and score. The goalkeeper wasn't expecting him to make it from that angle or distance, and he smashed his racquet against the floor in frustration.

Jeremy grinned over at Jean and said, "That makes up for the last fumble, right?"

"A solid play can't erase a critical mistake," Jean said. Jeremy rolled his eyes and sank back to his side of the couch. He was nearly settled when Jean said, "But most of the time you are very good."

It wasn't the words that set his heart tripping; Jeremy had heard variations of the same compliment for years from teammates and strangers alike. It was the heavy satisfaction in his tone that put a needy heat in Jeremy's stomach. Jeremy opened his mouth, closed it again, and settled on a bright, "Thanks! I try my best. Hey, want some water? I was about to go get some."

"Yes," Jean said, and Jeremy escaped the room before he said something they'd both regret.

He was putting the pitcher back when he noticed an odd brown square poking out from behind the fridge. A careful tug revealed a foot, and Jeremy laughed when he realized what he was looking at. He slid the standee out of its hiding spot and dusted the cardboard off with a careful hand. Barkbark looked none the worse for wear for the misadventure: whatever fit of pique drove Jean to hide it there, he'd at least been careful not to scratch the dog in the process.

He cupped both glasses in one hand, checked to make sure his grip was good, and carried Barkbark back to the living room with him.

"Look who wants to watch the game with us," Jeremy said, and put the dog on the empty cushion between them. The sidelong look Jean gave it said he was considering flinging it across the room like an oversized paper airplane, but he took his water without comment. Jeremy reclaimed his spot and settled down to watch the remainder of the match.

The second game was winding down when Laila popped into the doorway to give them a five-minute warning. She was already dressed to go in her black bathing suit, long legs on full display and hair pulled up into a pinned French braid. A few seconds after she left, the Trojans scored, but Jean didn't even react. He was staring through the TV like he'd forgotten where he was.

Jeremy couldn't help himself. "Must be nice, liking both. I bet it makes things easier."

"Stop dyeing your hair. The bleach is rotting your brain," Jean said, with more acrimony than Jeremy thought his comment warranted. "Why is she dressed like that?"

"I'll tell you in five minutes," Jeremy promised.

Jean grumbled something rude under his breath but let it slide, and they watched the final two minutes in silence. Jeremy found a new spot for Barkbark before leading Jean to their bedroom, and he explained their plans to spend the afternoon barbecuing and playing beach volleyball. Jean was predictably unimpressed with the plan, but he'd been soundly outvoted and wasn't going to stay home by himself. He changed into the coolest clothes he owned while Jeremy slipped into swimming trunks and a tee, and they found the girls waiting for them at the front door.

Cat snagged Jean's wrist and chucked her tote of towels and sunscreen at Jeremy. "We'll meet you there!" she said as she hauled Jean out the front door behind her. Jeremy caught the door with a foot and saw she'd already moved their helmets and jackets out to her motorcycle. Jeremy honestly expected a bit more resistance from Jean, but he hesitated only a moment before taking his helmet from Cat's outstretched hand.

They were gone before Laila had even locked the front door. Laila sent Jeremy a sidelong look and said, "Oh, surely this won't backfire on you at all."

"She can't even get in," Jeremy pointed out.

Laila only shrugged and followed him to his car. The rest of the floozies would head straight to the beach so they could stake out some sand, but Jeremy's group had a stop to make. Both Mathilda and Warren were at work today, and Bryson was in Edmonton. That left Jeremy's house unattended, so he'd offered the use of their grills for dinner. He lived only twelve minutes away from where they were spending the afternoon, so the food would still be hot by the time they lugged it down there.

Holiday traffic made the drive longer than he wanted it to be, and Cat had the advantage of being on a smaller ride. When Jeremy pulled up at his house, the motorcycle was alone out front with a helmet hanging from each handle. Cat didn't have a key to his place, and William was out of town for the holiday, so Jeremy assumed Cat and Jean were loitering in the backyard. Instead he found the grill burning unattended.

Jeremy only had a moment to wonder before Cat opened the back door and said, "About time! Did you guys walk here?" She noted the nonplussed look on his face and jerked a thumb over her shoulder. "Dallas let me in, said William told him you'd be by to make dinner. Of course he panicked."

She moved aside to let them in. The family chef was hard at work at the kitchen island, sleeves rolled up to his elbows as he shaped patties with his hands. The Trojans had decided on black bean burgers tonight so they could grill theirs and Ananya's all at the same time, and William must have passed that verdict on when enlisting Dallas to the cause. A small pile of cutting boards and knives were off to one side, evidence he had already diced up any possible topping he could think of.

"You should be home relaxing today," Jeremy said.

"When all the good food is here?" Dallas asked. "Give

104

me fifteen more minutes and I can start packing everything up for you."

"You sure you don't need a hand?"

Dallas's smile didn't even waver. "Get out of my kitchen, Jeremy."

Cat laughed and hooked an arm through Laila's. "Come on, Jean's in the dining room. The normal one."

She hauled Laila out of the room, and Jeremy had no choice but to follow. The door they were looking for was just two down, past the rear closet where the cleaning supplies were kept and the stairs down to the wine cellar. All six seats at the table were empty. Cat didn't look nearly as concerned as she ought to find Jean missing and instead went to pour herself lemonade from the jug sitting in the center of the table.

"That's weird," she said when Jeremy turned on her.

"You sent him on a tour," Jeremy guessed.

Cat clasped a hand to her chest. "Would I have been so bold?"

Laila pulled out a chair, silently ceding the search to Jeremy, so Jeremy left them to each other's company. Warren's office door was firmly closed, as was William's bedroom door. The laundry room was of course empty. Jean wasn't in the formal dining room or the day room either.

Jeremy was starting to think he'd gone upstairs or ducked into the first-floor bathroom when he found Jean in front of the sitting room fireplace. Most of the mantel was covered in tasteful knickknacks Mathilda's late mother brought home from her various sets, but the centerpiece was a family portrait from eight years ago. Jean was still as stone as he studied it.

"Pretty cool stuff, right?" Jeremy asked as he approached. He lifted a delicate pipe and showed it off. "This is from Eternally Yours. Nan's costar planned on taking it home, but he gave it to her as a parting gift when

105

he heard it was her last film." He set the pipe back and smiled over at Jean, but Jean didn't even glance his way. Jeremy tried again to distract him: "I don't know if I ever told you she was an actress? You hate movies so much I didn't think you would care. Angelica Laslo," he said, knowing it would garner no recognition from Jean.

Jean didn't even acknowledge that but said, "There are four." He couldn't mean people when there were seven faces in the portrait, except he did: "Cat said you only had three."

Siblings, Jeremy realized too late.

Jean lifted the portrait from its spot and tilted it toward Jeremy. Jeremy waited for him to ask, but Jean's finger settled unerringly on Noah's face. He'd seen the rest of the family portraits on his self-guided tour, then. This was the only one still on display that Noah was in. Mathilda packed the rest away years ago, claiming she couldn't bear to see his face staring back at her in every room.

Jeremy took the portrait from Jean's unresisting hands and put it back in its spot. "He's gone, four years this August." The hoarse edge in his words earned him a pensive look from Jean, but Jeremy feigned not to notice. He cleared his throat as he turned away. "Let's see how the burgers are coming along, yeah?"

He made it halfway to the door when Jean asked, "Does it get easier?"

He wished he could pretend he hadn't heard, but his feet betrayed him and went still. When Jeremy turned back, Jean was again studying the portrait like it somehow held all the answers. Why it was so important to him, Jeremy wasn't sure, but Jeremy had asked too much of him this summer to not at least attempt some honesty.

"No," Jeremy admitted, and Jean turned his distant stare on Jeremy. "Sometimes I get so caught up in everything else that I just—forget," he said, though it was such an awful thing to admit. "Then I remember and it's like it happened yesterday. But Dr. Spader said grief isn't supposed to get easier: you just become someone strong enough to weather it. You let the good things and the good days shore you up so the bad days can't tear you down."

Jean considered that, then slowly tapped his fingers to his thumb in turn: one, two, three, four. "I think I understand," he said, and started toward Jeremy at last.

They found the girls right where they'd left them. Cat looked between them, furrowed brows at odds with the teasing tone she affected. "Most people come back from Jeremy's house looking impressed, not like they stepped on some tacks. I thought you said Bryson was out of town this week?"

"Up in Edmonton," Jeremy agreed. "Ready to go?"

"Yes," Jean said, and Cat frowned but let it slide.

They returned to the kitchen to see Dallas packing a half-dozen Tupperware into a cooler. He glanced up at their approach and rattled off what he'd prepped, everything from avocado to two different kinds of onions and five condiments. There were four types of cheese beneath two kinds of lettuce, and fruit salad if they wanted a refreshing dessert. He needed a few seconds to layer more ice on top, then snapped the lid closed and set it near the end of the island. The burgers were packed separately to keep them warm, and he had three packages of buns in with an obscene amount of chips.

"Last but not least," Dallas said, taking a mailer off the top of the fridge. "William left this for you, Jeremy." Jeremy took it, mystified, but Dallas didn't wait for him to open it. "Off you go. Have fun, wear your sunscreen, no drinking and driving."

They left in a chorus of thanks and farewells. Jeremy passed Laila his keys so he could open his package in the passenger seat, and he laughed in delight at the sight of French language lessons. The set included a slim book, but the bulk of the lessons were spread across eight CDs.

He showed it off to Laila, who motioned to the radio. The drive was too short to make any real progress, but Laila and Jeremy were content to echo *Bonjour, salut* at each other as she circled for a parking spot.

Between the four of them it was easy to carry everything to where the rest of the floozies had managed to snag a volleyball net. Cody and Pat were squaring off against Ananya, Min, and Xavier. To make it even, if not at all fair, Min was riding on Xavier's shoulders.

They relinquished the net in favor of stuffing their faces, and Pat produced a football from his bag afterward. To no one's surprise, Jean refused to participate. Cody sat out with him, needing time to recover from the three burgers they'd eaten. The rest set to the game with glee, pouncing on each other and kicking sand everywhere. Cat managed to tackle Xavier before he could score to tie the game, and Jeremy scooped her up for a triumphant spin. As he was setting her down again, he caught a glimpse of Cody and Jean.

Cat noticed the immediate change in his mood and turned in his arms to look. Before Jeremy could decide whether he ought to go over there, Cody pushed off the blankets and started their way. Jean looked confused, not angry, but Cody's shoulders were tense. The floozies exchanged startled looks as they collapsed to a tight group, but Cody had eyes only for Xavier.

"Jean's pretty riled up about you getting knocked over, seeing how you're on a no-touch jersey at practice," Cody reported. "He asked if your heart recovered enough to take a hit like that and whether it was going to be a problem. Your heart! Turns out he's been operating under the assumption this was heart surgery." They waggled a hand toward the twin scars on Xavier's chest. "Do you want to handle it, or do you want me to run interference and explain it to him?"

"Oh, I've got it," Xavier said. "Sub in for me, will

108

you? Pat'll enjoy tackling you more, anyway."

"Jesus," Cody said, but obediently took the ball Xavier offered.

"Good?" Jeremy asked.

"Good," Xavier promised as he set off.

They got the game going again, but it was more for show than anything. They missed most of their throws, too distracted sneaking peeks at the other pair. Laila plucked the ball from Min's unresisting fingers and handed it directly to Jeremy. Jean looked baffled as Xavier tried to explain top surgery to him, which was worlds better than disgust, but then he gave a sharp jerk of his hand in violent rejection. Jeremy started that way automatically, but Xavier laughed as he got to his feet.

He jogged back toward them, and Jeremy met him halfway. Xavier paused long enough to say, "Since it has no impact on how I play, he says it's my prerogative to fix whatever's broken. He doesn't understand why he should have an opinion on my personal life one way or the other." He smiled, slow and bright, and said, "I like him, Jeremy. Let's keep him forever."

That Jean had grasped in seconds what it had taken some of the Trojans weeks or months to come to terms with left Jeremy almost dizzy with relief. "That's the plan," he said, and continued toward Jean alone.

Jean scowled as Jeremy dropped down beside him. "He said I didn't belong on the Ravens. That is not the compliment you all seem to think it is."

Jeremy smiled. "Sorry. We'll try to be better about that."

"I don't think you will," Jean accused him.

Jeremy drew a sun in the sand with his finger and admitted, "Probably not."

Jean sighed, tired and aggrieved, but let it slide without further comment. They watched their teammates cavort around until it was time to pack up and move for the fireworks. The cooler's ice was dumped in the gutter to melt while the empty bags were tossed into Jeremy's trunk, and Cody stole the last package of cheese slices to eat on the ride.

One of the local high schools had offered up their football field for people to party in, and the place was packed by the time they made it over there. Parking was free, but entry to the field had a fee. The attendant gave Jeremy a funny look when he asked about receipts, so Laila acquired yellow wristbands for everyone in his group. A security guard ensured all bands were in place before letting them through, and the Trojans pushed forward into the chaos and music.

Jeremy lost Xavier and Min first, then Ananya's group not much later. Cat and Laila came and went as the swelling crowd swept them this way and that. The first time a family almost pushed Jeremy away from Jean, Jean caught hold of his wrist in a death grip. Jeremy took one look at his tense face and hauled Jean closer. Jean would feel better when the show started and the crowd went still, surely, except the first crackling pop startled a violent flinch out of him.

Jeremy flicked him a worried look, but Jean's transfixed gaze was on the fireworks crackling to life above them. Surprised, not afraid, Jeremy decided, but he couldn't look away again. He watched colored lights dance off sun-reddened cheeks until Jean finally caught him at it. Gold peonies reflected in Jean's eyes as he turned a curious look on Jeremy.

Between the delighted crowd and the fireworks, it was too loud for Jean to hear him. Jeremy rocked onto the balls of his feet to say at his ear, "I'm glad you came."

"I could've watched three more matches in the time we've been gone," Jean said.

Predictable to a fault; Jeremy couldn't help but laugh. Maybe he ought to apologize for upending Jean's plans so thoroughly, but then Jean tapped idly at Jeremy's wrist. Jeremy glanced down, curious, but didn't get a chance to ask. Jean's lips grazed his cheekbone as Jean turned his head, and every coherent thought Jeremy had crumbled to dust. Jean had to feel Jeremy's pulse kick up beneath his thumb, but all he said was, "But I'd forgotten—I do not know them in English."

"Fireworks," Jeremy said.

"Fireworks," Jean echoed. He tipped his head back to study the sky once more, and maybe Jeremy imagined his, "This is good, too."

It was more than Jeremy had expected or hoped for, and he was still smiling when he went to bed that night.

-

On Thursday morning, Rhemann ruled in Jean's favor: effective immediately, Jean was allowed extra court time after practices with any Trojans interested in learning his Raven drills. Rhemann was generally trapped doing paperwork for an hour after his team left anyway, so it made sense to let them use it productively. All he wanted was a promise they'd clean up behind themselves.

Jeremy was glad for them—it was hard not to be, when Tanner was so stoked and even Jean looked satisfied with the outcome—but he quietly worried what would happen in August. Once classes started, he'd be living at home again. The trek home after afternoon practices would take nearly an hour. Staying here later might allow some traffic to clear up, but it was just as likely to work against him. He did the math on his fingers and found the numbers too uncomfortable to dwell on.

Either Laila caught him at it, or she'd been his friend long enough to sort it out herself. She waited until Tanner and Jean took the court Thursday evening before joining Jeremy on the home bench.

"Remember that Jean's our responsibility this fall, not yours," she said without preamble. "If you try and wait

111

him out, you won't get home until ten. I don't need you falling asleep on the road again."

"That was one time," he protested. She leveled an arch look at him, and Jeremy relented with a sheepish, "Three or four times. If I'd realized you would hold it over me this long I never would've told you about it. But thank you," he added before she could lecture him about his safety, and he tipped his head toward the court so she'd understand what he meant. "Have I told you yet you're perfect?"

"This week?" Laila considered it. "Not yet. Feel free."

"You're perfect," he said. "Must be why Mom wants me to marry you."

It startled a laugh from her. "You're joking. She can't even look me in the eye. It would make for such an awkward ceremony." She pressed her shoulder to his, and he was content to lean back. Laila held her left hand out so they could study her imaginary ring. "Tempting as the offer is, I will have to decline. Can I keep the rock?"

"Family heirloom," Jeremy said gravely. "I'm afraid I need it returned."

"Alas." Laila mimed slipping it off, but instead of pressing it to his hand she settled her fingers on the open book at his lap. There was no humor in her now, just quiet reluctance as she asked, "Are you sure about this, Jeremy?"

Jeremy refused to look down. This was his fifth time attempting the section on logical reasoning. Every time he made it further than two paragraphs in, his thoughts wandered off without him, and he didn't have the energy or willpower to call them back. Having a deadline would make it easier to focus, but every time Jeremy considered registering for an exam, he remembered Bryson's warning. The chances of it being an empty threat were slim to none, but Jeremy didn't have it in him to fail on purpose.

"Jeremy," Laila pressed when he took too long to answer.

"Yeah." Jeremy watched Jean obliterate cones at dizzying speed so he wouldn't have to see Laila's disappointed face. "I'm sure enough."

"Peas in a pod," Laila said wearily. "You're both terrible liars."

"He's so bad at it," Jeremy agreed, almost admiring. "Unexpected."

"Is it?" Laila wondered. Jeremy sent her a curious look, but she thought it over before trying to put it into words. "Jean's often said he's not allowed to talk to outsiders, but what about the Ravens? They were trapped in the Nest, bound to each other and the dark almost twenty-four-seven. How do you keep secrets in a place like that?"

She shrugged, as if warning him not to take her too seriously, but continued, "We're his team now, and you're his partner. Maybe he can't lie to us because we're his people."

Jeremy tested it out, liking the sound of that: "We're his people."

"It's just a theory."

"We're his people," Jeremy said again, and was heartened enough to return to his studies. He used a finger to follow along, then two when he kept zoning out. Laila was thumbing through something on her phone, but she still noticed how many times he flipped back to the first page. She grumbled under her breath and took the textbook from him.

"Listen," she said, and read it aloud.

This didn't make it any less awful or boring, but Jeremy appreciated Laila's help too much to tune her out. Every other paragraph she'd stop and wait for him to summarize it before continuing. Bit by bit they conquered the section. Just as Jeremy thought he'd finally make it out of this chapter, Rhemann stepped into the inner court with a piece of paper in his hands. Laila trailed off at his approach and used her thumb as a bookmark.

"That time already, Coach?" Jeremy asked.

"Schedule's in," Rhemann said, sitting down on Laila's other side. He folded his paper in half and tapped the corner against his palm as he thought. Nothing in their district would give Rhemann pause like this; Jeremy knew where the conversation was going before Rhemann finally said, "Arizona wants to get space reserved as soon as possible, so I need a banquet headcount by next Wednesday."

"Oh," Jeremy said. It was all he could manage.

Laila gave Jeremy's arm a firm squeeze. "You don't have to go."

"You don't." Rhemann's agreement was easy, like it wasn't the big deal they all knew it was.

The banquets were a mandatory team event. For a player—a captain, even—to miss them three years straight was otherwise unheard-of in the NCAA. Jeremy's saving grace was the Trojans' reputation and the unwavering respect the ERC had for Rhemann. Jeremy knocked the heel of his shoe against the ground and looked toward the court. If he was hoping for inspiration, he came back emptyhanded. Every word he ought to say was lodged somewhere in his chest.

Rhemann figured out nothing was forthcoming and said, "It's your senior year, so I thought I should at least ask."

Laila followed Jeremy's gaze and could guess where his thoughts were going. "Trust me and Cat to keep an eye on Jean for you. We'll introduce him around to the teams and make sure they understand he's one of ours now."

Jeremy kicked a little harder, until the jarring felt like it would shake his kneecap out of alignment. "By Wednesday?"

"End of day Wednesday," Rhemann confirmed, holding up his paper.

"I'll let you know, Coach." Jeremy took his book back from Laila, the schedule from Rhemann, and got to his feet. "Sorry, can you—?"

"I'll get him home," Laila promised, and Jeremy left without looking back.

It was an easy walk home so long as he refused to think about anything. He heard Cat's strident voice down the hall as he eased the front door open. She and Cody had left practice on time so they could log into their game and do some kind of event. Jeremy closed the door as quietly as he could, pushed his shoes into their place off to the side, and went down the hall to the kitchen. Careful hands smoothed the schedule out, as if that tight crease could be undone, and Jeremy stuck it on the fridge to consider it.

One game at a time, he added their matches to the calendar. More than a few made him smile. The Trojans were historically dominant in their district, but he liked almost all of their opponents: some because they made the Trojans work for it, others because their players followed the Trojans' lead and just tried to have a good time. The few bad apples were spaced out, and it was unfortunate that White Ridge would be the first team they faced, but Jeremy was satisfied overall.

"Hey," Cat said from the doorway.

Jeremy glanced back. "I thought you were playing?"

"Cody's connection is being a bit fussy, so they're resetting their router." She watched him put the pen away and toss the printout in the trash before getting to the point: "Laila texted me. What're you thinking?"

An easy question with no easy answers. Jeremy chased his ragged thoughts down their twisting paths, but they all dead-ended at a crossroads.

"It's my last year." Jeremy wouldn't think if he meant *as a Trojan* or *ever*. "I should go. I mean, I want to go. I

115

want to be there with and for my team." Cat hesitated, but then her cell phone gave the *pewpewpew* alert she'd given Cody. Jeremy smiled away her lingering concerns and insisted, "Thank you for worrying, but I'm good, I promise. Go enjoy your star thing."

"Celestial Nights," Cat supplied. "We're writing haikus. Cody's are *so* bad."

"Read us some at dinner," Jeremy invited her. "Speaking of, I'll go ahead and get it ordered. Jean should be wrapping up any minute now, so the timing should be perfect."

"Okay," Cat said. "Make sure they send us extra chopsticks? Laila broke another set in the dishwasher. I don't know how many times I can tell her to turn them upside-down first."

"Will do," Jeremy promised, and Cat slipped out of view.

He ordered enough food to feed a small army, texted Laila with the estimated delivery time, and sent a weary look toward his guidebook. He couldn't think of a better way to spend the time, so he carried it down the hall to the living room.

Ten minutes later he'd made no progress whatsoever. He went to chuck it, saw Barkbark watching him from across the room, and said, "Okay. Osmosis it is." The standee had no opinion on the matter, so Jeremy draped the book across his face and dozed until Laila and Jean finally made it home.

CHAPTER SEVEN
Jeremy

Lucas returned on Monday morning. Jeremy privately
thought it too early to be back on the court, but this had to
be Lucas's decision; the lineup was large enough
Rhemann could've approved just about any amount of
time to grieve. Jeremy attempted just once to catch him
alone, but Lucas refused to hear anything he wanted to
say. The junior put a hand up as soon as Jeremy said his
name and said, "Not you, cap. I can't hear it from you."

Maybe he should have pushed, with all the trite words
that only worked on perfect days, but Jeremy mutely
relinquished Lucas into Cody's care. If Lucas didn't want
his help, Jeremy would focus instead on Jean. Jeremy
wasn't sure anyone else noticed, as they were busy
smothering Lucas with careful, gentle attention, but Jean
didn't once get within ten feet of Lucas. How he pulled it
off when they had only a few lockers between them,
Jeremy didn't know. He wanted to ask Jean at break, but
there was no good lull in Cat's chatter.

When practice ended, Lucas didn't even stick around
long enough to shower. He peeled off his gear, yanked on
his day clothes, and was out the door with Travis and
Haoyu chasing him. The awkwardness of it all made the
showers quieter than usual, and Jeremy wasn't surprised
when his teammates were in and out faster than normal.
Cody and Xavier hung back, but Xavier waited until it
was just the three of them before finally cranking his
shower head off.

"He say anything to you?" Xavier asked.

"He didn't want to talk to me," Jeremy admitted.

"Do you blame him?" Cody raked both hands through

117

their brutally short hair. When they noticed Jeremy watching them, they gave an uncomfortable shrug and said, "How can you understand what he's dealing with? Maybe if it'd been Bryson—"

"What the hell, Cody?" Xavier interjected. "That's enough."

Cody winced but persisted. "I just mean it's not the same kind of loss. What Lucas needs to cope and grieve is going to be completely different from what worked for Jeremy. Remembering Grayson in his heyday won't help him when Lucas is so desperate to figure out the *why* and *who* he became while he was gone. It's not you he needs to hear from," they said again, with a glance at Jeremy to gauge his reaction. "It's Jean."

"That's not going to happen," Jeremy said. Cody frowned, so Jeremy put a bit more force in his words: "That's final, Cody."

Jean wouldn't even talk about Grayson with them; there was no way Jeremy was asking him to have a heart-to-heart with the man's grieving brother. Jeremy would never make Jean spell it out, but he knew what Grayson had done at Evermore. The truth was in Jean's fierce avoidance, in the way he dug at his own throat when Grayson came up in conversation, in the hideous bites Grayson had left on his skin when he hunted him down at the court.

That Laila put it together felt inevitable; that she'd done it so quickly made his heart ache. They'd barely made it into June when she cornered him for confirmation, and Jeremy couldn't lie to her when she spelled it out first. He assumed Cat found out while Laila was processing this horrific news, but the rest of the floozies didn't have the same easy access to Jean's life. Maybe if they'd seen Jean's injuries, they would figure it out, but Jean was careful to keep his neck covered at practice.

Cody was studying him thoughtfully, so Jeremy

finally said, "I'm sorry."

Cody waved that off. "You know him best. I'll follow your lead."

"Thank you," Jeremy said, and the three left the showers at last.

They dressed in their separate rows, and Jeremy saw them off before moving to the inner court with his books.

Jean had acquired a second student, it seemed: Mads was out with Tanner at the half-court line. Jeremy wasn't sure what they were trying to accomplish, but from Jean's body language the drills were obviously not going well. Jeremy would understand if the freshmen gave up and retreated, but the two simply waited until he finished chewing them out before trying again.

When Mads completely butchered the exercise a third time in a row, the Raven in Jean threatened to come out at her. It was lucky for all of them that Mads was laughing at something Tanner said, as neither of the freshmen saw it when Jean's hand went back with every intent to strike. Jeremy's heart gave a startled lurch as he came off the bench, mouth open on a warning that would come too late.

Jean remembered himself just in time. He aborted the swing so forcefully he had to take two steps back and turn away, and he stormed off toward the first-fourth line. Tanner and Mads turned at his abrupt retreat, confused. Jeremy thought he heard Tanner's voice echoing off the wall, but Jean only waved him off with a quick flick of his racquet.

The freshmen jogged off to gather their scattered balls, but Jeremy had eyes only for Jean as he paced short lines back and forth. On one of his laps, Jean finally noticed Jeremy on the sidelines. He came to stand across from him with only the wall between them. Walking it off had taken some of the tension from his shoulders but none of the frustration out of his face. Jeremy idly wondered how much of that was at his trainees for failing, himself for

119

wanting to hurt them, or Jeremy for keeping a close eye on him.

They'd always known the Ravens were capable of extreme violence, and Jeremy had seen more than a few clips of the ugly brawls Jean got into on the court, but somehow, he'd still forgotten. Jean had been working hard to curtail his aggression on the court these last few weeks, courtesy of the contract he made the Trojans offer him. He slipped up now and again—throwing Jeremy off his feet, leaving bruises all down the arch of Derrick's foot, and slipping in a nasty trip here and there when he wasn't thinking—but this felt different.

Jeremy wondered what the trigger was behind this near-miss: was Mads really that offensive in her performance, or was Jean so caught up in Raven drills he'd forgotten who and where he was? After everything he'd seen of Jean this summer, Jeremy leaned toward the latter, but he would have to have a serious talk with Jean later. Jeremy wouldn't put his teammates at risk no matter how badly Tanner wanted to learn the Ravens' tricks.

He wasn't sure Jean could hear him, both through the wall and his helmet, but Jeremy enunciated "Be nice," and hoped Jean could at least read his lips. Judging by the way Jean scowled, Jeremy figured he got the message. It wasn't the most encouraging response, but Jeremy needed to believe it was enough. More importantly, he needed Jean to know that Jeremy trusted him to do the right thing. Rather than push Jean for more concrete reassurances, he held up his French book where Jean could see it and offered a cheery, "Salut!"

It didn't matter if Jean could hear him—the look that crossed his face when he realized what Jeremy was holding was more than enough. He looked genuinely thrown, like he hadn't believed Jeremy was being serious about learning, and his confusion was enough to finally take the lingering irritation out of him. Jean treated

Jeremy to a searching look, and Jeremy tipped his head to indicate the freshmen who were waiting for him.

"Have fun!"

Jean rolled his eyes as he turned away. Jeremy laughed as he retreated to the bench to study, reassured that Jean's mood was steady enough to continue. He set the book aside in favor of his LSAT guide, and he flipped to where he'd left off. Five minutes later he hadn't read past the first sentence, so Jeremy dropped it over his shoulder and went back to studying French.

-

July slowly settled into a routine. Lucas and Jean continued to avoid each other, unable to reconcile their differences when Grayson's suicide sat unresolved between them. By the end of his first week back, Lucas was no longer rushing out of the court after practice. By Tuesday of the second, he was talking to everyone except Jean, but his hollow performance on the court gave lie to his feigned normalcy.

Jean, meanwhile, collected two more Trojans for his daily drills: Sebastian and Dillon. Since Cat and Laila would have to plan around these lessons in August, Jeremy volunteered to stay with him at the stadium that summer. It should have been perfect, an hour of focused study time before he was distracted by his friends at home, but after three days of staring at the same chapter header Jeremy dusted off his portable CD player and brought his French CDs to the court. He walked laps as he talked to himself, stumbling his way through unfamiliar phrases and tricky pronunciations. When Jean was finally through, they headed home together.

Sometimes the four of them crowded the island as they ate, cheerfully meandering from one topic to the next as they reveled in each other's company. Jean excused himself the nights they watched movies, more interested in picking through the Trojans' matches on his laptop.

Convincing Jean to use the living room when Laila had no game shows on took a bit of work, as Jean was keenly aware the TV was not his. Jeremy stuck with him those nights, as much to relive his team's best plays as to hear Jean's unfiltered opinion.

Once a week Jean called Dr. Betsy Dobson—supposedly. Jean made his calls from the study but never bothered to close the door; aside from a simple greeting Jean said nothing else. He sat at his desk with his phone at his ear, toying with his wristband from the 4th of July party and a sand dollar he'd picked up at some point. Jeremy had no idea how Dobson was filling the time, but whatever she had to say was more than enough to ruin Jean's mood the rest of the night. Jeremy got used to taking him for a late run on Tuesdays; he could think of no other way to bleed the anxious rage out of his rattled teammate.

A few times a week Cat kidnapped Jean for motorcycle lessons: sometimes getting out of the house before morning traffic became too much of a snarl, other times taking advantage of the long days and heading out after rush hour slowed down a bit. The first few times they went, Jean looked a bit like he regretted the life choices that had brought this down on him, but each successive lesson made him a little less reluctant to leave the house.

On the 22nd, Jeremy finally settled on the simplest message he could think of for Kevin: "We're keeping Aaron in our thoughts this week. How is everyone holding up?"

"They lost focus a week ago," Kevin sent back.

Whoever said texts couldn't convey tone had never messaged Kevin Day. Jeremy couldn't help but smile as he tapped out a quick, "Who can blame them?" Knowing exactly what the answer would be, Jeremy followed up with, "Let us know if you need anything at all, okay?"

Keeping up with the trial that week was a task and a

half. Reporters couldn't get inside, but they could track who came and went to the courthouse. Andrew was among the first called to testify, and it was unbelievably lucky that Dr. Betsy Dobson arrived right behind him. Jeremy had two seconds to appreciate finally having a face to go with Dobson's name when someone was heartless enough to put a camera in Andrew's face. Andrew threw it halfway across the street, and the look on his face said he had every intention of sending the journalist after it. Dobson somehow got him inside without further carnage.

Another reporter stopped by Palmetto State for a comment, but Coach Wymack had absolutely no patience for vultures. Security barricades went up at the stadium the same day, and every other picture snapped of the Foxes that week was taken from about a hundred feet back.

Kevin was due at court that afternoon, but Jeremy was on lunch break before he saw the photograph in his news feed: Andrew going down the stairs as Kevin went up them, as far apart from each other as they could be on the stairwell. Caught halfway between them was Neil, standing still as a stone as if he wasn't sure which one of them he was supposed to be following. Jeremy found the answer by accident, when Cat showed him a news clip later: Andrew left by himself, and Neil accompanied Kevin inside. Jeremy went through six different drafts before finally texting Kevin a simple, "Are you okay?"

He knew Kevin couldn't respond until he was freed for the day, but by eight that night he gave up waiting. The silence was answer enough. Jeremy winced and set his phone aside.

Laila muted the end credits of her show and said, "That bad?"

"That bad, I think." Jeremy saw the look on her face and reached for her, and he let her crush the blood from his fingers. He willed her to believe him when he said, "It's going to work out, Laila. I promise."

"That would be a first," was all she said.

The only other Fox called on to testify that week was Nicholas Hemmick, who got into a spectacular confrontation with his parents when they arrived at the courthouse the same morning. Security had to practically body him up the stairs, but it set the tone for the rest of the day. The press continued to dutifully spy on the courthouse and report back names, but Jeremy recognized no one else. Character witnesses, he assumed, who could vouch for Aaron Minyard. The odd one out was the girl reported as Aaron's girlfriend, a cheerleader who'd been notably absent the first day but showed up every single day after that.

Jean's quiet, "No verdict," distracted Jeremy from his endless scrolling on Wednesday.

Jeremy glanced up, looking first to Laila where she was reading in her chair, then to Jean where he was supposedly watching a match on the far end of the couch. It was the first time all week Jean acknowledged what was happening with the Foxes. Jeremy had wondered if it was apathy or avoidance, considering Aaron was on trial for murdering a rapist, but he'd resisted asking. This felt like an answer a few days too late, and Jeremy set his phone aside.

"Not yet," he admitted. "Maybe tomorrow?"

Laila set her book aside and left. Jeremy wondered if he should follow, but she was back less than a minute later with her brush. She lightly bopped Jean on the head with it before retaking her seat and saying, "Come here." When Jean just stared at her, not following, she pointed an imperious finger at the ground in front of her. "Sometime today, preferably."

Jean was clearly suspicious of her intentions, but he settled on the floor in front of her. As soon as she put the brush to his unruly black hair, he tried to take it away. "I can do this myself."

"I know you can," she said, moving it out of his reach.

"It's almost grown out," he said next, thinking perhaps that was what was bothering her. Despite that sullen defensiveness, he reached for the spots that had been so jarringly mismatched when he moved to California in May.

"Barely noticeable," she agreed. When Jean didn't drop his hand, Laila batted at him and said, "You see me and Cat do this with each other all the time. Watch your game and stop overthinking it."

Jean reluctantly subsided, and Laila set to work. Judging by the tense line of his shoulders, Jean spent the next several minutes trying to sort out her motives instead of watching the match. If Laila noticed, she gave no sign of it: at an outward glance she was completely focused on the Trojans' match. Only the lack of a smile at a spectacular save from Cat gave her away. Jean's silence was equally telling, and finally Laila couldn't take it. She set the brush aside in favor of working her hands through his hair instead.

"If you don't learn how to relax, you're going to snap in half," Laila said. "Tell me about the match."

"You're watching it," Jean pointed out.

"I'm obviously distracted."

Jean grumbled a bit in annoyance but obediently started breaking down the match thus far: reiterating and expanding on some earlier observations, then moving to real-time commentary as things started heating up on the screen. It still took the rest of the period for Jean to forgive the feel of her hands on his head; every time she shifted her grip his shoulders tightened for a blow that never landed. Only in the last minute of play did he stop noticeably reacting. Laila sighed and leaned forward, winding her arms around his shoulder in a slow hug.

125

"You'll be the death of us, Jean Moreau."

"I won't let me be," Jean said. He offered her the remote over his shoulder and said, "I will not watch the rest."

An unsubtle attempt to escape her, but Laila knew to cut her losses. She took the remote and freed him, and Jean left without looking back.

The Trojans were halfway through a scrimmage Thursday afternoon when the news broke: Aaron Minyard had been cleared of all charges. Rhemann stepped onto the court to let them know, and Jeremy was off the court to message Kevin as soon as he got the okay to leave. He had to go all the way back to the locker room to find his phone, and he tossed his gloves aside halfway there so he could handle the tiny buttons.

"Just heard the news—that's fantastic! We're so happy for him!!"

Kevin's response took only a minute: "Unexpected, if I'm being honest." Then, "Andrew would have burned the judge's house to the ground if he turned on Aaron. Maybe he knew that?" Jeremy idly wondered if that was a joke. He was halfway through a reply when Kevin sent, "They've been a nightmare to deal with all month with this hanging over them. I'm glad it's finally over."

The last, "Coach canceled practice tomorrow" was unnecessary, but Jeremy laughed.

"Good! Take the time to take care of each other."

He set his phone away before Kevin could answer and jogged back down to the court.

-

On August 3rd, Rhemann came to Lyon to collect his team. Rather, he came looking for Jeremy and then went in search of Jean as soon as Jeremy peeled away from his machine. Never in Jeremy's four-plus years had Rhemann interrupted the morning workout like this; even Coach Lisinski looked on edge as she watched him steal two players out from underneath her nose. That Rhemann didn't simply pull them into the next room did nothing to put Jeremy at ease. They went all the way outside, and only when they'd put about twenty feet between them and the fitness center did Rhemann turn on them.

"I've spent the last hour on the phone with Edgar Allan," he said without preamble. "More accurately: I've split the time between them and a hauling company trying to figure out how best to resolve the matter. The Ravens have sent you a gift," he explained, studying Jean with disquieting intensity. "They've dropped a car off at the Gold Court for you."

Jeremy stared. "They bought him a car?"

"Sent it over with the title," Rhemann said, and Jeremy glanced over to see what Jean thought of that. The too-blank look on his face wasn't encouraging, but Rhemann only gave him a few seconds to react before saying, "Supposedly you left it in West Virginia, so they covered the costs of getting it transferred over."

Jean looked ill, not surprised, so Jeremy connected the dots as best he could. "It's really yours, isn't it?"

"All Ravens are given cars when they sign to Edgar Allan," Jean said slowly. Jeremy belatedly remembered Kevin saying something similar: they'd given him a car, and he'd used it to flee Evermore when Riko broke his hand. "They should have destroyed it when they destroyed everything else. Why didn't they?"

Jeremy thought of Jean's notebooks and folded his arms tight across his chest. "Too expensive to be that careless with, perhaps?"

"It's nicer than mine," Rhemann agreed. Jeremy could have told him that everyone had a nicer car, but Rhemann had inherited that ancient station wagon from his late father and would rarely tolerate jokes about its obvious decline. "Someone paid a pretty dime to ensure it made it directly to you. They refuse to leave it at the court without your permission, and I already tried twice to reschedule delivery, so I need you to ride over and sign off on the delivery."

"They spent all of spring stirring up trouble," Jeremy said. "Why this? Why now?"

"Uncharitable best guess?" Rhemann shrugged and motioned them toward his car. "Jean's interview is next week, and Edgar Allan knows they're going to be a hot topic. This is an unsubtle bribe to keep his mouth shut and smile away any prying questions."

Jean would never argue with a coach, but Jeremy saw the look on his face as he and Jean climbed into the backseat. "You disagree?"

"They know I will not speak against the Ravens," Jean said.

"Maybe Coach Moriyama knew that." Jeremy didn't miss the way Jean flinched at his name. "They're under new leadership now, and Coach Rossi is tasked with trying to somehow salvage their reputation. He'll start with the carrot."

He let Jean mull over that for the first half of the ride, then said, "You could, you know. Turn on them, I mean," he added when Jean refused to look at him. "You're not a Raven anymore; you're not beholden to their contracts and expectations. You have the right to speak out about what happened to you."

Jean made a rude noise in his throat. "There is nothing to say."

"I'm not saying you should tell people more than you're comfortable sharing, but you should establish and protect your own boundaries. Stop letting them tell your story for you."

He waited, but Jean continued to stare out his window like he wasn't even listening. Jeremy swallowed a sigh and said, "You don't even have to make it personal, if you don't want. Even just some insight into what's wrong at

Evermore would help start the conversation again and make people question what they've so blindly assumed about you. The Ravens' training schedule, the way you're forbidden to interact with outsiders, the ironclad meal plans..." He trailed off, hoping Jean could fill in the blanks from there.

Jean asked, "How long have you known Kevin?"

"Uhhh?" Jeremy blinked, thrown. "Three years, give or take? No, closer to four. He and Riko weren't on the team yet, but they attended our semifinals match with the Ravens my freshman year. They came by the bench to say hello afterward. Why?"

"Four years," Jean said, "and you heard about the Ravens' schedule from me. Their dietary restrictions, their synchronized majors, contrition, from me. Not once in four years did Kevin bother to explain himself to *you*, and you think I would say such things to a camera?"

Jeremy grimaced at the back of his head. "He's been more honest since he transferred you to us. Maybe he's almost ready to open up about it."

"Sometimes you are unbearable."

"Easy, both of you," Rhemann said from up front.

His tone was calm, but Jean's shoulders still hunched a bit at that hint of displeasure. The last minute of the ride passed in uncomfortable silence, and as they finally arrived at the stadium Jeremy saw the car hauler that was taking up an extraordinary amount of room. That the driver had made it through Los Angeles was genuinely impressive; that he'd made it around the tight turns at Exposition Park was a miracle bordering on ridiculous. Why he hadn't switched to a smaller rollback when his load was only one car, Jeremy didn't know.

The driver's door was open. The driver himself was standing in the opening, leaning back against his seat while he smoked and played around on his phone. He looked up at their approach and zeroed in on Jean immediately. He flicked his cigarette aside, missed it completely when he went to step on it, and dragged a clipboard off his seat. A gesture toward his face indicated Jean's tattoo, and he held the clipboard out when they were close enough.

"Marrow," he said. "Sign here to accept delivery."

"Moreau," Jeremy said.

"That's what I said."

Jean didn't seem to notice, too busy reading the short form he'd been handed. It looked like a standard workup from the hauling company; the top half was split between pick-up and delivery locations, and the bottom half had instructions on who it was to be released to. The next pages were the aforementioned title and associated paperwork, and a sticky note on the final page noted the car was no longer insured.

"Anytime this morning," the driver said. "I'm an hour behind schedule."

Jean slowly scrawled his name across the highlighted lines, and the driver scooped the clipboard back as soon as he lifted the pen. Jean's keys were on the dashboard. The delivery driver handed them over without fanfare before going to get the car unloaded. Jean stared down at where the pair sat in his palm, looking very far away from here.

Getting the car offloaded only took a few minutes. Rhemann ushered his Trojans aside so the truck could finally pull out. While it would have been entertaining to watch it navigate out of the park, Jeremy was more interested in the sleek black car it left behind.

"Is that an S4?" he asked. "Not bad."

Jean said nothing, so Jeremy went over alone to inspect it. The cross-country drive left it in dire need of a wash, but otherwise it looked brand new. The tires were in good shape and there wasn't a single dent to be seen. The only sign it'd ever been driven was a small scrap of paper on the dashboard. Jeremy peered at it through the windshield, trying to read it upside down. It was a ticket stub for short-term parking at an airport.

He stepped back as Jean and Rhemann moved up alongside him. The distant look on Jean's face made Jeremy think he hadn't come over by choice, and he still was holding his keys like he was two seconds from catapulting them across the lot.

"Hey," Jeremy said. "What's wrong?"

"I don't want it," Jean said. "I don't want anything from them."

Jeremy knew that warmth in his chest was inappropriate, considering Jean was distressed, but for him to unhesitatingly reject Edgar Allan's overtures was heartening. He hummed a little as he thought, then said, "You could sell it, but maybe give it a week to make sure you're sure. I just don't know what to do with it in the meantime," he admitted, glancing it over. "We don't have room at Laila's place to store it so long as my car's there, and it can't really stay here."

Rhemann gave Jean a minute to think it through before saying, "I could park it at home until you decide to trade it in." Rhemann couldn't miss the way Jean went so tense and still, and he sent Jean a sidelong look. "But I'll only take it if you're comfortable with me driving it."

"I won't let it be a problem for you, Coach," Jean said. "I will figure something out."

"If it was going to be a problem I wouldn't have offered," Rhemann said. "Just loan me a key until Monday so I can move it. Jeremy knows the way if you change your mind and want to come get it, but otherwise it can stay there as long as it needs to. I won't even know it's there."

"Trust me," Jeremy said. "Coach has room for it."

Jean wasn't reassured. "I can't—" he started, but even he couldn't think of a better solution. He fidgeted with his keys with a nervous restlessness, unable to impose on

Rhemann's generosity. Jeremy put his hand out but kept it out of Jean's space: a silent offer rather than a demand. At length Jean grimaced and relinquished his keys with a quiet, "I'm sorry, Coach."

"You shouldn't apologize for something I suggested," Rhemann said.

"Yes, Coach. Sorry, Coach."

Jeremy exchanged a pained look with Rhemann but only asked, "Shouldn't we drive it over there, though? If you take it, what about your car?"

"Adi and I can pick it up this weekend."

Jeremy nodded acceptance and passed him the keys. "Thanks, Coach. We'll brainstorm our options and get it out of your hair as quick as we can."

Rhemann pocketed the keys and checked his watch. "They've only got about thirty minutes left at Lyon. Rather than drag you back there, let's have you do tens and twos until it's time for break."

Rhemann held the gate open, and Jeremy motioned for Jean to precede them to the door. The Monday after Grayson's visit he'd made sure Jean knew what the code was, and since then he'd let Jean handle it even though they always traveled here together. He never again wanted Jean to be in a position where he couldn't escape.

The three of them went to the locker room together. Rhemann went on ahead of them to his office, and Jean and Jeremy went to the inner court to alternate two laps around the court with ten flights of stairs. By the fourth set Jean had successfully locked away the entire problem, judging by the new calm on his face.

Cat could have undone all of that when the Trojans made it back to the Gold Court for lunch, but luckily for everyone she was smart enough to corner Jeremy alone.

"There's a Raven car out front," she said without preamble. At the bemused look Jeremy sent her, she shrugged. "Not my fault you don't keep up with enough

Raven conspiracy theories! One for every Raven on the team, but they never leave Evermore. And get this, they have to be identical. Every time there's a major body style change that would cause a freshman's car to stand out, Edgar Allan simply sells back and replaces all of them. Absolute freaks," she said, almost admiring.

"It's Jean's," Jeremy admitted, "but he's pretty rattled about it, so let's just be careful how we talk about it with him? We'll have to get it insured and registered sooner than later, but for the time being it's going to hide out at Coach's place."

"I'll talk to Laila," she promised. "We'll figure something out."

None of them brought up the car over lunch. Aside from a few curious questions from the Trojans about missing morning practice, no one else put it together enough to ask. Jeremy was half-afraid Lucas would recognize the car, at least, but he didn't seem to notice it. Jeremy was relieved, but beneath that was a dull ache. Grayson would have had a car just like this, but the brothers were such strangers Lucas didn't even know that.

Jeremy waited until after practice was over and Jean was busy with drills before messaging Kevin: "Edgar Allan sent Jean's car to the Gold Court."

"Mine arrived two days ago," Kevin answered a few minutes later. "My textbooks and notes, too. I'd assumed the coaches sold them back to the school, but they're all accounted for."

"Oh, nice!" Jeremy returned, and meant it, but he couldn't resist a, "They weren't damaged?"

Kevin responded by sending a picture: a crammed shelf in the background, and one textbook open to about the third-way mark on a pale desk. Aside from the expected highlights and notes in the margins, the book looked otherwise unscathed. Jeremy teetered between responses, but it wouldn't be fair to diminish Kevin's delight over a cruelty he'd had no hand in. Rather than bring up Jean's destroyed schoolwork he wrote, "That's great!"

"They are scared of us," Kevin noted.

Kevin agreed, then: the cars were an attempt to buy the perfect Court's discretion. "Should they be?"

Kevin took his time responding, and then just sent, "Remains to be seen."

"Then I will see you in a week," Jeremy sent, and set his phone aside to watch Jean play.

CHAPTER EIGHT
Jeremy

Jeremy sat perched on the trunk of his car at Los Angeles International, picking through his empty takeout cup for an ice chip to suck on. His phone dinged in scattered intervals as the floozies went back and forth, but he didn't try to keep up. The only alert that needed to be addressed with any urgency was the funky little fox bark assigned to Kevin's number. It'd been hours since the last message came in, but Jeremy gamely resisted the urge to check the time.

The air rumbled as a plane took off, and the persistent honking from the clogged traffic out front of the airport was temporarily drowned out. Jeremy found another piece of ice to crunch on, wiped his fingers on his shorts, and gave in to temptation. A quick poke at the buttons lit his screen up, and Jeremy sat up straight when he saw the clock. It was close enough to Kevin's expected arrival time to risk heading in, so he dumped the rest of his ice onto the concrete to melt in the heat.

He was almost out of the garage when he finally heard from Kevin. Jeremy stopped off to one side to send an enthusiastic message back, and he picked up his pace as soon as his phone was safely tucked away again.

Even now, it felt impossible that Kevin was coming here. Theirs had always been an unconventional friendship, in large part due to the sheer distance between their schools. He'd been face-to-face with Kevin a half-dozen times at most: last spring against the Foxes, and then in semifinals and finals against the Ravens his freshman and sophomore years. Every other conversation happened over text, checking in on each other after games

135

and sharing insights on the opponents they would both face in their climb to the top. Kevin had dropped out of contact for over a year after breaking his hand, but Jean's transfer had brought him back in force.

This was the first time they were meeting when there wasn't a game to play, but it still wasn't a social visit. Kevin was here to help introduce Jean to the world and assist with overdue damage control. He was in town for two nights only, and Sunday morning he'd be on his way home again.

Jeremy understood why it was such a tight turnaround, but he wished Kevin would stick around longer. He wanted to show Kevin the best Los Angeles had to offer. If this trip went well enough, maybe he could convince Kevin to fly out again. Maybe he could go out to South Carolina, though the last time he'd looked up Palmetto State there'd been a genuinely impressive lack of things to do in the area.

It was a short walk to baggage claim. Jeremy had a printout in one pocket with Kevin's flight information on it, but he'd skimmed it so many times he had the details memorized. He scanned the screens over the luggage carousels out of habit, knowing it was unlikely Kevin had checked anything for such a short trip, and moved to where he could get a better look at the incoming crowd. It was a funny bit of déjà vu, as Kevin was on the same airline Jean had used a few months back.

Thoughts of Jean had him checking his phone for any individual texts from Cat or Laila. Jean had been moodier than usual this week, and Jeremy honestly wasn't sure if he was more uptight about the interview or Kevin's visit. Jeremy had almost asked a half-dozen times, but every time he had the chance, he remembered the angry honesty in Jean's *"I wanted him to die."* The best he could do was keep an eye on them both and hope they made it through the weekend unscathed.

Jeremy forcibly turned his attention to the incoming crowd instead and was rewarded a minute later when he spotted Kevin coming down the tunnel. Jeremy knew Kevin wasn't alone, but he couldn't yet tell who'd been assigned as his traveling partner. Even if Kevin hadn't admitted this summer that he wouldn't travel off-campus by himself, he'd said "we" this morning when he was boarding his flight at Upstate Regional. Jeremy hadn't asked because it honestly didn't matter; he'd happily chauffeur the entire Fox lineup around the city if it meant Kevin was here with Jean for this.

He raised a hand to get Kevin's attention, and Kevin motioned to his companion before changing course. The crowd finally shifted enough to reveal the Foxes' impossibly short goalkeeper. Jeremy clapped Kevin on the back as soon as he was within reach and offered Andrew Minyard a cheery nod. Andrew's bored gaze slid past him almost immediately, so Jeremy turned his full attention on Kevin guilt-free.

"Good to finally have you here!" he said. "How was your flight?"

"Unremarkable," Kevin said. "My phone hasn't updated yet. What time is it?"

"Half past seven, give or take a few. I can swing you by the hotel first if you want to check in, otherwise you're welcome to come unwind with us. Not sure if you were able to eat on account of what time your flight was," he said, and waited for Kevin to shake his head. "Great! Dinner it is. We've got water and beer at the house, or do you prefer something else?"

"Vodka, generally," Kevin said, "but I can work with beer."

"I know where we can get some," Jeremy assured him. "No other bags? All right, car's out this way."

The two had a single hard-sided carry-on between them, and Andrew took it from Kevin at the crosswalk so it could sit in the backseat with him. As soon as Kevin buckled up in the passenger seat, Jeremy got them on the road back to USC. He started the AC but motioned for Kevin to adjust the vents as he liked. Jeremy tried to keep his attention on the road and not the pale scars on the back of Kevin's left hand, but knowing now who'd broken Kevin's hand two years back put an anxious knot in Jeremy's chest.

"Tell me what's new," Jeremy said. "How's the team?"

"Dreadful as always," was the sour response. "But they are twice as worthless off the court as they are on it, so I will suffer them for two more years."

Jeremy felt compelled to say, "It wouldn't hurt to cut them some slack, you know? They are your teammates."

Kevin waved that aside with an impatient hand. "That makes their countless failings less forgivable, not more. The Foxes have always known how little I think of them; I will not sugarcoat facts to spare their feelings."

"A boring broken record," Andrew said. "They'll learn to tune you out like I did."

Kevin flipped down the mirror on his visor to give Andrew an arch look, and there was a heated accusation in his, "You tried," that had Jeremy glancing at his rearview mirror. He studied the cool expression on Andrew's face, wondering what he was missing, but at last Andrew looked away. Kevin snapped his visor back into place with a smug smile.

"You're very good," Jeremy said over his shoulder, hoping to ease the new tension in the car.

Kevin nodded. "He will be Court."

Jeremy glanced back once more to see what Andrew thought of that assessment, but the goalkeeper appeared unmoved. He was gazing out the window like he'd already checked out of the conversation, and Jeremy idly wondered if that boredom was real or an attempt at modesty. If it was anyone else in his backseat he would've

138

gone with the latter, but he'd heard enough rumors about Andrew over the last couple years he hesitated. It should be impossible for someone with such a phenomenal reputation to care so little, but Jean was equally complicated.

"Jean hates Exy, too," he said.

"It doesn't matter," Kevin said. "He has no choice but to play."

"For two more years," Jeremy agreed. "I wonder what he'll do after graduation?" He waited a few moments to see if Kevin would speculate with him, but of course Kevin had nothing to add. Jeremy let it slide and said instead, "He thinks we have a real chance to take first place this year."

It worked like a charm. Kevin latched onto the new topic with enthusiasm, and they spent the rest of the ride picking through the list of potential contenders to the throne. There were only two schools in USC's home district that posed any threat during the fall season, and neither one could do enough damage to keep the Trojans from making championships. Getting to the finish line was not the problem; it was only at the very end that the Trojans choked year after year.

The Ravens were an unknown factor now that they were self-destructing, but Jeremy wasn't quite ready to write them off. They'd been on top of the world for too long to give up now. Surely they would find a way to pull together and salvage their reputation, if only to spite those who celebrated their overdue comeuppance.

Penn State was an obvious threat, but the Foxes were the biggest question mark where Jeremy was concerned. Wymack might have caved to pressure to recruit a larger team this year, but he would never change his recruiting policies. Whether last year's unprecedented synchrony could survive six new tumultuous teenagers was anyone's guess.

"Only if Neil develops a tolerable personality," Kevin said when Jeremy asked, and Jeremy tried to pass a laugh as a cough. The sidelong look Kevin sent him said he wasn't fooled, but Kevin didn't waste his time being offended. "The freshmen have united against him, even that pathetic excuse of a striker he fought so hard for. If he can't win their respect, the Foxes might as well throw their racquets in the trash."

Jeremy filed that important insight away for later but only said, "Speaking of Neil, I'm surprised he didn't come with you. Not that we're not happy to have you," he added over his shoulder at Andrew, "but I assumed he'd want to visit Jean again."

It took him a minute to realize he'd said something wrong. He made it past another exit before realizing Kevin was staring at him. Jeremy studied his curiously blank expression and realized he'd finally gotten Andrew's undivided attention.

Jeremy forced his gaze back to the road, bewildered. "Is it something I said?"

"What do you mean, visit Jean *again*?" Kevin asked.

"What do you mean, what do I mean?" Jeremy returned. "He was here in June."

Kevin twisted in his seat to stare at Andrew. Jeremy risked a glance at the rearview mirror, but Andrew was gazing out the window again with a distant look on his face. Kevin gave him a few moments to come up with something before settling in his chair with a curse. He had his phone out and at his ear a moment later. Whoever he was calling picked up within a couple rings, and Kevin tore into them in furious French.

Jeremy put a warning hand out toward him and interjected with a firm, "Is that Jean?"

"Neil," Kevin said, and went back to chewing out his teammate. Whatever Neil had to say on the matter did nothing to improve Kevin's mood. It was a blessedly short

140

call, but Kevin looked fit to throw his phone after he hung up. Luckily he remembered whose car he was in before he followed through. He subsided somewhat grumpily, holding his phone in a white-knuckled grip.

Jeremy considered giving him time to calm down, but he couldn't help asking, "How did you not know?"

"Neil didn't tell us where he was going, but we assumed we knew based on who he was supposed to be meeting. He never said Jean was involved." Over his shoulder Kevin said, "He refuses to explain himself over the phone."

"Typical," Andrew said, unconcerned.

Jeremy cast about for a way to ease the tension. "It worked out for the best," he offered. "That was the same weekend Grayson Johnson passed away. Before they ruled it a suicide, the police wanted to hang Jean out to dry as the most obvious suspect. Neil's visit is the only reason he had an alibi they couldn't refuse."

Kevin was not at all reassured, judging by the way he buried his face in one hand.

Andrew pushed the back of Kevin's seat. "Raven backliner. Who was he to Neil?"

"No one, as far as I know," Kevin said. "He had... history with Jean."

That hesitation made Jeremy ill, and he couldn't stop a quiet, "Did you know?"

"Not here," Kevin warned him. Not with Andrew in their backseat, he meant, and it was answer enough.

Jeremy let the last few miles slide away in miserable silence and was glad to pull up behind Laila's car. They left the carryon in the back, since Jeremy would take them by their hotel later, but Andrew dug a pack of cigarettes out of it before getting out of the car. He gave it a shake and held it up toward Kevin.

"Is there a corner store nearby?" Kevin asked Jeremy. "He had to toss his lighter at security."

"Oh, I've got one you can borrow," Jeremy said, and slipped past Kevin to reopen the passenger door. Kevin arched a brow at him when Jeremy dug a pack of clove cigarettes out of the glove compartment, but Jeremy only smiled disarmingly. "I've picked up more people at bars by having a lighter handy than I have by being charming. Just walk it off before you come in?" he asked, shaking the lighter free and passing it into Andrew's waiting hand. "Laila is really sensitive to the smell."

Rather than answer, Andrew glanced at Kevin. Kevin nodded and motioned to Jeremy, so Andrew set off down the street.

"Something I said?" Jeremy asked when Andrew was out of earshot.

"It's California, not you," Kevin said. "Too many memories, especially this soon after Aaron's trial. He'll be in a foul mood all weekend."

Jeremy locked his car and led Kevin up the stairs. Kevin followed his lead when Jeremy toed out of his shoes. Cat and Laila were waiting for them in the living room, tangled together on the couch, and Cat pumped her fist in enthusiastic greeting.

"Hail, Queen. Was starting to think you'd never visit us."

Jeremy only half-listened to their easy chatter. He caught Laila's eye, and she gave a quick tip of her fingers. Jeremy leaned back, looking down the hall toward the kitchen. Jean had to have heard the door; even if he missed it, Cat's greeting was too loud to be missed. But he failed to appear, and Jeremy wondered if he should slip away from Kevin to check on him. Would it be rude?

Cat saw his distraction. "There's coffee, if you need a pick-me-up for the jet lag."

"Thank you," Kevin said, and Jeremy had no choice but to lead him to Jean.

Jean was leaning against the sink to drink his coffee,

and Jeremy didn't think it a stretch he'd gone there to put a whole room between himself and his unwanted guest. His mug stilled halfway to his mouth when they walked in, and his gaze went right past Jeremy to Kevin. Jeremy searched his face, looking for any hint of violence or anger, but Jean's expression was curiously blank. He didn't move as Kevin crossed the room toward him.

Kevin took his mug from unresisting fingers and set it aside. "You look better. California agrees with you."

Jean curled his lip. "You could sound less proud of yourself."

"Why?" Kevin asked. Jean reclaimed his mug instead of answering. Kevin let it slide in favor of giving him a onceover. "Your hair's grown back enough the cameras shouldn't pick it up, but you could have at least trimmed it to the same length." He was uncowed by the deadly look Jean sent him and insisted, "We won't have time to fix it in the morning, and I doubt anyone is open this late."

"It blends in enough now to give him a layered, wind-tossed look," Jeremy said. "Carefree summer break kind of style. I like it."

"You're not helping," Kevin said, and motioned to Jean. "Show me what you're wearing tomorrow."

Jeremy quirked a brow at him and counted off more appropriate greetings on his fingers. "It's good to see you, been a while, hope you've settled in okay, heard your team loves having you around."

Rather than take the hint, Kevin stole Jean's coffee again. Jean barely gave him time to set it aside before pushing Kevin out of his way. Jeremy had to move to let them pass, and he followed them down the hall to the bedroom. Jean tugged open the closet door, gestured wordlessly to his half of the closet, and sat on his bed to wait for Kevin's decision.

Kevin started at one end and made his way to the other, a small frown on his face. Jeremy refused to believe he was that disappointed in their options, since Laila had handpicked almost everything Jean now owned, but then Kevin lifted a shirt off the rack and said, "I can't imagine you in color. Seems unnatural."

"You've doomed me to wearing gold this fall," Jean said. "Deal with it."

Kevin settled on four shirts and brought them to Jean to try on. Two he rejected as soon as he saw Jean in them. The third gave him pause, and he folded his arms across his chest as he considered it with a serious look on his face. Jeremy wasn't sure what the problem was; Jean looked just as good in this shirt as he had the last two.

He almost said as much, but managed to censor himself at the last moment: "What's up?"

"It's a closed studio," Kevin said. "The lighting will be significantly different than if it was built for an audience. We'll have to see what this looks like in morning sunlight to know for sure. Try the last."

Jean muttered something rude under his breath but obediently changed. As soon as he dropped his hands Kevin reached out to fix his collar and tug the top two buttons loose. Kevin hesitated, then hooked a finger under the silver chain around Jean's neck and pulled it free.

"This is Renee's," Kevin said, but Jean only stared him down in silence. Kevin didn't press him for an explanation but withdrew. "Let it show. The people who are most likely to have a problem with you will be the ones most comforted by such a symbol. You need all the good favor you can scrape together right now."

"I don't care," Jean said, moving to tuck it away again.

Kevin caught hold of his hand to stop him. "We're trying to sell you to them. An image of you, rather. Don't make it harder for us than it needs to be." He waited a beat to see if Jean would argue, then withdrew and motioned to the shirt. "Keep this one with the other. We'll compare

144

them in the morning."

He draped the third shirt on Jean's bed before carrying the rejected two back to the closet. Jeremy assumed Jean was used to Kevin's bossiness after so many years together, but he glanced at Jean's face to gauge his mood. The look on Jean's face, there and gone again in a heartbeat, was almost enough to startle him off the doorframe. Jeremy had no time to dwell on this sudden understanding; Jean felt Jeremy's stare on him and was thoughtless enough to return it.

Maybe Jeremy should have schooled his surprise, but he wasn't expecting Jean to flinch like he'd been struck. Jean turned sharply away, a vain attempt to hide his reaction, and yanked his buttons loose with a force that should have ripped at least one off its threads.

"With a little more care," Kevin said, aggrieved. "We might need that tomorrow."

"Get out," Jean warned him. Kevin made a disapproving noise but left the room. Jeremy lingered for just a moment, but the hint of panic in Jean's second, "*Get out*," had him beating a hasty retreat after Kevin.

Confusion left Jeremy rattled, and he was glad to subject Kevin to Laila's and Cat's enthusiastic questions so he could think. Jean hadn't denied his sexuality the first time Jeremy brought it up, and he'd been more annoyed than anything when Jeremy teased him about Laila last month. He'd gotten caught checking them out more than once this summer, but he was always quick to retreat into his own space afterward. It always felt more like caution and avoidance than fear or self-loathing. Jeremy couldn't imagine why Kevin alone would inspire such a vehement reaction.

Whatever it was, it wasn't enough to keep Jean away for long. He came looking for them just a few minutes later, and Cat gleefully relocated everyone to the kitchen so she could start on dinner.

Jeremy noted the clock as he stole one of the stools and asked, "Should you check on Andrew? He's been gone a while."

Laila perked up. "Oh, is he here?"

"Ravens do not travel alone," Jean said.

"Can you point at the Raven in the room?" Cat asked without looking up from her mixer.

"He likely won't come back until I tell him we're on the way to the hotel," Kevin said. "It's better that way."

Laila sighed in disappointment. "I'd love to talk to him one day. He's very good."

"He will be Court," Jean said.

"So will you," Kevin said.

Such an unhesitating endorsement from Kevin Day would have knocked anyone else off their feet, but Jean's expression went smooth as stone. Jeremy chipped in with a quick, "If you want to be."

"I am perfect Court," Jean said, inflectionless and quiet. "I will play where I am signed."

Cat picked up on the dip in Jean's mood immediately. "Kevin! Help us with the arepas. Jean will show you how." She nudged him with her elbow. When Jean scowled silent refusal, she jabbed him again and said, "Make the Queen roll up his sleeves, it'll be good for him. Nothing's better than a meal you've had a hand in."

"I can also—" Jeremy started.

"Touch nothing," Cat said, brandishing her knife at him.

Kevin arched a brow at him, but Jeremy sliced a hand across his neck in a desperate *Let's just forget it*. The mischievous look on Cat's face said she was two seconds from listing off his various disasters, but then Jean dragged his bowl to where Kevin could reach it. Jeremy watched as Jean showed Kevin how to shape the arepa dough around slices of fresh mozzarella. Kevin's first attempt was messy but serviceable, but Jean took it away from him to press it into a cleaner shape. Kevin watched him work with a distant gaze.

"When did you learn how to cook?" he asked.

"Cat is teaching me," Jean said. He could have left it at that, but after a beat, he admitted, "I like it. It makes everything else go away for a while."

He'd never hesitated to join Cat in the kitchen, but this was the first time he'd offered such an unguarded opinion of it. The smile that curved Cat's lips was gentle; the look Laila sent Jean was fond. Kevin studied Jean like he wasn't quite sure who he was looking at: not with any trepidation, but quietly reevaluating a man he'd known for so many years. For a moment Jeremy felt the history between them and was dizzy; in another he was keenly aware there was too much there for him to ever understand.

Kevin offered Jean a second arepa, waited for Jean to reach for it, and said, "I'm glad."

Jean went still with his fingers on the dough. His jaw worked for a moment as he weighed his possible responses. In the end he said nothing, but when he finally curled his fingers around the little flatbread he pressed his knuckles into Kevin's palm. Maybe it was optimistic, but Jeremy interpreted it as a silent *thank you*.

Maybe not, or maybe that was as vulnerable as Jean felt like being tonight, because Jean turned to Jeremy a few moments later. "He's underfoot. Take him away and show him your most recent match against Arizona."

"I don't think Kevin wants—" Laila started.

Kevin didn't even hear her. "It was a phenomenal game," he said, eyes alight.

"Maybe *he* will forgive your fumble," Jean added, and Jeremy made a face at him.

"Against Faser," Kevin said. The fact that he knew exactly what play Jean was talking about was equal parts mortifying and fascinating, and Jeremy could only stare at him. Kevin made an annoyed sound and said, "You are his better in every way. You should have slammed him into the wall."

He had, later that night at the hotel room, but Jeremy didn't think Kevin needed to hear that. He gamely ignored the *I-told-you-so* look Jean sent him. "That's the trouble with playing opponents you're familiar with. They know how best to distract you."

"A rookie excuse," Kevin said derisively.

"We can't all be perfect," Jeremy said with a smile.

Kevin shrugged that off. "You are close enough to count."

Jeremy had all of one second to revel in that praise before Jean sent Kevin a sullen look and said, "Jeremy is studying for law school."

Kevin's jaw dropped. "No."

He rounded on Jeremy, and Jeremy barely beat him to the punch. "If it's all the same to you, I'd rather not get into it tonight. I'm not asking," he added when Kevin wasn't so easily deterred. Kevin continued to stare at him like Jeremy had personally betrayed him, but he wisely kept his peace. Satisfied, Jeremy changed the subject with, "What's the plan for tomorrow?"

At length Kevin said, "To somehow present Jean as someone to root for. A thankless task," he said, and ignored the withering look Jean flicked him. "So long as we stick to the script, everything will be fine."

"Good," Jeremy said, smiling at them in turn. "Nothing to worry about, then!"

"Put a jinx on the whole thing, why don't you?" Cat lamented. "Go knock on wood."

"Elsewhere," Jean added pointedly.

Jeremy pushed away from the island. "Kevin and I are running up to the store real quick, then. Do we need anything?" He waited while Cat gave the fridge a cursory inspection and answered a negative, then caught Kevin's eye and started for the door. They paused at the entrance to put their shoes back on. Kevin took the keyring from Jeremy after he'd locked the door behind him and inspected the Traveler keychain.

"I wish you'd come to USC. It would've been fun to play with you all these years."

"I would not be me without Edgar Allan," Kevin said, returning Jeremy's keys. "Everything I am and have today is because I grew up at Evermore."

"Up to and including the broken hand," Jeremy said quietly as they set off. Kevin rubbed the back of his left hand and said nothing. Jeremy was loathe to kill the good mood they'd fostered in the kitchen, but with the Ravens on the table it was hard to resist. He drummed his hands against his thighs in a nervous beat before finally asking again, "Did you know about Grayson?"

Kevin didn't hesitate. "All Ravens know a variation of the story."

Don't ask, Jeremy thought, but how could he not? "Did he ever—were you—?"

"They had no reason." Kevin caught his poor wording even as Jeremy rounded on him. "That's not what I meant," he said with a grimace, and Jeremy stared him down as he searched for a better way to phrase it. "The Nest thrives on violence, but every punishment doled out is calculated and executed with purpose. Unsatisfactory times on drills, missed shots, failure to block a striker or failure to outstep a defenseman, there is always a triggering factor."

Jeremy refused to listen to this. "There is nothing that justifies what happened to him."

Kevin opened his mouth, thought better of it, and looked away. Jeremy honestly wasn't sure what was worse: that the Ravens thought themselves right for hurting Jean so horrifically, or that Kevin knew what their excuse was. He felt ill as he demanded, "Why didn't you

149

say something this spring when they were tearing him apart?"

"Because I know better than to put Jean's back to the wall."

"I don't understand."

"You do," Kevin said.

"The hell I do."

"Jean cannot betray them. He doesn't know how. He will always betray himself first. If I had spoken out this spring and accused Edgar Allan of fostering such abuse, Jean would have felt compelled to undermine me. He would have embraced the Ravens' lies no matter how much it killed him to accept the blame. I have heard it before," he insisted when Jeremy started to argue. "I will not listen to it again."

Jeremy wanted so badly to refuse that. He thought of Jean flinching away from every mention of Coach Moriyama and Riko, of how easily and quickly and stridently he insisted he deserved everything that had happened to him. He thought of Jean's haunted stare and hoarse, *"You cannot save me from what came before, and you help neither of us by trying to dig up those graves."* It was so cruel Jeremy couldn't breathe.

"You can't tell me that not a single Raven would support him if he spoke the truth. I won't believe that."

"You don't even know what his truth is," Kevin said, frustration bleeding into his voice.

"I don't care." Jeremy waved that off with a sharp jerk of his hand. "He was sixteen."

Kevin grimaced at him. "It's the age of consent in West Virginia. Without a complaint, there is no crime, and there will never be a complaint."

Jeremy had to walk away, but he didn't get far. Kevin caught his arm to drag him to a stop. Jeremy yanked out of his grip to stare him down, but Kevin's "Jeremy—" was followed only by miserable silence. Jeremy studied the

150

tension in his expression and shadows in his eyes and knew Kevin was fighting to confide in him. Jeremy wasn't sure which side he wanted to win. He didn't want Kevin giving away Jean's secrets, but he desperately wanted to understand the Ravens' wretched mentality.

At last Kevin only said, "Silence is the only way Jean has a voice. He does not have to participate in his own downfall. It is not kind or fair, but it is the best we can do."

"He deserves more than that," Jeremy said. "You know he does."

"He deserves peace. That's why he's here."

"That's not enough."

"It is more than he has ever gotten."

Jeremy studied him in silence. "And what about you?" he asked at length. "They've wronged you too, more than I think you've let on. A couple sly words in spring," he said, tapping his fingers to the back of Kevin's hand, "but nothing since then. I would've guessed it kindness, to avoid starting a fight while Edgar Allan grieved Riko's death, but I don't think that's it anymore. You won't fight them either, will you?"

"I have no reason to fight," Kevin said. "Everything I want and need still lies ahead of me; it is a waste of time to look back so long as that holds true."

"Justice is not a waste of time."

"I don't care about justice. All I want in life is to play the perfect game." After a beat he added, "And to know why you are applying to law school. You belong on the US Court with me, but they can't sign you if you're not contracted to a professional team. Don't say you want to quit. I will not believe you."

"That topic was already vetoed for the night," Jeremy reminded him. "Let's focus on one nightmare at a time."

It was an inexcusable slip. Maybe later he'd forgive himself for being careless, considering the conversation they'd just had, but right now the look Kevin turned on him had Jeremy taking two steps back. The chirping crosswalk gave him an excuse to turn and walk away, and he made it all the way to the front door of the liquor store before Kevin caught up with him. Jeremy gestured for Kevin to precede him inside, but Kevin stopped beside him.

"Jeremy," Kevin pressed.

"Promise me you'll protect him tomorrow," Jeremy said. "That's all I'm asking."

The look on Kevin's face said he wasn't going to let this slide for long, but at last Kevin said, "I promise."

Jeremy couldn't manage a smile, but he knew Kevin didn't expect one from him. "Thank you. You're a good friend, Kevin. I hope you know that."

"He and I are not friends."

"But you're mine," Jeremy said, and said again, "Thank you."

It took Kevin only a few minutes to get the bottle he needed, and the walk back to the house passed in dead silence. Rather than take his drink inside, Kevin stopped beside Jeremy's car and said, "It is for tomorrow." Jeremy unlocked the doors so Kevin could stow the bottle in the passenger seat footwell, and they continued into the house emptyhanded. Jeremy feigned not to see Laila's curious look when they returned without bags but settled in next to her at the island.

"Smells great," he said, motioning for Kevin to take the last seat beside him.

"Of course it does," Cat said cheerily. "We made it. Check this out."

Jeremy only heard every other word as she showed off the recipe they were trying, but that was all right. Here it was warm and safe, and Jeremy could use that to hold the rest at bay for at least a little while.

CHAPTER NINE
Jean

Jean and Kevin were due at the station at half-past nine on Saturday morning. Kevin had gone over what to expect over a light breakfast, but nothing he said could make Jean feel better about this. It wasn't a live segment, but the turnaround time for it to be aired was only expected to be a few hours. They could each bring one guest to wait in the wings—Andrew for Kevin and Jeremy for Jean—but other than that it would just be them and the crew in the studio. Kevin had gotten a written promise there'd be no other guests.

The whole setup was a complete turnaround from every other appearance Kevin had agreed to. Jean wasn't sure if Kevin had set such strict rules for Jean's sake or in response to how badly Kathy Ferdinand's show went last fall. He was honestly a little surprised the station went along with so many demands, but Kevin hadn't spoken to anyone since finals. Perhaps the exclusive right to finally ask Kevin about Riko's death was worth any concession.

Jean had been trying to hold that thought at bay for weeks, but with them five minutes from leaving the house it hit like a bag of bricks. He glanced across the living room at Kevin, who was trying to hug himself out of existence near the bay window, and felt his stomach give a violent lurch. He barely made it to the bathroom in time to throw his entire breakfast up, and his hands were trembling so badly afterward he could barely sip water from the sink.

"Oh, babe," Cat said, combing her fingers through his hair as he tried tearing the hand towel in half. She traded him a glass of water for the towel. "You can do this. I

153

know you can."

"I can't. I won't go."

"You can," she stressed. "Kevin and Jeremy will be right there with you, and Laila and I will be cheering you on from here."

"Pretend you're talking to us," Laila added from the doorway.

"I can't talk to the press. I'm not allowed. And I can't—" *listen to Kevin lie about Riko.*

"Maybe you should have a drink, too," Cat mused. Jean didn't think it would at all help, but he drained half of the glass she'd brought him. Cat clarified a moment later with, "I mean vodka. I know it's not your style, but Kevin seems a bit more settled since he knocked some back. It's kind of funny; I hadn't thought him the type to get stage fright."

Jean stared at her, waiting for her words to make sense, but the best he managed was, "Vodka."

"Genuinely impressive how fast it went down," Cat said. "I think you were getting dressed when—oh?" She scrambled to catch the glass he pushed at her hands, and Laila almost didn't make it out of Jean's way in time as he stormed out of the bathroom. Jean made it halfway to Kevin before Andrew appeared in his path. Jean moved to shove him out of the way, but Andrew gave his arm a brutal wrench that almost took him off his feet.

"Hey," Jeremy said, coming off the couch in alarm. "What's going on?"

Jean scowled at Andrew. "Get your hands off me, Doe."

"Still the best you have to offer?" Andrew asked. "Boring."

Kevin was closest, so he caught hold of Andrew's wrist. "Don't. He's not going to hurt me. He doesn't know how." Kevin ignored the scathing look Jean flicked him, intent on staring down his tiny teammate. The tilt of

154

Andrew's head said he was considering it, but his iron grip didn't waver. Kevin's knuckles went white as he squeezed. "I need him today, and I can't put him in front of a camera if you break him."

Andrew let go and stepped aside, and Jean immediately shoved Kevin. Kevin leveled a vicious look at him, unimpressed with his attitude after Kevin had intervened on his behalf, and Jean lit into him in furious French:

"You're drinking? *You*? What is wrong with you?"

"You of all people don't get to ask me that."

Jean went to shove him again, but Kevin caught a fistful of his shirt. He slammed Jean into the wall almost hard enough to knock the breath out of him. Jean was dimly aware of the Trojans standing still as stone, startled by the sudden violence and an argument they couldn't understand.

"I'm the one who's going to get us through this," Kevin warned him. "How I do it is up to me."

"Kevin." That was Jeremy, pushing past Andrew like he didn't even see him. He caught hold of Kevin's elbow and dug his fingers in when Kevin wouldn't be pulled. Jeremy's tone was every inch a warning when he said, "Kevin, back off. Right now." He waited for Kevin to let go and step back, then planted a firm hand against Jean's chest when Jean moved to follow. "No. We are not doing this, not now and not like this. You two can talk it out like civilized adults when we get back from the studio."

"You let him drink," Jean accused Jeremy.

Jeremy returned his frustrated glare with a calm look. "He's not driving. If he says he can handle it, that's his decision to make."

"He's not handling it."

"And you are?" Kevin demanded.

"Enough," Jeremy said, snapping his fingers in their faces until they both looked at him. "We don't have time

155

for this. Pack up your differences and put them away for now. We need to get moving. Go on," he said, motioning for Kevin to put more space between them. "You know where my keys are. Take Andrew out to the car, and we'll be out in just a sec."

"Kevin," Andrew said, and started for the door. Kevin flicked one last cool look at Jean before following.

Jeremy waited until the front door closed before dropping his hand from Jean's chest. The look he turned on Jean was serious, but his tone was careful when he said, "You've got to get through this interview, Jean. Forgive and forget or whatever it takes; you can't bring this fight into the studio with you. They don't know anything about you outside of what the Ravens have been saying. This is your best and only chance to set the story straight. Okay?"

A dozen furious rebuttals chewed at his throat. Jean worked his jaw and said nothing. Jeremy only gave him a minute before insisting, "Jean."

"It's in my contract," Jean finally said, because what else could he do but bite his tongue and bow his head? "I agreed I wouldn't misrepresent the Trojans in public. I will behave."

"Thank you," Jeremy said, moving out of his space at last. "Just get through this, and then you and Kevin can sit down and try to make things right."

It was so optimistic, so naïve, to think such thing was possible, but Jeremy was right: this was not the time to get into it. Jean closed his eyes and counted his breaths until he felt a little calmer.

Jeremy waited until he opened his eyes before asking, "Good?"

"No," Jean said. "Let's go."

Cat met him halfway to the door to fix his shirt and give him a tight hug. "One question at a time, okay?"

"Yes," Jean said, and followed Jeremy out to the car.

Andrew and Kevin were in the back, so Jean took the passenger seat. The twenty-minute drive to the news station passed in uncomfortable silence, as even Jeremy wasn't interested in idle chatter. There was a row of parking spaces for studio guests, and Jeremy held the front door to let them all precede him inside. Kevin went to chat up the receptionist, his pleasant persona already locked in place, and Jean studied the lobby with growing unease.

Kevin beckoned them over to show off their IDs, and they passed around a sign-in clipboard while the receptionist called them an escort. A youthful aide came out to greet them only a minute later, all bright smiles and rapid-fire greetings. Her handshake was more a quick squeeze than anything else, and Andrew didn't even look at her when she turned on him last.

Kevin's smile didn't waver as he said, "Please excuse him."

"Of course," she said, spinning on her heel. "Right this way!"

She buzzed them through a set of doors, then led them down a long hallway filled with awards and colorful posters. The elevator was quick to arrive, and she swiped her badge to get them to the third floor. She didn't stop talking the entire time, but Jean let most of her chatter flow right through him. It leaned toward the inane fawning Kevin tended to bring out in people: how thrilled they were that Kevin and Jean agreed to come by, how excited she was for the upcoming season, and some quick facts about the woman who'd be interviewing them today.

Another desk was right outside the elevator doors, but one of the two staff stationed there was on the phone and the other was battling a fax machine. Their guide— Amber? Amy? Jean had already forgotten—scooped a folder off the desk without slowing. She opened it as she walked, withdrew two packets to hand Kevin, and led them into a small lounge.

"Nothing you haven't seen," she said, motioning for them to sit. "If you want to take a moment to read through and initial everything, I'll go check in with the team."

"Thank you, Amber," Kevin said, and she was gone.

A cup of pens sat in the middle of one of the coffee tables. Kevin passed one of the packets to Jean before settling down to skim his own. Jean tilted his so Jeremy could see it, but Jeremy only nodded. The first page was a list of studio policies, and the second a contract giving the studio permission to edit and use today's footage however they pleased. The last was the expected list of topics for the day, including a dozen-odd example questions. Jean only read three of those before flipping quickly back to the front.

"Just sign it," Kevin said. "It will take you too long to read it."

"No one asked you," was Jean's sour response as he scribbled his signature across the bottom of the first two sheets. Jeremy knocked his knee to Jean's in silent question, and Jean said, "My year of English lessons were predominantly oral. I learned to read after the fact so I could pass my classes. It is an offensively ugly language," he added, skimming the endless paragraphs on the page. "No personality whatsoever."

Jeremy smiled. "Good thing I'm learning French, then."

Kevin looked up, startled. "Are you?"

"Trying," Jeremy amended. "It's not going so well."

Kevin glanced between them. Jean very much did not want to hear whatever he had to say about that. Luckily for all of them, their aide swept back into the room to check on them. She collected their packets, waited for them to return the pens to the cup, and motioned for them to follow. They detoured by the studio first to drop Andrew and Jeremy off, and Amber took a few moments to introduce them to the crew. Jean glanced across the room toward the small stage. A recliner and loveseat were angled toward each other with a pale table between them. A vase of vibrant flowers was the only bit of decoration.

"This way," Amber said, and Jean dragged his stare away to follow.

He and Kevin were handed off to two women, who busily set to work fixing their hair and applying just enough makeup to offset the studio lighting. Jean kept his hands folded tightly in his lap and fixed his stare on an empty corner of the mirror.

"You've got some scarring here," his attendant said as she checked his scalp. "Does this hurt?"

When Jean didn't answer, Kevin had to: "Thank you, but it's an old injury. He's fine."

"Just let me know," she said, and went back to work.

They were nearly done when Hannah Bailey came in to greet them. Jean recognized her from watching the news this summer; she usually helmed the desk for the evening sports broadcast. She was taller in person, and her makeup was jarringly severe face-to-face, but her hand was powder soft as she offered them each a lingering handshake.

"Good to have you here," she said. "I'm Hannah Bailey. Do you have any questions for me before we begin?"

Kevin charmed her with an ease that was irritating to listen to. He'd watched some of her segments online over the years as he followed the Trojans' seasons, so he was familiar with her style and some of the larger stories she'd covered. Whether he genuinely meant any of his vapid praise, Jean didn't know and didn't care so long as he warmed her to them and held her attention. It kept her distracted the entire walk to the studio, but as she showed them to their seats, she finally turned a considering look on Jean.

"I'm aware this is your first public appearance," she

said. "Try to forget about the cameras and think of it as just a conversation between the three of us. We'll keep it as straightforward as we can, and we'll send you a copy of the final edit when it's set to go on air. Sound like a plan?" Jean stared at her in silence until Kevin cleared his throat, but Hannah beat Jean to speaking. "Forgive me for how this comes across, but we've heard mixed reports on how fluent you are. We can provide an interpreter if it would make you more comfortable."

A rumor started by the Ravens last fall whilst they were destroying his previously nonexistent reputation, and which had worked to his benefit at least once since moving to California. Jean saw no reason to upend it now if he could keep hiding behind a language barrier. He glanced at Kevin, but Kevin motioned meaningfully to Hannah. He wasn't going to help this time, so Jean fought back a scowl and said, "Kevin will help me."

"As you like," Hannah said. "We've just got one or two things to set up and we'll get started. I'll begin by introducing the segment, and you'll know when the camera has panned out to include you when I do this." She turned a warm smile toward the camera and gestured to indicate her guests. She glanced their way afterward to ensure they understood their cue and dropped her hand to her lap. "Would you like some water?"

"That would be great," Kevin said.

Hannah motioned to her team, but the faint frown that tugged at her mouth had Jean following her gaze. Amber was huddled with the camera crew around a laptop, both hands over her bulky headphones as she stared in slack-jawed fascination at whatever was happening on the screen. Hannah cleared her throat, offered a quick, "Excuse me," and went to corral her team. She made it halfway to them before one of the men rushed to meet her and pull her aside. Jean heard the murmur of voices but couldn't make out any words, but Hannah hurried to

160

Amber's side only moments later.

"That bodes well," Jean said in an undertone.

"Unlikely to have anything to do with us," Kevin said.

Despite that easy dismissal, he glanced across the room toward Andrew and Jeremy. The pair were also watching the fuss, but Andrew only needed a moment to feel Kevin's gaze on him. He waved it off, looking unconcerned. Jeremy caught the gesture as well. When he saw the question in Kevin's stare he checked his phone. His helpless shrug a few moments later ought to be reassuring: if the floozies weren't blowing up his phone with rumors and gossip, then Kevin was right about it not being their problem. Another headline for Hannah to chase as soon as she got them out of here, perhaps.

Amber lowered her hands and nudged her pair of headphones ajar to free an ear. She gestured wildly at the screen as she explained what she was looking at, and Hannah clasped her shoulder in either thanks or encouragement as she stepped away. Her "Keep an eye on it and keep me posted," carried well enough as she started back toward her chair. She was almost back before she remembered why she'd left, and she called, "We'll take water, and then we'll get started."

She turned an apologetic smile on her guests as she got comfortable, but the new light in her eyes made Jean deeply uncomfortable. Whatever new story was unfolding put a hunger in her that was likely to make her tactless and greedy as she rushed through this for the next big thing.

"I'm sorry about that," she said. "Shall we begin?"

Since Amber was busy, one of the men had to bring glasses of water over, and he arranged them on the table within reach. Then he hurried back to his spot between the cameras. As soon as his crew motioned their readiness, he waved an okay to Hannah and counted them off.

"Good afternoon, Los Angeles, and welcome to a special segment of Bailey's Breaking News," Hannah

161

said, brandishing her perfect smile for the cameras. "I'm Hannah Bailey. As of this morning, we are two weeks out from the start of the NCAA Exy season. Join us this evening at eight-thirty for our weekly check-in around the nation. With some last-minute coaching changes in the Midwest, we're bound to see some shakeups heading into the year. Minnesota and Iowa will both be dialing in with the latest updates, and you won't want to miss it.

"Today we've got something special in store," Hannah said, pointing her gaze toward the other camera. "I have with me today two of the biggest names from Class I Exy, Kevin Day of Palmetto State University and Jean Moreau of the University of Southern California." She motioned broadly to them. Jean kept his stare on her, aware that Kevin had glanced obediently toward the camera with a smile and an acknowledging tilt of his head. "These former Ravens are here to help us pay an overdue homage to a legend and to prepare us for what's to come this season. Kevin, Jean, thank you for joining us today."

"Thank you for inviting us," Kevin said, with a warmth that made Jean's skin crawl. "And thank you, and your viewers, for being so patient with us this year. The privacy you afforded us this summer was immeasurably kind."

"Of course, of course," Hannah said, reaching toward him like she meant to clasp his hand. "I cannot even begin to imagine what this summer has been like for you. We have all grieved," she said, including Jean in her sorrowful stare, "and I know we pressured you to grieve with us, but obviously our relationship with Riko Moriyama is so far removed from what the two of you had with him."

"We stepped back, but we weren't completely sheltered," Kevin said. "We've seen the tributes and well wishes, and the forums dedicated to his best plays. It's been—" he paused, searching for the right words. Jean wasn't sure if it was for show or if Kevin was fighting to

162

find the kindest lie. "—heartening, in the best and worst way, to know how deeply we've all been affected. That we're not alone as we contemplate his loss."

Jean tasted blood. He wasn't sure if he'd chewed through the inside of his cheek or if it was the sour tang of brutal memories. He started to reach for his face to check before remembering there were cameras. He pressed his fingertips to his lips instead of shoving them into his mouth. The movement was enough to attract Hannah's attention, and she turned a sympathetic look on him.

"Thank you especially, Jean, for being with us here today," she said. "We've asked a lot of you by bringing you on today, tying your debut interview so intricately to such a grave discussion, but we are glad for the chance to finally hear from you."

If he spoke, he'd likely throw up his stomach lining, but he'd promised to be here and to behave. Jean swallowed hard against his nausea and said only, "Yes."

"Can we start with Riko?" she asked, looking between them. "A bit grim, to be sure, but it seems kinder to begin on a tragic note and end on the brightness of your respective futures."

"Of course," Kevin said.

"This story begins at the end: a controversial showdown between the undefeated Edgar Allan Ravens and the Palmetto State Foxes. Absolutely brilliant performances all around," Hannah noted, extending a hand toward Kevin, "with a last-second win clinched by none other than Kevin Day. We could spend all day dissecting that game, but as we are pressed for time we will have to focus on its unexpected conclusion."

"A curious choice," Kevin said. At her gesture, he clarified, "Calling it unexpected. The Foxes had undeniable momentum leading up to that match, including one of the best win-loss ratios across the nation. Once we were able to defeat USC, the Ravens should have known to take us seriously."

"No offense intended," Hannah said belatedly. "The Foxes won, the Ravens' perfect streak was destroyed, and Riko Moriyama was hospitalized with a shattered arm." That she left off how and why he was injured wasn't surprising, and Jean understood in a heartbeat who she'd cheered for in that match. Still, it was a ballsy omission when Andrew was standing across the room. "A few hours later, Edgar Allan reported that his body had been found in one of Evermore's towers." She paused there to let that reminder breathe, then asked, "Were you able to speak with him after the match, Kevin?"

"No," Kevin said. "We exchanged a few words during the game, but nothing after."

"It feels indelicate to ask, but take us through it," Hannah said. "How did you find out? What was it like, hearing he was gone?"

Renee's voice at his ear, asking Jean to turn off the TV and wait until she could reach him. Jeremy's text, Jeremy's call, *He's gone.* For a moment Jean remembered the weight of the coffee table as he threw it into the TV, and he dug his nails into the back of his hand. He felt fuzzily hot in one moment and clammy in the next. In quiet French he said, "I should not be here for this."

Kevin put his hand over Jean's to hide the half-moon marks Jean was tearing into his skin. "Stay with me," Kevin said, just as soft, and Jean forcibly relaxed his death grip. Kevin looked toward Hannah, who was watching them with exaggerated sympathy, and finally said, "It was devastating."

She made a sympathetic noise, and Kevin withdrew his hand as he sorted through his troubled thoughts. The best he managed was a slow and careful, "He was my brother. Growing up, the only thing that mattered was the future we were going to carve out together. We'd drifted apart after my injury and transfer, but he was still

164

undeniably important to me. For him to be gone feels impossible, even now."

"If the Ravens had won, or if he hadn't lost his arm," Hannah started.

That put a little more life into Kevin, and he smoothly cut in to say, "I would prefer not to entertain such hypotheticals. I know it's not your intention, but it puts the burden of his death on us: the Foxes for their spectacular victory or Andrew for doing what was necessary to save Neil's life. And I will not argue on that last point," Kevin added when Hannah looked a bit taken aback. "Neil's life was very much in danger."

"You genuinely think Riko was aiming for him and not the court floor," Hannah said, with obvious skepticism.

"Yes," Kevin said without hesitation. Rather than linger and argue that point with her, Kevin leaned her way and motioned for her to follow along. "I grieve him, but I reserve my outrage for the system that led him to his death. You do not understand what it is like to be a Raven: the unrelenting pressure to perform to perfection, the suffocating legacy that weighs down your every move. It is that environment which cost Riko his life, as it did so many other Ravens this summer."

"A tragic year on many fronts," Hannah agreed. "Wayne Berger, Colleen Jenkins, and Grayson Johnson also took their lives over this summer. Four lives destroyed by a legacy. Nearly six, if the rumors are to be believed," she added with a glance toward Jean. "We heard some upsetting news out of Palmetto State this last April. I will not be cruel enough to ask if they were true, but I will say I am glad to see you still with us and that I hope you are in a better place now."

"Yes," Jean said. Kevin's heavy stare was a lingering weight, so Jean made himself add, "Thank you."

"The fifth, of course, would be Zane Reacher,"

Hannah said. "Details have been relatively scarce on that front, but we have come across some new information that ought to be addressed. Namely, your role in the affair, Jean."

She didn't know about January; she didn't know about broken promises. She didn't. She couldn't. "I don't understand."

"We reached out to Edgar Allan's staff this past June to see how the Ravens were adjusting to their new coach. Unsurprisingly close-lipped," she noted with a glance toward the camera, "but we were able to get something interesting from head nurse Josiah Smalls: he only called the Reacher family that day because you told him Zane needed help." She waited a beat to see if he'd respond unprompted, then asked, "How did you know he was in danger?"

Kevin motioned for him to answer, so Jean offered an evasive, "I just did."

"Jean," Kevin said.

"I won't answer that," Jean said in French. "It isn't right to share their business with outsiders."

Kevin's stare was heavy as he followed Jean out of English. "How did you know?"

Jean flicked a furtive look at Hannah. "He was in love with Colleen. He was different after—" It caught in his throat, sharp and violent enough to break him. Jean swallowed hard and tried again: "Finding out she was gone after everything else that happened would surely destroy him, or so I thought. I had to try."

Kevin considered that for a moment, then turned on Hannah and said in English: "Colleen and Zane were in a relationship." If he noticed the accusatory look Jean sent him for betraying them, he didn't deign to acknowledge it. "Jean feared how Zane would handle the news of her death, especially considering the Ravens' instability this summer."

"Oh, what tragic new insight," Hannah said, pressing her hand to her heart as if the truth was distressing to hear. "I'm sure his family is enormously grateful you were looking out for him. Have you been able to speak with him since he was discharged from the hospital, Jean?"

"No," Jean said.

She waited a beat, like she was expecting more than that. When Jean only stared at her, Hannah took a more aggressive approach: "Forgive me for the way this comes across, but why did you save him?" She put out a calming hand before he could respond and said, "We are all of course immensely grateful that you did, but the Ravens have gone out of their way to make you a public spectacle this year. You could have simply looked away. No one would have known."

"I do not care what they are saying about me," Jean said, too offended to watch his tone. "They have every right to hate me for transferring when and where I did. I do not hold it against them, and I do not believe they should die for it. Who are you to suggest such a thing?"

"Jean," Kevin said, with a smile that said Jean was trying his patience. To Hannah he said, "Forgive him, he is passionate when he gets going."

"It was an unkind question," Hannah said, unapologetic. "The fault is with me. But it is curious, isn't it? The unmitigated aggression," she clarified when neither man responded. "Kevin also transferred away from Edgar Allan, albeit over winter break. The Ravens' crusade against Palmetto State University is a well-known grudge—further exacerbated by the end of this last season—but they never turned that outrage on Kevin specifically."

Kevin turned a serene stare on her. "You're leading up to a 'why'," he said, and it was almost impressive how pleasant he could make an accusation sound.

Hannah smiled and admitted, "Guilty. Some of the

167

rumors are fairly damning, if you'll excuse my Fr—
language," she finished with a glance at Jean. "Would you
feel comfortable addressing those with us today to help
clear the air?"

Jean teetered between kneejerk refusal and the
bewildered suspicion he was supposed to allow this. If he
denied her the answers she craved, would he be
considered combative? Would that break his contract and
his promise to behave in public? He had only a couple
dizzying seconds to war with it before Kevin gave a quiet
"Huh" at his side. It was just loud enough to get Hannah's
attention, and she glanced away from Jean.

Kevin didn't wait for an invitation to speak but said,
"I'm sorry; it's just an unexpected line of questioning.
You're the last person I expected to buy into the Ravens'
sensationalism, especially seeing how you've covered the
Trojans for the last six years. USC's endorsement should
be more than enough to settle the debate, I would think."

"Even an ardent fan such as yourself must admit USC
is not without its missteps," Hannah pointed out. "Part of
the Trojans' undeniable charm is in how enthusiastically
they recover and work to improve."

"The misstep here is not theirs," Kevin said. "The
Ravens are out of line, and I am out of patience with their
tedious antics. They should spend less time dragging Jean
through the mud and more time rebuilding their
nonexistent defense line. They've lost their major
players," he insisted. "Zane graduated, Jean transferred,
and Grayson…"

Kevin didn't bother to finish that thought but gave a
slight *what can you do* wave of his hand. Letting a camera
see this heartless side of him was unprecedented; Jean
wasn't sure whether to blame the vodka or Hannah's dig at
the Trojans. He stepped on Kevin's foot in silent warning,
but Kevin persisted with, "They have no one of value
left."

Hannah drummed her fingernails on the arms of her chair as she considered him. "A rare treat to see you so protective of someone, Kevin."

"I lost Riko this spring," Kevin said. "Jean is the only brother I have left."

It stung more than it should this many years later, but Jean only had a moment to seethe. Across from him Hannah said, "Speaking of brothers, let's backtrack to Grayson Johnson."

Jean stopped breathing. At his side Kevin said, "It is perhaps a little too soon."

Hannah nodded to acknowledge that but didn't give up. "Every other Raven we lost this summer chose to— leave," she said after a brief search for the best euphemism, "from their own hometowns. Grayson is the sole exception, as he drove two hours north to Los Angeles from San Diego. By all accounts, Grayson's younger brother Lucas—also a Trojan—and Jean were the last two people he spoke to before he died." She gave Jean her undivided attention. "What did he say to you, and did you know then it was a cry for help?"

"I know where you play. I know where you live."

Jean couldn't feel his face. "I don't want to talk about Grayson with you."

"The report filed with campus security stated that you got into an altercation with Grayson outside of the Gold Court but that you chose not to press charges. Coach Rhemann, however, filed a complaint to ban him from school property. An unusually decisive and aggressive move from USC, don't you think? Must have been quite the confrontation. What did you two fight about?"

Teeth, Jean thought. He was distantly aware of Kevin's bruising grip on his wrist, as Kevin tried to pry Jean's nails free of his throat without being too obvious about it. Whether or not the camera could pick it up mattered little; Hannah was studying Jean's hand with an unhealthy

169

amount of interest. Jean sucked in a slow breath and held it, looking past a cruel *"Who is going to protect you now?"* to a too-calm *"Grayson will never bother you again."* Jean forced his grip to relax and let Kevin press his hand flat against the couch.

The Trojans would beat him black and blue for standing his ground so rudely, but any agony would be better than this. "I won't talk about him with you. Do not ask me again."

"I just think—"

"Hannah," Kevin said, in a tone that shut her up immediately. "That is enough."

She looked between them, weighing her options. Jean didn't trust the look in her eyes one bit, but at last she nodded and sat back in her chair. "Then we will talk less about the Ravens and more about you. Jean Moreau," she said, as if testing the sound of his name for the first time. "Formerly of the Edgar Allan Ravens, now a member of the USC Trojans. From a three to a twenty-nine, save the lingering beauty mark." She gestured to her left cheekbone. "You've been a recognized member of the perfect Court since you were first spotted at Edgar Allan, but Coach Moriyama sheltered you from the pressures of public appearance. Language barrier?"

It was as good a lie as any. "Yes."

"Born in Marseille," she said, counting off facts on her fingers. "You immigrated to the United States at the age of fourteen to study under Tetsuji Moriyama, and you joined the Raven line-up at the tender age of sixteen. As of last year, you officially hold dual citizenship with the US and France. A necessary step, I assume, if you hope to play alongside Kevin on the US Court." She waited a beat to see if he would weigh in, then said, "When is the last time you were home?"

"This is my home," Jean said.

"But your family is still in France," she noted. "Your

170

parents, Hervé and Chloé, and your younger sister Elodie." Hearing her name here was so unexpected and uncalled-for it knocked the wind out of him. He stared numbly at her as she studied his face for a reaction. "I find it a little curious, perhaps a little sad, that you haven't taken time to visit them. A lot can happen in five years, can't it?"

"Did you think you were special?"

"Ravens do not have families," Jean said. "It was not my choice."

Hannah looked genuinely thrown by that comment, so Kevin slipped in a quick, "As you know, Ravens are contractually obligated to stay at Edgar Allan over breaks. It doesn't matter if you're from France or DC; you are asked to set everyone else aside and focus only on your team until graduation. It is an unforgiving schedule meant to ensure a total dedication to the team."

"An incredible sacrifice," Hannah said, and sent Jean another intent look. "Have you at least had a chance to speak to them over the phone?"

There was a reason she was pushing this angle. Jean knew it, but he had no idea what she was building toward. The roiling in his stomach said it wasn't going to be good, but all he could do was say, "No."

Hannah steepled her fingers together and tapped her index fingers to her chin. She was weighing how far to take this, gauging if this was the moment to push it, and finally went still to ask, "Are you aware your parents were arrested by Interpol an hour ago?"

Oh, Jean thought. *Oh no.*

He was going to be sick. He could feel it chewing up his stomach, shredding his lungs on the way to his throat. In frantic French Jean protested, "I can't answer that accusation yet. I don't know how much they know."

And Amber said in flawless French, "We've got Le Monde pulled up on our laptop if you'd like to step aside

171

for a minute and read the article. As far as we can tell, it hasn't yet made it to international news."

Jean stared at her, refusing to believe what he was hearing. She misconstrued his alarm as surprise and smiled brightly. "I was asked to be on hand for this interview in case you needed an interpreter, but you deferred to Kevin." She motioned again for him to approach her and said, "Would you like to take a break and review it? Because this interview is recorded, we can edit the clip to be a seamless transition."

Jean rounded on Kevin and did the only thing he could: he slipped into Japanese and said, "Don't make me do this."

"Oh," Amber said in startled English. "That's not French."

Kevin ignored her and answered in Japanese, "Have Jeremy take you outside for some air. I will inform Hannah we will not be answering any of these questions. If she refuses to back down, we will leave. I will message Jeremy with the decision either way."

Jean didn't have to be told twice. Amber turned toward her computer when he got up, thinking Jean was giving in to curiosity, but Jean went straight for Jeremy without slowing. Jeremy moved to meet him halfway, looking more than a little alarmed, but Andrew got there first. A quick hand on Jeremy's chest pushed him back out of the way, and Andrew started for the door. Jean honestly didn't care who went with him so long as someone did, so he fell in line behind Andrew and followed him out of the studio.

Jean had no idea how they made it from that room to the parking lot. He didn't remember the elevator. He didn't know if Andrew had to sign out at the front desk. He was just suddenly aware that his hands were planted on the hood of Jeremy's car as he fought to suck air into his collapsed lungs. Every breath seemed to snag in his throat. Maybe he'd suffocate out here and finally be free of this wretched existence.

Andrew's fist came down on the square of his back with a solid thump, and Jean finally managed to take a deep breath. Andrew listened to him breathe for a few moments before saying, "*History*," with such a ferocious edge Jean knew he was mocking someone else's poor word choice. Fingers in his hair forcibly turned his head so Andrew could see the bloodied marks on the side of his throat, and Andrew demanded, "Did Johnson ever touch Neil?"

Jean didn't want to talk about Grayson, but that beast was the only thing big enough to smother the bone-deep ache of his shattering family. Hannah knew about Elodie, but how much did she know? Did Le Monde report her missing, or did they know she was—

"No," Jean said. Andrew only stared him down, weighing the veracity of that simple refusal. Jean took his sister and shoved her as deep as he could go, feeling how it tore his heart asunder to bury her again. "No. It would have been an inappropriate punishment for someone like him. His unforgivable crime was his willfulness and defiance in the face of his betters."

"Implying it would have been appropriate under other circumstances." Andrew's stare was heavy enough to crush him. Jean knew in a glance it was less concern for Jean himself and more a visceral reaction to the violation. Perhaps Andrew's nerves were still raw this close to the trial, but Jean assumed Neil's imagined near-miss was the more likely culprit. Andrew's tone when he said, "Enlighten me," was steady, almost bored, but Jean wasn't fooled.

"You of all people should not have to ask." Jean dug his thumb into Andrew's wrist and slid it up the length of his arm toward his elbow.

Andrew snatched his hand back, and Jean was finally

173

able to straighten. He rubbed the new ache from his neck before smoothing his hair with unsteady fingers, and he didn't miss the way Andrew's gaze flicked to his throat once more. Jean, in turn, dropped his stare to the arm bands Andrew never went without. He missed the days he hadn't even noticed such ridiculous accessories.

Jean remembered well the thick satisfaction in Riko's voice as he told Jean what he'd dug up in California. Who, rather: a long-lost brother who could feel the law closing in on him and would do anything to break free of the investigation. Getting him to South Carolina was easy, and Drake Spear knew what to do from there.

Destroying the goalkeeper Kevin was so fanatically invested in had sustained Riko for weeks. After the news of Andrew's assault broke, Riko obsessively collected every article he could find on the attack and hung them over his bed. Getting a full report from Proust in January had made him even happier. For a moment Jean felt a razor taking ghost-thin strips off his back; Riko's hungry *"Read it again from the top,"* was so loud at his ear Jean automatically looked for him over his shoulder. The memory of fingernails biting at his scalp, pushing his face closer to the dreadful file, was sharp enough Jean checked his hair for blood.

He couldn't stay in these thoughts, so he said, "You stole Kevin from us."

"He stole himself."

"You called him yours to Riko's face. 'My things'," he reminded Andrew. Jean hadn't gone to Kathy Ferdinand's interview, but the distance hadn't saved him. The long hours back to Evermore had done nothing to soothe Riko's fury, and Jean had missed two days of practice to recover. "You had no right to covet him. I could have—" Somehow he bit off *told you how that'd end* just in time. Jean clenched his hands into fists and forcibly refocused on Andrew's cool expression.

174

The silence that settled between them felt brittle, and then Andrew said, "Spoil the surprise for me. Did Neil kill Johnson while he was in town?"

It was an untimely reminder that the Foxes knew the truth of the Moriyamas through Kevin. Jean shouldn't be surprised that this fair-haired rat would know Neil's secrets, too, but he still cast a wary eye at Andrew as he weighed how to respond. Lying was the only sensible response, but it wouldn't get him anywhere here.

At last he grudgingly said, "He hired his uncle's people to handle it."

Andrew didn't have the good sense to look at all concerned. He turned away and dug a pack of cigarettes out of his pocket. Jean swiped at them, but Andrew moved out of his reach just in time with a calm, "Your one and only warning: you will lose the hand if you try again."

"You are an idiot," Jean accused him. "You were barely fast enough to save him last time. The next time someone takes a swing at him, you and your brisket lungs will have to watch him die. I wouldn't have given him to you if I'd known you would just throw him away so carelessly."

"Filing that one under the list of things no one asked you," Andrew said as he lit up.

Jean scowled at him as he pulled his phone out. He hadn't bothered to save Neil's number, but it was the only unregistered one in his call history. Jean stared at it, warring between necessity and his desire to avoid this conversation at all costs. At length he closed his eyes and dialed out. It took three rings before Neil answered with a simple, "Neil."

"We're nowhere near the trial," Jean said in French. "Why were they arrested already?"

Neil said nothing for a moment, then offered only a confused, "What?"

Jean explained Hannah's ambush, then said, "They are

175

supposed to be what connects me to you, but the Butcher's investigation is still ongoing. What am I allowed to say if I cannot point the finger at him yet?"

"Can't claim ignorance now if they're going to use you as a witness later," Neil mused. "It'll cast too much doubt on your credibility. Demand privacy as you come to terms with their arrest and avoid making a proper statement as long as you can, perhaps. I'll reach out for some answers."

Not a perfect solution, but it would have to do. Jean hung up as Andrew's phone beeped. Andrew skimmed his latest message before placing the phone near Jean's hand. It was Kevin's update: Hannah promised to stay on track with her questions for the rest of the interview, and she would send Amber down to collect them from the lobby.

Jean would've preferred she held her ground so they had an excuse to leave, but there was nothing he could do about it. He pushed away from the car and started for the door. Andrew was slow to follow, buying time to get through his cigarette, but he caught up at the entrance and they went in together. Amber was waiting near the desk with her cheerful smile still locked in place, looking for all the world like Jean hadn't walked out on them.

The trek back to the studio was too short, and Jeremy caught Jean's eye as he stepped through the doorway. Jean would have to apologize later for misbehaving after promising to properly represent the Trojans, but for now he went back to his spot on the couch and sat once more at Kevin's side.

In weary Japanese Kevin said, "Our damage control needs damage control. I will never do an interview again."

"Don't lie. You like the sound of your voice too much to give this up."

Kevin conceded with a light shrug. "Are you ready?"

"Would it matter if I said no?"

Kevin didn't waste his breath responding but smiled

over at Hannah, who was watching them closely. "We're ready to try again."

"Good, good. And apologies for dropping that without warning," she added, as an afterthought. "Kevin and I already filmed a few cutaways for commercials, so let's take it back a few steps and try a new angle." She waited for Jean's nod, then motioned to her producer. He counted them off, and Hannah turned her winning smile on the camera. "Welcome back to Bailey's Breaking News. When last we left off…"

CHAPTER TEN
Jean

Twenty-five minutes later they were finally freed from
Hannah's clutches, but getting out of the studio only
solved one problem. Everything they'd set aside for the
sake of surviving the interview had to be addressed, and
Jean didn't miss how quickly Jeremy's smile faded as
soon as they were out of that wretched building and in the
parking lot.

Kevin snagged Jean's sleeve halfway to the car and
said, "Give us a minute, Jeremy."

Jeremy turned toward him immediately. "Let's hear
it." When Kevin gestured between himself and Jean,
Jeremy lifted his chin and fixed Kevin with a steady look.
There was nothing aggressive in his stance or tone, but
Jean heard the easy challenge in his: "Sure. Look me in
the eye and tell me this is going to cause no problems
whatsoever for my team, and I'll wait in the car while you
two talk it out. Can you promise me that?"

Kevin's hesitation was all the answer Jeremy needed,
and Jeremy turned toward Jean next. "Obviously this is
not something either of you wants to talk about, and I
wish I could respect that. But whatever is happening here
will have ramifications for all of us, so let's find a way to
tackle this together."

Jean fixed his stare across the parking lot. "You don't
know what you're asking."

"You asked me to help you survive whatever comes
next, and this is part of it," Jeremy said. "I'm standing
here as your friend and your captain, and I'm asking you
to be honest with me. Look at me, Jean," he said, and
waited until Jean dragged his attention back to Jeremy's

178

face. "Can you trust me, or can't you? I need to know."

No was the easiest answer, but it wouldn't get him out of this conversation, and Jean knew it wasn't true. He studied Jeremy in silence, this bottle-blond sunshine captain who could force Kevin into submission without raising his voice or hand. Chances were good Jeremy would regret digging into this, but did Jean really have a choice? Whether he told him now or when Nathan's trial started, Jeremy was going to get the same version of the truth.

That didn't make it any easier to say aloud, but Jean held Jeremy's stare and said, "My parents were business partners with Nathan Wesninski."

There was a heartbeat of startled silence, and then Jeremy asked, "The so-called Butcher? Neil's father? That Nathan Wesninski?" At Jean's tense nod, he glanced past them at the studio and said, "Hold that thought after all; this is not something we should be talking about here. Let's head out before they get the wrong idea."

Jean expected to be harangued the entire way back home, but Jeremy said nothing until they were nearing their neighborhood. When the streets started looking familiar, Jeremy asked, "Do you want to do this at home or at the stadium?"

With or without an audience, he meant, but the only thing worse than having this conversation at all was having it multiple times. "Home."

Jeremy accepted that without argument and took the turn he needed to get them to Laila's house. Within seconds of him parking at the base of the driveway, the front door was open. Cat and Laila stepped out onto the porch to greet them. Cat's greeting was cheerful, but Laila's gaze as she looked from Kevin to Jean was intent. Looking for a sign they'd made it through the ordeal unscathed, Jean guessed. A pity he was going to have to disappoint her. Her stare landed on Jeremy last, and

179

Laila's expression went grim.

"How bad?" she asked as they started up the stairs.

"This conversation needs coffee," Jeremy said. "Let me set some up first."

Kevin had gotten dressed before Jeremy picked him up at the hotel this morning, so he had nothing to change into, but Jean made a beeline for his bedroom as soon as he'd gotten past Cat. He knew it was his imagination that his clothes smelled like the studio, but he had to get out of them and into something else before he tore his skin off.

He felt a split second of resistance as he yanked the second sleeve off his arm but realized too late what had caught on the shirt's pale buttons. The sight of Renee's necklace on the ground had his heart skipping in his chest. He snatched it up with unsteady fingers, looking for the break. It had snapped right at the clasp, leaving both loops hooked together on the same end.

"Hey." Cat gave the hair at the nape of his neck a gentle tug as she came up alongside him. "Are you okay? Kevin's already drinking again, and even Jeremy looks uptight. I'm assuming the interview did not go well."

"Hannah Bailey is a rancid bitch."

Cat's eyebrows went up. "Tell me how you really feel." Her humor died as she got a better look at his face, and she gave his arm a brief squeeze. "I'm sure it's not as bad as you think. And if it was... Well, we've had to clean up and smooth away a few things over the years. We'll get through this one way or another. Oh, your cross!"

He turned it over to her waiting hand, and she hummed as she inspected it. "The chain's a loss, but Laila should have something thin enough to replace it. Can I borrow this while I dig around?"

"Yes," he said, and she hurried away.

Jean was in no rush to follow, but he didn't need anyone else to come looking for him. He traded his slacks for dark jeans before digging through his closet. In the end he settled on the black USC shirt Jeremy bought him in May. Maybe they would hate to see him in it when they found out the truth, but there was a slim chance the familiar logo would be a subliminal calming influence. Jean would take any edge he could get for this conversation.

The coffee maker didn't have a large enough carafe for all of them, but it worked out. Andrew didn't want anything from them, Kevin was drinking straight vodka from a glass, and Cat opted for a beer when she saw how much Kevin was knocking back. The kitchen was too sterile a place for this conversation, so as they got their drinks, they headed down the hall to the living room. Jean wasn't sure if it was intentional, but he and Jeremy were the last to leave.

Jeremy was leaning back against the counter as Jean poured his coffee, and he touched careful fingers to Jean's elbow. "I'm sorry," he said. Even though everyone else was at the far end of the hall, he pitched his voice for Jean's ears alone. "I hate to do this the same day she tried so hard to hurt you, but I know her type. She's not going to edit that out if it means she's the first to report on it this side of the ocean."

"You are protecting your Trojans," Jean said.

"You are one of my Trojans," Jeremy reminded him, low and insistent. "This isn't me picking them over you. I need you to know that. I'm trying to look out for all of us."

Jean had to step back so Jeremy could finally pour his drink. The ache in his chest was now hooked in his throat as a boiling knot. He knew what he had to say to them, and he knew what he couldn't say without it killing him. He'd spent two months burying Elodie beneath everything he could find, only for Hannah to drive a spade right into her festering grave. For a moment Jean felt far away from here, and in his desperation he reached out. He planted a

181

hand against Jeremy's chest as Jeremy took the first step to the door.

"Jeremy," he said, and it sounded so much like *please* that Jeremy went still as stone. "Do not ask me about her. Anyone but her." Jeremy stared up at him, looking more than a little lost. Jean couldn't say her name, but Jeremy had no idea who Jean was talking about. Jean swallowed hard against a rush of bile that tasted far too much like blood and said, "My sister. I can't—" The panic biting at his chest threatened to tear him open, and Jean looked away as Jeremy's gaze shuttered. The best Jean managed was, "I can't talk about her. I won't."

He thought he heard Jeremy's soft, "I'm sorry," but his heart was pounding so loud he might have imagined it. Jean dug his nails into his own chest, trying to force his heart to a calmer pace, and fought his grief back with everything he had. Jeremy waited with him, but he was kind enough to aim his heavy stare elsewhere and say nothing else. Jean closed his eyes anyway and looked for the box he'd shoved his nightmares into. He visualized forcing it closed and wrapping it in chains, layer after layer until he couldn't see the wood anymore. A problem for later, with the hope "later" never came.

He felt steadier when he opened his eyes. "I am ready."

Jeremy wasn't crass enough to ask if he was sure but led him out of the room. Kevin had taken the far corner of the couch while Andrew sat cross-legged on the bay window where he could watch all of them. Laila had claimed her papasan chair, and Cat was sitting on the floor in front of her. She had a wad of tangled necklaces in one hand that she was picking at. She held it up when they arrived and said,

"I'm trying my best, but Laila apparently doesn't know how to use a jewelry box. Found these in a baggie under the sink."

"Oops," Laila said, unrepentant.

Jeremy motioned for Jean to take his seat first, and Jean opted for the other end of the couch. It left a cushion open between Kevin and himself that he assumed Jeremy would fill, but Jeremy knelt on the ground on the far side of the coffee table. Jean supposed that was the best place for him if he wanted to look both Kevin and Jean in the eye without having to turn back and forth.

Jeremy followed Jean's lead in emptying half his mug. When he set it down, the click sounded final. Jeremy only waited another moment before asking, "Why did Neil come to Los Angeles in June?"

It was probably meant for Jean, but he didn't mind that Kevin was a touch faster on the draw. "He had to meet with the FBI to discuss complications with his father's investigation. We incorrectly assumed he would head to Baltimore for it," Kevin added, with a sidelong look at Jean. "Why they chose to meet here is beyond me."

"Because Jean is here." Jeremy turned his head toward Cat and Laila, meaning his next words for them, but kept his gaze on Jean's face as he said, "Because Jean's parents worked with Neil's father, the alleged Butcher."

"Not alleged," Jean said, even as Cat's startled, "What?" nearly blew out his eardrums.

Cat and Laila rounded on him, Laila looking taken aback and Cat's mouth so wide it was a wonder she hadn't dislocated her jaw. Cat found her voice first, but all she managed was a strident, "You're not serious."

Jean quietly picked his way through the truth, looking for the answer he was allowed to give them and the details that would best explain this fiasco to Kevin. He turned an unwavering stare on Jeremy and said, "The wrong people were asking why Neil came back from Evermore different. He'd spent years on the run; for him to throw away his disguise when his team was the talk of the nation

183

was unforgivably reckless.

"If they turned too long a look on Evermore, Neil thought it inevitable they would find me. He came here to warn me and to force a preemptive strike. Where Neil goes, the FBI follows. We wanted to come clean on our own terms rather than be blindsided down the road."

Laila put it together first: "You were with the FBI when Grayson died. The local office vouched for you with the LAPD."

"Yes."

Jeremy looked toward his friends then and finally explained, "Jean's parents were arrested by Interpol a few hours ago. It hasn't made the news here yet, but Bailey's crew must have put flags on his family as they researched his background for the interview. They had a French speaker on hand to help interpret if Jean needed it, and she found the article on a foreign press site."

"She didn't ask you about it," Laila said. She saw the answer she needed in the look on his face, and the edge in her voice was all righteous fury. "With no warning?"

Jean held onto his mug like a lifeline and stared down at his dark coffee. It was a minute before he thought he could trust his voice, and then the best he had to offer was, "I promised I would represent the Trojans appropriately, but I walked out. I will apologize to Coach Rhemann as soon as I am able."

"You didn't attack or insult her," Jeremy pointed out. "Even your anger when she made that awful comment about Zane will work out in your favor, as it was a genuine burst of empathy. No one associated with our program is going to have a problem with how you handled yourself today. I'm glad you walked out," he stressed when Jean didn't react. "It was unbelievably cruel of her to spring it on you like that. It wasn't what you'd agreed to talk about."

Cat was still staring at Jean. "Your parents are French

184

gangsters? Like for real?"

"Yes," Jean said.

"Don't take this the wrong way, but what are you doing here?" Cat asked, tossing her clump of chains from hand to hand as she looked for a new loose end to pick at. "Why'd they let you come all the way to America where they couldn't keep an eye on you? After how they treated you and what they did to you, that's either some serious self-delusion or some unbelievable trust, that they thought you'd keep their secrets when you were so far away."

Neil had come up with this part of the story, though it was anyone's guess if it would hold up. "It is hard to run an empire with a child underfoot," he said. "I was a liability, a potential bargaining chip to be taken and used against them. I was rarely allowed to leave the property if not for games and practices, and I was forbidden to interact with anyone outside of their crew. It was better for them if I simply went away. So long as I kept my mouth shut and sent money home after graduation, they would never come for me."

"*Two* children underfoot," Cat said, frowning at the inconsistency in his story. "You told me you—"

"Cat." That was Jeremy, in a tone that would brook no argument. "Let's not."

Cat flicked him a startled look but wisely went quiet. Jean knew she'd work through it on her own, and he could only pray she'd go to Jeremy for answers instead of him. He squeezed his mug until he thought it might crack between his palms.

Jeremy bought him time by turning on Kevin, but the question he presented was one Kevin didn't have the scripted answer for: "Did you know about them?"

"He found out at the banquet last fall," Jean said. "Neil and I recognized each other and panicked. We were too busy trying to figure out if we were safe with one another to remember that Kevin could also speak French."

185

Uncomfortable silence settled in the room for a minute as they each tended their own thoughts, and then Laila said, "It's not the sort of thing to come up in casual conversation, and you've only known us for three months. I can't hold it against you for keeping it from us." She let that sink in before continuing, "That said, this has potential to blow up in a bad way. How can we help?"

"I don't know," Jean admitted.

"I have people I can talk to," Laila promised him. "I will make sure you are safe."

Jean didn't understand, but Cat couldn't hold out any longer. This was exactly the kind of gossip that would get her going for days, and the gleam in her eyes was unbridled fascination. "Not alleged, you said. Then you've met the Butcher before? Ouch!" she complained when Laila thunked her temple. "Am I supposed to ask about his family instead? 'Hey Jean, wow, what was it like?' We've seen him naked, Laila, we know the answer to that." She waggled a hand at her chest, indicating the scars Jean had blamed on his father. "I was trying to be considerate."

Jean half-tuned her out as his thoughts wandered. The official story he and Neil settled on had him meeting the Wesninskis in France when he was young, but Jean had never been face-to-face with Nathan. He knew the Butcher had come by Evermore years ago, but only Kevin had been snatched into the Moriyamas' embrace then.

Jean hadn't met him, but he had met the man's murderous cleaner Lola Malcolm. He still remembered the easy way she held herself, like the master and Riko were worth less than the heels she strode in on. Jean had found it horrifyingly offensive up until the master gave ground without hesitation. If Lola wanted Nathaniel, she had the master's word the Ravens would relinquish all rights to him and stay out of her way. After that easy submission, Jean had been so blindingly afraid of her he'd barely slept for a week. Riko had counted it as a victory despite his

186

uncle's violent fury later, since Neil was guaranteed a slow and agonizing death.

"Oh, you did," Cat said.

Jean wasn't sure what she saw on his face, but he managed a rough, "Yes."

Kevin finished his drink and reached for the bottle. Jean seized his wrist in a bone-creaking grip and said, "I will break it over your head."

"You know it's normal for college students to drink now and again, right?" Cat asked, lifting her can of beer and waggling it at him. "One day you really ought to try some, or maybe a little…" She made a pinching gesture near her mouth that he assumed meant cigarettes. She wasn't cowed by the look he sent her but said, "Something to take the edge off before you snap out of existence. I know someone who's got a medical card."

Kevin tried pulling free, so Jean turned to glare at him. Kevin considered Jean with blasé amusement. He was well and truly drunk, then, and that only made Jean's mood worse. Jean stabbed an accusatory finger at him and demanded, "You're Queen of the US Court—for now. How long can you hold it when you're drinking poison?"

"Always," Kevin promised. "The last person who tried to take it from me died. Checkmate."

And if the angry satisfaction in his voice wasn't bad enough, Kevin had the nerve to smile. Jean let go like he'd been burned. He grabbed his empty mug on his way off the couch and left the room, needing to put space between them before he tried to claw Kevin's eyes out.

He didn't want more coffee, but setting up another pot gave his unsteady hands something to do. He gave up right before hitting brew and started digging through the cabinets instead. The sight of food left him queasy and out of sorts. He pushed the doors shut and turned back toward the coffee maker, only to realize he was no longer alone.

He hadn't heard Kevin come in through the pounding

in his temples, but Kevin was seated on the middle stool at the island. He'd refilled his glass before leaving the living room, and he was working his way through it as he watched Jean. Jean wanted to put it through the window.

"You are supposed to be better than this," Jean said, a quiet accusation.

"You have always known what I am."

Kevin had been a ward of the Moriyamas for most of his life: spending most of his early summers with Riko while his mother traveled, then moving in for good once Kayleigh Day was removed from the equation. Once the cage doors slammed, he was forbidden to put even a door between himself and his beloved, loathed brother Riko until the night Riko finally threw him away.

He'd grown up with the master's unforgiving violence, the first body upon which Riko could practice his fledgling cruelties. The frequent public appearances demanded of the Raven pair could stay Riko's knives but not his malevolent hunger; most of Kevin's scars were branded into his heart and mind. By the time Jean was thrown at Riko's feet, Kevin had mastered the art of putting mental walls between himself and whatever Riko was doing.

Jean had hated him for months. Incapable of stopping Riko's sadism and forbidden to leave the room, Kevin had simply stepped as far back as he could and feigned normalcy, arguing Exy drills and statistics while Riko pressed burns into Jean's pale skin. A soulless puppet who survived by hitching everything he was to his dream, or so Jean had believed, until the day Kevin leaned in and asked to learn French. It was the first hint he still had a personality of his own, that some part of Kevin Day existed separate from Riko Moriyama. It was proof that surviving Evermore was possible. Jean simply had to let go and stop fighting.

Now they were both free—of Riko, at least—but

Kevin would still do anything he could to avoid processing the horrors of the Nest. Jean shouldn't hold it against him, seeing how desperately he was struggling to keep his own nightmares at bay, but Kevin had always been the stronger of the two of them. Kevin's defenses had been unshakable up until Riko broke his hand, and then they'd shattered to dust.

Why he'd turned to vodka instead of rebuilding those walls, Jean didn't know. Maybe there was too much rubble to build atop, but Jean didn't have to like this solution. If he was this far out from Riko and Evermore and he still couldn't face what he'd been through or what he'd done, what hope was there for Jean?

"*You* are supposed to be better," Jean insisted.

"We are what they made us," Kevin said. "It is unavoidable."

Jean went to him and put his hand flat over the top of Kevin's glass. "Why did you even tell that doctor all of our secrets if you were still going to destroy yourself like this?"

"Coach had me in her office three to four days a week at the start," Kevin said. "Saying nothing was more maddening than being honest."

"Dad," Jean mocked him.

Kevin hunched his shoulders a bit. "That's—that doesn't sound right."

Jean tried to take the glass away, but Kevin caught it with both hands. Jean would have pulled, but Kevin flicked a defensive look at him and said, "I don't know if I would have survived my transfer without her. But there are days that her words aren't enough, and I can't hear her past…" He risked letting go of his glass to tap his fingers to his temple. "Best not to think at all."

"You are a fool."

"And what have *you* told her?" Kevin asked in quiet challenge. The look he turned on Jean said he didn't need an answer, but Jean still looked away. Kevin let the silence settle between them for a minute, then dug his nails in so hard his knuckles went white. "I can still hear him. Can you?"

"Don't." Jean pried Kevin's hand free and smashed it flat on the island. "We are not talking about him. I won't. I can't."

"Even with me?"

"You least of all," Jean said. Kevin managed an unsteady frown, but Jean refused to believe him surprised by the rejection. "My words are not safe with you. You have confessed to your doctor, your father, and your team. How long until your truths make it back to mine? You cannot deny it, you ruinous wretch. You told them who broke your hand." He dug his nails into the back of Kevin's hand and demanded, "What were you thinking?"

"I have known Jeremy far longer than you have, Jean."

"It is not just him," Jean argued. "Cat and Laila were there."

"You don't trust them," Kevin concluded. Jean faltered, and Kevin took advantage of his silence to press on with an impatient, "I can because he does, and because I know how important Dermott is to him. I am not afraid of what she does or does not know about me. She cannot betray him, so she will never betray me."

Kevin reached for his drink, but Jean grabbed it first. He upended it in the sink, pushed the cup aside to wash later, and took a clean glass down from the cabinet. There was filtered water in the fridge, crisp and cold, but Jean was annoyed enough to fill the glass from the tap.

"Fair is fair," Kevin said when Jean set it in front of him. "Talk to Betsy."

"I didn't agree to that." When Kevin said nothing, Jean insisted, "You are not my captain or my partner. You cannot make me."

190

"Yes, I can," Kevin said. Unspoken: *you cannot refuse me.*

"I hate you."

"Sometimes you do. I don't care."

Jean glowered at him, looking for a way out of this, and nearly jumped out of his skin when Cat knocked on the doorframe. She glanced from him to Kevin, gauging the mood in the room, as she held up a slender silver chain. Renee's cross glinted in the light as it gently spun, and Jean moved to meet Cat at the door. Rather than turn it over to him, she undid the hook herself and reached up to fasten it behind his neck. Jean gave it a gentle tug to check it, but he only managed a "Thank—" before Cat wound her arms around his neck.

She hugged him, slow and fierce. Comfort for surviving this morning's ambush, he thought, except the bite of her fingers into his shoulders was almost desperate. This was grief, he realized. She'd put the pieces together herself or demanded the truth from Jeremy in his absence.

Jean wanted to shove her away, because how could he ignore this wretched ache if Cat was drawing attention to it? Instead, he dug bruises into her back, knowing he had to be hurting her but unable to let go. She smelled of jasmine and vanilla, not blackberries and sea salt. He latched onto that to keep himself here and now even as his heart wanted to swallow him whole.

"I'm sorry," she said. "I shouldn't have asked. I didn't know she was gone."

Stuart's bored voice haunted him: *"A mild term for it."*

"Don't," he said, burying his face against her shoulder.

His heart was going too fast, so he focused on the beat of hers against his skin and counted himself back to the safety of their kitchen. It felt an eternity before he could relax his grip on her, and Cat was slow to let go after. She pressed a lingering kiss to his jaw before backing out of

191

his space.

She tapped Renee's cross, which now sat lower on his chest, and cleared her throat before saying, "Laila says the chain is yours to keep, if you like. If you're not happy with the length, we can pick a better one out next time we're shopping."

"Thank you," he said. "It is good like this."

Cat nodded and glanced between them. "Are you ready to come back? Jeremy needs to get ahold of Coach. It's probably going to take a few calls," she warned him with an apologetic grimace. "We haven't gotten the final cut that's airing, but once we know how she's spinning everything we'll have to revisit the game plan."

Staying here with Kevin was almost as miserable an option as hashing this out again from the top, but putting off the latter would only save him for so long. Jean motioned an okay toward the doorway, so Cat stepped aside. Rather than follow him into the hall, she gave his back a quick pat and went to distract Kevin. Andrew was missing when Jean made it to the living room, and Jeremy had moved to the couch. Laila got up at Jean's approach, gave his hand a brief squeeze, and left. Jean sank onto the cushion at Jeremy's side and stared at the dark TV.

"Do you want me to do the talking?" Jeremy asked. "You'll have to answer any follow-up questions, but if you're not comfortable saying these things to Coach I can repeat what you've told me. Just correct me if I get it wrong," he added, and waited for Jean's short nod. "Okay."

Maybe Jeremy had messaged Rhemann a warning they needed to talk, or perhaps the coach just had his phone handy in case the interview went poorly. Either way, he picked up halfway through the first ring. Jeremy put the phone on speaker but held it near his face, and Jean let his gaze wander the room as Jeremy laid it out for Rhemann. He started a few steps from the actual problem,

192

commenting on her pursuit of Grayson's story and her ugly speculation regarding Zane, before finally making his way to the subject of Jean's family.

Rhemann didn't say a word the whole time Jeremy was speaking. Jean could only imagine how furious he was, finding out Kevin and Wymack had dumped such a mess on his hands without warning. The smart thing for USC to do was transfer him to a different school before his worsening reputation dirtied theirs, but perhaps they would save face and money by keeping him as a sub. They could present themselves as tolerant and supportive while ensuring he didn't sully their name further. Either way—

"Moreau," Rhemann said.

"Yes, Coach."

"Are you all right?"

"Yes, Coach."

"It's a rare honest day for you," Rhemann said, sounding weary. "Attempt not to break the streak, please. I asked if you're all right."

Jean squeezed his hands together so hard his knuckles ached. "Yes, Coach." At the pained look Jeremy sent him, Jean added a, "Thank you, Coach." It still wasn't the answer Jeremy was looking for, judging by his quiet sigh, but Jeremy only reached out and tugged lightly at his wrist until Jean relaxed his grip. Jean tried again with, "I'm sorry, Coach."

Rhemann didn't push it. "I'm not sure if you had plans for the afternoon, what with Kevin being in town, but it's probably best to stick close to home while this makes the rounds. Any idea when you're supposed to get a final copy?"

"It's supposed to air at twelve-thirty, so I think she promised to have it to us by noon," Jeremy said, and tipped his phone so he and Jean could see the clock. It was just past eleven now. "Want me to forward it to you when it arrives?"

193

"The second it does," Rhemann confirmed. "I'll get a conversation started with my team and the board. In the meantime, I need the four of you to contact your teammates. I don't think you want to be fielding calls the rest of the day, so what details you give them are up to you, but they at least need a warning that we're going to be getting a lot of attention for a while so they know to keep their heads down. You and I can touch base after we've seen how much she gives away."

Jeremy nodded. "I'll let you know when we've heard from Neil, too."

"Good. If anyone tries to get a statement, smile and send them on their way. Direct them to the authorities if they want to keep pressing but keep them away from Jean at all costs." He waited for an affirmative before saying, "There's a lot more to say on the matter, but let's get the ball rolling while we can. Let me know if any of you need anything."

"Will do," Jeremy said, and hung up.

Jeremy collected a notepad and pen on their way to the kitchen, and it took only a few minutes to figure out the most concise way to warn their teammates. Cat had the best handwriting, so she was put in charge of writing out drafts as Laila and Jeremy suggested them. Jean only had to stick around long enough to approve the final version, and then he and Kevin were sent on their way while the other three divvied up the Trojans between them.

Jean wasn't sure what else to do, so he led Kevin to the study and pulled up one of the Trojans' games on his laptop. He didn't know how much they'd get to watch before they were needed back in the kitchen, but it was better than risking another conversation.

Kevin got distracted as it was buffering and plucked up the yellow wristband Jean had set on the shelf. He twirled it between his fingers, frowning a little as he tried to sort out its significance. Jean took it away without bothering to explain where it was from and dropped it in his desk drawer. As he was sliding the drawer shut, Kevin caught hold of it to stop him. His free hand darted in and came back with one of the postcards Jean had hidden in there.

Jean kept his gaze on the computer screen while Kevin stared down at the vandalized card in his hand. He was slow to set it aside, and he did so only to pull two more out. Jean wasn't going to sit here while he checked every single one, so he finally said, "They're all like that."

Kevin chucked the cards aside and went to collect a second chair from one of the other desks. He was drunk enough to be clumsy, and after dropping it a second time he settled for dragging it the rest of the way. "They have always been boorish assholes. I never understood why you liked any of them."

"You wouldn't," Jean said. "Your world revolved around the two of you; you didn't have any space or time for them. But I knew them."

"Or thought you did," was the cool response.

Jean ignored him in favor of turning the game on. It was enough to shut Kevin up for about twenty minutes, and then the camera briefly cut to the Trojans' bench. Jeremy was in an animated conversation with Ananya and Shawn as they watched their teammates play. At the first glimpse of Jeremy, Kevin muttered a disbelieving, "Law school."

"He called it family tradition."

The noise Kevin made gave his opinion of that. "His grandfather's fault, most likely." He said nothing else, so Jean dug his elbow into Kevin's side in a silent demand for an explanation. The Trojans scored, and the teams reset. Kevin sat back with a satisfied smile before finally saying, "Arnold Wilshire is a sitting senator for Texas. It was mentioned in most of Jeremy's early interviews, and I know I showed you those. Did you read any of them, or were you too busy fawning over his phot—"

Jean elbowed him again as hard as he could and checked the empty doorway. "I couldn't read well enough to bother with so much text. It gave me a headache."

"They were supposed to be a warning, Jean. If you didn't read them, you missed the entire point of me sharing them." He waited like he expected Jean to ask what lesson he'd missed and sighed when Jean refused the bait. "You can't tell me his family hasn't come up a single time this summer."

Jean thought of the vacant smile Jeremy wore for hours after visiting home, the insinuation that his brother Bryson was a bastard, and the way Jeremy had cracked when Joshua messaged him in June. Jeremy's quiet, *"Felt like I'd been waiting forever, so it wasn't at all fair to come from her first"* had been jarring enough to center Jean when nothing else could, but he'd thought he misunderstood until he saw Jeremy's house. So much larger than Laila's, but so lifeless, it was more a showroom awaiting a staged photoshoot than a home. How someone so warm had survived such a cold place, Jean didn't know.

"We don't talk about family," Jean said.

Kevin only shrugged and let it slide. They were able to get through the next fifteen minutes uninterrupted, and then Kevin got a call from the studio that a link to the final cut had been forwarded to his email. Jean ceded his laptop to Kevin and went to collect his teammates, but he stayed in the kitchen as they left. When Cat hung back to wait for him, he only shook his head.

"I do not want to see it."

She nodded and left without argument. Jean cleaned out the fridge to keep himself busy. He'd scrubbed down half of the cabinet fronts when the others made it back to him. He heard their shoes and the scrape of the stools, but he kept his attention on his work so he wouldn't have to see their faces. The ruse lasted only until Jeremy came and crouched beside him. Jean dropped his hand to his thigh and waited.

"Bad news is she kept the bit about your parents," Jeremy said. "The whole thing is cut to make it look like that's why the interview was stopped, which—not the best look when done that way, but anyone who doesn't understand why you walked off is beyond our help. The rest of it is surprisingly well stitched, and she added a bit of commentary at the end where she tries to break down some of your responses. That, too, is generally in your favor. I was right: your reaction to Zane's bit looks perfect on camera. Loyalty and grief despite the Ravens' crusade against you."

"But," Jean said.

Jeremy wagged his hand, undecided on whether his *but* was negative or not: "The microphones were on the set itself, not you. They couldn't catch everything you and Kevin said to each other, but what they did hear, they made sure to translate and subtitle. At the very least it establishes that Kevin knows the truth about your parents."

"And that you speak Japanese," Cat piped up. "I was so far off with my guesses."

"An interesting choice, learning Japanese before English," Laila said, studying Jean with disquieting intensity.

Jean hadn't prepared an answer for that, and he felt that misstep keenly. Luckily for him Kevin was used to lying to cover for the Moriyamas, and he answered with a dismissive, "Unsurprising. Exy started in Japan and the master was Japanese. I doubt Jean was the only obsessed child who picked up the language along with the sport."

"Good lord." Cat scrubbed at her arms. "Don't call him that. Queens have no masters." When Kevin only lifted one shoulder in a shrug, Cat turned a considering

197

look on Jean. "Wonder what happened to him, anyway?"

"If we're lucky, we'll never know," Kevin said. He took a swig from his cup, grimaced when he remembered too late it was only water, and flicked Jean a mean look.

Jeremy nudged Jean's knee before standing. "I've got to update Coach. Are you ready for round two?"

"No," Jean said, but he got to his feet and washed the cleaner off his hands.

Jeremy smiled. "One more call, and then we're done for the day, okay? We've done all we can for now. Let Coach handle the rest of the fallout without us. We'll pretend this morning didn't happen and attempt to have a little fun before Kevin abandons us for South Carolina. The rest we can deal with tomorrow, yeah?"

Jean would always be a fan of emotional procrastination, so he said, "Yes."

This call was much shorter, as they were just tweaking their earlier approach to account for what did and didn't make it into the cut. Rather than ask Rhemann if it was okay to leave the bulk of the aftermath to him, Jeremy simply said they'd be going dark the rest of the afternoon. The audacity was enough to have Jean leaning away from him on the couch, but Rhemann agreed it was for the best.

And then Rhemann asked, "Have you warned your parents yet?" and Jeremy's easy smile faded right off his face.

Jeremy tapped the butt of his phone against his temple for a few moments, then admitted, "No. Once they hear about it, I'll have to go home, and if I do that I won't be back tonight. Kevin's only in town one more night, so…" He trailed off as if expecting an argument. When Rhemann said nothing, Jeremy said, "I'll deal with them after I've gotten Andrew and Kevin on the plane."

"It's your call," Rhemann said. "I assume you'll be turning off your phone, then."

"Think I'll have to, yeah."

"Then I'll call Laila if I need to follow up with you. Do you need anything else from me before I let you go?" Rhemann said, and waited for a negative before stressing, "Stay safe and look out for one another."

Jean studied him as Jeremy turned off his phone. It wasn't his business or his place to press; Ravens weren't supposed to talk about families when they weren't allowed to have any. But he wasn't a Raven, was he? He waged a quiet war with himself until Jeremy turned a too-calm look on him. Jeremy said nothing, but his expression was expectant. He knew Jean was working himself up to something, but he said nothing to dissuade him.

It was permission enough, so Jean said, "You won't play in Texas because your grandfather is there."

"He is not—" Jeremy caught himself, but Jean quietly stored that automatic rejection away to mull over later. "He's my stepfather's father; that doesn't make him family. But yes—and no. He's been living in DC since he was elected to Congress, so he's not in Texas now, but he'll have to go back sooner or later."

Jean's American geography hinged on knowing where important teams played, but even he knew roughly where Texas was. "It is a long way from California."

"He moved out there twenty...one?" Jeremy glanced at his hands as if he meant to count on his fingers, then shrugged and continued with that best guess, "years ago, when his wife's father fell ill. Settled in her parents' house and just never came back. Guess the culture suited him better." Jeremy shifted like he was readying to get up from the couch, but he hesitated long enough to say, "I've asked you a lot of questions today that I knew you didn't want to answer, so it's only fair to ask: is that enough?"

"It is not my place to ask you for more."

"You're my friend. Just because I don't talk about my family doesn't mean you can't ask."

"You are my friend," Jean returned, testing the way it

199

sounded aloud, "and you don't want to talk about them. I won't ask."

Jeremy's smile was slow and radiant, and Jean had to look away. He needed to leave before he got himself in trouble, but of course Jeremy followed him to the kitchen.

Luckily there were three other people to serve as a distraction, and Cat was halfway through making lunch. Food wouldn't sate this gnawing hunger, but Jean would take what little relief he could get.

They were nearly done eating when Neil got back to him. Browning didn't want Jean talking about it yet, so if anyone pressed him about his parents he was simply to deflect: the arrest was tied into an ongoing investigation, so he was not at liberty to speak about it. It was a flimsy defense, but it was better than nothing. With that settled, Jean turned his phone off and put it aside to forget about for a while.

For a few hours it was like the interview had never happened. The Trojans and Kevin could carry a conversation without any help from him, so Jean watched with quiet interest as they got to know each other properly. It was inevitable that Exy would come up again and again, but Cat and Laila were good at steering Jeremy and Kevin to other things when they were at it for too long. It was a surprisingly pleasant afternoon until someone started pressing nonstop on the doorbell.

They'd gathered in the living room for board games and gossip, but at the echoing tones they all went quiet. Laila motioned for everyone to stay put as she got up. She disappeared long enough to check the peephole and came back with her face a thundercloud. With a finger to her lips, she said, "It's Bryson. Sit tight while I get rid of him."

It was almost impressive how quickly Jeremy's expression went blank. Jean glanced at him as Laila left, then the empty doorway, and got to his feet. Jeremy caught his wrist before he'd taken the first step away. Jean heard the locks clacking undone on the front door as he turned a cool look on Jeremy. He wasn't sure what he could say that wouldn't be picked up by those at the front door, so he leaned down into Jeremy's face and murmured, "Let go, captain."

"She can handle it," Jeremy said, barely loud enough for Jean to hear.

"—at the stadium with Kevin," Laila was saying down the hall. "You're welcome to wait outside the Gold Court for him if it's that important."

A haughty voice said, "I will wait here."

Jean caught hold of Jeremy's chin and forced his attention away from the doorway. Jeremy looked thrown, like he'd already forgotten Jean was standing there. Cat hadn't oversold it, then; Bryson was a problem. Jean dug his fingers in and insisted, "I am your partner. It is *my* place to assess and handle threats against you, not hers. Let me go."

Wood hit flesh with a dull thud in the hallway, followed by Laila's fierce, "I didn't invite you in. If you're going to wait here, you can sit in your car."

"Exactly the sort of hospitality I'd expect from a sand ni—"

Jeremy hurried to speak over his brother's awful words: "I've got to go."

He had to let go of Jean to get to his feet, and Jean was out of the living room in a heartbeat.

Jean got Laila out of the way with a quick hand on her shoulder. She was all that was keeping Bryson from getting inside, but Jean caught a fistful of his shirt as he stumbled through the doorway into the hall. He had a half-second to take him in: Jeremy's caramel hair, Jeremy's brown eyes, the same cheekbones and jawline, and then he threw Bryson off the porch with everything he had. The sickening crunch of glass as Bryson hit the windshield of

201

Laila's car said Jean owed her a thousand apologies, but Jean didn't slow on his way down the steps.

Bryson was spitting outraged curses as he tried to roll off the hood of Laila's car, but Jean caught the collar of his shirt and threw him into the glass a second time. This time he put his weight behind it, choking off Bryson's air.

"Be still, or I will break your neck," Jean warned him, and Bryson froze.

Laila appeared at his side. "Ease up."

Jean didn't see why he should let go, but he forcibly relaxed his grip on Bryson's shirt. Bryson choked on the first breath he managed and coughed dramatically like he'd somehow forgotten how to breathe. He was stupid enough to try sitting up, so Jean used a hand on his forehead to slam him back down. Laila's grip went bruising, and he didn't miss the way she cast a quick look around the empty street. "*Enough*, Jean."

"You don't know who you're messing with," Bryson said, glaring up at Jean. "I'm a Wilshire. Who the fuck are you?"

"I am Jean Moreau," Jean said, and Bryson tensed up so fast it was a wonder he didn't crack a bone in the process. It was a curious thing, being feared off the court; normally only his opponents regarded him with any measure of dread. Jean assumed Bryson had watched the interview and heard about his parents' supposed connections. He brushed the speculation aside and said, "You're trespassing."

"I'm looking for my brother," Bryson said. "You assaulted me unprovoked."

"Did he?" Laila asked. "I promise I can find a dozen witnesses who'll say you vandalized my car after I wouldn't let you inside."

"You bit—" Bryson lost the rest when Jean shoved him hard into the cracked glass.

"Like I said: wait in your car or leave," Laila said. "If

202

you set foot on my property again, I will file a restraining order against you. I don't care how many Wilshires are on the force; none of them are stupid enough to take your word over mine."

She waited to see if he argued, but Bryson only glared at her. Jean made a quiet note to figure out the hierarchy between their families after he figured out how to fix her broken windshield. Satisfied by his silence, Laila motioned for Jean to follow. "Leave him. He isn't worth the headache."

"One swing with a racquet would shut this half-baked baguette up for good," Jean suggested, but Laila only tugged at his shirt until he finally backed away from Bryson.

Bryson didn't say a word as they went up the stairs and inside. Laila kicked her security bar into place as soon as she'd done the locks, and the two of them went into the living room together. Jeremy was standing frozen where Jean left him. Cat had her arms out and waiting, and the look on her face was only a shade too anxious to be murderous. Laila folded herself into Cat's tight embrace without hesitation. Jean stopped in front of Jeremy and waited with his gaze averted.

"Someone please remind me to talk to our neighbors," Laila said, muffled against Cat's shirt. "I need to bribe some witnesses with a few months' reduced rent in case he wants to start a proper fight."

"Will do," Cat promised.

"We heard glass," Jeremy said, looking between them. "Everyone okay?"

"Everyone important," Laila said, turning her head to peer at him. "Bryson jumped on my car and cracked the windshield in a dozen places, but Jean and I are all right."

"Jumped." Jeremy's stare was heavy, but Jean refused to return it. "Jean?"

"The contract I signed says I must represent the

203

Trojans appropriately in public. This is private property."

"That's a thin line to argue." He didn't sound pleased, so Jean checked the line of his shoulders. He was tense, but not coiled to strike. Jean didn't realize how obvious he was about it until Jeremy continued with a weary, "You know it is, or you wouldn't be avoiding me right now. I won't lie and say I'm not disappointed, but the fault is mine for not following you to the door."

Jean dragged his stare to Jeremy's face. Jeremy said nothing, seemingly content to study Jean's guarded expression, and then Laila lifted her head from Cat's shoulder to say, "For the record, it was the sexiest thing I've ever seen, and I don't even like men. It would have done you so much good to see that bitch humbled, Jeremy."

It was enough to startle a laugh from Jeremy, and a wry smile crept across his lips. "Thank you for defending her, but be more careful, would you?"

"Yes," Jean said, and followed Jeremy's lead in getting settled again. He was acutely aware of Kevin's considering gaze, but Jean refused to acknowledge him. Kevin was at least smart enough not to say anything, and they went back to their game as if nothing had happened.

CHAPTER ELEVEN
Jeremy

After four years with the Trojans, Jeremy had lost
count of the ways his teammates made him proud. There
were some standout moments to be sure: the way they
rallied around him his freshman year, how quickly most of
them had given Xavier their unwavering support when he
chose to start transitioning his sophomore year, and their
commitment to the Foxes' imperiled team last year that
culminated in their spectacular showdown at semifinals.

The week following Jean's interview earned a near-
immediate spot on the list. Few of them were comfortable
with this development, but the tone of the nonstop
messages Jeremy and Xavier fielded that weekend leaned
more toward curiosity and concern than anger.

Finding out who Jean's parents were couldn't erase
what they'd seen with their own eyes all summer; it
simply added a critical piece to the Jean Moreau puzzle.
No one would deny he was standoffish and often rude, but
Jean wasn't the vicious transfer student they'd expected.
They'd seen his countless scars, and they'd all noticed
how quickly Jean retreated when challenged by his
coaches. How could they fear a man who couldn't even
look Rhemann in the face two months into summer
practices?

Monday's practice started with a team meeting, but to
Jeremy it felt more like a formality. The Trojans had had
plenty of time over the weekend to hash it out over texts
and calls and to watch the interview as often as they
needed; their minds were made up before they set foot in
the Gold Court on August 13th. The coaches went over the
more pertinent details, such as the increased risk of

scrutiny and trespassing journalists. After-practice Raven drills were temporarily canceled until the coaches could assess the blowback.

After they covered their necessary talking points, they opened the floor for questions, but the Trojans steered clear of the actual interview content in favor of more light-hearted gossip: did Jeremy and Kevin combust when they saw each other out of uniform, had Jeremy convinced Kevin to transfer to the Trojans for his fifth year, how many languages did Jean really speak, and so on.

Lisinski let them joke around longer than Jeremy expected her to, but maybe she knew Jean needed to see his teammates' uncowed support of him. She finally called for them to wrap it up, and they got to their feet in a cacophony of sliding chairs and laughter. How Jeremy heard Lucas's accusation, he wasn't sure, but the weight behind his words punched through the rest of the noise:

"You're nineteen."

Slowly the Trojans went quiet. Lucas was the only one still seated, arms folded across his thighs as he stared down at his shoes. It was the first time Lucas had acknowledged Jean since his brother's death, and Jeremy wasn't sure which way this was going to go. Jean had refused to throw Grayson under the bus when Hannah gave him the opportunity, but the way he'd reacted to Grayson's name and news of Rhemann's unprecedented banishment got people talking. No consensus yet, according to Cat, but she'd keep an eye on it.

Lucas said nothing else, so finally Jean said, "Yes."

"Then you were sixteen when—"

"Do not," Jean warned him.

Jeremy didn't trust Lucas to let it drop, but the Trojans didn't need to be here for this. He caught Xavier's eye as he said, "Let's keep it moving, guys, we're behind as it is."

Lucas, unsurprisingly, didn't budge. Neither did Jean,

and Jeremy wasn't sure if he was honestly willing to hear Lucas out or if he knew Lucas would chase his exit with louder demands. Lisinski helped Xavier herd the rest of the Trojans out of the room, though she lingered just out of the doorway in case she needed to intervene. Jeremy remained at Jean's side and kept his eyes on Lucas' bowed head.

"Did they know?" Lucas demanded, still staring at the floor like he wanted it to swallow him whole. "They had so much shit to say about your freshman year, but did they know you were just sixteen? When he—" Lucas made a noise like he was about to throw up, but somehow he managed to fight it back. His voice was hoarse when he said, "You're younger than I am. Did Grayson know that?"

Jean was digging bruises into the side of his neck, but his voice was steady when he said, "They all did." Lucas flinched like he'd been struck, and Jean forcibly loosened his grip as he started for the door. "Trade racquets with Ananya today. You are dead weight on a heavy, and I will not tolerate it any longer."

Lucas said nothing, so Jean was able to slip out of the room. Jeremy lingered long enough to test the water with a careful, "Lucas." He thought about Cody's warning and forcibly changed what he was about to say, eschewing useless comfort in favor of facts: "You are not your brother, and you are not responsible for what he did. Stop trying to carry that weight in his absence. It will only crush you."

Lucas scrubbed a rough hand over his face but gave no sign he'd heard. Jeremy glanced toward the door and nodded when Lisinski motioned to him. She'd keep an eye on Lucas; he needed to catch up with his team and get them over to the fitness center.

The Trojans filed out of the stadium in a straggling line. The reminder that Jean should be a sophomore had taken some of the cheer out of them, or maybe that was Lucas's abject misery infecting the rest. How long it would take them to realize what Lucas was referring to, Jeremy wasn't sure; they'd all heard rumors about how Jean made the Ravens' lineup, but they'd moved on from such outlandish gossip months ago. Hopefully it would stay forgotten, and they'd get too distracted by Lucas's grief and Jean's parents to worry about the crueler details.

Lucas was only twenty minutes behind them in making it to Lyon. His teammates were heartened by his arrival, assuming he'd sorted out whatever was bothering him, and rallied around him with good cheer that sounded less forced by the minute. The mood was almost normal when they finally left, but getting intercepted on the way back to the stadium by a handful of reporters didn't help. Luckily Shawn and Shane didn't need to be asked, and they ran interference with too-bright smiles and easy reassurances.

Knowing the press was around had Jeremy's group sticking to the locker rooms at lunch. They'd just gotten settled in one of the huddle rooms when Ananya came looking for them. She folded her arms across her chest as she said, "Your continued crusade against my racquet is admirable but unnecessary. I told you I like lighter racquets."

That Lucas had passed on Jean's demand was unexpected, but Jean seemed more annoyed than pleased as he pushed his rice in agitated circles. "This time it is about his mistakes, not yours. He relies too much on power and not at all on finesse. He would be stronger in the long run if a lighter touch forced him to rethink his style. If you won't come to your senses at least loan him one of your spares today."

Ananya considered that for a few moments, then sighed and set a box of Band-Aids near his bowl. Jean went still to frown at it, and Ananya motioned to it as she stepped back. "Emma was too afraid to bring you these herself since she wasn't sure how you'd react. They're for your fingers," she explained, crooking her fingers at him to show him her painted nails. "In her wrap-up Hannah mentioned how you hurt yourself whenever she made you uncomfortable, and it made Emma think about how often she's seen you at it this summer."

"Oh, I like it." Cat upended the box and started stripping paper off. "Pick a hand to start with!"

"You aren't serious," Jean said.

Jeremy didn't think Jean would let her get away with this, but then Cat pressed a careful thumb to the fresh scabs on his throat. Jean muttered something rude in French but offered his left hand. Ananya nodded satisfaction as she left to finish her own lunch, and Cat made short work of the task set before her. She covered each of Jean's fingers with two Band-Aids, one over the nail and one around the fingertip to hold the first in place. Jean considered her handiwork with distaste as she carried her trash away, but he didn't bother to peel any of the bandages loose.

Afternoon practice felt a little stilted, leaving Jeremy to wonder how much his teammates had been gossiping over lunch, but no one was cruel enough to voice their speculations on the court. The only real fuss came from Derek and Derrick, who started gleefully referring to Jean as "lil bro" during the final scrimmage. Jean tripped them both so violently he was almost pulled from the line, but they defended him stridently enough that White simply switched them to mark Cody and Pat.

It bought Jean only forty minutes of peace, as the pair hounded him all the way to the showers after practice for a French equivalent to call him. Jeremy idly wondered if he ought to intervene, but Jean seemed more confused than distressed: offended by their excitement over his age and bewildered by their persistent good humor in the face of his caustic irritation. He obviously wasn't used to being teased, or maybe it was the complete lack of maliciousness behind their jokes that threw him off his game.

Xavier finally arrived at the showers and took stock of Jean's predicament in a glance. A helpless smile twitched at his lips as he announced, "I see the bazonga line is in full menace mode today."

"Wow," Derek protested. "I thought we moved past that nickname like two years ago."

Derrick clocked Jean's lost look and made an exaggerated gesture near his own chest. "Derek and Derrick, double D? Jillian really thought she was funny with that one. A step up from being the Oreo line, at least." He reached past Jean to thunk Derek in the shoulder. "Speaking of bazongas, don't forget to show Jean a picture of Cherise. I would literally slit my throat for her. Please tell her I said that."

"You ever figure out where her eyes are, I'll tell her," Derek said. "Hey, Jean, how do you say bro in French?"

Between them Jean cranked his shower off, done with this conversation and their unflagging nonsense. Jeremy half-expected them to try and stop him, but Derek and Derrick let him go with exuberant farewells. As soon as the door closed behind him, Derek turned an arch look on his line partner and said, "Anyway, you better pray I don't introduce Jean to Cherise. She would choose him over you in a heartbeat."

Derrick staggered like he'd been hit. "That's heartless, dude. I thought we were friends or something, brother from another mother?"

"If you're my brother, you definitely should not be checking out our cousin."

"No longer brothers," Derrick was quick to say. "Never even met you before in my life."

Sebastian frowned over at them. "Does he even like

girls? He got scooped up by the floozies so fast. Ouch, what was that for?" he protested when Shawn stepped on his foot. Shawn sent a quick gesture toward Xavier, and Sebastian blanched when he realized his misstep. "Hell, sorry, didn't mean it like that. Maybe he's like Cody, then. What's that kind of queer that likes both chicks and dicks?" He yelped when Shawn got him again. "Jesus, *sorry*. I just mean that he—never mind, I give up."

It was a familiar struggle by now; Sebastian had come to them from a conservative upbringing in Birmingham and was prone to taking one step back for every two steps forward. He leaned more toward confusion rather than Lucas's grudging tolerance, but once he started fumbling, he had a hard time finding his feet again. The clumsiness was a bit painful sometimes, but Jeremy was glad he was trying.

"What are we going to do with you?" Cody said, more amused than offended, but immediately changed tracks as the door opened to let Lucas's small group in. Jeremy assumed they'd been hanging back until Jean was out of the way. "Heya, Lucas. We're taking a head count to go see the new Bourne movie this week. Are you in or did you go already?"

Jeremy couldn't even imagine the effort it'd take to get Jean into a movie theater; just the thought made him smile as he cut his water off. He'd left his towel on a numbered hook near the door, and he gave himself a cursory scrub before winding it around his waist and heading out into the locker rooms. It shouldn't surprise him that Jean was already fully dressed and waiting on the strikers' row for him, but he was honestly impressed with how fast Jean could move when he wanted to get out of here. Jean glanced up at his approach but was quick to drop his gaze to the apricot cradled in both hands.

Jeremy took his time drying off and getting dressed, knowing Cat and Laila would be a few minutes more.

211

When he was done, he straddled the bench at Jean's side and started pulling up news on his phone. He was only distantly aware of strikers coming and going as he tracked the day's fallout. Someone had caught up to Kevin, it seemed, but Kevin staunchly refused to speculate or elaborate on Jean's family. The more interesting development was that Edgar Allan had nothing at all to say. It seemed someone had finally been smart enough to put a muzzle on the Ravens.

After Jean refused to talk about his family Saturday morning, Hannah had turned her focus back to Riko's career and death, and she'd seamlessly pieced together a worthy tribute for the fallen King. Between that touching piece, the revelation that Jean had saved Zane, and Jean's scandalized defense of his former team, a bit of ill-timed malice from the Ravens might finally turn the tide of public opinion against them. It was perhaps too much to hope they'd apologize for their antagonism this spring, but Jeremy had seen stranger things.

Cat and Laila finally stopped by, but even now they couldn't leave. Laila didn't want reporters following them to her house, which meant leaning on the Trojans' sheer size as a shield. Laila, Cat, and Jean would follow their teammates back to the dorms, and they'd hide out with the floozies until they felt safe enough to sneak home.

Jeremy wished he could go with them, but avoiding his family this weekend had brought about the expected consequences: he was to stay home this week. His parents couldn't keep him from attending practice, but they knew what time it let out and roughly how long the drive would take. Jeremy didn't regret choosing Jean and Kevin over their prying oversight, but he was sorry he had to leave his friends to deal with this chaos alone.

"Be safe," Jeremy said, getting to his feet.

"Drive safe," was Laila's easy response, and Jeremy had no choice but to walk away.

Laila's quiet *pin-pon* alert dragged Jeremy out of a light doze Thursday night, and he pushed his books aside to pick up his phone. He could imagine Laila's disgruntled tone as he skimmed her message, and it was enough to bring a helpless smile to his face: "Cat and Jean dipped out, my fiancé abandoned me, and my show tonight is a rerun. Barkbark is refusing to bring back the ball when I throw it. I am bored out of my mind."

"You're welcome to come hang out with me," Jeremy sent back.

"At your place? I don't love you that much."

"But I'm studying fallacies. It's very exciting."

"Liar. What's today's French lesson?"

"Objects around the house." Jeremy sent her a picture of his desk, which was now covered in sticky notes of vocabulary terms. Laila's subsequent crack about his handwriting was to be expected, and Jeremy gave a put-upon sigh as he obediently rewrote a few of the messier ones. He was trading out the papers when Laila came back with,

"Think you'll be home tomorrow?"

Home, she said, knowing he was technically home already. Jeremy toed at the leg of his desk and let his gaze track his room. The bedroom was frozen in time, a tidy snapshot of the son his parents wished they had, with serious books lining the bookshelves and a well-made bed in boring beige. He'd hung a dozen-odd pictures of his friends and teammates on his wall, but he'd made sure to only choose photographs where they were out of uniform. His Exy awards and trophies were tucked away in the closet behind a monochromatic slew of uncomfortable clothes.

"I don't know," he finally typed out. He hadn't asked yet, hoping that a week of quiet obedience would smooth away the lingering edges of his mother's anger. "She

213

might fight it, especially since school is starting so soon."

"Hard at work, I see," Annalise said from his doorway, and Jeremy jumped so hard he dropped his phone. "Who are you texting?"

"Laila," Jeremy said as he collected his phone again.

"The Egyptian."

"Her mother's Lebanese," he said, but Annalise ignored the correction. Jeremy tugged his study guides closer and neatly stacked the LSAT book on top of his French notes. Annalise was less likely to rat him out than Bryson was, but it was best not to take any chances. "Her father's been reassigned to Thailand. Maybe she'll let me go with her next time she visits him? I could scratch Bangkok off the bucket list and pop around Asia for a week or two."

"With what money?" she asked, but didn't wait for him to react to that unkind dig. "Oh wait, irrelevant. You don't have a passport."

Jeremy held onto his smile for all he was worth. "Somewhere I do."

Mathilda had always kept the family's most important documents in a fireproof cabinet in her home office, but she'd removed most of Jeremy's paperwork years ago. His medical records were still there, but his passport, social security card, and birth certificate were nowhere to be found. Jeremy had turned every room in this house inside-out more than once looking for them. If he could just find them, he could hide them in Laila's safe, but he always came back emptyhanded. He had to assume his mother had moved them to a safety deposit box; they were gone until she felt like giving them back.

Annalise's accusation was quiet: "You don't want to go to Thailand, anyway. You just want an excuse to visit Seoul. Why? Dad won't see you."

"Osan." Jeremy took his phone apart and put it back together. "Maybe he would. Could he really turn me away if I was right there?"

She said nothing. For all that had broken between them four years ago, Trent Knox was an open wound they would always share. They'd been cut in different ways by his long absences and abrupt departure, and Annalise would always take their mother's side first, but they didn't have the heart to really fight about him.

At length Annalise beckoned imperiously to him. "Get the door for me. My hands are going to be full with my laundry."

Annalise was the only one of them allowed to live on her own year-round, a reward for being the least disappointing child. She avoided coming home whenever possible, but her washer was acting up for the fourth time this week and she was in dire need of clean clothes. Jeremy was idly surprised she hadn't just gone out and bought more to hold her over until maintenance could come by, seeing how she still had unfettered access to her college fund.

Jeremy pushed such thoughts away as he stood. "I'll carry it down for you."

Annalise stepped back to let him out of his room and pointed to where her laundry basket was waiting off to one side. Jeremy scooped it up and followed her to the stairs. They were halfway down when the doorbell rang, and Annalise sent a disapproving frown at her watch. It was late to have guests, but Warren's rotating schedule at the hospital made for an unreliable social life.

William reached the door only seconds before they did, and Jeremy drew up short when he saw Cat on his front porch.

"William!" Cat said, beaming at the butler. "Hey, sorry to drop by unannounced. Just trying to steal Jeremy. Is he—heyyy," she said as she spotted Jeremy over William's shoulder. "Come chat with us real quick."

"Does she know what time it is?" Annalise asked as

215

she snatched up her purse and keys.

"Bit late, but you're all awake," Cat said with unflagging cheer. "Gorgeous as always, Annalise. Smile just lights up the room."

Annalise, who was decidedly not smiling, only motioned for Cat to get out of her way. Jeremy smiled apologies at William as he followed his sister onto the porch, and then Annalise rocked to an abrupt stop. Jeremy had to lurch back to avoid slamming the laundry basket into the small of her back. He thought perhaps she'd forgotten something, but Annalise was staring at Jean where he stood only a few steps back from the porch. Jeremy moved up alongside her, mouth open on a quick reassurance, but Annalise looked more startled than afraid.

Maybe it was the night that put that color in her cheeks, or maybe it was the way Jean was studying her with unabashed curiosity and no little interest. He wasn't the first to look at Annalise like that and he wouldn't be the last; she had a face born for stardom and had pursued modeling gigs until her accident. Jeremy knew she was beautiful, and he knew Jean liked women and men equally. He didn't know why the laundry basket was now digging permanent creases into his fingers, but his tone was friendly and light as he introduced them.

"Jean, this is Annalise. She's studying polisci at UCLA. Annalise, Jean Moreau, our newest backliner."

"The Raven," she said, toying idly with the strap of her purse. "After all of the horror stories, I expected something… less," she finished after a moment's pause. Jean continued to gaze back in silence, unbothered by that backhanded compliment, and Annalise sent Jeremy a sidelong look. He smiled in the face of her scrutiny, trying to radiate innocence, but Annalise only said, "I was right, wasn't I? You really are going to make the same mistakes all over again."

"Good night, Annie," Jeremy said.

The look that crossed her face ruined her pretty features. "Don't call me that."

Jeremy jostled her laundry basket at her, and Annalise led the way to her car. She got the back door for him, and he wrapped the seatbelt around the basket to keep it from sliding around on her journey home. He held the driver's door open until she was buckled, then stepped back to watch her pull away. Only after her car was gone did he finally rejoin Cat and Jean near the fountain. William had been sent away at some point, and the front door was closed, so Cat caught Jeremy's hand and planted a kiss on his knuckles.

"Long way from home," Jeremy said, looking between them.

Cat smiled and swiped sweaty bangs out of her face. "We were in the area. Rode out to Thousand Oaks and figured we might as well come back this way. Jean needed to talk to you, anyway."

Here she sent Jean a meaningful look, but Jeremy's front door opened before Jean could say anything. Mathilda stepped out onto the porch alone, expression frosty and arms folded tight across her chest. She would have heard from William who was at her door this late; that she'd come out here herself to shoo them off said worlds for how displeased she was by their boldness.

Cat was uncowed but hurried toward her with a gushing, "Mrs. Wilshire, sorry to stop by so late, but oh my god, your hydrangeas—?"

Jeremy glanced toward Jean, arching a brow in silent question, but Jean only looked away. Jeremy wasn't sure how much time Cat could buy them, so he pressed, "What's on your mind?"

"I need a ride on Saturday," Jean finally said. "From you, not Laila."

"Where are we going, and when?"

Jean scowled but said, "Doctor, ten-fifteen."

217

"I'll see what I can do," Jeremy promised. Jean didn't look at all reassured, so Jeremy said, "Mom's a doctor—an OB anesthesiologist," he elaborated at Jean's small frown, "so I can't imagine she'll refuse if I tell her we're going to a hospital. I'll talk to her as soon as I get inside and let you know tomorrow, okay?"

"Jeremy," Mathilda called, so Jeremy had to leave Jean there. He passed Cat on his way to the front porch, and he obediently took up a spot at Mathilda's side. He and his mother watched as Cat and Jean pulled their helmets back on. The quiet roar of their motorcycles coming to life had Mathilda muttering rudely under her breath.

It wasn't the noise that had her so riled up; as soon as Mathilda knew she'd be heard she said, "You do have *some* white friends, I assume."

Jeremy's smile froze on his face. "You just saw one of them."

"I didn't recognize him."

Asking if she could recognize any of the Trojans was a surefire way to get on her bad side, so Jeremy only said, "A friend introduced us. I'm pretty sure he has a crush on Laila," he added, before she could ask him what sort of friend Jean was. He waited a bit to see if she'd call him out on it, but either she hadn't been paying nearly enough attention to the news or the night and distance had hidden Jean's tattoo from her. "Before all this happened, I'd agreed to take him to the hospital this weekend, so he needed to know if I was still free. Won't be steady enough to ride afterward," he added.

"There and back again," she said as she turned toward the door.

He should take his victories and let it go, but Jeremy had to try. "I've only got one week left of break, and then it's my last year at university. Can't I spend it with Laila? Not the school year," he was quick to say when she flicked him a severe look, "but just this last week."

"That foreigner teammate of yours put your brother through a windshield," Mathilda reminded him.

"Supposedly," Jeremy said. "All of Laila's neighbors say differently about what happened with Bryson."

"He needed stitches," Mathilda reminded him. When Jeremy said nothing, she continued, "You shouldn't associate with a criminal. It reflects badly on us and your grandfather."

Jeremy bit off his kneejerk rejection in the nick of time: "He is—not his parents. Jean came to America to get away from his family's crimes and carve out a life of his own. Doesn't that play into the narrative Arnold's always leaning into? The American dream," he emphasized when Mathilda paused to think it over. "The chance to become more than what you're born with. If we're part of that success story, doesn't that make us look good?"

"It doesn't change the fact he's dangerous."

"If he was, USC couldn't have signed him," Jeremy reasoned. "My team has fought to maintain a legacy of kindness and acceptance. We wouldn't have brought him onto the line if we thought he'd ruin our reputation and undo years of hard work." He waited a beat for her to make up her mind, then motioned toward the stairs and said, "Can I help you with anything before I head back up? If not, I've got a chapter left to get through before bed."

"Have you signed up for any exams yet?" she asked.

"I set an alarm for tomorrow morning so I wouldn't miss the next registration period."

"Good." Mathilda straightened his shirt with a neat tug and briefly cupped his face in her hand. "Show me the confirmation email and you can stay with that girl next week."

"Thank you."

"Thank me when you've done it," Mathilda said, and

219

gestured toward the stairs. "Go on."

Jeremy headed back upstairs to his room and grudgingly traded out his French book for his LSAT guide. Despite what he'd told his mother downstairs, he only made it two pages further before he was so bored he had to call it a night. He was up at eight the next morning so he'd make it to practice on time, and he refused to think about how his first alarms would be set to four o'clock once the school year started.

His laptop went with him to the stadium. The increased presence of reporters wandering around campus and Exposition Park this week had them taking their lunches in the locker room. Today it worked in his favor, as he could use the wi-fi to find an exam slot. He forwarded his mother a copy of the confirmation email and tried not to notice the look Cat and Laila exchanged. Jean's heavy stare was a harder weight to shake, but Jeremy only smiled as he put his laptop away. He'd be back at Laila's house tonight; did it really matter that he couldn't taste his lunch?

They stayed up far too late that night playing card games, but Jeremy got the best sleep he'd had all week. On Saturday morning Jean showered while Jeremy brewed coffee, and Jean put together breakfast burritos while Jeremy washed up. Cat and Laila slept through breakfast, which meant there was more than enough coffee for Jean and Jeremy to take with them. Only when they were buckled up in Jeremy's car did he ask where they were going, and Jean checked a printout for an address.

It was an easy drive, up Vermont to Olympic then over, and Jeremy found parking in an associated garage. He lingered long enough to drain the last of his coffee before collecting his study guide from the backseat. They took the side exit out of the garage and went around to the front of the building. Jeremy held open the front door to let Jean precede him into the lobby.

Jean hesitated only a few steps inside to consult his notes again. "Fifth floor."

Jeremy pressed the call button for the elevator. This time of day it was quick to arrive. Jean started to follow Jeremy on, only to retreat as soon as he was two steps into the car. Jeremy was so startled he almost didn't catch the doors in time, but he managed to shove them back open and rejoin Jean in the lobby. Jean looked rattled as he watched the doors slide closed.

"I will take the stairs," he said. "You go."

Jeremy looked from him to the lift. "I'm sorry, I didn't know you were claustrophobic." Jean didn't answer, so Jeremy looked around for a sign. "Over here," he said, and pushed open the door that would let them into the stairwell. Flight after flight they made their way up, and Jeremy let them into a pleasantly boring waiting room drenched in white and cream. Jean hesitated with one hand on the door like he was considering going back downstairs before finally checking in at the front desk.

Jeremy found them a spot to sit and asked, "Checkup?"

"No." Jean clenched his hands together and pinned them between his knees. Jeremy took the hint and let it drop, but Jean grudgingly explained, "Dobson cannot teach me how to swim again from so far away. She arranged a referral to a local specialist." He frowned down at the floor as he thought, but the best he managed was a hesitant, "Exposure therapy?"

He was here to see a psychiatrist, Jeremy realized, but Jeremy's surprise was quickly washed away beneath a dizzying warmth. Jean had been forced into therapy against his will when the Ravens started spiraling, and he'd rebelled against that by sitting silent as the grave on his weekly calls to Dr. Dobson. Jeremy wasn't sure what had inspired him to finally talk to her, but it left him

221

buzzing with equal parts hope and relief.

He didn't realize he'd reacted until Jean scowled at his hands and said, "Stop looking at me like that."

"Can't I be proud of you?" Jeremy asked. "It's not easy asking for help."

"No. You should be annoyed that I've missed so many workouts this summer," was the sullen response. The elevator dinged as another patient arrived, and Jeremy didn't miss the way Jean's shoulders went tense. Every inch of him screamed readiness to get out of here, but Jean held his ground and stayed where he was. "I am Jean Moreau. I am perfect Court. I refuse to end this year as second line, but I can't even participate in practices twice a week."

"You haven't been idle," Jeremy pointed out. "You've found other ways to fill the time."

Jean ignored him. Jeremy accepted his temporary defeat and flipped through his guidebook in search of where he'd left off Thursday night. All the coffee and the joy seeped out of him by three sentences in, and Jeremy swallowed a sigh when he realized he was already skimming without reading. He went back to the start and marked the line with his finger, trying to force himself to read along. Progress was a little better this time, up until he had to turn the page and Jean said,

"Wilshire."

Jeremy checked the waiting room instinctively, but he saw no one he recognized. Jean slanted a look at the LSAT guide and said, "The senator is a Wilshire. Your mother took the name; Cat called her such. But you are a Knox."

"For better or worse, yes." Jeremy slowly flipped the book closed. "I kept my father's last name when Mom remarried. Back then I think it was about holding onto the family I wanted us to be, but then it was this, I don't know, teenage rebellion kind of thing." Jean's quiet snort gave his opinion of that, and Jeremy couldn't help but laugh. "Is it so surprising? I'll have you know I'm Mom's biggest headache."

Jeremy studied the painting hanging across from them as he mulled it over. "I never want to be a Wilshire, but if I'm honest, this hasn't worked out much better." Too many people wielded 'Knox' as an insult, a reminder he would never fit in with his family. "I've thought about changing it to something new, but I'm not sure if it would jumble my college stats to have them logged under two different surnames. Besides, I don't know what I'd change it to. Maybe I'll put together a poll for graduation and let the floozies vote on it."

"Deny a vote to whomever named the dog," Jean said.

Across the room the receptionist called, "Jean?" and Jean's expression went blank as he got to his feet. Jeremy watched until he was through the back door to where the offices were, then opened his study guide once more.

He got more napping done than reading; no amount of caffeine could counter how wretchedly boring this chapter was. Each time he stirred he saw new faces in the room. The last time he woke it was to the quick touch of fingers to his temple. Jean only lingered a moment to make sure he was awake before heading for the exit. He was two flights down by the time Jeremy entered the stairwell, moving at a pace that should have had him tripping forward into a broken neck, and Jeremy ran to catch up. Jean made it all the way to the car before finally collapsing into a crouch.

"Hey," Jeremy said as he squatted beside Jean. "Are you okay?"

Jean dug the heels of his hands into his eyes. "Yes."

He really was a wretched liar sometimes. Jeremy didn't waste his breath arguing but sat with him until Jean sounded less like he was shredding his lungs on every inhale. There was still a tremor in Jean's hands when he got to his feet, so Jeremy took Jean on an impromptu tour instead of heading home. They drove up and down the streets of downtown Los Angeles, with Jeremy pointing out buildings and restaurants he recognized. Only when the ghastly pallor finally left Jean's face did Jeremy turn them south toward campus.

Jeremy parked before asking, "Will you be going back?"

Jean dug lines into the back of his hand. "Once a week for the next three to four months."

From him it sounded like a death sentence. Jeremy caught his little finger and tugged in a silent demand to stop hurting himself. When Jean obediently loosened his grip, Jeremy said, "Then I'll make sure you get there. One week at a time, okay?"

The girls were in the living room, Laila hunched over a crossword puzzle while Cat watched one of her ghost hunting shows. Cat was too transfixed by whatever weak evidence the crew was currently discussing to look their way, but she waggled her fingers in silent greeting. Laila tapped her pen twice against the corner of her mouth, filled in another row, and pointed to the other end of the coffee table.

"Mail for you, Jean."

Jeremy was closer, so he scooped the postcard up and held it out in offering. Jean stared at it like he wasn't sure what he was looking at, so Jeremy took a moment to study the simple design taking up the entire front. A white crescent moon and palmetto tree sat against a deep blue background, with a pale white border following the edges.

"This looks familiar," Jeremy said. "I just can't quite place it."

"It's the South Carolina state flag," Laila said, scribbling in another answer.

Jean finally reached out with both hands to take the card, but he was slow to turn it over. It took him only a few moments to read the short message penned on the back. Jeremy wasn't sure what it said or which Fox had sent it, but it was enough to take the tension out of Jean's shoulders for the first time that day. Jean's tired, "I hate him," as he left the room narrowed down the potential list of senders to one, but Jeremy wisely didn't comment on that transparent lie.

Later that afternoon Jeremy spotted the postcard hanging on the wall over Jean's desk. Laila found him leaning against the doorway to the study room and propped herself up opposite him. Jeremy smiled at the questioning look on her face and said, "I think we're in for our best year yet. Are you ready?"

"Last year," she said. "Last chance. Let's finish it."

They hooked their pinkies together in silent promise, and Jeremy let Laila tug him down the hall.

CHAPTER TWELVE
Jeremy

For all that Jeremy loved mornings and sunrises, four o'clock was a dreadful hour to be awake. He yawned so hard his jaw popped as he pulled on a USC tee and white shorts. The lamp on his desk felt obscenely bright this morning as he clicked it on. He'd packed his bag last night, but it was a long way back if he forgot anything, so he pawed through it as he counted off books and notebooks. His CD player was in the smaller pocket with his pens and gum. After a moment's debate he dug extra batteries out of his drawer and tossed them in on top.

Satisfied he had what he needed, he dug his sneakers out from under his bed and laced them up. A small tote bag on his desk had what he'd change into after he was done at Lyon this morning, so he plucked both bags up and cut the lamp again. He immediately ran into his chair in the dark and grimaced as he made his way out of the room. The railing helped him get downstairs in the dark.

By the time he reached the landing he'd readjusted to the shadows, only to promptly blind himself again when he cut on the kitchen light. Jeremy set his things on the island, glanced toward the coffee maker where it was finishing up a delayed brew, and went to get breakfast out of the fridge.

Going forward he'd be eating at Laila's place, since he had to leave his car there anyway, but Dallas insisted on making something for the first day back. He didn't care if Jeremy was nine or twenty-two; he was sticking to tradition until Jeremy finally moved out. Jeremy was the only one left Dallas could do it for, since Joshua lived with Arnold, Annalise had her own space, and Bryson

226

would be back in Connecticut by the end of the week.

Jeremy peeled foil off his plate, laughed at the stick figure horse Dallas had drawn into his pancakes, and got his food into the microwave as the coffee maker beeped completion. William had only prepped half a pot, enough that Jeremy could have a mug here and pack some to go. Jeremy clung to the mug for dear life as he watched the clock. The coffee was gone long before his food was, but eventually Jeremy could pile everything into the sink and get his plate soaking.

He plucked up the travel mug William had set out for him and hesitated when he saw what was hiding behind it: William had moved his keys in here so he could go out the side door if he wanted. Beneath the ring was an index card that simply said, "Drive safe," in William's tidy handwriting. Jeremy pocketed the note with a smile, grabbed his bags and coffee, and snatched up his keys on his way to the door.

The extra caution was unwarranted: Bryson's car wasn't out front. Where he'd gotten off to this early in the day was a mystery, but Jeremy would take his blessings where he could find them. He dropped his things in the passenger seat, put his coffee where he could reach it, and started the trek east toward campus. This time of day there was little traffic to contend with, and the morning was cool enough Jeremy could put the windows down while he drove.

Laila had left the porch light on for him. Jeremy parked behind her car, grabbed his bags, and took the stairs up two at a time. There was a piece of paper taped to the front door as he reached for the handle, and he hesitated at the sight of a crudely drawn guillotine. Laila's neighbors hadn't expressed any reservations about Jean's presence this summer, even in the days following the interview, so this was an unexpected rudeness. Jeremy tugged it loose, checked it all over for a message or any

227

hints as to who'd left it, and brought it inside with him.

The bicycles that had been tucked into the back corner of the living room all summer were now moved to the living room doorway, their tires eating up half the hallway. Cat and Laila tended to ride to campus during the school year, both to make the trek between classes faster and so they could grab groceries on the way home from practice. Last year they'd set a slow enough pace to campus he could run alongside them as a warmup, but this year he'd be walking to Lyon with Jean. Since the morning workout ran until seven-thirty and the first class of the day started at eight, the Trojans were set to rendezvous directly at the fitness center at six.

Jeremy found his friends sitting shoulder-to-shoulder at the kitchen island, munching their way through overnight oats with bleary eyes. He took up a spot opposite them and set the paper down where they could all see it. It took a second for them to register what they were looking at, and then Cat and Laila went perfectly still. Jean's eyes narrowed a bit in annoyance, but he kept eating.

"It was taped to the door," Jeremy said, glancing over at Laila. "No visitors last night?"

"None that we heard." Laila pushed her bowl aside in picking up the piece of paper. "I'll talk to Gary about getting security cameras set up out front, but I'm not sure how useful that will be. I don't think it was a neighbor— no sane person would risk losing their lease now that school is underway."

"Man…" Cat took the drawing when Laila moved to set it down. She glanced at Jean's face to gauge his mood, but he was more interested in his food than this new complication. "We were so careful to cover our tracks. No one should know he's here except us and the Foxes. Who else could it be?"

"Someone idiotic," Jean said. "We haven't used the

228

guillotine in thirty years."

"Almost exactly thirty," Laila agreed. "September 1977."

"I like that you two just know this off the top of your heads," Cat said dryly. "Nerds."

A glance at the clock showed he had some time to linger, so Jeremy cracked his drink open and set to inhaling it. Cat and Laila went back to their oats, but they kept glancing toward the artwork with moody stares. Cat was scraping the last spoonful into her mouth when her phone dinged. She scooped it up, opened her new message, and said "Oh!" so loud Laila nearly jumped out of her skin.

Cat dropped a quick kiss against Laila's shoulder in apology before turning on Jean. "You get to meet the water kids today! Angie's already setting up at Lyon." She set her phone aside so she could count them off on her fingers. "Angie's a grad student studying biokin... etic... uh."

"Biokinesiology," Laila supplied, "with an emphasis on sports science."

Cat pointed at her. "Yes. That. Thank you. You'll only really see her at Lyon or on game nights. Tony and Bobby are the undergrads. They alternate afternoons but will also come along to all our games. Tony takes a bit to warm up to new faces, but Bobby's the most scatterbrained sweetheart you'll ever meet. She's also desperately in love with Diego, so don't be tempted by her cute face."

"Our mascot," Jeremy said, assuming Jean wouldn't recognize the name.

"A useless expenditure," Jean muttered into his coffee.

"Next you'll say the Ravens didn't have cheerleaders," Cat said, then paused as she thought. "You didn't, did you? I honestly can't remember ever seeing them at your games."

"Our fans came to watch us, not a wasteful side

229

show," Jean said, putting out a hand for her bowl. Cat passed hers and Laila's over, and Jean went to rinse them out in the sink. Jeremy looked at the clock, chugged the rest of his coffee, and set his mug aside to collect on his way home that evening. The artwork was slipped into his backpack so he could show it to the coaches, and he slung his bag over his shoulder.

Cat got up and straightened their shirts with exaggerated seriousness as Jean and Jeremy tried to pass her for the door. "Oh, my darling sons, off to their first day at school. Mwah!" she added, kissing the air near Jean's cheek. "Do Momma proud."

Jean looked to Laila and said, "Handle her."

"Oh, I do," Laila said into her coffee.

Jean looked two seconds from willing himself out of existence, but Jeremy only laughed and turned him toward the front door. He toed back into his shoes while Jean detoured to the bedroom for his own bag. They were out of the house a few minutes later, and Jeremy breathed in the crisp morning air with a wide smile. As rough as getting up had been, there was something undeniably glorious about starting a new year. He simply had to quiet every yammering voice that reminded him this was his last year.

The peace lasted only until they reached Exposition Boulevard, and then the blinding smatter of flashing lights took a few years off Jeremy's life. He put a hand up instinctively to shield his face, but before he'd sorted out what was going on there were three older men in their personal space. Jeremy rapidly blinked spots out of his eyes as he tried to get a good look at them.

"Jean Moreau," one said, and Jeremy would give him points for getting it right if not for his follow-up question: "We've got a few questions about your parents."

"Good morning, friends," Jeremy said, dropping his hand to Jean's elbow and giving it a careful nudge. Jean kept pace with him as he set off toward campus, and of course so did the journalists. "Thanks for your interest, but it's not a good time. We're trying to get to morning practice."

"A word about Grayson's visit," a second said, undeterred.

"Clarify your age for us," the third said, earning a dirty look from the second for interrupting. "Hannah Bailey revealed that you're currently nineteen years old, and we were able to dig up supporting evidence." He put a hand to his notepad, checking his work, and said, "Here it is: Jean-Yves Moreau, fourteen at time of immigration. That's you, I assume; only Jean Moreau to enter the country that year as far as I could find."

Jean rocked to a stop but said nothing. Jeremy filed it away for later—much later, if the look on Jean's face was anything to go by. The man scribbled a note even as Jeremy tried again to get Jean moving. Jean didn't need encouragement but set off down the sidewalk at a brisk pace. "Based on the timeline, that means you would've been sixteen when you enrolled at Edgar Allan." He checked Jean's face for confirmation. Jean kept his stare pointed forward like he couldn't even hear them. "Two years is a tight turnaround to get a high school degree, especially in a new language and school system. I would've thought you'd lose years, not gain them."

"Agreed," the first admitted, studying Jean with interest. "I'm impressed you pulled it off but curious as to why it was approved. Starting you at Edgar Allan so young was Coach Moriyama's greatest mistake." Jean's flinch was full-body, and Jeremy saw all three men take notes. Rather than comment on it, the man bulled on with, "I'm not denying your talent, but the numbers your freshman year don't back up his faith in you. It's not until we put them alongside your own age group—high school sophomores and juniors—that the gap widens to something phenomenal. I want to know: why the hurry to throw you up against Class I schools, rather than let you gradually age onto the lineup?"

When Jean said nothing, the third asked, "Is he even following any of this?"

"He understood Hannah just fine," the first said. "Hello, Moreau, we are talking to you."

"It's too early for heavy conversations," Jeremy said, showing them his watch. "Perhaps you can ask Coach Rhemann to set something up at a more reasonable time and location."

"Just a few more questions," the third said, flipping through his pages again. "Need him to weigh in on a couple rumors for us. Not the usual ones," he said, and found the spot he was looking for. "See, I think it's interesting that we've somehow got so many criminals at play here. This spring we got a heads-up about Neil Josten's relationship with both the Wesninski and Hatford families, and now here come the Moreaus from left field. It's a little hard to believe, don't you agree?"

When Jean gave no sign he'd heard, the reporter lengthened his stride to get ahead of the pair. Jean sidestepped him, but the reporter grabbed the strap of his bag to drag him to a stop. "At least listen to the working theories before you refuse me."

"That is enough, thank you," Jeremy said, catching hold of the same strap. Jean felt the weight of his hand and slipped free of his bag, letting Jeremy step forward to fill the space between them. Jeremy held the reporter's challenging stare and said, "I would like to remind you that no one here is at liberty to speak about the ongoing investigation."

"The people have a right to know who USC has on their roster."

"Sure," Jeremy agreed. "This is Jean Moreau, a transfer from Edgar Allan who'll be wearing the number twenty-nine this fall. He is a valuable addition to our defense line, and we are all excited to have him on board."

"And you're not worried about him?" was the skeptical accusation.

"I have no reason to be," Jeremy said. "He is my friend."

The second man nudged the first and muttered, "Like Dexter was."

Jeremy gave the man his undivided attention and his most pleasant smile. "Sorry, I didn't catch that."

"I think you did," the man said, even as his companion said, "Don't swing at a Wilshire, man. It isn't worth it."

"On your left!" came Cat's cheery cry, and she dinged her bell nonstop as she rolled up on them. She kept her collision course, forcing the reporters to give ground to her, and pulled up alongside Jeremy so close their sleeves brushed. Laila came up on Jean's other side with her phone at her ear. Both girls had to dismount, as this pace was too slow to stay balanced, and Cat gave one of the reporters an enthusiastic clap on the shoulder. "Nice! Up and at 'em at dark o'clock! Good to see you're as excited for the season as we are. You've seen the schedule, right?"

And off she went, chattering about the Trojans' first game at a speed and volume they couldn't compete with. It was an unfortunate topic, considering it was the Bobcats' former star the reporter meant with his dig, but Jeremy would take anything at this point. Every attempt to interrupt her was simply talked over, as if Cat was too excited to notice their words. Jeremy quietly passed Jean his bag back, and Jean fell in alongside him as they continued toward campus at last.

"Jeremy," Laila said, and he followed her stare. A few security guards were at the corner of Vermont and Exposition. Laila held up her phone to get their attention before hanging up and tucking it into her pocket. The guards came out into the crosswalk to meet them as soon as the pedestrian light turned on.

"Okay, next time then!" Cat said, waving farewell as the reporters were practically bodied back across the street. Once they were out of earshot, she grimaced over at Jeremy and Jean. "I thought mosquitos were diurnal. Where'd they even come from?"

"Caught up with us at the end of your street," Jeremy said.

"Address has definitely been compromised, then," Laila said, and looked from Jeremy to Jean. "Are you okay?"

Jean waved her off with a sharp jerk of his hand, and Laila let it drop. The turnoff to take them to Lyon wasn't much further, and the girls chained their bikes up out front before following Jean and Jeremy inside. Angie was working with Xavier when they reached the Trojans' weight room, watching the way he twisted and turned. She added a couple notes to his file before sending him on his way with her blessing.

"Jean Moreau," she said when Jeremy led Jean over to her. "I've heard a lot about you."

"Good here?" Jeremy asked. "I'm going to catch up with Coach."

"I've got him," Angie promised, so Jeremy left Jean in her care.

Lisinski was going through a folder, trusting Angie to get the Trojans started, but she set her work aside when Jeremy stopped in front of her. "Someone's figured out where Jean lives," he said as he tugged the artwork out of his backpack. "Found this on Laila's front door this morning, and we had a couple opinionated reporters escort us to campus."

Lisinski frowned down at the guillotine drawing. "Fantastic."

"Laila's uncle will set up cameras at the house, but…"

"I assume you'll be driving to campus going

234

forward?"

"If they persist, I might have to," Jeremy said, with a quiet sigh. "It'll be harder to track when they lose interest and move on to bigger topics, but better safe than sorry."

"If any of you stop feeling safe, you let us know immediately."

"Yes, Coach."

She clipped the artwork to her file, supposedly so she could show it to the rest of the coaching staff while the Trojans were at class, and turned a searching look on him. "Anything else? All right, let us worry about this for a bit," she tapped the paper, "and you focus on getting through today."

Jeremy accepted her dismissal at face value and went to join his designated group. Summer practices had put them here for two hours, so shaving off half an hour for class made the time fly. Those that had eight o'clock classes hustled through the showers afterward, gamely ignoring their teammates' jokes about finding a nice place to nap instead, and Jeremy passed Jean off to Shane out front afterward.

"I'll see you after," he promised, and went his own way.

He'd had this professor before, so he had a good idea how his first class would go. He was pleased to be right: she distributed syllabi, updated her roster with preferred nicknames, and did the world's quickest Q&A as to what she expected from them this term. Although she personally didn't care about attendance so long as her students did the work requested of them, Jeremy was required by the university to be in class unless he was at a game or on death's doorstep. Today was a happy exception, because she didn't want to see any of them again until Wednesday.

"You are between me and my lox bagel," she said, pointing toward the door. "Goodbye."

235

Jeremy had half an hour before he had to collect Jean from Shane. He was briefly tempted to go in search of coffee, but he got comfortable on the steps near the fountain and sent Jean a quick heads-up text as to where to find him. The bag holding his gym clothes wasn't quite thick enough to be a proper pillow, but he was happy to put his head back and doze anyway. A light kick to his shoe roused him sometime later, and he smiled up at Shane.

"Thanks," he said. "How'd it go?"

"Exhilarating," was Shane's dry response. "I really should've changed my major."

He technically still could, except after his fifth year he'd be off the team and out of a scholarship. Any additional years to compensate for wasted credits would be on his own dime.

Jeremy got to his feet, slapped some dust off his jeans, and looked to Jean. "Ready?"

Shane went one way while they went the other, winding through a campus that was still slowly waking up. It was an easy walk, but most of their pottery classmates were already present. Jeremy had expected long tables and standing room, but the reality was a circle of twelve chairs with a single table in the middle. Each spot had an electric wheel in front of it, and Jeremy scanned the room for two chairs together. There weren't any, but he paused on a familiar face.

"Oh, Eli," he said, lifting his hand in greeting.

Elias Chisolm looked up from where he was trying to shove his backpack under his chair and smiled. "Jeremy! Didn't know you were taking pottery. Then this is uhh, the Raven," he said, fighting an uncooperative memory as he gave Jean a discreet onceover. "John? Sorry, sports aren't really my thing. Here, here." He snagged his bag and shifted down one spot, and just like that there were two seats side-by-side for them.

Jeremy smiled gratitude as he took the one between them and tucked his bags behind the chair. Since Jean didn't see fit to answer, he said, "Jean, yeah. Jean, this is Elias. He's studying fine arts; I met him when I took a photography class last fall." He arched an eyebrow at Jean and waited, silently willing him to remember his manners.

Jean held Jeremy's stare for ten seconds before offering up an unenthusiastic, "Morning."

Elias let it slide with an easy nod and returned his full attention to Jeremy. The slow head-to-toe he treated Jeremy to was less subtle than the quick scan he'd given Jean. Jeremy kept his eyes on Elias's face, content to wait him out. Elias only grinned at being caught and said, "You almost look rested. How long will that last?"

"Oh, I'd give it a week," Jeremy said, and went quiet as their professor moved to the center of the room.

"Good morning, good morning, good morning. And to you," he added as the last girl came rushing in. "Can you get the door? Thank you, thank you. Good morning! I am Adrian Gracie. You can call me Adrian. Let's make sure we've got everyone." He turned in a slow circle, counting heads with his finger, and gave a satisfied nod. "Okay! This semester we're going to be studying basic wheelwork using electric wheels.

"Fair warning: you are going to get messy. We do have aprons you can borrow," he pointed to where they hung on hooks against the far wall, "but they can only stop so much. I would strongly warn you against wearing anything you'll hate to see ruined. If you can bring a change of clothes with you, great! Class is technically scheduled until eleven-fifty, but we'll be done with the wheel by twenty after, so you have time to clean your stations and change if you so desire. Good? Good! Let's begin.

"Each station should have a bag of clay and a bucket, yes? Let's get the clay out of the way and see what we're

237

working with." His own station was only a few spots down, and he went to overturn his bucket. A small pile of tools fell out, and Jeremy pulled his own out as Adrian went over the purpose of each.

From there it was a quick introduction to the wheel itself, from the pedal to the removable bat. He sent them to the sink to get water for their buckets before having them gather around the table. There were a few circular plywood trays scattered across the surface, as well as a lone bag of clay, so Adrian tugged what he needed closer.

"Let's talk about clay," he said, and launched into an easy explanation of what type of clay they'd be using, what size chunks he wanted them to start with, and how to wedge it so it was ready for the wheel. He worked as he talked, kneading his own clay into something manageable, and showed it off when he was done. "Easy, right? Let's center it. With me," he said, and got comfortable at his station.

He made it all look easy and got so distracted answering basic questions and giving his credentials that he ended up with a small pot. He hummed as he considered it before taking wire to it and freeing it from his wheel.

"Okay, let's get to it," he said. "I'll come around and help out, so flag me if you need anything before I reach you."

Jeremy wasn't sure what he'd expected this clay to feel like, but the reality gave him pause. It was the dryer side of sticky, and prying off a chunk to work with was a little harder than he expected. Jean looked equally displeased by the texture of it, if his slight scowl was any indicator, but he wordlessly followed Jeremy to the table. There was a distinct lack of any energy or interest in prepping his clay until the girl across from them said, "Oh, like kneading bread!"

"Close enough," Adrian said, scraping residue from

his bat.

Jean considered that in silence for a moment before getting back to work with a little more focus, and Jeremy tried not to smile at him. The more Jeremy worked his clay, the better it felt under his hands, or maybe he was just getting used to it.

The real fun began when the class had to practice centering. Elias forgot to remove his tools first and sent them flying when he hit the pedal too hard, and more than one startled yip around the room said their classmates' clay was trying to make a similar escape. Adrian made a slow circle, studying each student in turn and offering advice. Jeremy tried listening to all of it in case it proved useful. The first time was a success for all of five seconds; when Jeremy tried a second mound just to test it, he cupped his clay so hard he squashed it. He glanced over to see how Jean was doing.

"What do you think?"

Jean showed off his filthy hands, but he checked how far away Adrian was before muttering, "This is repulsive."

"A little," Jeremy agreed, tapping his sticky fingers together. "I'm going to make a dog bowl for Barkbark."

Jean stared at him in disbelief and immediately lost control of his clay. He cracked his knee into the wheel in his hurry to catch it, and he scowled at Jeremy's helpless laughter. Adrian caught up to them then, briefly killing their conversation. He checked their posture and their grip, showed Jean how to brace his elbows against his legs so his arms were better locked, and gave them a stamp of approval before moving on.

"Everyone's looking good," he said. "Let's move on and practice pulling. Nothing fancy, okay? Not yet, anyway. We'll save that for midterms."

Jeremy had severely overestimated what could get done in a class this long. The entire period was a series of failures. Sometimes the clay cooperated, and Jeremy could manage a lopsided little cup; others it wanted to wilt and cave in on itself for reasons he couldn't always guess. Jeremy was just as likely to send his sponge flying at the two-hour mark as he was in the first two minutes, and Adrian hadn't lied that the aprons could only protect him so much. He had splatters all the way up his forearms and a half-dozen more on the knees of his jeans.

Adrian treated their lack of progress with an easygoing patience. Now and then he'd settle down and crank out a vase or plate like it was nothing, but he spent most of his time floating from station to station. He could tell in a glance what had gone wrong with each attempt, and he had a half-dozen easy ways to explain how to improve on the next go. Jeremy considered his latest collapsed mess in some consternation and sat back to wait on Adrian's arrival. There was no point calling him over when he was only two students down, so Jeremy glanced over at Jean instead.

Jean was every bit as messy as Jeremy was, with a few streaks on his cheek where he'd unthinkingly tried to get his hair out of his face, but for the first time this class his expression was calm. His foot was off the pedal as he gazed down at his wheel, his hands sitting relaxed and limp a safe distance from his clay. Afraid to mess with his piece any further, perhaps, because Jean had somehow gotten a three-inch cup to hold together.

"Oh, hey," Jeremy said, pleased. "Nice!"

"It is a lot of mess for a little thing."

It lacked the annoyance Jeremy expected to hear. Jeremy idly wondered if he was secretly pleased with his progress or if he was just relieved to have finally pulled it off; Jean's face was too guarded to give the game away. Jean turned his hands out so he could consider his palms, and he tried in vain to scrape them on the edge of his bucket. Adrian was in front of him in a heartbeat, offering distracted apologies to Elias and Jeremy as they were temporarily passed over, and he leaned over to inspect Jean's cup.

"Nice," Adrian said. "Sides look thick enough to hold up in a kiln. Have you checked the base?" Jean obediently pricked the bottom of his cup and held up his needle for the teacher's inspection. Adrian was satisfied with the results, and he scooped up Jean's wire for a quick demonstration in the air. "Like so, easy does it."

Jean's wire went through the base of his cup smooth as floss, and Adrian stepped back with a proud smile. "Great! Go ahead and drop that off on the shelves so it can dry. On the bat," he quickly added when Jean reached for his cup. "Good. Find your name tag on the shelves and, if you're feeling up for going again, there are fresh bats in the cabinet right beside it. Good, good. Where was I?"

"Here," Elias said, waving him over, and Adrian hurried to his side.

Jean lifted his bat from the wheel and considered his cup at eye level. Jeremy thought he heard a quiet, considering "Hmm" before Jean got up and carried the cup to its designated shelf. Jeremy turned a wry look on his own disaster, but Adrian was by a moment later to help him salvage it. He managed to end the class with one unsteady cup-like object, and he put it with his classmates' creations to dry. Maybe it'd be funnier at the end of the semester than it was now, when he—hopefully—could judge his progress by it.

Cleanup took longer than Jeremy thought it would, and there was only so much he could do to tidy himself. Jean picked at the spots on his own shirt with an agitated scowl as he followed Jeremy back to Hoffman. Cody was waiting for them out front, and they looked from one to the other with obvious amusement.

"I see we had fun."

"I think I made negative progress, but yeah, it was great!" Jeremy scratched idly at one of his new stains and

241

checked his watch. "I'm done with classes for the day, so I'm going to find a sunny spot to nap for a half-hour or so. I'll kidnap Jean when you're done with him."

"Nah, we're good," Cody said, waving him off. "I'll get Jean fed and see him down to the stadium on time, so don't rush back. Right?" They made finger guns at Jean, who only gave a serious nod. Jeremy was heartened by Jean's easy acceptance of Cody's company, and he returned Cody's grin with a grateful smile. Cody motioned for Jean to get a move on and said, "All right, let's get in there before we're late. I've heard horror stories about this man, and I don't want to start the year off on his bad side."

They headed inside, so Jeremy turned away and considered his options. He really did want to sleep, whether it was on the lawns here or on a bench at the Gold Court, but this morning's run-in with the press meant he should deal with his car first. He walked back to Laila's place alone, went in long enough to grab his travel mug, and drove his car over to the stadium. With that done, he let himself into the locker room and lay down on the strikers' bench to nap. It was probably the least comfortable thing he'd attempted, but he slept until his teammates arrived.

Raven drills were still on hold, so Jeremy was able to drive all three of his friends home after practice. Someone was waiting on the steps for them, idly tapping a pen to his notepad, but he perked up as Jeremy pulled up behind Laila's car. Jeremy motioned for Jean to stay put but got out and approached the stranger with an easygoing smile.

"Evening," he said. "Can I help you?"

"Jeremy Knox," the man said, pointing his pencil up at Jeremy in recognition. "Hoping to have a couple words with your teammate. You told my colleague to come back at a more reasonable time, so here I am."

"I asked him to arrange something with Coach,"

Jeremy clarified as he settled in at the man's side. "I don't begrudge you trying to do your job, but I've got to put the safety of my teammates first. Having unknown faces show up at their home at all hours is a little off-putting, don't you think?"

"The sooner he talks, the sooner I'll be on my way," the man said.

Jeremy followed the man's gaze to his car. Jean wasn't even looking at them; he was looking over his left shoulder toward the backseat. Cat's hands were moving as she talked, and Laila had her phone at her ear. Laila hadn't trusted the police since high school, so he assumed she was talking to her family. Jeremy offered the reporter a conspiratorial smile as he tried to get his attention back.

"If you don't mind me asking, how did you even know he was here? We really thought we were sneaky."

"Don't ask me. Came through as an anonymous tip."

"Oh? That's interesting." Jeremy got only a shrug in response. "But I really do have to ask you to leave. First day of school's always a bit of an adjustment, yeah? Everyone's tired and hungry; we haven't even been able to have a proper dinner yet. I can give you Coach Rhemann's number if you want to try and contact him tomorrow for a possible interview slot."

"It's three questions," the man said. "It'll be faster if he cooperates."

"Perhaps," Jeremy allowed, "but you're not going to talk to him tonight."

The man shrugged and pointed his pen at Jeremy. "How do you see this working out? If you keep asking me to leave, and I keep saying no, then what? I don't imagine you'll call your uncle on me, Knox."

"I've been rude," Jeremy said. "I never asked your name and association."

It earned him a cheeky grin. "No offense, but I'm not that stupid."

243

Laila got out of the car and came to stand in front of them. She clasped her hands together in front of her and offered the reporter her politest smile as she said, "Good evening. I'm afraid I'm not comfortable with unfamiliar men loitering outside of my house, so I'm going to ask you to leave. Preferably before my security team arrives in the neighborhood."

"Ah, Miss Dermott. One or two questions for the road?"

"Do you need Coach Rhemann's contact information?" Laila asked.

"I'll take that as a no."

He got to his feet, dusted off his pants, and went to where he'd parked halfway down the street. Jeremy watched for him to leave before accepting Laila's hand up. He answered her questioning stare with a helpless shrug and, "Said the address was an anonymous tip. Wouldn't give up his employer but works with at least one of this morning's guests. Security a real thing?"

"Gary installed the cameras and alarms around lunch," Laila confirmed, glancing past him toward her front door. "And yes, he hired some private security to sit on the house overnight for a week. Hopefully once the press realizes we're serious about not sharing our time they'll give up and we can go back to normal."

She motioned an all-clear to the others, and Cat and Jean finally got out of the car. Jeremy tweaked Laila's hair and asked, "Do you want me to stay a while just in case?"

"I want you to *stay*," Laila said, with a meaningful look. "Good night, Jeremy."

He waited until they were all inside, then got back in his car alone and started the long drive home alone.

CHAPTER THIRTEEN
Jean

Jean's first week at USC was a bit of a mess, but at least it was an eye-opening experience. Laila had secured them a pair of private security guards to watch the house and escort them to class in the morning, but there was always one or two reporters following along. They couldn't approach, but they snapped nonstop pictures just to be aggravating and called their intrusive questions over to Jean the whole walk.

By Tuesday the hungry press had figured out campus was where they were most vulnerable, and they started camping outside of Lyon to follow the Trojans to class. Rhemann immediately filed a complaint with the university. By the following morning half of the campus entry points were barricaded and security desks guarded the rest. Anyone needing entry to campus needed a written invitation from the faculty or a student ID. It successfully locked the reporters out, but the extra steps for access were unpopular with Jean's teammates.

Around that bit of chaos, Jean was learning how to be a college student. It was a curious thought to have when he was starting his senior year, but it wasn't until Wednesday afternoon that he truly understood how narrow his view had been. The Ravens' lives had been tightly controlled, with dedicated instructors and compact classes tailored to work around their shortened schedules, so he'd never really spent time on campus. He remembered towering buildings and boring lectures, the shuttle that would rush the Ravens back to the Nest, and little else. Now Jean was trapped on campus from six to half-past two five days a week.

Monday and Wednesday were a series of easy hand-offs, Shane to Jeremy to Cody. Jean always had a lunch prepared, since he and Cat put together a week's worth of meals, but Cody sought out one of the on-site dining halls for their own food. Afterward the pair found a sunny spot to settle down, and Cody drifted between easy conversation and comfortable silence until it was time to head to the stadium.

Tuesdays and Thursdays proved to be a bit more complicated, but Jean hoped it would get easier with time. Now that the school year was underway, Jean's permanent schedule with Dobson settled into place. It was a wretched way to start the day, having to call her right after morning practice, but at least it got her out of the way. Somehow every single one of the floozies had a class during that period, but Tanner was free and willing to study at the library while Jean holed up in one of the study rooms for his call. As soon as Jean was free Tanner had a million questions for him about the Ravens, most of which Jean ignored unless they had to do with drills.

Jeremy had gotten permission to sit in Jean's business microeconomics class so long as he wasn't disruptive. He didn't have to pay attention, but on Tuesday he gave it a good attempt out of some semblance of curiosity or solidarity. By ten minutes in his eyes had glazed over from boredom, and five minutes later he was fast asleep. Since he was quiet at rest and he was only attending for Jean's sake, Jean let him sleep and focused on his own notes. Jean's next class was in the same building, so he sat tense in his classroom until Shane caught up with him. Afterward Cody came by to snatch him up.

On Thursday Tanner thought to bring his laptop and a headphone splitter to campus, so he and Jean watched part of a Raven match after Jean hung up on Dobson. Tanner pointed out every instance he spotted the kind of shot Jean's drills were slowly teaching him. Seeing it in action

246

and knowing what he was working toward pulling off seemed to light a new fire in him. Tanner wouldn't have any court time this year, as the USC Trojans recently started red-shirting their freshmen, but he was trying to cope by looking ahead.

"No one's going to see me coming," Tanner said, sounding pleased. "They'll know my high school stats only and not that I was getting one-on-one training from the perfect Court."

"Assuming you can ever learn the drills," Jean said.

"I can!" Tanner made a face at him. "I'm trying."

"Sometimes you do. Most of the time you are a walking disaster."

"Rude! Sorry I wasn't born creepily gifted, or something? But I can do it. I'm not gonna stop until I figure this one out." He checked his watch before shoving his laptop into his backpack, and he hesitated to turn a serious look on Jean. "Hey, I was talking to Lucas about your drills. You sticking him on a light racquet, and all, I wondered if these would help him figure it out, but he said he couldn't come. You two still fighting?"

"My personal opinion of Lucas is irrelevant," Jean said. "He is a Trojan."

Tanner kicked idly at the leg of Jean's chair before getting to his feet. "That's not really a yes or no, you know."

"The drills do not have an invite list."

"That's still not—" Tanner gave a disgruntled sigh as he started toward the exit.

Jeremy was coming from class, so they reached Hoffman first. Tanner had another open period, since he'd stacked most of his classes on Mondays and Wednesdays, so he was in no rush to leave. Tanner practiced swings while he waited, complete with unnecessary "whoosh" sound effects. Jean tried not to hold his form against him, since Tanner was obviously doing this more for entertainment than proper study, but it was still irritating enough he had to look away. Luckily Jeremy was by to save him only a couple minutes later.

"He really likes you," Jeremy noted as they got settled in their classroom.

"He likes the muzzle you have put on me," Jean returned. "If I could treat him honestly, he would have walked out weeks ago."

"And would that make you happy?" Jeremy asked, studying him with a steady look. "Treating him like a Raven, I mean, with your contrition and anger and perfectionism. Would you enjoy it? Because I don't think you would; I think you're just so caught up on the results that you'll accept whatever process will get you there fastest. He's a kid, Jean. He's got five whole years ahead of him."

Jean was saved from answering when the teacher stood up from his desk to start class, but the question chased him as he filled his pages with notes. *"Would you enjoy it?"* He imagined driving the butt of his racquet into Tanner's back or hitting him across his padding hard enough that Tanner would feel it for days, and he drew agitated circles in the corner of his page. It would be for Tanner's benefit, obviously; a couple good hits and the man would either step up or give up. Jean was doing him a grave disservice being so tolerant with his mistakes. Tanner's future and the Trojans' success were more important than anyone's individual happiness.

And yet.

The Trojans placed second in the nation more often than they did third, and they'd given the Ravens a good run this spring. Slow and steady and unserious was working for them, for the most part. With a little more grit and a little more blood, maybe they could have already closed that gap and seized the victory they claimed they wanted. Instead, they'd settled into their role of being second place. Objectively, they were a failure of a team, a squandered collection of phenomenal talent.

Even still. Jean curled his fingers into a slow fist, looking for pain that had long since faded. When the season started next week and he could see firsthand how they handled their opponents, he would know for sure how wretched this year was going to be.

-

Friday was the messiest day of the week to handle, as the only one of Jean's classes to carry over was his eight o'clock business writing class. He had nowhere to be until afternoon practice started at three. The absence of ceramics meant Jeremy was also free, except he had to leave campus for therapy on Friday. Cat should have been available for at least part of the morning, but she had meetings with her advisors to discuss changes to her program. Shane left Jean with Xavier and Min instead, who turned him over to Nabil an hour later, and then Emma and Mads came to steal him away. Jeremy returned only ten minutes before Cody could stake a claim on Jean's time.

"You showered again," Jean said as Jeremy got settled at his side.

Jeremy stared blank-faced at him. "Uh?"

"Different cologne." Jean dragged a highlighter over a relevant section of his notes. "This one does not suit you whatsoever."

Jeremy tugged at his shirt to sniff it. "Oh, I didn't even notice. Not mine," he explained when Jean glanced his way. "I bumped into a friend on my way back to campus. Is it really that offensive?"

Knowing it had come off another man's body made it twice as terrible. "Yes."

"Sorry," Jeremy said, sounding more amused than apologetic. He scooted out of Jean's space, then moved again when he realized he was upwind of Jean. His smile

249

was irreverent when he asked, "Better?" and Jean refused to humor him with a response. Jeremy didn't press him for an answer but flopped back on the grass with a satisfied smile. Jean highlighted the same section again with a little more force.

Jeremy looked at peace, but Jean found the silence grating. Cody's arrival a few minutes later finally broke the tension, and the older backliner dropped into the empty space at Jean's side. Today they had a little carton of strawberries with them, and they held it up in offering. Jeremy made a face at the sight, and Cody rolled their eyes before divvying it up between just the two of them. Jean ate his slowly, savoring the tang, and was only halfway through when Cody looked between him and Jeremy.

"Ready for tomorrow?" they asked.

The western district followed the same schedule as the northeast: the first weekend of the year was reserved for the fall banquet. It was an easy meet-and-greet before the season got underway, a chance to assess one's opponents without the sourness of a first game already muddying the atmosphere. The south and central districts put anywhere from one to three matches on the schedule first, which Jean had found annoyingly backwards last year.

This year the University of Arizona was hosting. Laila guessed it would be an eight- to nine-hour drive once breaks were accounted for, and she'd taken him out last week to find something appropriate to wear.

"Yes," Jean said, before adding, "I do not know these teams except on paper."

"Oh, I guess you wouldn't. Most of them are pretty cool—to us, anyway. Quite a few have serious issues with each other. The only one who wants to beef with us in public is White Ridge." Cody hummed thoughtfully and tugged idly at the grass. "Normally we just kill 'em with kindness until someone else intervenes or they embarrass

250

themselves by being awful, but I don't think it's gonna work this time. Not if Jeremy's going, I mean."

Jean stilled with his last strawberry halfway to his mouth. "If."

Cody misunderstood and flicked Jeremy a keen look. "Unless you changed your mind?"

"No," Jeremy said, staring up at the sky. "I'm still going."

Jean frowned at them both. "It is a mandatory event. Attendance is required."

Cody looked at Jean like he'd grown a second head; Jean stared back and waited for someone to explain this new insanity. After a few uncomfortable beats Jeremy finally pushed himself up on his elbows and explained, "I haven't been to a banquet since my freshman year. Coach has always excused me."

"If the ERC finds out you've been skipping—"

"They know," Jeremy cut in, with a smile Jean didn't believe for a second. Jeremy didn't explain but tugged at his shirt and said, "Didn't notice this cologne until you drew attention to it, but you're right, it's unbearably strong. I'm going to go scrub it off and put on something that doesn't smell. You mind getting him down to the stadium later?" he asked Cody.

Cody's mouth thinned to a hard line, but all they said was, "Yeah, I've got him."

"Thanks!" Jeremy hopped to his feet and left.

Cody watched him walk away, and Jean studied Cody's serious face for any clues. At length Cody gave a sour, "Bright as a broken bulb and still in the running for valedictorian. I will never understand it," and scooted so they were facing Jean. "You really don't know? Even if he hasn't said anything, it was all over the news a few years back. Oh, wait." They hesitated and counted years on their fingers. "I guess you weren't in college yet. We wouldn't have been on your radar."

251

It was only half-true. Jeremy had started his freshman year one year ahead of the perfect Court, but Kevin tracked the Trojans' seasons too obsessively to miss his arrival. Maybe Kevin knew what Cody was dancing around, but Jean had never bothered to read the articles Kevin shared with him that year. Like he'd told Kevin, his reading hadn't been strong enough to try. And like Kevin had accused him, Jean had been ultimately more interested in the accompanying photographs than whatever the text might have said. Jean pushed such thoughts aside as useless and forcibly focused on Cody.

"You weren't," he lied.

Cody muttered unintelligibly as they scrubbed at their face: stalling, Jean guessed, as they figured out what to say on the matter. At length they gave an explosive sigh and dropped their hands to their lap. "Well, most of it is public record. I can give you the press-friendly story now, or you can wait to see if Jeremy is feeling truthful later. Either way, we at least need to talk about Noah. There's a non-zero chance some asshole will bring him up tomorrow, and I know Jeremy won't want to talk about him."

"Former Trojan," Jean guessed.

Cody winced. "Jeremy's baby brother."

A new name; the missing piece. Jean remembered the child who appeared in only one photograph in Jeremy's house; he remembered the hoarse edge in Jeremy's voice as he confirmed his brother's death. *Four years this August,* he'd said, and Jean knew how this story would end. He almost told Cody he didn't want to hear this story, but Cody was already picking through an uncomfortable explanation.

"Noah was Jeremy's plus-one at our freshman banquet—not by choice, but I missed a couple details on how he got saddled with him. Polite enough kid, but very obviously not okay. Any time Jeremy got distracted by

252

anyone or anything else, he just kind of…" Cody passed a hand back and forth in front of their face and affected a vacant stare before finishing with, "…checked out. Jeremy said he was just tired and bored out of his mind, so I let it go. Not the kind of guy you wanted to get in an argument with back then, you know?"

Jean had no idea what that was supposed to mean, but this wasn't the time to get sidetracked. He tucked that comment aside for later as Cody continued. "Jeremy got invited to an exclusive afterparty, so he sent Noah back to the hotel alone. Probably figured he'd watch TV or go to sleep early, but Noah went up to the roof instead. Security footage had him at the rooftop lounge for about three hours." Cody rubbed away a sudden chill before saying, "When he finally got up, it was to go over the railing."

He'd known it was coming, but Jeremy's jagged, *"He's gone,"* echoed in his thoughts as Jean stared at Cody. "He jumped."

"Officially, no. The press release said he was trying to get a picture of the skyline and leaned too far, or some weak excuse like that. Since the footage was never released, the Wilshires could spin the story however they liked—and what they liked was to farm his death for pity points and privacy. Needed something to counteract Jeremy's disastrous evening. Coldblooded, if you ask me," Cody added. "Jeremy needed help, not damage control. I really thought we were going to lose him for a while there."

It was so unexpected Jean could finally shove Noah and Elodie from his thoughts. Cody grimaced at the sharp look Jean sent them and gave a helpless shrug. "To really get into that, we'd have to talk about the rest of the night. Do you want that story from me or Jeremy?"

"He said I can ask," Jean said. "I will ask."

"Your call," Cody said. They checked their watch and collected their trash. "Just promise me you'll keep an eye on him tomorrow. Most everyone who was a problem back then should've graduated by now, but I know at least one who's still around. These kinds of grudges don't go away so easily."

"He is my partner," Jean said. "I will protect him."

He'd gotten Neil through three weeks at the Nest; dragging Jeremy through one banquet would be easy. Having to behave would be the only difficult part.

-

The west-coast fall banquet was a dinner affair, scheduled to start at six mountain time. Rhemann wanted his team in Tucson an hour ahead of time, which meant they were due at the stadium by half-past eight for a nine o'clock departure. A charter bus and its driver were waiting for them in Exposition Park. Loading their overnight bags and dinner clothes into the storage compartments was easy work. White and Jimenez took a head count in the parking lot, and Rhemann and Lisinski did another once everyone was on board.

There were enough seats that the coaches could each sit alone and a few of the Trojans could similarly spread out. Derek and Derrick, unsurprisingly, packed in side-by-side. Jean's four students sat together, one pair in front of the other. Jean's satisfaction was short-lived, as there were also five strangers in their midst.

"Dates are allowed," Jeremy reminded him when Jean voiced his disapproval. Despite his reassuring tone, there was a telltale smile tugging at his mouth. Jean scowled at him and slid into the next available seat. Jeremy settled in beside him and said, "Fair warning: there'll be more of them this December. It's just rough finding people this early in the year. First weekend, you know? Everyone's still getting settled."

"All the more reason to forbid it," Jean insisted, but Jeremy only laughed.

With Jean, there were nine bodies in the so-called

floozy group. Cody was the odd one out, but they were quick to fill the empty space beside them with a bag of snacks. Pat and Ananya had the seat behind them, and Cat and Laila the one in front. Jeremy and Jean were across from the girls, and Xavier and Min claimed the spot behind them.

Jean was content with his spot on the outskirts, and he only paid their cheerful conversation half a mind as he watched Los Angeles slide by out the window. He'd loaded a few matches onto his laptop last night, but it wasn't likely to do him much good. He'd learned early on that reading or watching anything while traveling made him wretchedly carsick. He'd spent most away games with the Ravens simply sleeping away the hours, desperate to make up for time lost at the Nest.

The first few hours were easy, sliding in and out of a doze while his friends laughed and chatted about anything under the sun. He woke to find Cat and Cody now sharing a seat, both hunched over handheld game devices, while Laila solved a crossword puzzle. Jeremy was on his knees facing backwards so he could talk to Xavier and Min; trust the man to never run out of anything to say.

Jean planned on going back to sleep, except he was too rested to drift off. That was annoying and unexpected. He wasted half an hour trying before he gave up and started counting teams on his fingertips. He named as many strikers as he could think of, half-heartedly quizzed himself if they were right-handed or left, and mentally assigned them his best-guess at jersey numbers. He was halfway through the list when Jeremy realized he was awake, and the captain broke off his conversation to settle down at Jean's side.

"Good news," he said, with a touch too much cheer. "Three hours down, six to go."

Jean flicked him a withering look. "I will leave you behind at the next rest stop."

Jeremy's smile was radiant and unafraid, and Jean had to look away even before Jeremy said, "You wouldn't."

"Maybe not," Jean said, "but I'll think about it."

Jeremy laughed. "Did you not bring anything to do?" Jeremy asked. When Jean only waved that off, Jeremy said in French, "Hello! My name is Jeremy Knox. What is your name?"

The sound of his language on Jeremy's lips was enough to give Jean pause. He counted his heartbeats as he studied Jeremy's face, committing the textbook-perfect sounds to memory, and finally said in English, "I am not an ideal practice partner for you. I am from Marseille," he added, when Jeremy looked ready to argue. "You are learning Parisian French."

It took Jeremy a moment to catch on, and he looked delighted. "You have an accent."

"Yes."

"So do Cody and Sebastian," Jeremy pointed out.

"You already understand the language they are speaking," Jean said. "You know how to compensate for unexpected pronunciations without risking your own progress."

Jean took one look at Jeremy's stubborn expression and swallowed a sigh. Explaining the difference between his mother's nasal 'proper' French and the twang of his father's dialect was not how Jean planned on spending this ride, but with six hours ahead of them Jean would make an exception. He broke it down as simply as he could, explanations followed by examples, and Jeremy listened with unwavering fascination. Jeremy tried sounding a few words out despite Jean's best attempts to discourage him. The self-study course Jeremy had settled on would contradict these lazy vowels and lingering sounds; practicing it Jean's way would only set him back.

Jeremy shrugged off Jean's warnings. "Maybe I can find a tutor from Marseille."

"No one will take you seriously if you learn French with a southern accent."

"Does that really matter?" Jeremy asked, studying Jean with a stare that felt prying. "I'm not learning French for anyone but you."

Getting kicked in the chest would be a little less painful. Jean desperately wished he'd sat with Cody; sitting thigh-to-thigh with Jeremy while he said such things so seriously was cruel. When Jean took too long to answer, Jeremy leaned into him to dig his phone out of his pocket. He dictated his message to his butler as he typed it out, perhaps buying Jean time to argue with him. Jean should, but the words caught somewhere between his lungs and teeth. He wanted to trace the memory of Jeremy's weight down his side.

Rescue came from an unexpected corner: a hollered "Hey, bro!" from near the back of the bus jarred Jean from his frozen contemplation. He refused to believe it was for him until it came again in French, and he muttered darkly under his breath.

"I did not teach them that," he said when Jeremy sent him a sideways look. Derrick was the next to call him. The last two voices Jean wasn't sure about; he was too busy being offended by how terribly they butchered the pronunciation to sort it out.

"We do have French instructors on campus they could have asked," Jeremy reminded him as he moved into the aisle. "Good luck!"

Jean made his way to the back of the bus. Shawn and Shane were in the very last row, each with an unfamiliar girl in tow. Derrick and Derek were in front of Shane, with Ashton and Emma across from them. Lucas' group was next, Lucas alone and Travis with Haoyu opposite him. Jean let his gaze slide right past Lucas without hesitation and turned a disparaging look on the so-called double-D line.

"Do not mangle my language," he said.

Derrick immediately pointed past Jean at Sebastian. "That was him. Anyway, look." He elbowed Derek, who was already turning his laptop so Jean could see the screen. Derek had a photo album open, and he tapped to bring up a picture of him with two other people. Neither of the strangers was wearing Trojan colors, but Jean had only a moment to question their relevance to him when Derrick stabbed a finger at the beautiful woman tucked under Derek's arm.

"That's my future wife," he said proudly.

The oft-touted Cherise, then. Jean understood in a glance why Derrick was keen on her, but he wouldn't give the man the satisfaction of agreeing. He turned a steady stare on Derek and said, "This is not why you called me back here."

"That's about it, yeah."

Jean turned to go, but Derrick came off his seat to snag Jean's sleeve. "They get you all the time. You should stay and gossip with us." It was a ridiculous demand when there was nothing to gain from his company this far from a court. Jean flicked him a suspicious look, but Derrick was already motioning wildly to Lucas. "Move your stuff, man, let him sit down."

There was no chance Lucas would allow this, except after a brief hesitation he pushed his bag to the floor. Derrick turned a winning smile on Jean and said, "I won't even talk about the Kings. Cross my heart, hope to die, pray the Sharks all up an' die, et cetera et cetera."

"What do you have against sharks?" Timmy asked.

"Why is everyone on this bus so uncultured?" Derrick complained.

Shane ignored him to address Jean: "We'll be stopping for a break in an hour or so. I know you can tolerate us for that long."

Jean couldn't guess an ulterior motive, but they were

258

his teammates. He would go along with this for now. Jean obediently sat in the spot Lucas had cleared for him, keeping his back to the other man and putting his legs in the aisle. Derrick hung off the back of the seat to ask, "What do you want to talk about?"

"This was your idea," Jean reminded him.

"What do you normally talk about with them?" Derrick tried.

"I mostly listen."

Derek's dry, "That works, because Derrick loves to talk," only made Derrick laugh.

He wasn't lying; as soon as Derrick had permission to speak he was running his mouth without any breaks for breathing. Jean was content for now to lean against the back of his seat and listen.

Save for Shane, who was in three of Jean's classes, Jean rarely saw these Trojans outside of practice. With Jean living off-campus and no Nest to bind them together, perhaps it was inevitable, but this was a rare chance to see how they interacted without Exy in the mix. There was an easy familiarity to the way they treated each other as they bounced from topic to topic without cease. They were quick to tease one another, but it lacked the biting edge and sly grievances that stained too many of the Ravens' conversations.

"What're you thinking about?" Derek asked, poking at the top of his head. "You've got a serious look on your face."

There was no point lying, so Jean said, "The Nest."

"Y'all's Away locker room is horrible," Sebastian said. "Can I say that now?"

"'Y'all' nothing," Shawn spoke up. "He's not a Raven."

Sebastian grimaced. "Yeah, I just—the point stands. I hated it. Did you really live there?"

Jean thought of dark walls and red lighting, rows of

259

identical rooms, and the way his blood looked black on Riko's bedroom floor. The same few meals over and over, the same callous faces day-in and day-out, and the court where the Ravens could finally spread out and breathe. Harsh laughter, wild violence, and the crick-crack of fracturing bones. Jean flexed his fingers, needing to know they worked, but the lack of pain was as unsettling as it was comforting.

"Yes," Jean said, because they were still watching him.

Dillon leaned past Sebastian. "What was it like?"

A living nightmare, Jean thought. Aloud he said, "The Nest was a critical factor in our success as a team."

"Stronger than me," Sebastian said, looking to Dillon for agreement. "I'd've gone mad."

"Who says they didn't?" Lucas asked.

It was the first thing he'd said since Jean sat down. Shane stood, looking ready to intervene if needed, but Jean wouldn't deny it.

He considered it, then sent a sidelong look over his shoulder. "What is it in English, the colored glass at church?" Lucas hesitated before answering, and Jean couldn't fight back a faint scowl at the sound of it. "Stained glass. English continues to be a hideous invention. *Stained glass.*" He flicked his fingers, trying to erase it from his memory, but said, "That is what the Ravens are: sharp-edged and shattered, and fused together into a new whole. You cannot take them apart again."

"You and Kevin left," Derek said.

Kevin was forcibly broken off and Jean was stolen, but there was no point getting into that with these people. "We are perfect Court," he said. He was closer to the Ravens than Kevin and Riko had ever been, as the King and his brother existed on a pedestal, but his entire tenure at the Nest he'd been a half-step apart. Jean dug his fingers into his tattoo until his cheekbone ached. "We are

260

not the same."

Jean hadn't realized the freshmen were paying attention, but Chuck popped up in his seat to stare at Jean. "Are you going to keep that?" he asked, pointing at his own face. "Isn't it a little weird? All the others being gone, I mean."

"Ignore him," Derek said. "His mama didn't raise him right."

Chuck made a face. "I'm not the only one who wants to know!"

"You could probably find a better way to ask," Nabil said from a row or two up.

Haoyu hissed at Chuck to get his attention. His stage whisper wasn't quiet enough for Jean to miss his "Riko!" warning, and Jean glanced over in time to see Haoyu slice a finger across his own throat. Chuck blanched at the reminder and dropped out of sight as soon as he realized Jean had seen them. Haoyu glanced over, warned by Chuck's reaction that something was wrong, and dropped his hand to his lap as quickly as he could.

"Pop, and he was gone."

They weren't at a rest stop yet, but Jean wasn't staying back here any longer. He pushed out of his seat and started for the front of the bus. Chaos followed in his wake: forced cheery farewells from Derek and Derrick, and a flurry of hushed accusations and frantic self-defense: "What did you do?", "Why would you say that?", "I'm sorry, I didn't mean it!"

Jean tuned it all out in favor of reclaiming his spot at Jeremy's side. Jeremy got up to let him back into the seat, and his smile dimmed a bit as he got a look at Jean's face. Jean didn't miss the way he glanced toward the back of the bus, but Jeremy stayed with him rather than investigate.

"Hey," Jeremy started as he settled at Jean's side.

Jean didn't want to hear it. "I will teach you a phrase,"

261

he said, digging in as hard as he could against the memory of Riko's hands on his throat, in his hair, clawing lines into his face. "You will use it at the banquet if you need to leave. Yes?"

The speed at which Jeremy's expression went from concern to delight to caution was almost impressive. He half-expected Jeremy to ask him what he knew, but after a minute's silent contemplation Jeremy finally nodded. Jean sounded it off for him: first at a normal speed, and then in bits and pieces as Jeremy echoed it back to him. Jeremy stumbled a bit over it as he tried putting it all together, but Jean mercilessly bullied him until he got it right. Only when Jean was satisfied did he turn his stare out the window.

He and Jeremy didn't talk again for another three hours.

CHAPTER FOURTEEN
Jeremy

The University of Arizona had rented space at a convention center three miles off-campus for the banquet, and Rhemann had secured rooms for his team at the hotel adjacent to it. Their driver pulled up outside the hotel long enough for everyone to disembark and collect their things from the storage compartment. Rhemann waited for a headcount from both White and Jimenez before sending him on his way, and the man promised to be back by eleven the next day to collect them. There were too many of them to follow Rhemann inside, so Jeremy and Xavier helped keep watch over the team while Rhemann and Lisinski checked them in.

Rhemann passed out keys and instructions to be back by half-after before letting them into the lobby. With four elevators it would be easy work to get the team up to their floor, but Jeremy looked from the room number printed on his key to Jean. He quietly told himself it'd be a nice stretch after so many hours on the road, and he almost believed it. Flagging Laila down was easy work, and he motioned Jean over from where the other man was hanging back.

"Can you take our bags on the elevator?" Jeremy asked Laila as he held up his change of clothes. "Jean and I are taking the stairs."

Laila looked from Jeremy to Jean and back again. "It's eight flights."

"We do more than that at practice," Jeremy pointed out.

He half-expected her to push the matter, but at last she held her hand out for their things and said, "Better you

263

than me."

Finding the stairwell took a bit of work, as there wasn't a sign for it in the lobby, but soon enough Jeremy and Jean were on their way up. Jeremy waited until they rounded the third-floor landing before looking back at Jean and asking, "What's the cutoff before you start feeling claustrophobic? You seem fine in cars, and you've mentioned it's airports you're not comfortable with, not airplanes. How small does it have to be before it bothers you?"

"I don't like being in boxes."

Either something got lost in translation, or Jean was being vague because he didn't want to talk about it. Jeremy let it slide in favor of counting steps in French. Jean said nothing about his pronunciation, but Jeremy knew he was listening. He could feel Jean's steady gaze on him, a comfortable weight against the back of his head. Since Jean had nothing to correct there, Jeremy next attempted a basic monologue on his way to the fifth landing.

"My name is Jeremy Knox. I am from Los Angeles. I am studying English at USC. Today I am in Tucson for— uh." He faltered as he overestimated his vocabulary. Jean sighed but obediently supplied the missing word. Jeremy didn't have to ask what it meant; its intonation was different from its English equivalent, but it was still close enough to understand. "—a banquet." He looked back at Jean for his approval, but Jean's annoyance was plain. Jeremy finished with a quick, "Thanks!"

"You aren't going to law school," Jean said in English.

Jeremy stared at him, thrown, then assumed Jean made the mental jump from his major to his ill-advised plans for grad school. He smiled in the face of Jean's disapproval and said, "There's no harm in taking the exam."

Jean was as swayed by the argument this time as he

was the last, and he stubbornly insisted, "It is your fifth year. They will put a camera in your face and ask you what your hopes are for graduation. If word gets out you are considering other careers, it will jeopardize your chances and shrink your prospective pool. What recruiter will fight for a man who is already looking elsewhere?"

How easily Jean laid bare that gnawing fear in Jeremy's bones. Jeremy looked away, but not quickly enough. Something showed on his face, judging by the edge in Jean's insistent, "*Jeremy.*"

Jeremy stopped on the seventh landing to face him. Jean wasn't expecting it, and he nearly ran Jeremy over when he lengthened his stride to catch up. Jeremy dug his feet in, refusing to budge, and Jean caught his chin so he could get a good look at Jeremy's face.

Jeremy offered him a wry smile. Keeping an easy tone was second nature, but it did nothing to take the frustration out of Jean's stare. "It's important to my parents that I at least consider it, so I will. It'll be fine, Jean, I promise. The test itself isn't a commitment. Even if Harvard accepts me, I have until spring to make a final decision."

Invoking his parents was the right move; Jean gave ground to higher authority too readily to encourage rebellion in his captain. After a few tense moments Jean let go of him, and Jeremy was able to turn away unchallenged. He took the last flight up and let them out onto the eighth floor. A glance from their room key to the signs on the walls had him turning right down the hallway.

The Trojans were scattered across two or three floors, but Rhemann had attempted to keep friend groups as close together as possible when handing out keys. Cat and Laila should be on his hall somewhere, but Jeremy had forgotten to ask their room number. He texted his own to Laila instead, and he'd just toed out of his sneakers when she rapped on the door. Jean was closer, so he let her in.

She was half-changed out already, dark tights under a knee-length skirt and only a pale camisole on top. Jeremy didn't miss the way Jean pointedly stared at the ceiling as she carried their clothes over to the nearer bed.

"Iron's on the shelf in the closet if you need it," she said. "We'll see you downstairs."

"Thanks," Jeremy said, and Laila left. Jeremy went to investigate the state of his clothes while Jean contemplated his life's choices near the door. Jeremy's thoughts wandered as he dressed: Laila, to his sister, to Renee's picture that had disappeared from Jean's desk shortly after they teased Jean about her. None of the three looked anything alike, leaving Jean's taste in women an utter mystery. Jeremy considered asking, but instead he said, "Mom thinks I should marry Laila."

It was enough to get Jean's undivided attention, at least until Jeremy peeled his tank top off. Jean immediately found something else to stare at, like he always did when Jeremy was in varying stages of undress. It was horrifically inappropriate fighting for Jean's attention like this, Jeremy knew; shame was a prickling heat eating away at his satisfaction. He was quick to tug his shirt on, a simple white button-up with a snazzy tie to brighten it, but Jean didn't move until Jeremy was buttoning his slacks.

"Ridiculous," was all Jean had to say as he unzipped the bag with his clothes.

Jeremy sprawled on his bed to wait for Jean, but in the silence his thoughts threatened to wander. He slung an arm across his eyes and said, "I wonder if they've got the Foxes' game on demand. Maybe we can watch it when we get back to the room tonight."

He'd seen the score last night but not the match; the three-hour time difference and a long afternoon practice saw to that. It was easier to keep up with on game nights, since afternoon practice was scratched in favor of short, low-level warm-ups. Jeremy could put it on as background noise in the locker room and at least catch the first bit. The Foxes had won their first match, but only by a single point. Jeremy was curious to know if that close call was due to the skill of their opponents or their combative freshmen fracturing the lineup.

It was inevitable his thoughts would turn from the Foxes to their archrivals, and Jeremy asked, "Are you worried about the Ravens?"

"No."

The south kicked off the season last night, but the Ravens hadn't played. Coach Rossi claimed most of his lineup was out sick with a stomach bug, and Edgar Allan provided testimony from a half-dozen professors to support his story. A makeup match was scheduled for Thanksgiving week. Another string of bad luck for the beleaguered team, Jeremy had said to Kevin, but Kevin had no patience for the Ravens' lies.

"Not a single one is ill," was Kevin's response. "They are simply failing to adapt, and Rossi is desperately trying to buy time."

Kevin would know better than he did, and Jeremy had to admit it was suspicious. The southern district had their fall banquet next weekend. By missing last night's game, the Ravens had set themselves up for a spectacular comeback: their first game of the season would now be their rematch against Palmetto State on Friday, September 14th.

Weight on the bed had him drawing his arm back. Jean was leaning over him, one hand braced on the mattress beside Jeremy's head. His charcoal dress shirt was only half-buttoned, and Jeremy instinctively followed the line of his throat down to his exposed collarbone. From anyone else this would be an invitation, but this was Jean. Too many others had put their hands on him and shattered his trust. Jeremy couldn't make the first move here no matter how desperately he wanted to tug a few more buttons loose.

Don't, he warned himself, even as he studied the pale scars crisscrossing on Jean's skin.

If Jean noticed his distraction, he gave no sign. His expression was serious as he said, "Tell me the phrase."

Jeremy would be lucky to know his own name when Jean was standing between his legs like this. He put his arm across his face again so Jean could only see his smile and guessed, "I take it Cody told you about my catastrophic introduction to USC? I thought they might when I walked out on you two yesterday. It's fine," he hurried to add. "Saves me the embarrassment, if nothing else."

"It is an incomplete story," Jean said. "Cody is trying to protect you."

How far they'd come from such an uncomfortable beginning. Jeremy let his fondness bleed into his, "They're a good bean."

"I said I would ask you for the rest, but Cody insinuated you'd be dishonest." Jean waited a beat to make sure that hit before leveling a quiet accusation at him: "You would, wouldn't you?"

Jeremy ran his tongue along the backs of his teeth, chasing the memory of alcohol and sweat. Fast on its heels was a bitter taste he could never forget. He flexed his hands, working away a tremor that might only be in his head, and bit the inside of his cheek until the only voice in his head was Spader's. He had her home number saved on his phone out of necessity. He'd likely have to call her in the morning for a quick check-in, but maybe he'd end up calling her tonight.

At last Jeremy remembered to say, "No. Not to you." He moved his arm so he could see Jean's face. The Frenchman looked unconvinced and unimpressed. Jeremy held his stare and willed Jean to believe him. "I told you all summer I want you to trust me and feel safe with me, didn't I? Lying to you would undo everything we've worked so hard to build. I'd rather lose face than lose your confidence."

Predictable to a fault: such an earnest appeal had Jean retreating out of his space. Jeremy was finally able to sit up, and he reached out to snag Jean's wrist. "I mean it. If you want to ask, just ask. I will never lie to you."

Jean stared him down in silence before finally saying, "White Ridge has a vendetta against you."

"For a few years now," Jeremy said. "I destroyed their captain's career and reputation. It's a hard thing to forgive."

By the look on his face, Jean had no idea what to do with that information. Jeremy waited patiently for the obvious follow-up, but Jean only pulled free of him and said, "No. The details cannot matter tonight. You are my captain and my partner; that is all I need to know. I will stand with you against them."

"You and me against the world," Jeremy mused, delighted despite himself. "But it's not just me on trial tonight, so take what time you need to steel yourself. They've likely heard all the rumors and watched your interview backwards and forwards; they'll have a lot of opinions and a lot to say. I'm obligated to remind you this is a public event and that you'll have to play nice, but if you watch my back, I'll watch yours."

"Tiresome charade," Jean muttered.

He moved away to finish buttoning his shirt, and Jeremy went in search of his dress shoes. Jean was still fiddling helplessly with his tie when Jeremy was completely ready, so Jeremy went to him and put his hands out in offering.

"Let me," he said, and Jean relinquished it to him. Jeremy wound it around Jean's neck and hesitated, trying to imagine the movements on someone else and distracted

269

by the weight of Jean's unblinking stare. Jeremy went through the motions slowly as he waited for muscle memory to kick in. It took two attempts before he figured it out, and he smiled triumph as he smoothed Jean's tie flat.

"Easier on—" he started to say, but Jean's fingers on his neck killed his train of thought.

"Horrid creations," Jean said as he fixed Jeremy's collar. "No better than a noose."

Jeremy meant to laugh or agree. What he said was, "You look good." When Jean went still as stone, Jeremy hurried to correct himself with, "It looks good on you, I mean. But I get it—not the most comfortable thing to wear." He was saved when his phone went off with Laila's alert, and he retreated to a safe distance to check her message. "Looks like most everyone else is downstairs already. Shall we go?"

Jeremy passed Jean one of the room keys on their way out of the room. He kept an easy pace down the stairwell, as it was hot as the devil's buttcrack in Tucson and he didn't want to sweat through his dress shirt before dinner even started. They caught up with the Trojans out front and wriggled through the crowd until they found the floozies. Cody had put both Cat and Laila between themselves and Pat and Ananya, and Jeremy didn't think it was the heat that put that flush in Cody's cheeks. Ananya's expression was calm as she stared into the distance, but she had her arms crossed so tight she'd leave wrinkles in her dress.

"Easy," Jeremy said, tweaking her sleeve.

"I can't make it any easier," Ananya said in a low voice.

It was and wasn't true, but it wasn't Jeremy's fight.

Finally all twenty-nine Trojans and their accompanying six dates were accounted for, and Rhemann led them over to the convention center.

Check-in was smooth, and each player was given a lanyard in USC's colors. The laminated cards hanging off the hooks featured prominent jersey numbers, with surnames and positions printed below them. Their room wasn't much further along, two turns and a short hall, and then a set of fire doors that were currently propped open.

One of Arizona's assistant coaches was sitting just inside the door. She stood to shake hands with USC's four-man staff before lifting a microphone to her mouth. Judging by the crowd and the noise, Jeremy guessed at least five teams were already settled, but the coach had set her mic to carry over the chaos: "USC Trojans now in attendance. Coach Rhemann, Coach Lisinski, Coach White, Coach Jimenez. Captain Jeremy Knox, vice-captain Xavier Morgan." She flicked her mic off and leaned closer to Rhemann as she pointed. Jeremy was close enough to hear her say, "You'll be at tables thirteen and fourteen in the gold quadrant."

"Thank you, Coach," Rhemann said, and set off in that direction with his team a long line behind him.

Jeremy's heart was a hummingbird trapped in his throat. He loved the chaos and noise and crowds of game nights; having the western teams all under one roof was an even greater gift. There was so much talent in this room Jeremy felt electric, but beneath that current was the sizzling snap of too many memories. Jeremy let his gaze wander: looking for familiar faces, looking for faces that would've moved on years ago. How desperately and fervently he'd dreamed of events like these, and how swiftly he'd destroyed it. There was comfort in knowing he was not that person anymore, but it was a hollow accomplishment.

As one of the largest teams in the west, USC could have easily dominated an entire table. Instead they were put back-to-back at neighboring tables so they could converse with other teams. One table was split with

271

Arizona's Wildcats, and the other shared with Boise's Broncos. Both teams got on well with USC outside of matches, so Jeremy was pleased with the arrangement. He caught Xavier's eye and tipped his head toward the Wildcats. Xavier motioned from himself to Boise's table in response. Each opponent would get a captain's attention to avoid the appearance of favoritism, and the floozies would divvy themselves up appropriately.

Spotting Arizona's captain was easy work; Jeremy could find his former teammate in any crowded room. Jeremy feigned not to see the question in Alejandro Torres's stare as he held out his hand. Torres didn't hesitate to give his hand a firm shake, but the faint smile he managed didn't reach his eyes.

"Jeremy Knox, I think," he said as Jeremy sat opposite him. "Last I checked you were a brunette. Senioritis giving you a midlife crisis?"

"Something like that," Jeremy said with a laugh. "Congrats on making captain. I should have texted when I saw the roster update."

"Implying you didn't delete my number years ago?" Torres asked, and Jeremy could only shrug. The Wildcat didn't care enough to pursue it but turned a considering look on Jean. "The infamous Jean Moreau, then. Heard a lot about you."

"I don't know you," Jean said.

"This is Alejandro Torres," Jeremy said. "He and I went to high school together. He's one of the cleverest dealers I know, and he's got a great team here. Playing in Arizona is always a treat: their fans are phenomenal, and the facilities are gorgeous." To Torres he added, "Jean's still learning the western teams. It might take him a bit to put names to faces."

Torres understood what Jeremy didn't say. "I suppose he wouldn't know us. We've always been irrelevant to the Ravens."

"You had a really strong season last year," Jeremy said. "I'm excited to see how you've built off of that and kept the momentum going."

Whatever Torres had to say on the matter was drowned out by the next announcement: "White Ridge Bobcats now in attendance. Coach Jones, Coach Caper, Coach Hatcher. Captain Thomas Ennis, vice-captains Peggy Walter and Adam West."

Jeremy's stare went unbidden to the newest arrivals. The largest team in the west, there were thirty-three Bobcats on this year's roster. With a dozen-odd dates in the mix, the line seemed to go on forever. Jeremy wasn't surprised to see them seated a safe distance from USC, as Arizona saw no benefit to stoking antagonism this early in the season. The Bobcats had placed second in the district almost as many years as USC placed first, and it was always a toss-up as to who'd win their fall showdown.

Torres didn't seem to notice his distraction. He still had his eyes on Jean as he asked, "How are you liking the Trojans? Bit different from the Ravens, I assume."

"Yes," Jean said, and didn't elaborate.

The seat across from Jean was already taken, but another Wildcat approached to steal it. When her teammate didn't immediately get up, she rapped him on the shoulder with an impatient, "Move." He heaved a put-upon sigh as he relinquished the spot to her, and she almost hip-checked him in her hurry to sit down. It took Jeremy a moment to recognize her without her gear on, but the number hanging from her neck confirmed her as one of the Wildcats' goalkeepers.

The Canadian, he remembered, a half-second before she launched rapid-fire French across the table at Jean. Jean stared at her in dead silence for several moments before answering, and it was her turn to size him up with a fierce frown. Jeremy looked from one to the other, idly wondering how he could police Jean's rudeness if he couldn't understand what he was saying. Both players looked equally annoyed, but not enough to call it off.

"You two good?" Jeremy asked.

"Probably talking mad shit about us," Torres said, nudging his goalkeeper.

"His is hands down the worst accent I've ever heard," she said.

Jean's scandalized, "*Mine?*" startled a laugh out of her, and they went back to harassing one another. Torres offered Jeremy a helpless shrug, and Jeremy sat back to listen. He'd assumed Jean was naturally introverted, not hesitant to speak, but the easy way he held his own against this stranger was eye-opening.

Jeremy mulled it over, trying to make sense of it. Jean had always been a touch defensive about his English proficiency, even as he was willing to hide behind the excuse of a language barrier when he didn't want to speak to someone. Five years of immersion in the US should have given him a bit more confidence, except even as Jeremy thought it, he felt the missing pieces fall into place. He'd told Jeremy at Hannah Bailey's office that he'd learned reading and writing via his coursework—the same day he'd said, "my year of English lessons."

"I was not allowed to speak French at the Nest," he'd said. He'd been allowed a single year to study English before being shoved into the deep end at Evermore. Jeremy wondered how patient the Ravens had been with the bewildered foreigner dropped in their midst. Not very, he assumed, and it made him ache. On its heels was renewed determination to master French, and he checked his phone to see if William had secured him a tutor yet. The last message he'd received was a simple promise that he would look.

A text came in from Ivan Faser as Jeremy was about to put his phone away: "Where you staying tonight?" Jeremy glanced down the length of the table to where the backliner was sitting. The junior offered him a rakish, hungry smile when their eyes met, and Jeremy teetered between need and revulsion. Faser was very good and very enthusiastic, but Jeremy didn't know if he could drag someone to bed here without tearing open too many memories.

"Ask me later," he sent back. "I might have other plans."

"Lame," was the response, followed by a string of frowning faces.

Jeremy shrugged an apology at him, and Faser turned his attention to the Trojans across from him. The arrival of two more teams back-to-back brought an end to Jean's conversation; the goalkeeper's face lit up as the second one was announced and she excused herself from her seat to hurry away. Jeremy didn't ask, but Torres saw his nonplussed look and said, "Her boyfriend plays for Nevada."

Jeremy nodded easy acceptance. "How many are left to arrive?"

Torres tipped his head back to think. "With Nevada and San Francisco, we should be at ten teams, so... three to go? Couldn't tell you who, though, I wasn't paying enough attention. Make that two," he added as he was interrupted by another announcement. One of the Wildcats players came over to speak into his ear, pointing across the room, and Torres caught Jeremy's eye before tipping his head. Jeremy nodded understanding, and the two Wildcats left together.

Jeremy gently knocked his knee into Jean's and gestured to where a pair of men were standing in the middle of the room. "Representatives from the ERC," he said. "Schumaker's been around forever, but I don't remember the younger one. Willis? Williamson? Uhhh... Laila?"

"Whitney," she said without hesitation.

"I could live a hundred lives and never be as smart as you," Jeremy said.

"Maybe if you would learn to read," she returned.

Jeremy put a hand over his heart. "I read for class. That counts for something."

"Company," Jean said, a half-second before something fell past Jeremy's face. Jeremy hadn't even heard someone move up behind him with all the rest of the noise, but he stared down at the candy scattered on his placemat with some consternation. He started to turn in his seat to see who'd brought him such an odd gift when Torres's chair was pulled out across from him.

"Jeremy Wilshire," Rusty Connors said as he sat, and Jeremy forgot all about the man at his back. "We were taking bets on whether you'd show this year. JJ here said you wouldn't dare, but I had faith. Last year, and all. No way you could resist."

Jeremy smiled at the Bobcats' goalkeeper. "It's still Knox, actually."

Connors had a fistful of the same candy JJ Lander had given Jeremy, colorful paper sticks packed to the brim with powdery sugar. He tore the end from one, knocked it back, and showed Jeremy the new blue stain on his tongue. "Well, you know us, always glad to have you around. We're even going to have a little get-together afterward for old time's sake. You should come."

He tore the top off another stick, but instead of eating it he dumped it in a slow line across the tablemat in front of him. Beneath the table Laila dug bruises into Jeremy's thigh. Jeremy dragged his attention back to Connors' face and kept it there even as the man made another tidy row. The rest of the sticks he chucked across the table toward Jeremy, adding to his small pile. He licked a fingertip, tapped it to one line, and tested it on the tip of his tongue as he held Jeremy's stare.

"Appreciate the offer," Jeremy said, "but I'll have to

pass this time."

"Real shame," Connors said. He nudged the Wildcat next to him and said, "This kid used to be quite the partier, you know?"

"Cool," the backliner said, with no enthusiasm or interest, and motioned to Jeremy. "If you're not going to eat those, can I have them? My sister's an absolute fiend for them. Thanks," he added when Jeremy started collecting the scattered sticks. "She'll be singing your praises when she's bouncing off the walls later."

"Did you bring her with you?" Connors asked.

"What? Here? Nah, man, she's eight."

"What about you?" Connors asked Jeremy, and Jeremy froze with his hand halfway to the Wildcat player. "I mean, you've still got a couple siblings left, don't you?"

"That's more than enough," Laila warned him. Jeremy heard the words but didn't hold onto them; he was stuck somewhere between his heartbeats. He found Laila's hand under the table and she immediately let go of his leg to lace her fingers through his. "We didn't come here to fight with you. Keep it civil or keep it moving."

"Who's fighting?" Connors asked, and turned an expectant look on Jeremy. "I'm just making conversation."

Jeremy finally managed to let go of the candy and withdraw. "Sure," he said, with an evenness he wasn't feeling, "but I'm not interested in talking about my family with you. Come up with a different topic or go back to your own table."

Connors ignored that to say, "There's what, at least two, right?"

He looked past Jeremy at his teammate for confirmation. Jeremy assumed Lander nodded, because Connors gave a triumphant gesture as he returned his full attention to Jeremy. He leaned forward: daring Jeremy to take a swing, knowing Jeremy wouldn't. "You could've brought at least one. Word is you're staying at the Knight's Rest, same as us. Didn't you know? Guests don't have rooftop access there."

It was enough to put a hole in his chest, but Jeremy only managed a hollow, "What," before Jean's fist came down between them hard enough to rattle every set of silverware on the long table. Conversations faltered around the room; within moments the only sound was the squeak of chairs as curious athletes turned to watch this confrontation. Jeremy was keenly aware of the ERC's judging stares, but he couldn't look away from Connors long enough to grimace an apology at them.

Connors studied the hand that had come dangerously close to taking his nose off before turning a shrewd look on Jean. "You missed."

"Only once," Jean warned him.

"Jean," Jeremy said, and hoped he heard the *Don't* in Jeremy's clipped tone.

He didn't have to understand what Jean said to know it was rude. Jean leaned into his space but kept his cold stare on Connors as he asked in English, "This is White Ridge. Yes?"

"Yes," Jeremy said. "Connors is their starting goalkeeper."

"And you're Jean Moreau," Connors said, sizing Jean up. "I've heard so much about you. My condolences, of course, that you ended up with the Trojans. Whose idea was it to put a rhino in a tea shop?" Jean looked at Jeremy, blank-faced, and Jeremy drew horns in front of his face with a finger. Connors understood the issue immediately and said, "A brute like you needs a team that will encourage your talents. You should have come north."

"To Pennsylvania?" Jean asked.

"To Spokane," Connors stressed. The noise Jean made put a sharp edge in Connors' smile, and the goalkeeper could fill in the blanks easily enough: "You don't think

278

we're good enough for you, but USC doesn't even appreciate you properly. Slotting you into the second line? How embarrassing."

"Better to be second line here than traded to a dead end there," Jean said. It took the smile off Connors' face, but Jean wasn't done. He gave a dismissive flick of his fingers and said, "I have heard enough about you to know you are no different from Penn State or Edgar Allan. You rely on size and aggression to win your games. It is easy and satisfying, and I have seen it all before. If I am to improve, I must try something new. This is the only team that matters."

"That's bullshit," Connors said.

"I am perfect Court. I cannot be wrong about Exy."

"No one here actually believes this, right?" Connors looked at the Trojans and Wildcats that were watching this exchange with tense interest. Connors waved expansively at the two men sitting across from him and insisted, "We all know the real reason you're at USC. Don't we, Wilshire?"

Jeremy knew better than to take the bait, but he still said, "Enlighten us, Connors."

Luckily for all of them, Torres returned then. "Ass out of my chair."

Connors shrugged him off. "I'll go in a second."

"One," Torres said, and gave his chair a hard shake. He kept his stare on Connors' head but pointed across the table at Lander. "Rethink whatever you're about to say. I will beat your ass six ways from Sunday in front of God and the ERC if you two don't get away from my team. We assigned you across the room for a reason."

Connors made sure to slam the chair into Torres as he stood up. More than one Wildcat got up, ready to throw hands if needed, but Connors kept his stare on Jeremy's upturned face and only said, "Good seeing you again. I'll tell Dex you said hello."

279

"Give me his new number and I'll tell him myself," Jeremy suggested, and Laila nearly crushed his hand in warning. Jeremy ignored it, more interested in the venom bleeding into Connors' expression. Jeremy finally found his smile again and affected an easy tone to say, "We'll see you on the court next week. I'm sure it'll be fun."

Torres barely waited for Connors to move before taking his chair again, and he frowned down at his placemat. "The hell is this?" he demanded, pointing to the lines of sugar Connors left behind. "Who's doing blow at my table, or do I even need to ask?"

His backliner laughed and showed off his collection of sticks. "It's candy, cap. Look!"

Jeremy had practiced Jean's phrase to perfection, but it was all a jumbled mess now. The best he managed was a casual, "Bum one?" to Torres as he yanked free of Laila and got up from his seat. He half-expected his former teammate to refuse, but after a beat Torres passed his pack of cigarettes over. It was heavy enough Jeremy knew the lighter was inside, so he smiled his thanks and turned away.

Jean snagged his wrist. "Do not."

Jeremy tested his bruising grip. "Walk with me."

The look on Jean's face said he didn't want to humor this tantrum, but at last Jean let go. Jeremy set off without waiting for him, and the weight of too many stares followed him to the door.

CHAPTER FIFTEEN
Jeremy

The sweltering heat outside did nothing to improve Jeremy's mood, but at least he could breathe easier. A charter bus pulled up to the door as he pushed through it, dropping off the second-to-last team at the convention center. Northern Arizona, most likely; Jeremy couldn't think of any other teams close enough to travel in their banquet clothes. He lingered only long enough to hold the door for Jean, then headed down the length of the building as quickly as he could go.

Halfway down he finally stopped and sat on the curb. Jean immediately stole the cigarettes from him and chucked them to one side. Jeremy sighed and shifted to go after them, but Jean clapped both hands down on his shoulders to hold him still. Incredulity and disapproval put a harsh bite in his words when he insisted, "You are not this stupid."

"Are you sure?" Jeremy asked.

Judging by the hard line of Jean's mouth, it wasn't the answer he expected or wanted. Jeremy was able to push him back and get up. Jeremy kept his distance as he lit up and studied the curling smoke so he could move downwind of Jean. He killed a third of the cigarette in one long drag, prayed the nicotine would do its job, and grimaced at the irritation in Jean's, "Jeremy."

He'd get an earful from Laila later; he didn't need one now. "Thank you," he said, and took advantage of Jean's confused silence to clarify, "for not hitting him. I know you wanted to, and I know you could have. Thank you for choosing restraint."

Jean made a cutting gesture in his peripheral vision.

"Let me fight him. I will make sure he never plays again."
When Jeremy only shook his head, Jean promised, "I will
do it with no witnesses."

"It'd be his word against yours," Jeremy said, with a
wan smile. "They'd take his without hesitation. Not
because anyone honestly thinks he deserves the benefit of
the doubt, but because it'd be more satisfying to believe
the Trojans finally cracked. They're getting bored of us, I
think," he admitted as he flicked ash aside. "They're quick
to congratulate our good sportsmanship, but they crave the
drama of a hard fall from grace."

"As fiercely as you resist it," Jean said. "I do not
understand your obsession."

Jeremy had tried explaining it before. All of that was
still true—the joy of a good game, the message his team
hoped to send—but the same excuses and reasons
wouldn't get him anywhere today. There was more to it
and Jean knew it. Jeremy turned his hand this way and
that, watching the cherry blur as he made his cigarette
dance, and offered up a quiet, "Redemption, perhaps."

It was enough to earn him a long stare, but Jean said
nothing. Jeremy looked across the parking lot to where a
crowd was slowly gathering. The last team was nearly
here. Jeremy sighed regret and finished his cigarette as
quickly as he could. He crumpled the butt against the curb
and tucked it into his pocket to throw away on the way
inside.

They were halfway to the door when Jean said, "Dex.
Dexter? Your friend."

Jeremy rocked to a startled stop. "Cody wouldn't have
called him my friend."

"No," Jean agreed. "Reporters said it on the first day
of class. I do not know this name."

"Dexter Rollins was the Bobcats' captain for three
years straight," Jeremy said, "but he was a fifth-year my
freshman year, so I only met him once. At the fall

282

banquet," he confirmed when Jean glanced past him toward the building. That Dexter's name hadn't come up in Cody's tale was puzzling. "What exactly did Cody tell you?"

Jean hesitated before answering, "Noah."

Jeremy's chest went tight in grief, but Jean didn't elaborate. Jeremy had never liked him more. He sucked in a slow breath, willing his heart down from its frenetic pace, and asked, "What about the party?"

"Only that you went to one."

Temptation was a ravenous beast. He'd said he wouldn't lie to Jean, but the truth was a many-tiered mess with so many irrelevant avenues. Omission wasn't dishonesty, but that didn't explain the heavy sickness chewing up his throat as he considered it. He didn't realize he'd looked away until Jean caught hold of his chin and turned his head back.

Jean's warning was quiet: "You promised."

"I promised," Jeremy agreed, "but this isn't the time to get into it." When Jean didn't let go of him, Jeremy motioned toward the approaching team and tried again. "You said the details can't matter tonight, so we'll talk about it tomorrow. Okay? I'll get us some coffee and tell you anything you want to know."

Jean said nothing, but he let go. Jeremy got them back to the conference room only a few steps ahead of the last arrivals. As expected, Laila and Cat had switched seats in his absence. Jeremy refused to take it personally but passed Torres's cigarettes across the table.

It took only a few minutes for the thirteenth team to find their seats, and then Arizona's head coach stood up to offer introductions and greetings. A catering crew rolled carts up and down the rows as he talked, handing out plates. Jean surveyed his meal with obvious distrust until Cat leaned behind Jeremy to give him an okay. Jeremy didn't miss the curious look Torres sent between them, but the Wildcats' captain didn't comment.

Either Connors got what he wanted with that brief meet-and-greet or someone filed a complaint with the organizers in Jeremy's absence; either way, the Bobcats stayed far away from him the remainder of the night. Jeremy was able to focus on the rest of the teams, and he did his best to introduce Jean to everyone he knew. As expected, Jean's proficiency in English appeared indirectly proportional to how personal the conversations got. Jeremy did his best to steer the conversation back on track every time it strayed to Jean's family or the Ravens.

It took half the night before he realized how much work the Trojans were putting in on Jean's behalf. Derek and Derrick brought over a gaggle of friends they'd made over the years, excited to show off their infamous teammate, and Jeremy heard Tanner hyping him up at one of the freshmen's meet-and-greets. Ashton made sure to introduce his sister, a senior at Oregon State, and she flagged down several of her backliner teammates to inspect Jean up close. A couple players who'd studied French in high school or were currently taking it sneaked over to practice with Jean, and Jean gave them his undivided attention.

Finding reasons to celebrate their teammates and opponents was the well-known Trojan way, but the sincerity of the team's unabashed enthusiasm and Jean's reserved demeanor did worlds for his image. Over the course of the night, conversations slowly shifted from prying curiosity and indelicate gossip toward cautious sympathy: on top of everything else that had gone wrong this summer, news had gotten around that USC was overrun with paparazzi. That they'd had to bar the campus gates just a week into the school year was utterly ridiculous.

Despite the evening's awful start, Jeremy considered the banquet a rousing success. Jean was less enthused, judging by his sour, "I will not speak to anyone else for a week," when they finally made it back to the hotel lobby that night.

Cat laughed and looped an arm through his. "You did good! I think they like you."

"I do not need them to."

"Isn't it nice, though?" Cat asked, trying and failing to drag Jean toward the elevators. "After how cruel everyone was this spring and summer, isn't it nice to finally see those rumors get ignored in favor of the real you?"

"They did not meet the real me, since you will not let me tell them how irrelevant they are on the court."

"Jean, treating other people with respect is just a part of life," Laila said. "If you say they cannot know you when you are being polite, what does that say about us? Are we forever strangers to these teams, or do they just see the best parts of us that encourage them to be the best parts of themselves?"

Jean waved her off, but Laila refused to give up. "What good does ridiculing someone do? Giving someone advice that will improve their overall performance or keep them from repeating a mistake is helpful. Harassing someone for messing up when we all have off days gets us nowhere. Or will you tell me you can't pinpoint your mistakes without someone riding you?"

"It is part of the process."

Cat weighed that in silence before asking, "Do you want to hit me? When I get outstepped at practice, when my passes get intercepted, if I can't stop my marks from taking a shot at goal, I mean. Do you want to break your racquet over my back?"

Jean looked taken aback. "No."

"But don't you want me to improve?"

"Yes, but—" Maybe he was imagining it: Cat's upturned face covered with bruises, blood drying at the corner of her mouth. He reached for her, testing her head for nonexistent lumps, and Jeremy's heart ached. Cat's gaze went soft, and she tugged Jean's hand around where she could kiss his palm. Jean finally said, "Not you. Not like that."

"So even you know it's not necessary," Laila said.

Jean looked away and said nothing. Rather than push him to admit it himself, Cat tried tugging him toward the elevators once more. Jean immediately dug in his heels and said, "No. I will not ride that thing. I am going to take the stairs."

"We'll meet you up there," Jeremy told the girls.

Laila caught hold of Cat's sleeve, and the girls exchanged a long look. Cat peeled her heels off and hooked the straps over her fingers. "Which way is the stairwell?" she asked. As soon as Jean gestured, she set off with a cheery, "Race you to the top!"

Jeremy started to follow, but Laila snagged his back pocket. To Jean she said, "See you in a bit," before hauling Jeremy behind her toward the elevator. There was no chance of getting a car alone with a half-dozen teams sharing this hotel tonight, but they were the only two to get off on the eighth floor.

Despite stopping five times to let other athletes off, they beat Cat and Jean to the room. Laila sat on the edge of Jeremy's bed while he wrestled his tie loose. When he cast it aside, Laila held out her arms, and Jeremy stepped into her fierce embrace. Without twelve other teams to distract him or Jean to keep an eye on, it was inevitable he'd slide back down memory lane. Jeremy tangled his fingers in Laila's dark hair and stared past her at the far wall.

"I'm glad I came," he said.

"Are you?" was Laila's quiet challenge.

He didn't have an easy answer for that, but the trill of his phone distracted him from miserable thoughts. Laila leaned back so he could dig it out of his pocket. He knew who it'd be even before he opened his texts, and for a fleeting moment he was tempted to block Faser's number. He read the man's message twice through, weighing common sense against his threadbare nerves.

He made up his mind when the lock at the door popped undone, and Jeremy tapped out a quick response as Cat and Jean moved into the room. His only clean clothes were what he was due to wear tomorrow, so Jeremy peeled off his shirt and pulled on this morning's tank top. He feigned not to notice Laila's disapproving frown as he went in search of his shorts.

"Not PJs?" Cat asked as she flopped at Laila's side. "I figured we'd get room service and watch the Foxes' game, or something."

"I'll catch it later," Jeremy said. "I'm heading out for a bit."

Faser's next text came in before Cat could quiz him further, and she laughed at the familiar alert. "Oh. Tell him we said hi."

"Probably won't," Jeremy admitted. He grabbed his keycard from the nightstand on his way out. Jean's unblinking stare was a weight he refused to return, and he lingered at the door only long enough to ensure the lock caught. He bypassed the busy elevators in favor of the stairwell and hurried down to the ground floor. Faser was parked over at the convention center where there'd be fewer prying eyes, and the passenger door was already unlocked.

The seat was laid back all the way so Jeremy could stay out of sight of any passersby, and Faser chucked a hat into Jeremy's lap before he even had the door closed. Jeremy tugged the ballcap low over his face and fumbled for his seatbelt.

Faser ran an appreciative hand up his thigh. "Didn't think you'd come. Glad you changed your mind."

"So am I," Jeremy said, and if it wasn't entirely true, it

at least sounded convincing. "Let's get out of here."

"Hell yeah," Faser said, and nearly brought the asphalt with them.

The last time they'd hooked up was a home game in Los Angeles, so Jeremy wasn't sure where Faser's apartment was from here. At five minutes he figured they'd gone far enough to be safe, and he tossed the hat into Faser's backseat. The other man didn't protest when Jeremy sat up, but he did finally draw his hand back. Ten minutes later they rolled into a dark complex of a half-dozen squat buildings.

"Told my roommate to beat it," Faser said as he parked and killed the engine.

His place was on the first floor, three doors down on the left. Jeremy toed out of his shoes, earning an amused look from Faser as the man set off deeper into the apartment. Half of the walls were covered in movie posters, and the cloying scent of air freshener couldn't quite cover up the lingering smell of weed. If Faser's roommate really was gone, he'd left very recently. Jeremy waited near the door while Faser scoped the place out.

"Just us," Faser called from out of sight.

Jeremy followed his voice to a cramped kitchen. The other man was setting out a string of shot glasses. The top of his fridge was littered with booze bottles, and Faser pawed through them until he found the one he wanted. Jeremy put a warning hand to his shoulder and said, "Easy. You've got to drive me back later, you know."

"Easy," Faser returned as he poured, careless and content. "Take a taxi back, rich boy."

Jeremy could imagine how poorly that conversation with his parents would go, but that was none of Faser's business. He forced himself to let go and smile, and Faser set the bottle aside to kiss him. His "Let's have some fun," was barely a murmur against Jeremy's lips, but Jeremy didn't need to hear the words when Faser's hand was shoved into the pocket on his shorts. His knuckles were an insistent weight against Jeremy's skin. Jeremy would have to figure it out later; for now, he took the offered shot glass and knocked it back.

"Good," Faser said, as he started his drinks from the other end. "Tell me about your Raven."

"You really want to talk about Jean right now?" Jeremy asked.

"He got between you and Connors real quick," Faser said. If he noticed Jeremy stopped after his second shot, he didn't comment but went down the line with impressive speed. "Just wondering how I'm supposed to read into it. I heard what they were saying about him this spring, and we both know you're a shameless slut."

"Says the man who invited me here," Jeremy said, cool enough that Faser laughed.

"Can't make up my mind. Either he's as a big a whore as you are, or the Ravens are using your history to destroy his reputation. Who'd question it once USC got involved, you know? They put up with your mess, so of course they'd take on someone like him." He drained his last shot and chucked the glass to the counter. "Shine a little light on the mystery. You fuck him yet?"

Jeremy pulled Faser's hand free. "I didn't come here to gossip about Jean. If that's all you want from me, I'll just leave."

Faser shook loose and cradled the back of his skull in a firm grip. The look he favored Jeremy with bordered on pitying. "I don't think you will," he said as he ducked in for a kiss. His free hand went down the back of Jeremy's shorts to squeeze his ass, and he pulled Jeremy flush against him. Jeremy caught his wrist again in a crushing grip, and Faser rolled his eyes at that silent warning. "Keep your secrets, spoilsport, but lose the clothes."

"I'm not going down on you on linoleum."

Faser didn't need to be told twice, and he hauled

289

Jeremy after him down the hall. Alcohol made him clumsy and needy, but Jeremy could use that eagerness against him easily enough. He put Jean and Connors from mind and focused on the hungry heat of Faser's embrace.

Faser was snoring only minutes after Jeremy finally rolled away from him, and Jeremy contemplated the ceiling as he weighed his options. The easiest thing to do would be to borrow Faser's car and make it his problem; surely a teammate could take him back to the convention center tomorrow to retrieve it. But Faser drove a stick shift, and Jeremy wasn't entirely sure he wouldn't stall it out within a couple blocks. Walking back was out of the question, considering how long the drive had been. The only sensible solution was to call a taxi and deal with his parents' disgust when they saw the charge hit his account.

He rolled off the bed and got dressed. His phone wasn't in his pockets anymore, but he found it where it'd fallen out near the bedroom door. Jeremy stared down at the clock. It was a quarter to one, but his friends might still be awake. All of tomorrow's meetings were for the coaches: meet-and-greets with the referees, a panel with the ERC's representatives, and other such boring things. The Trojans had nowhere to be until it was time to leave Arizona, so they could stay up as late as they wanted tonight.

Jeremy prayed for a little luck and sent, "Awake?"

Laila answered immediately. "Yes."

He passed his phone from one hand to the other, fighting a silent war, and finally texted, "He's too drunk to drive me back tonight." He sent a final look at Faser's slack face before heading down the hall toward the kitchen. Laila's response came as he was ransacking Faser's fridge for water, and Jeremy put the bottle back in favor of hunting down mail. There was none by the door, and the junk mail in the recycle bin was too shredded to be helpful, but he finally found a pizza ad on the coffee table. He sent her Faser's address and sat down to wait.

It took almost half an hour, but finally Laila messaged him a summons. Jeremy couldn't lock the door behind himself, so he quietly hoped Faser's roommate would be back soon. Getting outside was easy enough, and he went straight to the taxi parked at the curb. Laila was waiting in the backseat. She said nothing when he got in, knowing better than to get into it when the driver could hear everything. Jeremy still risked a sheepish, "Sorry," as he buckled up.

"Back to Knight's Rest?" the driver asked.

"Yes, thank you," Laila said.

It was a quiet ride, and Jeremy listened for the total charge when they were dropped off. He wasn't sure he could free up enough cash to pay her back, but he'd find a different workaround that would fly under his parents' radar: covering her groceries, perhaps, or buying her a gift card for the local bookstore. He didn't have a pen to write the number down, but he texted it to her so he could find it again. Laila automatically checked her phone when it beeped at her, but she didn't comment.

The silence lasted only until they were on the elevator. At this hour, they had the car to themselves. She turned a serious look on him and said, "Were *you* drinking?"

Jeremy watched the numbers tick up above the door. "Only a little. Two shots," he said when she continued to stare at him. "I know my limits, Laila."

"I don't think you do."

He flicked her a wounded look, but she didn't return it. Her attention was on his throat, and she closed the distance between them to press careful fingers to his neck. Even that faint pressure hurt. Jeremy remembered Faser's bruising grip as Jeremy teased him to madness. At the time it'd been easy to ignore, as Faser's desperate, breathless swearing had been far more interesting than any discomfort. He fidgeted with his shirt, but a tank top

291

couldn't save him from her heavy stare.

Laila was relentless. "I don't like him, Jeremy. Don't see him again."

"You don't like any of them," Jeremy muttered.

"With good reason. Would it kill you to fuck someone who respects you?"

The edge in her words warned him not to argue. Jeremy should let it go, but he crossed his arms over his chest and looked away. "Faser blames me for Jean's rumors. Said I'm the reason the Ravens could say such vile things about him after he transferred." He tapped an agitated beat on his bicep and risked a look at her. That she didn't look surprised by this theory made all of it worse. "Everyone can believe that he slept his way onto the lineup and the perfect Court because we're the ones who signed him. I set the precedent for what USC will stand by."

"Jeremy," Laila said, but bit her tongue when the elevator slowed to a stop. The hall was empty when they stepped out, but Laila took a long look around before turning back to him. Her hands were gentle when she finally reached for him, and she tugged him close so she could press her forehead to his. "The next time you go home with Faser I will take your balls off with my fingernail clippers. Understand?"

Jeremy flinched. "Jesus, Laila."

"I said, do you understand?"

"Yes, yes," he hurried to say, and Laila looped her arm through his with a satisfied nod.

She knocked on his hotel room door, but Jeremy fished his keycard out of his pocket and swiped it over the reader. Cat was already halfway to the door when they stepped through, and she ground to a halt to stare at him. "Tell me those are hickeys," she said, sharp and disbelieving. Jeremy motioned for her to keep it down even as Laila hurriedly closed the door behind them.

"What the fuck, Jeremy?"

Jeremy waved her off. "Don't worry about it." He glanced at Laila and gestured over his shoulder toward the bathroom. "I'm going to take a quick shower. Will you two still be here when I get out or are you ready—"

The slap of a hand against wood nearly startled three years off his life, and Jeremy stared blankly at the arm barricading the bathroom doorway. He hadn't even heard Jean get up, but now the other man was standing only inches away from him. The look on Jean's face almost crushed the breath from Jeremy's lungs, and far too late he thought of bloody bites and Jean's fingernails digging lines into his own throat.

"Give me a name," Jean said. "I will kill him."

"Babe, wait." Cat reached for Jean, and Jeremy moved without thinking. He almost wasn't fast enough, but somehow he caught Jean's arm halfway through its instinctive swing and dragged Jean toward him. Recognition set in a second too late, and Jean flicked a quick look at Cat.

She put her hands up, not in self-defense but in conciliation, and retreated out of his space. "I'm sorry. That's on me. I'm sorry."

"Jean," Jeremy tried, but Jean was slow to face him again. Jeremy let go of him before asking, "Are you okay?"

Incredulous anger returned in a heartbeat with a flat, "Am I?"

"I'm okay," Jeremy stressed. "She's okay. Are you?"

"A name," Jean insisted.

"No," Jeremy said, and ignored the scowl that refusal earned him. "It's fine, Jean. This is not—this isn't the same as—" He floundered in search of a delicate way to finish that statement. The best he managed was an insistent, "He didn't mean to hurt me. He just had a bit too much to drink, so he got a bit heavy-handed. That's all it

293

was. I would tell you if it was something to be worried about, I promise."

"You promise."

Jeremy heard the accusation in that. "If you won't trust me, trust Laila. She hates all my partners; she wouldn't protect them from you."

"True," Laila started to say, but Jean's fierce, "They are not your partners," was louder. Jeremy could only stare at him, and Jean said something vicious in French as he finally stepped back. He moved Cat out of his way with a quick hand to her shoulder and crossed the room like he could barely stand to be in Jeremy's space anymore. The silence that fell in the room was uncomfortable and tense, and finally Laila nudged Jeremy.

"Shower," she said. "Leave your phone with me; I'm going to block his number."

Jeremy relinquished it to her before retreating into the bathroom at last. He stayed under the spray until his fingers were raisins and the steam made his lungs feel syrupy. Scrubbing dry in there was an exercise in failure, so he wound a towel around his waist before leaving.

Halfway to the beds he realized the girls were gone, and he wasn't sure whether to lament their absence. Jean was sitting cross-legged in the center of his bed, phone in his hands but gaze pointed across the room at nothing. He didn't move at Jeremy's approach, and he said nothing as Jeremy pulled on a pair of sweats. Only when Jeremy chucked his towel at the nearest corner did he finally stir.

"Tell me about the cocaine."

Jeremy froze.

The warmth of the shower was immediately forgotten; Jeremy felt cold all over as his heart left cracks along his ribcage. Every second of silence that stretched between them felt heavier, and then Jean said, "Torres said it at the table tonight. The candy," he said, as if Jeremy didn't remember the moment with agonizing clarity. Jean drew two lines in the air with his fingertip and looked Jeremy's way at last. "He didn't name you, but he meant you. Didn't he?"

"Yes." It was so quiet Jeremy wasn't sure Jean heard, so he tried again. "Yes."

Jean looked away. It was the answer he'd known he would get, but it wasn't the one he wanted. Jeremy laced his fingers together and squeezed until he thought he'd break his knuckles. It did nothing to help his nerves.

Jean said again, "Tell me."

Jeremy looked at his bed, where someone had already pried the blankets up from the corners, and went to sit on Jean's. Jean had to shift to make room for him, and they settled down facing each other. Jeremy looked past him and watched the time change on the clock. One minute, two minutes; he still wasn't sure where to begin. The banquet was obvious, but the truth had older roots.

At three minutes, Jeremy said, "The summer after Bryson graduated high school, he totaled his car. Cracked his skull in two places and shattered Annalise's hip."

Those long days watching over them at the hospital still haunted him. His siblings had been so pale and worn they were strangers to him. It had taken months of therapy to get them moving again. Neither had fully recovered: not from their physical injuries, not from what Mathilda had demanded from them in the aftermath.

"They were both prescribed some pretty good pills during recovery," Jeremy said, "and Bryson just… never stopped taking them. I'm still not sure how he got ahold of them when his prescription ran out, since Mom and Warren both work at the hospital, but I never asked him. I didn't care," he added, forcing the words out as they tried to stick in his throat, "because he always had a bottle or two that he was willing to sell me for cheap."

"You were also injured?"

"No." Jeremy lifted one shoulder in a listless shrug

295

when Jean fixed a piercing stare on him. "But Bryson said the pills would make everything at home easier to handle, and I was desperate enough to believe him. They did and didn't. But then Christmas my senior year he came home with something better for me to try." Jean already knew what was coming, but that didn't make it any easier for Jeremy to say: "Cocaine."

Jeremy picked idly at the sheets. "I should have said no, but that year was... rough." Nan's death, Leo's betrayal, the ceaseless arguments about Exy and his sexuality, the daily traffic stops by cops wanting to push the Wilshire agenda on Warren's behalf—it all seemed so childish and self-centered compared to Jean's more brutal tragedies. Further proof that he was a soft-spined failure, as if his mother needed any more evidence to make her case against him. Jeremy crushed that line of thinking with everything he had and said, "I just wanted something that would keep me together until summer practices started at USC. And it did, mostly."

"Mostly," Jean echoed.

"I made a lot of friends," Jeremy said. "I lost a lot more. And the Trojans knew something wasn't quite right." It was a weak way to say they hadn't trusted him, and that the other freshmen had kept as far from him as possible. Rhemann had sat him down for a dozen careful lectures as he tried to sort out his recruit's mood swings and unpredictability. Shame had Jeremy swallowing back a rush of bile.

Jean said nothing. Jeremy could only stand the silence for so long before he had to press on. "Colorado's vice-captain had spent a few years quietly ferreting out gay players in the western district, yeah? Every year they'd meet up at the banquet and sneak away somewhere to let loose. I was recklessly indiscreet in high school, so he knew I was safe to invite. Said there'd be drinks and weed and crackers, pick your poison kind of thing, so I brought

296

enough coke to share. It was a big hit," Jeremy said, "up until Noah—"

Jeremy hugged his arms tight to his stomach, desperate to keep that black hole contained. "Police came looking for me after they identified him. Took them a while to finally pinpoint where I'd gone, but when they showed up…" He raised his hands in a helpless *what can you do* and said, "Only two of us were out of the closet back then; the other seven were cruising along as carefully as they could. But there we all were, drugged and drunk and tangled up with each other in this little hotel room. Officers called it in to dispatch as a 'faggot orgy' before any of us really understood what was going on."

The night was a fractured mess, but parts of it were clear enough to cut. The dizzying rush of an overdue high, the harsh taste of scotch on Dexter's lips, the weight of too many hands looking for a little release and comfort. Equally sharp: skinning his knees on the rough carpet when a cop hauled him out of bed, the bruising pressure of a boot on his spine to keep him down, the pinch of handcuffs snapped too tight. The officers were so horrified by the debauchery they'd stumbled upon they almost forgot to tell him about Noah.

"Dexter was the obvious fall guy, since he was the only one old enough to buy the alcohol, but my parents knew he'd bring me down with him. They cashed in every favor they could and spent a literal fortune trying to protect the Wilshire name. The alcohol and sex were already out there, courtesy of the first responders, but the drugs got swept under the rug. Dexter lost his captaincy and his prospects, but he didn't face charges, and my parents covered his remaining tuition in exchange for his silence."

"He wasn't silent," Jean said. "Connors knows. So does Torres."

"Torres went to high school with me, so he knew

297

when I started doing drugs," Jeremy said. "Connors was at the party. Like most of the others, he'd been closeted until then. Soon as word got out that he was getting drunk and shacking up with other men, his parents publicly disowned him and kicked him out of the house. Safe to say he still hates me for that."

"Did you sleep with him?"

Jeremy stared at him. "No."

"Then it is not your problem."

"It is," Jeremy said. "Jean, I—half of those guys never saw court time again, at least outside of practice. Fowler had to transfer down to a Class II school to get away from his team's relentless bullying. That's my fault. The police only found out about them because they were looking for me."

"You are not the one who jumped."

It was blunt enough to crush Jeremy's lungs to his spine. He shifted to get up, needing to put space between them, but Jean's hand came down hard on his shoulder. Jean's, "Did you know he would?" was probably meant to be a gotcha, but Jeremy flinched so hard Jean recoiled from him. Jeremy put a hand over his chest, desperate to keep his heart from breaking out, and wished he'd been smart enough to bring one of Faser's bottles back with him.

It came out barely louder than a whisper: "We all knew."

That wasn't quite true, but maybe that was worse. Bryson stopped caring about any of them after his accident, and Annalise couldn't see Noah's pain past her own. But Joshua and Noah were Irish twins and the best of friends, and Joshua knew his brother was in trouble. He'd begged Jeremy for help when every appeal to their mother failed. Jeremy tried, off and on for months, but neither of his parents wanted to hear it. Warren had no patience for Noah's bottomless sadness, and Mathilda only said, "All boys are strange at that age." She'd blamed him for setting such a poor example for his younger brothers.

She'll listen when she loses him, he'd thought, angry and defeated and so, so tired.

He hadn't meant it, not really, but—

A rush of nausea left him dizzy and hot. "I don't want to talk about Noah anymore."

Jean didn't push it. Jeremy closed his eyes and counted his breaths: four seconds in, seven seconds out, over and over until his roiling stomach finally calmed down. It did nothing for the loss gnawing through his chest, but at last he opened his eyes again.

He moved to get up, but Jean's hand on his knee warned him to wait. "Tell me you are clean now."

"I'm clean."

Not by choice, at first, but that wasn't worth getting into. The guilt and heartbreak had almost destroyed him, and he'd wanted nothing more than to spiral completely out of control until he couldn't feel anything. Mathilda refused to endure any further embarrassment on his behalf, however, and forced him into a rehab facility near the northern border of California. USC received a seven-digit donation from his share of the inheritance, and he'd done his first five weeks of classes long-distance.

"Look at me," Jean said, and Jeremy obediently dragged his stare to Jean's face. Jean's expression was inscrutable as he studied Jeremy, but his tone was firm: "You are my partner. My success is your success; your failure is my failure. Do not ever backslide, Jeremy. I will not forgive you."

"I can't," Jeremy said. When Jean appeared unimpressed by that immediate reassurance, Jeremy insisted, "I walked away from my brother, Jean. I knew he wasn't okay, and I knew he needed me, but all I cared about was having fun and getting high. I left him behind, and I never saw him again. I'd rather die than ever be that person again. Believe me."

"You are you," Jean said, simple and unhesitating. "I believe you."

It wasn't the first time he'd declared unwavering faith in Jeremy's character, but to hear it after sharing such a miserable story took the last ice out of Jeremy's chest. A quiet "Thank you," was sorely inadequate, but for now it would have to do. He waited to see if anything else was forthcoming, then glanced past Jean at the clock. "It's getting late. Is there anything else you want to know, or are you ready to get some rest?"

Jean pressed a thumb to the bruises on Jeremy's throat. "His name."

"I can't give you that," Jeremy said, scooting toward the edge of his bed. "I told you it was an accident. He was just worked up and drunk."

"I don't believe you. Cat has never bruised Laila like this."

"Maybe Laila's not as good with her tongue."

It took him a moment to realize what he'd said, and he and Jean were left staring at each other. Jeremy didn't trust himself to speak, but one of them had to break the silence. Luckily Jean found his voice first. Maybe that wasn't a crack in his voice; maybe it was just his accent coming on stronger than usual. Jeremy forgot about it when the words registered:

"I will tell her you said that."

"God, please don't," Jeremy said, flinging one of his pillows at Jean. "She'll kill me."

Jean turned away from him. "Unfortunate."

"I'm going to buy you decaf tomorrow."

Jean scoffed. "No, you won't."

"I'll think about it," Jeremy promised as he went to get the lights. He hit the nightstand on his way back to bed and grimaced at the shadows as he clambered onto the mattress. Getting comfortable was easy, but a waste of his time: Jeremy's thoughts were too tangled to let him rest, and he stared at the ceiling in silence until dawn.

CHAPTER SIXTEEN
Jean

The first week of September was short, as classes and practices were canceled for Labor Day. Despite that wasted day, Tuesday had a few unexpected bright points: Bryson moved back to Connecticut for school finally, buying Jeremy a bit of peace at home, and the press did a last-minute sweep of the western teams. A final check-in before the season got officially underway, supposedly, except every single team was asked about Jean.

If they were hoping for gossip, they were sorely disappointed, and Cat's glee over the banquet finally felt a bit justified. Every team save White Ridge had a positive response to offer. Quiet and serious, most said, and unfailingly polite. More than one spoke of the obvious respect Jean and the Trojans had for one another, and those who had gotten a bit more of his time—Ashton's sister, for one, but mostly the French speakers—had only good things to say. They would all reserve final judgment until they faced him on the court, but they were pleased.

Isn't it nice? Cat had asked Saturday, and Jean had only shrugged her off with exhausted impatience. But after five years of being stepped on and half a year of nastiness he couldn't defend himself against, it was... unsettling, to see complete strangers take his side so enthusiastically. He admitted as much to Cat when they went for their ride Wednesday night. In response she tugged him down by his shoulders so she could kiss him square in the middle of his forehead.

The peace couldn't last. Thursday evening Cat came to pick Jean up from Raven drills on her motorcycle, and even with her helmet on Jean could tell something was wrong. He was slow to take his helmet from her, studying her tense expression for any hints, but she shook her head at the question in his stare.

"I'll tell you at home," she said.

A short while later she led him into their kitchen, and Jean found Laila sitting on a stool with a sour look on her face. There was a pile of envelopes in the center of the island that Cat motioned Jean toward, and Jean slowly spread a few out to look. They were all addressed to him, from names he didn't recognize and states that held no meaning. On and on they went, some so thick they required multiple stamps but most paper-thin. Jean frowned at Cat, then Laila, but they could only shrug at him.

"Something tells me your address was officially leaked," Laila said. "It could be the same source who tipped off the press, escalating because he didn't get what he wanted, or perhaps someone local was asked to follow the press to you." She gave a helpless shrug and scattered a few more envelopes. "They could be fan letters, or they could be more drivel. Do you want us to help you go through them?"

"Perhaps," he said.

There were maybe sixteen to twenty of them, and it would take him forever to read them. Laila divvied them up into three smaller piles before passing them out, and for a few minutes the only sound in the kitchen was the rustling of paper. Laila was the fastest reader, and she'd already slapped two letters off to one side by the time Jean was finished reading his first.

"Any you don't want to keep, just stack here," she said.

Jean nodded understanding before adding his to the pile. It was a relatively tame letter, all things considered, but highly inappropriate: the sender wanted insider gossip on Riko's personal life. Jean was not going to indulge that.

303

One letter wanted to know if there were any differences in Exy between France and the United States, and another spoke of how disappointing it was to see the Ravens collapsing. The sender had watched Raven games for years, finding motivation in their flawless performances and unwavering dedication, and was horrified to see his idols falling apart. He didn't outright blame Jean for it, but he did reference spring as the beginning of the Ravens' end. The remaining few letters were less discreet. The variations on "He gave you everything and you betrayed him, he killed himself because of you," were to be expected, but every version Jean read left a sour tang eating away at his mouth and throat.

"If this keeps up, we'll perhaps look at getting you a PO Box," Laila suggested as she set her approved letters within reach. "We can set up mail forwarding for anything in your name."

"What if Kevin sends more postcards?" Cat asked, then passed Jean a letter from her pile with an, "Oh, you should handle this one."

The return address was Marseille, but the sender's name was the greater blow. Jean wasn't sure what showed on his face, but Cat kept her hand extended in case he wanted to reject the letter. Jean shook his head and slowly set to work peeling the flap up.

"A teammate from youth Exy," he explained, trying to picture her face. He'd been forbidden to spend time with anyone outside of practices and games and ordered by his parents to keep all conversations only to the sport, but she'd played alongside him for five years.

"To the arrogant loner of Sainte-Anne," her letter began, before whiling its way toward a more thoughtful message. It seemed she'd been keeping tabs on him since the master first revealed his imported Frenchman. She'd heard the news about his parents' arrest and was watching the ongoing manhunt for his missing sister. "Either my memory has been kinder to you than you deserve, or a lot of your strangeness finally makes sense," she said at the end. "I will keep you and Elodie in my thoughts."

Jean carefully folded the letter and set it aside. Cat studied his face for any sign of distress before tapping a finger to the envelope. "Can I ask?"

Jean looked where she was pointing. "It is my name. Was," he corrected himself as he flipped the envelope over. "I do not answer to it anymore."

"Bad memories?" Cat asked.

Letting her think that was easier than explaining the truth, so Jean only shrugged. Cat let it slide in favor of handing over two more envelopes she'd already vetted. Jean set hers atop Laila's. The discard pile they'd each come up with was significantly larger than the letters safe to peruse. The western teams might now be willing to give him a chance, but the Ravens' fans would forever be the greater and louder majority.

Jean wondered if he would always be the villain, if this mockery and hatred would chase him for the rest of his life. It didn't matter. It didn't; it couldn't. All that mattered was that he played to the best of his abilities and kept the promise Neil made on his behalf. But such thoughts couldn't sustain him, and the weariness that ate at him suddenly was bone deep.

"I am going to bed," he said.

"You haven't eaten," Cat said.

The gnawing in his stomach was nothing next to the sick chill eating through his chest, so Jean waved her off and left. He put the approved letters on his desk to deal with another day and shut himself in a too-quiet room. Barkbark was propped up on the windowsill, smiling its inane canine grin at him. Jean went to it, sure today would be the day he tore it in two, but he caught himself even as he started to tug. With an irritated mutter he put the dog on

Jeremy's empty bed instead. At least flat like this it couldn't watch him sleep.

It was hours before he could stop thinking long enough to drift away, and when he dreamed it was of the courts at Campagne Pastré.

-

Because the first game of the season was a home game, the Trojans were required to attend their Friday classes. Jean, who only had one morning class to sit through, tuned out the grumpy complaints of his less fortunate teammates. He expected today to follow the same pattern of handoffs as the first week, but Shane took him halfway across campus to rendezvous with Jeremy. Jean frowned at his captain but waited until Shane left to say, "You have therapy on Fridays."

"That was last week," Jeremy said, and didn't elaborate. "Good to head home for a bit, or do you need to do anything on campus?"

"We could practice," Jean said, glancing in the direction of the stadium.

"It'd be better to rest," Jeremy countered. "It's going to be a rough game."

Jean opened his mouth to argue, then took a closer look at Jeremy's face. When Jeremy was laughing and talking, it was harder to see, but in his quieter moments the shadows were more noticeable: he looked like he hadn't slept in two days. The strain of his commute, Jean supposed; he remembered their ceramics classmate making a crack about Jeremy's inevitable exhaustion. That someone outside the Exy team knew him well enough to know what was coming was annoying.

He gave in with a disgruntled, "Fine," and it was enough to make Jeremy smile.

They were nearly to Vermont Avenue when Jeremy's phone beeped with a coach's alert. Jeremy glanced at the crosswalk signal before pulling his phone out and

306

answering with a cheery, "Good morning, Coach, did we forget something?" Across the street, the light changed for them. Jeremy stepped off the curb, then seemingly forgot he was walking mid-step. He rocked to a stop so abruptly he almost fell over. Jean dragged him back to safety on the sidewalk, but Jeremy caught his wrist and hauled Jean after him across the street.

"Yeah," Jeremy said as they reached the other side. "Yeah, I'll tell him. Thank you."

He hung up but held tight to his phone, and although he let go of Jean, he said nothing to him to explain the call. Jean allowed him peace until Jeremy was turning the key in Laila's front door, and then he said, "Jeremy."

Jeremy motioned for him to come inside and pushed the door closed behind him. Only then did he look up at Jean. "One of the freshman Ravens is gone," Jeremy said. "A backliner named Harry Rogeson? Sounds like the Ravens found his body on a campus shuttle bus."

Jean didn't know the name. Maybe Tetsuji signed him after Jean's departure from Evermore, but it was equally likely Riko was too distracted by his vendetta to track the incoming Ravens. The *who* was less important than the *what*; every other Raven to die had been an upperclassman, robbed at the finish line of their hard-earned glory. A freshman who'd narrowly avoided the Moriyamas' violent control and the Nest's madness should not have shattered so quickly. Raven cruelty, perhaps: the old guard taking out their heartache and trauma on the new generation.

"I'm sorry," Jeremy said.

"It has nothing to do with me," Jean said, and toed out of his shoes. "Go sleep."

Jeremy lingered a moment longer, as if making sure Jean was honestly okay, and then headed down the hall to their room. Jean retreated to the living room to go over his morning notes, and he whiled away a few boring hours getting a head start on his homework. Cat showed up closer to noon with a handful of mail. She set his letters on the coffee table near where he was working, checked his expression with a pensive stare, and curled up in Laila's chair with her own work. Half an hour later she was quietly snoring.

Jean wondered if he should wake her, then dropped his gaze to his mail. The thought of having to sort through more vitriol was off-putting, but it had to be dealt with sooner or later. He moved the stack to where it was easier to reach and began going through them.

By the time Jeremy's alarm went off, Jean's mood was irrevocably ruined. Jean pushed the letters aside when he heard Jeremy's footsteps in the hall. Packing up his work was easy, and the noise was enough to rouse Cat. For a split-second she pretended to be engrossed in her studies, and then she woke up enough to remember where she was. She dropped her textbook off to one side to deal with this weekend and followed Jean to the kitchen.

They had time to eat lunch before heading back to campus, and Jean took those minutes to try and lock down every hateful accusation he'd read. None of this could matter right now; he had to get his thoughts back on tonight's match.

They could have gone straight to the stadium, but Jeremy led Cat and Jean on a path that would rendezvous with Laila outside the architecture building. Laila had a printout of the Bobcats' roster taped to the front of her three-ring binder, and she quizzed them on the walk to the Gold Court. Cat was more familiar with the upperclassmen than the younger players, but Jeremy was a lost cause. He knew names and positions, but nothing else, not even if they were right-handed or left.

"Why don't you know this?" Jean demanded.

Jeremy shrugged off his disapproval. "Stats are for coaches to stress over. I trust my gut."

"You're lying," Jean protested.

"It's worked this far, hasn't it?"

Jean couldn't deny that, but he didn't have to be happy about it. He subsided somewhat grumpily and followed his teammates across the street.

Exposition Park was unusually lively today, on account of the first home game. There were booths set up selling merch, and a few groups picnicking around blaring boomboxes. A couple people they passed were good enough fans to recognize the Trojans on sight; others were close enough to see the 3 on Jean's face and react to that. Cat and Jeremy accepted the fans' well wishes with good cheer and warm smiles, and soon enough they were safe inside the locker room.

The Trojans had a one-hour afternoon practice, then two hours off to eat and review tapes. Here the Trojans finally sounded like a Class I team to Jean. They still slipped in unnecessary compliments and praise as they reviewed the night's opponents, but they discussed the Bobcats' playstyle with unrelenting focus. There was a long history between the two teams, natural when both teams were so talented but further complicated by Jeremy muddying White Ridge's reputation a few years back. The Trojans knew these players backwards and forwards, and they knew it was going to be a fight all the way to the final bell.

"Literally," Xavier added, with a glance toward Jean. "They aren't quite as bad as the Ravens, but they're violent and they have the numbers to compensate for red cards. They'll likely try to injure Jeremy right out of the gate, but I wouldn't be surprised if they spent most of their energy on you."

"The weakest link," Shane said, and hastened to add, "As far as tempers go, I mean," when Jean flicked him a deadly look. "They'd love to see us get our comeuppance. If they goad you into a brawl in our season opener, they'll ride that high for years. You've gotten a lot better at practice, but we're not actively bullying you to test your restraint. Can you handle them?"

"Yes," Jean said.

When he left it at that, Jeremy smiled and said, "I have faith." Shawn looked like he might comment, but a crash down the hall and yodeling cry of despair distracted him. A helpless smile tugged at Jeremy's mouth as he called, "All good, Bobby?"

Roberta Blackwell appeared in the doorway. "Good," she promised. "Ignore that."

She was gone as quick as she'd come, though her yipped "Ow, ow, ow" echoed back to them a minute later.

The Trojans only had three assistants, but Jean would have guessed the number higher tonight. They were in constant motion, flitting this way and that across the locker room as they prepared for the match. Antonio Jones was in charge of loading the stick racks, and he took his time with each racquet before locking it into place: checking tension in the strings, inspecting the heads for any troublesome wear and tear, and fixing tape for the players who preferred wrapped sticks. Bobby had started off by delivering freshly-cleaned padding to each locker, using nametags to find proper homes for each piece, and then set to work filling the players' water bottles. Angie stuck by Lisinski's side, filling out forms with last-minute welfare checks.

A few months ago, Jean had found the concept of assistants ridiculous. The tasks they were assigned were ones the players or coaches could easily handle, and having extra faces in the locker room at practice was unnecessary. Tonight, he finally understood the appeal. Each nonsense task that Bobby or Tony took off his plate bought him a few extra minutes to focus on the lineup he'd be facing and the bodies he'd share the court with.

Traditionally the Trojans had rigid lineups for each

half: designated starters with assigned subs that would trade in halfway through. Jean had been assigned to the second-half lineup, which suited him just fine: second was where Jeremy, Cat, and Laila played, and it bought him time to study his teammates during the first half. Although Jean was officially a sub for Cat and Shawn's line until he could prove himself reliable, Rhemann was allowing him to start alongside Cat tonight. Anticipating trouble, Jean assumed—it would be easier to pull Jean if he acted out if Rhemann didn't burn up a sub putting him on in the first place.

A warning bell echoed throughout the locker room: they were an hour out from serve. Rhemann was meeting with the night's officials, so White collected the team and sent them to the inner court. The stands were a third filled already, and Jeremy looked positively gleeful as he took his team on a few easy laps. All the Trojans looked excited to be here, Jean realized as he glanced from one laughing face to another, and he felt the chasm between his heart and theirs keenly.

He couldn't remember the last time he'd looked at a court with any bright emotion. The Ravens had no time for joy. The game was all that mattered, the only place they had any real value, the stage upon which they would honor the master's investment in them. How could any of them truly love a cage? Not even Kevin was foolish enough to dabble in honest delight; his hunger for Exy was a greedy, all-consuming thing that dragged him ever onward.

Derrick's deafening "My wife!" jarred Jean out of his morose contemplation. A half-second later Derrick had him by the elbow and was dragging him out of the Trojans' line. The lowest row of seats in the stadium were raised four feet off the ground, with a barred railing keeping the fans separated from the inner court. During the game security guards would be stationed at each section to ensure no one fell or jumped down in their excitement, but for now the arriving fans had the run of the place.

Three women were standing at the railing closest to the Trojans' entrance, each wearing a cardinal red shirt emblazoned with a different letter from USC. The U was Cherise, easily recognizable now that Jean had seen her photograph. She leaned over the railing when Derrick reached for her, nearly falling out of her shirt as she did so. Derrick's fervent "I love you," was probably more for that near-miss than the smile she favored him with. He pressed a too-loud kiss to her knuckles before motioning to Jean. "Cherise, my buddy Jean Moreau! I've told him all about you."

"Only good things, I hope," she said.

"Please be the mother of my children," Derrick said, holding both hands up toward her in supplication. "We would make such beautiful babies."

"Charming as always," she said dryly. "Hey, Derek."

"Cherise," Derek returned as he came up on Jean's other side. "Hey, Tori, Denise."

"Derek." Tori leaned over the railing to smile down at him. "Looking good."

"I could say the same for you, T."

"You *could* say it," she said, with an expectant tip of her head.

Derek's smile was slow, but whatever he meant to say was interrupted by Bobby yelling down the inner court at them: "I'm telling Coach!" A half-second later she edited her threat to, "I'm telling Angie! Let's go, let's go, let's go!"

"Oh God," Derrick said, clutching at his heart. "Cherise, my love. Another day."

Derek used the railing to haul himself up, and Tori caught his face in her hands for a quick kiss. A group of fans six rows up erupted in hoots and cheers, and Derek

312

was grinning like a fool when he dropped back down to flat ground.

Cherise caught Jean's eye as he started to step back and said, "Look after our boys out there, will you?"

"Our boys!" Derrick yelled before taking off at full speed. "Our! Boys!"

"One of these days you'll figure out he's not joking about you," Derek warned Cherise. "Sort yourself out before you string him along much longer, would you? He's my brother."

"See you after," was all Cherise said.

Derek frowned at her but motioned to Jean and set off. They didn't try to match Derrick's speed but kept a slow pace, making it easier for the rest of the lineup to catch up with them. Jean settled in alongside Jeremy again. Somewhere behind him the Trojans were treating Derek like a returned hero, yelling and clapping and carrying on in the most embarrassing way. Jean idly wondered if they would ever shut up. The arrival of the Bobcats to the Away side finally earned a bit of peace, except now the Trojans shouted cheery greetings at them on their way by.

Jeremy and Xavier broke away from the line to pay respects to White Ridge's coaches and captains. Jean looked for Connors on his way by, but the Bobcats were still streaming out of the locker room. The Trojans made one last lap, collecting Jeremy and Xavier on their way by, and Jeremy took them to the locker room to change out. The teams were too big to share the court for warmups, but the Trojans would run drills first. It bought their visitors a little more time to shake out the stiffness of traveling.

Getting changed out was easy enough after nearly thirteen years dealing with so many layers. Jean was already wearing the gold shorts he needed for his Home uniform, so he sat on the bench to tug his shin guards into place. He yanked the straps tight, then kicked his legs out

313

one at a time and rolled his ankles to test them. Satisfied they'd hold in place without cutting off circulation, he pulled his socks on overtop. His shoes he left off to one side for now in favor of peeling his shirt off.

He tugged on his chest armor, strapping down his shoulders first before snapping the chest straps into place. His warmup jersey was tossed into his locker in favor of the gold-on-red one sized for sitting atop gear. It took a few quick tugs to settle it right over his padding, and he locked his neck guard into place before reaching for his gloves. There were two pairs: long cotton ones that would button up above his elbows and keep his arm guards from sliding or pinching his arms, and the bulkier set with armored fingers that would go on last. Jean tucked the latter into his helmet for the walk back to inner court and got his shoes on and laced up.

"Ready we ready we ready!" was the echoing war cry from the strikers' row, and it was answered with a ferocious "Fight on!" from nearly every Trojan. Cat gave Jean's hair an enthusiastic ruffle, her smile wild with excitement, and dragged him to his feet.

First-half players would practice on the Home side of the court, and second-half would take Away. The line-up for warm-ups on game nights had them alternating so they could peel off in different directions as they stepped through the court door. Jeremy had the front of the line, with Xavier right behind him, and the rest of the Trojans were arranged by court position. Although the freshmen weren't allowed to play, they could participate in drills, so they wriggled into the spaces their upperclassmen assigned them. Jean closed his eyes, listening to the way their laughter and upbeat voices echoed off the walls.

"Good?" It was Angie, pausing at his side.

There was no reason to tell her how strange it was to exist in such a moment and place, so Jean only said, "Good."

314

She continued on her way, counting players with her pen. Lisinski passed her going the other direction, and when Angie called, "Twenty-nine!" from the front of the line, Lisinski echoed it back. Tony and Bobby ran up and down the line, passing out racquets for warm-ups. Jean held his in the crook of his elbow as he pulled his helmet on and tugged his heavier gloves into place. Tony's "All out!" when they were done had Lisinski jogging toward the front of the line. Jeremy's whoop warned Jean the line was about to start moving, and even through Jean's helmet it was deafening when the Trojans joined in.

They jogged back to inner court in an unbroken, endless line. The stands had filled quite substantially since Jean last checked, and he felt the fans' roar like a weight against his bones. It was a smaller stadium than Evermore, with a far less rabid fanbase, but over the quieter summer months Jean had forgotten how loud game nights could get.

Rhemann had the court door open for them, and they ran through without slowing. The half-court line had four buckets of balls out and waiting for them. Jeremy took his group on two quick laps of their half, giving Laila time to get settled at her goal, before collecting them at half-court. He listed off the five drills he wanted them to work through, then passed them each a ball and sent them on their way with a loud, "Hey, hey!"

Jean forgot about the tacky uniforms and the crowded stands and the Bobcats that were making laps around the inner court. Only this mattered: the ball in his racquet, the team he was representing, the goal at Laila's back. Jean spared half a mind for Jeremy's callouts; everything else was focused on the way his body felt as it eased into too-familiar movements. He was well-rested and pain-free, sated from dinner and comfortable in armor that hadn't yet been bent and dented by heavy blows. He would perform well tonight.

Soon enough it was time to cede the court to the Bobcats. The freshmen and sophomores were in charge of collecting the scattered balls and refilling the buckets, which they left behind for their opponents to use. Rhemann was talking to two reporters when Jean followed Cat off the court. One of the two was watching for his jersey number, but Jean feigned not to hear his name over the noise of the crowd. Maybe Cat heard the call, too, because she immediately tugged at his sleeve and pointed to the Trojans' cheerleading squad. It was a well-timed distraction that would excuse him from having to speak to anyone, so Jean tried to care about what Cat was saying.

Not far from them was a young man in USC colors and a ridiculous plumed hat. He carried a broomstick that, in lieu of bristles, sported a plush white horse head. As Jean watched, he tucked it between his legs and went galloping wildly up and down the length of the court.

"Cat," Jean said, in a tone he knew she'd understand as *"What the fuck?"*

"Our Exy mascot!" Cat said as she hooked her stick onto the appropriate rack. Jean's racquet belonged only two spots down from hers, and he locked it into place before unstrapping his helmet. Cat pried her own off before asking, "You didn't see him last ye—uhhh, year before?"

"I was only looking at the court."

"Man," Cat said, almost pitying. "You really missed out."

"I don't think so," Jean said, and she only laughed.

The mascot—Diego, Jean thought—came galloping back their way to present Bobby with a carnation. It was missing half its petals, leaving Jean to wonder if he'd sneaked it down here in his pocket, but Bobby accepted it with a delighted laugh. Diego got a hug for his efforts, and he swung her into a deep dip for a kiss while the cheerleaders bounced around them. Bobby was flushed and giggling as she found her feet again, and Cat watched the pair with obvious fondness.

"Young love is the best," she declared, depositing their helmets on the nearest bench.

Jean couldn't make sense of it. From these outside distractions—Cherise, Tori, and Diego—to Cat and Laila, Xavier and Min, and whatever strangeness was going on with Cody, the Trojans seemed to fall in love so easily. He said as much to Cat as they collected their water bottles, and she peered up at him in renewed interest.

"Don't tell me you've never been in love," she said.

"Ravens are not allowed to have relationships," Jean said. "They can sleep around as they like to work out aggression and need, but allowing emotions into the mix could have catastrophic results on regulated partnerships and the overall hierarchy. The team's success must come before all else."

"That's not what I asked," Cat said.

Diego was taking Bobby for a ride on his makeshift horse. Jean couldn't hear her laughter from here, but he saw it on her face as she clung to him. Jean tasted bile and blood. He sucked in a slow breath through the aching burn on his tongue and said, "It doesn't matter."

When he dragged his stare back to Cat, the lighthearted teasing was gone from her expression. For a moment he thought she'd give up and grant him peace, but then she cautiously asked, "What happened?"

A knife at his throat; cruel fingers in his hair. *"Queers do not belong on my perfect Court. I will bleed this out of him within a week."*

Stupid, beautiful Kevin had tried his best to defend Jean. After all, he was blindingly obsessed with the Trojans; it was reasonable to assume Jean would also find a Big Three team captivating. He'd only dug Jean's grave deeper with that argument. Riko hadn't even known Jeremy was a factor then—it wasn't the Trojans he'd

317

caught Jean staring at with such unsubtle and idiotic devotion. Riko hadn't wasted his breath correcting Kevin, not wanting to give him any more reasons to protect their worthless third wheel. Jean hadn't tried either; what good would it do to confess to such an oblivious fool?

"Jean," Cat said, almost too soft to hear.

"I got caught," Jean finally said. "I do not want to talk about it tonight."

"Okay," she said, and looped an arm around his waist. "Okay. I'm sorry."

Jean moved without thinking, pressing a close-mouthed kiss to her temple the way she did whenever she thought he was unraveling. Cat's arm went so tight around him he felt two vertebrae in his spine pop, but the smile she turned on him was bright. If she had anything else to say on the matter, she was interrupted by Laila's arrival. Jeremy had gotten flagged down to speak to the reporters so Rhemann could return to his duties.

The Trojans drifted on their side of the arena, alternating jogging in place with slow stretches and easy twists. At ten minutes to serve, White took the offense line off to one side and Jimenez rounded up his defense. The freshmen listened with utter seriousness, never mind that his words weren't for them. With five minutes left to go, Jeremy was sent on court for a coin toss against the Bobcats' captain Thomas Ennis. He won serve, and Ennis chose the traditional Away court for his team's start.

Rhemann collected everyone as soon as Jeremy was back. "You've faced this team before. You know what they're capable of. They're fast, and they're good, and they're likely going to do their best to get under your skin. You know their game, and you know yours. One step, one push, one duck and weave at a time," he stressed. "You can overcome everything they throw at you. Trust yourself and your teammates, and don't hesitate to call for help where and when you need it."

He glanced from Jeremy to Jean at that, and Jean remembered Xavier's warning that the Bobcats would try to hurt them both. Jean wasn't concerned for himself; he could play through whatever these useless children threw his way. Jean assumed Jeremy was less reckless after having to deal with this team for the last four years, but he fixed a cool stare on Jeremy's face until Jeremy returned it. Jeremy's smile was lightning-quick and full of teeth, and Jean decided to trust him for now.

Overhead the announcer was going on at full volume, welcoming the fans to the Gold Court and declaring the game a sold-out success. With two minutes left on the clock, he finally read off the starting lineups, calling the Bobcats to the court first. Jean watched as they entered one at a time and took their places along the far-fourth and half-court lines. Xavier collected his first-half teammates and led them to the door.

"Starting line-up for your USC Trojans," the announcer said, and the crowd screamed so loud Jean could barely hear the roster. "On offense, strikers Derek Thompson and Derrick Allen. Starting dealer is your vice-captain, Xavier Morgan. On defense, backliners Cody Winter and Patrick Toppings. In goal, Shane Reed." Here he paused, knowing the band would launch into the Trojans' fight song.

One of the night's six officials was waiting at half-court, and he passed the ball to Xavier before exiting the court. Overhead the announcer was starting a twenty-second countdown. By seventeen, the entire crowd was counting along. The referee made it off the court at nine seconds to go, and he locked the door behind him. The Trojans' subs stood shoulder-to-shoulder, a few steps back from the wall so the referees could move back and forth as needed. Jeremy was smiling ear-to-ear, positively giddy, and Cat screamed "Let's go!" as the roared countdown went "Three, two, one."

As the bell sounded, Xavier tossed the ball so he could catch it and fire it up-court. The second it left his hand both teams were moving, Trojans and Bobcats flying in opposite directions to find their marks and open themselves for passes. For the first few minutes, the match was clean, and then Ennis threw Cody into the wall so hard Jean swore he felt it secondhand. Cody had to use the butt of their racquet as a prop to stay on their feet, and they took off after the Bobcats' captain. The ease with which they stole the ball from his shallow net was brilliant enough to give Jean pause: even Ennis didn't realize he'd been robbed, and he tried to pass a ball Cody had already heaved across the court to Pat.

Jean took his time studying each line: the way his strikers battled the Bobcats' violent backliners, the dealers' constant struggle in the middle, and the backliners' solid defense against White Ridge's rowdy strikers. The Bobcats' aggression was familiar; Jean watched his teammates stumble as they were tripped or grabbed. The Bobcats tried again and again to steal the Trojans' racquets, sometimes with violent twists between plays and usually paired with more brutal checks. The Trojans knew better than to hold on and risk wrist injuries, but they only let go with one hand, executing easy twists to get their racquets safely out of reach.

Jean had written the Trojans off as lackadaisical pushovers for months. Seeing them in an actual match when he wasn't playing for the other team was enough to give him pause at last. This was what he'd been looking for all summer, the truth he couldn't see when it was Trojans against Trojans in scrimmages. Derrick had tried explaining it a month ago: *"We're faster and slicker and we move better on the court."* At the time Jean was too annoyed with him to take it to heart, but tonight he understood. The Trojans gave ground when needed, but they never ceded control. Every step relinquished simply put them in a better position to regroup. It was a one-sided match from the get-go, whether White Ridge could see it or not.

To either side of him, the Trojans were cheering on their teammates, never mind no one on the court could hear them. None of them commented on the nonstop fouls or expressed frustration over missed calls against the Bobcats. Not ignorance, Jean realized; they knew exactly how many times their friends were crushed and thrown. It simply couldn't matter. The Trojans couldn't change how their opponents played, only how they performed despite the unchecked violence. Their game was more important than whatever their opponents brought to the table.

"You are very good," he said to Jeremy. "I finally understand why Kevin admires this team."

Looking at Jeremy was a mistake; Jean forced his attention back to the court so he wouldn't have to face that pleased smile.

"We," Jeremy said. "*We* are very good, Jean."

Halftime came with the Trojans two points up. As soon as they were back in the locker room, Lisinski, Angie, and the nurses moved through the first-half players, testing new injuries and studying the aches they carried with them. Derek stepped aside as soon as he could to unleash a flurry of blows on the punching bag down the hall, and Jean tried to tune it out in favor of the Trojans' easy chatter. Derek was back long before they were due back in inner court, and he smiled at Jean like he hadn't bloodied his knuckles.

"You've seen them in action now," he said, tugging his gloves on to hide his injuries from the press. "Ready?"

"I know how to behave when I must," Jean said.

More than one Trojan exchanged a skeptical look, but no one argued with him. Jean didn't bother to explain himself but followed his team back to the court.

"Let's hear it for the second-half lineups, starting with

your USC Trojans," the announcer said. "On offense, Ananya Deshmukh and your captain, Jeremy Knox!" He had to pause there as the stadium erupted in cheers. "Starting dealer: Min Cai! On defense, Catalina Alvarez and Jean Moreau!" Jean followed Cat through the doorway as the crowd yelled loud enough to rattle his teeth. In here he could barely hear the announcement for Laila, but he trusted her to be close behind him. He crossed the court to far-fourth and took his starting spot.

Spotting his mark up the court was easy work. Easier still was hearing the countdown as the referee handed White Ridge's dealer the ball for serve. The official left the court at an unhurried pace, and Jean silently continued the countdown as the door was bolted shut: *six, five, four.*

At center court the Bobcat dealer shifted his stance and raised his arm. Most dealers served by tossing the ball and throwing it from a high arc, but this man preferred the quick and dirty style of dropping it to his racquet. It meant he didn't have enough momentum to reach his strikers; he would likely pass it back to his backliners for a more forceful opening push. Jean mentally reviewed everything he'd read about the man in these past few weeks, calculating his chances of going left or right, and found them favoring Cat's side. Cat could hold off any transgressions into her territory, he was sure, so Jean turned his full attention back to his striker.

Three, two, one.

The bell sounded, the ball dropped, and Jean stopped existing for anything but the game at hand.

CHAPTER SEVENTEEN
Jean

Fear of violent retribution was a miraculous thing. The master was missing, the Ravens were half the country away, and Riko was ash and bone in a decorative urn somewhere, but tonight, the distance didn't matter. Jean locked down every brutal instinct of his beneath the simple understanding that acting out against the Bobcats would have horrific consequences for him. He would honor his contract no matter what and endure whatever was hurled his way. It was offensive to the core to let this inferior team push him, but Jean would rather be pushed than suffer his coaches' heavy-handed wrath.

Hinch went to trip him, but Jean had grown up laying teams flat on their back. He saw the telltale swing of the man's body and he moved in time, bracing his feet against the ground at an angle. The striker's foot slid off his ankle with minimal force, and the effort he'd put behind it thinking he would connect had him stumbling. Jean gritted his teeth behind a placid expression and caught Hinch's shoulder to steady him. He didn't need this arrogant bastard blaming his clumsiness on Jean when Jean had been warned again and again that Trojans couldn't trip their opponents.

The man had not yet stopped speaking. He had plenty to say about the Ravens' rumors and an abundance of theories regarding Jean's crooked parents. Jean did his best to tune it out. He had a game to play and a temper to throttle; he didn't have brainpower to spare for whatever rude drivel was being hurled his way. If Hinch wanted to burn up valuable oxygen speaking instead of conserving it for a long half, that was his problem.

"Jean!" Min called, before firing the ball in his direction.

The slide of a stick against his warned him what was coming. If Jean was a Trojan, he'd avoid injury by letting go, but Jean locked his wrists and held on for all he was worth. It sent a warning twinge up both forearms when Hinch gave his racquet a violent twist, but it would have been worse if he hadn't braced. Jean locked eyes with his striker, taking satisfaction in the moment of surprise on Hinch's face when he failed to disarm Jean, and said, "Did not work as intended."

Hinch answered with annoyed mockery: "Hon hon hon."

Jean tugged his racquet free, and the pair took off for the ball. Hinch could have caught up, but he seemed content to stay two steps behind. See-through intention of violence; Jean had done similar many times in his own career. Jean couldn't turn to see where his offense line was, but he had a clear shot to Laila, and he knew she would get the ball where it needed to go. He fired it to hit the ground a safe few feet from the edge of her goal. He had a second to see her move for it before his mark crashed into him.

Knowing it was coming helped; years of practicing full-speed impacts was better. Jean used the momentum to his advantage, crouching as he slid so he could use his racquet and free hand to steady himself against the floor. Instead of tumbling over, he skidded several feet and was back up and moving.

A few seconds later, Cat's mark ended up with the ball. Cat was too good a screen for him to risk a shot on goal, so he passed it toward Hinch. Jean had the longer reach; he knew how this would end. He had a half-second to look for Jeremy, and then he moved. He had to let go of his racquet with one hand to get the extra inches he needed, and he snagged the ball from the air just in time.

Hinch's racquet head missed Jean's stick by a hair, and Jean didn't wait for him to recover. He got his second hand on his racquet even as he turned, needing the momentum and force of a two-handed throw, and he heaved the ball as hard as he could.

The throw was good—of course it was—and Jeremy caught it with satisfying ease. That was as much as Jean saw, because Hinch slammed both hands into his chest to shove him. Jean forced his stare back to the man in front of him, who rewarded that attentiveness with another hard shove. This time Jean refused to give ground, silently daring the man to put a bit more effort into knocking him over. The unspoken challenge pissed the other man off; Jean could see the ugliness on his face. Jean desperately wanted to erase that disrespect. All it would take was a quick finger in his helmet grate to tug him closer and a headbutt the man would feel for days. Jean could already taste blood in his teeth from impact.

"You are very lucky they have me on a leash," he said in French.

"You're in America," the striker said. "Speak English, you illiterate fuck."

The buzzer sounded. The Trojans had scored again to put the teams at six-three. Jean offered his mark a thumbs-up and intoned in English, "Have a winning day."

Cat hadn't lied; the innocuous words earned him an immediate gloved fist in the mouth. Jean moved with the hit to save his teeth. The *Are you finished?* look he gave Hinch worked exactly as intended, and the striker dropped his racquet to launch at Jean. Jean thought of Tetsuji and Riko and let the blows land unanswered. The referees were likely on the court already, but the Trojans and Bobcats were closer. Cat wriggled in between them, taking more than one stray punch herself as she acted as a human shield. Jean wound an arm around her waist to pull her out of the way.

325

"That's enough," Jeremy said as he filled the space next. He put a hand flat to Hinch's chest to warn him off. "We're here for a game, not a brawl. Walk it off and let's get back to it."

"I'm doing you a favor," Hinch said. "Let me take out his teeth and he'll have an easier time sucking your dick."

"I'm sure I misheard you."

"I'm sure you didn't. We all know that's why you signed him—no chance in hell two fags ended up on the same western team by coincidence."

"Oh," Jeremy said, affecting surprise. "That's rude, considering your current roster. I hope you apologize to them later."

"The fuck did you just say?"

Hinch took a threatening step forward to get in Jeremy's face, but the referees caught up with them then and shoved them apart. Jean had only a moment to see the red card flashed at Hinch before Nurse Davis was in his face. Cat took advantage of the distraction to catch hold of Jeremy's elbow, and Jean heard the warning in her quiet, "Careful, Jeremy." If Jeremy said anything in response, Jean missed it, because Davis was speaking.

"Over here," he said, and Jean obediently went still so the nurse could inspect him. Light fingers touched his jaw and cheek, and Davis tapped a thumb to the swelling corner of Jean's mouth. "Bleeding?"

Jean swallowed it and lied, "No."

"Fingers?" Davis asked, holding two up.

"Two," Jean said, and then "Three," when Davis changed them.

The nurse flicked a quick penlight at his eyes before nodding and stepping back. "Line change in ten, then."

The referees wouldn't leave until both teams were at their starting spots, so the Trojans passed Jean one at a time to knock their sticks against his. Jeremy was the last to stop by. His smile didn't reach his eyes, and his stare

326

was intent as he studied Jean's bruising face. Jean kept his expression bored, but it did little to reassure his captain.

"All right?" Jeremy asked.

"I have had worse."

Jeremy winced and tapped their sticks together at last. "Not comforting, Jean."

Jean shrugged his indifference. Jeremy jogged toward the half-court line, and Jean returned to far-fourth. As he took his place, he looked down the court toward his new mark. The man was heavyset and broad-shouldered, but it took Jean a moment to recognize him: JJ Lander, Connors' friend from the banquet.

It was immediately obvious that Lander was better than Hinch. He didn't have Hinch's running commentary, but his aggression was better-timed and harder-hitting. The number of elbows he got right under Jean's chest pads was genuinely impressive; moreso was the deadly accuracy. Every single blow landed in the same spot on his diaphragm. The warning ache in Jean's chest was molten hot as it crawled up toward his lungs. It was a familiar burn that he could ignore and work through. He had to; he had no choice but to hold the line.

The eighth time Lander got him, he dug in hard enough to knock the breath from Jean. The need to break his racquet over the man's arm was so fierce Jean had to let go of his stick to avoid taking a swing. Lander laughed as he took off across the court. Letting his mark get such a lead on him was unforgivable. Jean pressed one hand hard into his side, digging in his gloved fingers like he could claw the air back into his crumpled lungs, and snatched up his racquet. Lander was halfway to Cat now; one side-step and pass from her mark, and Lander would have an unchallenged shot at goal. Jean had failed to protect the backline.

He couldn't fight Lander, so he did the only thing he could and slammed his racquet into his own shin guard

327

with a one-handed swing. Over the new ringing in his ears, he thought he heard fists beating on the court wall and a horrified "*Jean!*" from somewhere up-court, but Jean didn't stop to look. He ignored the raging fire in his leg and the burn in his side, and he chased Lander down.

Lander had the ball already, and he threw it at the goal with every ounce of strength he had in him. Laila dove for it, taking a swing with her paddle racquet, and somehow managed to catch the ball with the corner of her net. She hit the ground so hard she slid, but the ball was cleared— for now. It didn't have much speed when she'd only glanced it, and Lander went after it immediately.

Lander caught it and swung again, and Jean put his racquet up. He caught the ball two inches out of Lander's net and had to twirl his racquet to counter the momentum before the ball could pop loose. Lander turned on him, every inch a violent promise, and Jean spiked the ball off the floor. That got it clear of them when Lander slammed into him, buying Jean a few precious seconds to set up. He caught Lander's shoulder and used it to launch himself up and around the other man. He snagged the ball on a one-handed swing and dropped to his feet.

"Here!" Laila called.

Jean passed to her even as Lander used his shoulder and racquet to throw Jean. Laila cleared the ball with a ferocious swing, and Jean rolled on impact to protect his joints. He was up and moving as soon as he could brace his feet against the court floor, but the warning twinge in his side had him swaying on his first step. How ridiculous, to be so slowed by pain when he'd spent years playing through it. Had a few months of peace really made him so weak? He checked his glove for blood, was satisfied to find it clean, and slowed to a stop a few steps later when the buzzer sounded on a Trojan point.

A whistle from the court door had both teams turning to look. Rhemann had the Home door open, and he held up three fingers. He was subbing all three players at once: Nabil for Jeremy, Shawn for Jean, and Haoyu for Cat. Jean obediently started for the door, and Cat jogged to catch up with him. Rhemann stepped back to let them off, and the Trojans' three assistants were waiting off to one side. Each approached a different player, hands out for racquets and stray gear. Jean shoved his gloves into his helmet before letting Tony take his things.

Rhemann put a hand in Jean's path before he could step away. "You want to explain that hissy fit to me?"

"I'm sorry, Coach. He should not have gotten away from me."

"Not that," Rhemann said, aggrieved like it was the answer he'd expected but hoped not to hear. Jean wasn't sure what else he ought to apologize for, but Rhemann didn't make him guess. "I never want to see you swing at yourself again, do you understand? Everyone else is eager enough to hurt us; you don't need to do it for them."

"Yes, Coach."

Rhemann gave a jerk of his chin, and Jean looked to see Davis and Nguyen waiting to one side. "Get checked out and come back when you two are ready."

The two included Jeremy; Jean realized too late that Jeremy was favoring his left foot. As soon as Rhemann went back to watching the game, Jean fit himself against Jeremy's side. Jeremy offered him a grateful smile as he let Jean take some of his weight, and they followed the nurses back to the locker room. Jean got Jeremy settled in one of the nurses' offices before following Davis to the next. He peeled out of his jersey and chest armor when ordered, then his socks and shin guards when Davis pointed.

"You could have seriously hurt yourself," Davis said, crouching so he could test the line of Jean's shin with his thumbs. "What were you thinking?"

"I failed to control my mark."

329

"Would a fractured tibia make you run faster?" Davis demanded, and Jean stared down at him in silence. Davis stared back, waiting for the obvious to sink in, and finally removed his half-moon glasses so he could pinch the bridge of his nose. "The good news is your guard took most of the impact. You'll probably feel it for a while, and I'm sure you'll have some nasty bruising, but you didn't break anything. This time," he emphasized as he straightened and set to work on Jean's chest.

A quick scan showed nothing serious to be worried about, so Davis settled for wrapping an ice pack in a thin towel. "You'll probably want to put your glove back on for this," he said as he pressed the pack to Jean's bruising ribcage. "Send Tony or Bobby to get a new one when this one starts to get too warm, understood? Hold this," he said, and wrapped Jean's lower leg. At last Davis helped him get back into his jersey. It was too big without his chest armor, but Jean could fit an arm under the hem to keep the ice in place.

"Leave the gear here," Davis said as he passed over some pills. "I'll have Tony sort it out later."

Jeremy was waiting for him in the hall. Nguyen had wrapped his ankle and half his shin before fastening an ice pack over top of it. Jeremy offered Jean a smile in greeting. "All good?"

"Nothing serious enough to need all this," Jean said.

"I heard that," Davis said from the office.

Jeremy laughed and collected the crutch he'd propped against the nearest wall. At the severe look Jean sent him, Jeremy shrugged and smiled. "Nothing serious," he promised with cheeky irreverence, "but no point aggravating it further this early in the season. Ready to head back?"

They were almost to the door when Jeremy caught his sleeve, and Jean slowed to a stop. Jeremy's smile was gone, but his tone was earnest as he searched Jean's face.

330

"You were incredible out there. I know everyone else will say the same at the post-match roundup, but I wanted to say it first. And I know you're only going to get better from here, because I know you're still second-guessing this new style. I can't wait to see how far you can go this season."

"I was outstepped," Jean reminded him.

"Maybe," Jeremy said, "but you were never outmatched."

"He should have scored. That he didn't is a testament to Laila's skill, not mine."

"It's not about being perfect, Jean. It's about being better overall, and you were. You are in every way," he insisted when Jean tried to wave him off. "If I threw a rock into the chasm between your talents and his, I don't think I'd ever hear it hit bottom."

It was so uncharacteristically rude Jean could only stare at him. He didn't have to say anything; Jeremy grimaced and dropped his gaze. "Sorry, that was uncalled-for. I know better than to let them get to me, but they've always brought out the worst in me."

"It makes you more interesting," Jean said, and watched the way Jeremy's jaw worked on silent protests. That he wouldn't even defend himself said worlds to how disappointed he was in his thoughtlessness; he didn't want Jean to like this side of him. Jean finally took pity on him and explained, "Not your capacity for unkindness, but how fiercely you fight against it."

It wasn't the answer Jeremy was expecting, judging by the look on his face, but this was not the time or place to get into it. Jean held the door open so Jeremy could hobble through it first, and their return to inner court was hailed with a round of cheers from their teammates. Emma hurriedly made space on the nearest bench so they could sit. Angie flagged Bobby down to say something at her ear, and the sophomore took off at full speed. She was

331

back just a few minutes later with hard foam blocks from the weights room, and she set them up so Jean and Jeremy could elevate their injured legs a bit.

"Thanks, thanks," Jeremy said, and Bobby shaped her hands into a heart for him.

Lisinski came by briefly to check on them, and she accepted Jeremy's version of the nurses' assessment with a serious nod. After she left, Jimenez shooed an enthusiastic Tanner out of his way so he could study his injured defenseman. Jean fixed his gaze on the buttons of Jimenez's red-and-gold polo as the defensive line coach said, "You hit yourself like that ever again and I'll bench you for two months. Do you understand?"

"Yes, Coach."

"Brilliant otherwise," Jimenez said. "They wanted a fight; thank you for not giving them one. Just tell me if we've got damage control to do—I know something set Hinch off. What did you say to him?"

Jean glanced past him to where Cody and Cat were hovering. "I told him to have a winning day."

Cody whooped loud enough to send Derrick staggering dramatically away from them, and Cat used Cody's shoulder for support as she bounced up and down. "That's my boy!" she yelled, wild with shameless delight. "Hell yeah, let's goooo!" She thought better of jumping at Jean and instead took off on a lap down the length of the court. Her "Let's go, Trojans! Fight on!" carried back easily enough, and the stands nearest her picked it up with rowdy enthusiasm.

"All right, all right," Jimenez said, motioning to the Trojans who'd gathered close. "We're still in the middle of a match here, so let's keep our eyes on the prize."

The subs obediently scattered to where they could keep an eye on the game, leaving Jean and Jeremy alone on the bench. Jean didn't have to look at Jeremy to know he was smiling; he could practically feel the warmth radiating off his captain.

"Did you really?" Jeremy asked.

"He took it personally," Jean said.

Jeremy laughed. "They usually do! Cat struck gold with that one."

They'd wasted ten minutes with the nurses, so there were only fifteen minutes left on the clock. Jeremy and Jean watched the rest of the match side-by-side, comparing notes on the players battling back and forth across the court.

Shawn had been put against Lander, as he was closer in skill and weight class than Haoyu. Either he knew Lander better than Jean did from painful experience, or he'd been watching them very carefully, because Shawn fought tooth and nail to keep space between their bodies. When they had to get close and he didn't need his racquet ready, he kept it crosswise over his chest. It made it harder for Lander to hit him, though it wasn't a perfect defense. Even through the court wall Jean could see his pained grimace when Lander broke through to drive an elbow home.

The match ended at nine-six, Trojans' favor, and Jeremy gave Jean an enthusiastic shake. "Best gap we've had on them in years!"

"Ass on bench," Lisinski said when Jeremy started to get up.

"Agh, Coach," Jeremy protested, but he obediently settled down again. The rest of the Trojans were allowed onto the court to celebrate with their teammates and go through a quick handshake, and Jeremy settled for waving both hands over his head in solidarity. Rhemann led the coaches onto the court to meet the Bobcats' staff, leaving just the three assistants to keep an eye on the bench.

It was perhaps inevitable that a reporter would swoop in as soon as the coast was clear. She stole the open spot on Jean's other side as her cameraman crouched across from them.

"We're here at the Gold Court with Jeremy Knox and Jean Moreau," she said, beaming at the camera. "The final bell's just sounded on a nine-six victory over longtime district rivals White Ridge Bobcats. A fantastic start to the season, with stellar performances all around. How are we feeling tonight, boys?"

"An exciting opener," Jeremy agreed with a toothy smile. "I couldn't be prouder of my team for the effort they brought to the court tonight. You never know what to expect from a first match, right? Summer practices can only prepare you so much for the season, so snagging a win here feels unbelievably good. And against such a talented team?" he added, looking toward the court once more. "We're going to have so much fun this year, Ingrid. I can't wait."

"And you?" Ingrid asked, turning her smile on Jean. "I have a confession, before you answer that: I've never really been a Raven fan." She briefly hid her face as if this was a shameful secret to air, then tossed her curls out of her face and leaned into his space. "I've watched Edgar Allan, of course, but I grew up in Anaheim. The Trojans will always be my first love. I was a vocal naysayer when your transfer was first announced, but *wow*. Consider me a convert."

There wasn't a question there, but she tipped the microphone toward him anyway. Jean wondered if he could simply get up and leave. Jeremy gave him an expectant look, and Jean barely managed to fight off a scowl. He refused to look at her when he said, "The Trojans deserve your devotion. They are very good."

He could imagine Jeremy's tired *we*, but there was no easy way Jeremy could correct him with an audience.

"I'm happy to be wrong," Ingrid promised him. "You're a natural fit for the team, and it's clear your team adores you. There's this—I'm going to butcher this, I'm

sorry—this joie de vivre when they're around you."
Butchering it was an understatement. Jean bit the inside of
his cheek to bleeding so he wouldn't comment on her
pronunciation, but Ingrid wasn't waiting for a response.
She said, "Speaking of teammates, though, we couldn't
help but notice one in attendance tonight. I hope you don't
mind that we invited him down here for the postgame
interview?"

Jean refused to believe another Raven had come this
far, but then a familiar voice spoke up with a simple,
"Johnny."

Jean stopped breathing, but he was already turning. In
no world could he ignore that voice; they had been
partners for too long. At the end of the bench was a
security guard, and at his side stood Zane Reacher. Four
months away from the Ravens, he was still dressed head-
to-toe in black, but even from here Jean could see how
much weight he'd lost. He looked ghastly enough to
knock Jean's heart out of rhythm. Jean was on his feet
before he realized he was moving, but he wasn't sure if he
meant to approach Zane or retreat.

Ingrid was introducing Zane to the camera, but the
security guard didn't wait for her to finish. He looked
between Jeremy and Jean and said, "What's the verdict? I
can escort him back to the stands if you don't want him
down here."

When Jean took too long to answer, Jeremy said,
"Reacher, good to see you on your feet. I'm sorry for your
losses this summer."

"Talk to me again and I'll break your other ankle,
Knox," Zane said.

Jean put himself between them. "Do not threaten my
captain, Zane."

Zane dragged his stare back to Jean's face. "Or what?
Are *you* going to stop me?" He didn't miss the onceover
Jean gave him, judging by the mean smile tugging at his

mouth. He knew Jean was doing the math, weighing his chances against Zane's diminished state. The lazy challenge in his, "Try me," warned Jean not to press his luck.

"Jean," Jeremy started.

"Johnny's busy," Zane said, holding Jean's stare.

"I was," Jean agreed, tipping his hand toward Ingrid.

"I came all this way. You owe me your time."

"I don't owe you anything."

"No?" Zane demanded, heavy and hateful and angry.

Next to talking to Zane at all, doing it with an audience was the worst thing Jean could think of, so he waved for Zane to follow. "Locker room."

Jeremy reached for him. "Are you sure?"

Jean caught and held his gaze for a moment, but he had no easy answers for the questions in Jeremy's searching stare. The best he managed was an uncertain, "I don't know." Behind him Ingrid was getting up off the bench, intent on following him and Zane out of inner court. Jean motioned at her, and Jeremy nodded a silent promise to run interference. Zane fell in at Jean's side with the ease of long practice, matching stride and pace like they'd never spent a day apart. It was familiar enough to turn Jean's stomach.

The locker room door had barely closed behind them before Zane said, "You've got to be fucking kidding me, Johnny." He yanked hard at Jean's sleeve, a fierce scowl cutting his face in two, and said, "You were a stranger out there. No fight, no bite. You let that team run over you like you have a fetish for getting bullied. The master would beat you within an inch of your life for such a cowardly performance."

Jean braced for a blow that didn't land and instinctively looked to see if the master was about. Of course they were alone, so he gritted his teeth and said, "Perhaps he would, but I am not one of his Ravens

336

anymore. I signed a contract with the USC Trojans, and I am required to uphold their standards. If that means throwing a fight on the court, then that's what I will do."

"Toothless bitch," Zane accused him.

"We are not in public anymore," Jean warned him.

Zane got a hand around his neck easy as breathing, and Jean hit the wall so hard he lost one of his ice packs. Zane looked his fill, searching for something familiar in the red-and-gold clad man he'd spent so many years protecting. The disgust on his face said he came back empty-handed, but Jean was not the only stranger here. Once upon a time, Jean would have taken Zane's disappointment personally, but Zane had burned every bridge between them. He was not Jean's teammate or his partner anymore; his disapproval was worth less than a fly's tiny shit.

"The sunshine court," Zane said, thick with derision. "*You*. Aren't you embarrassed?"

"Says the man found in his own puke this summer."

Zane's fingers dug in so hard Jean knew he'd be bruised by morning. He didn't try to fight back. Zane had always beaten Grayson in their brawls, and Jean had never stood a chance against Grayson. He settled for glaring at Zane as he waited for Zane's grip to ease. At last Zane snatched his hand back and vigorously wiped it off on his shirt.

"Asshole," Zane said at last, heated and hoarse. "You should have let me die."

"I should have," Jean agreed, with a vehemence that had Zane stepping back from him. "But you were my partner, once. That meant something to me even if it meant nothing to you."

"It meant *everything* to me," Zane exploded, hot with rage. "Do you know what it cost me to stand at your side? Do you? The mockery I ignored for defending you, the punishments I suffered every time you couldn't keep up,

337

the side-eyes and sly remarks from our coaches and teammates? Every fucking day was a miserable fight, but I stuck with you because we were going to be something incredible together. And then you threw me away."

"I had nothing to do with that."

"Tell me you didn't want Josten to have my number," Zane demanded. "I saw your interview, Johnny. The Wesninskis and the Moreaus? You can't convince me it's a coincidence that two European crime lords got their sons into Class I Exy. You knew who he was all along, and you wanted him as your partner instead of me. I came here because I need you to say it to my face. Am I wrong?"

Jean couldn't deny it; all he could do was stare at Zane in mute defiance.

Zane got the answer he needed in Jean's silence, and he hit Jean hard enough to take him off his feet. The backliners' bench broke Jean's fall, and the pain that lanced through his already injured chest was enough to turn his stomach inside-out. Jean gritted his teeth and pushed himself back to his feet. It was almost impossible to hear Zane through the new cotton in his skull, but the hatred in Zane's voice helped his words carry:

"You destroyed everything I fought for. I wish I never met you."

"I am not the one who inked him!" Jean shoved Zane and asked, "What was I supposed to do, argue with Riko? Rip the pen out of his hands when he tried to put it to Neil's face? Tell me!"

The look on Zane's face was answer enough. The Ravens didn't know how to deny Riko anything. He was the centerpiece of their world, the venomous heart that bound the team together. January had carved indelible caverns into Zane's soul but had done nothing to dim his unwavering, unquestioning loyalty. Zane had screwed up, and he'd paid the price owed. The unhinged cruelty of his punishment didn't matter because it still balanced out in

338

Zane's desperate, broken calculations.

"You of all people know how much the King hated me," Jean said. Zane tried waving him off and turning away, but Jean caught hold of his shirt and held on for dear life. "You don't honestly believe I could have talked him into elevating a disobedient shit-stain to the perfect Court on my own. You knew it had nothing to do with me, but you betrayed me anyway."

"Fuck alive." Zane pried his hands off and pushed him away. "Get over it."

Get over it, because that was the Raven way. Cruelty was integral to the Nest; violence was necessary to ensure everyone stayed in line and performed to their best abilities. Aggression and talent determined the pecking order, and the only way to survive Evermore was to understand and believe that everything they suffered served a purpose.

But January was different; it would always be personal. The insinuation that Jean could ever forgive or forget had him seeing red, and he swung at Zane with everything he had. They were so close he couldn't miss. Zane crashed into the lockers behind him, and Jean followed to grab his shirt collar in both hands. Zane pressed a thumb to the blood at the corner of his mouth, unimpressed by Jean's anger even as Jean twisted hard enough to cut off his air.

"Tell me why." It didn't matter; it couldn't matter. Nothing Zane said could fix what had shattered between them. But it didn't stop him from trying again. "Tell me why. You were the only person left I—" Jean choked on his words and had to try again. "I trusted you."

For a moment the man staring at him was achingly familiar. A half-second later he was the stranger January made of him. Zane dug cruel fingers into Jean's wrists, forcing him to let go, and shoved Jean out of his space again. But his hand was still on the knife in Jean's back,

339

and Zane couldn't resist giving it one last ugly twist: "You should be thanking me for setting you up. Couple years without any ass? You must have been about to burst. I did you a favor."

Jean's fist went back again when a new voice from the doorway piped up with an uncertain, "Jean?"

USC had four coaches, three assistants, and twenty-nine Trojans, but somehow the one person to walk in on them was Lucas fucking Johnson. Zane went still as stone to stare at him, and Lucas sent a bewildered look between them. Jean put an arm out, knowing there was next to nothing he could do if Zane wanted to kill Lucas but needing to try anyway.

"Get out," he said, right as Zane launched himself at Lucas. Jean had to use his entire body to knock Zane off-course, but his shoes slid on the polished floor as Zane tried to surge past him. He wouldn't be able to hold him for long, but he dug in his feet as best he could and tried again: "Out, get out, *get out*."

Zane lost valuable seconds throwing his punch at Jean instead, and Lucas bolted from the locker room at full speed. Jean spit blood off to one side and fixed Zane with a deadly look. "That's Lucas, not Grayson. He's Grayson's younger brother. Leave him alone."

"Not Grayson." Zane rubbed his arms; his sharp and terrible laugh sent a noticeable shudder along his shoulders. He checked his knuckles, maybe looking for Grayson's blood. He'd beat Grayson halfway to death in January because there was no chance in hell Grayson would let himself get mounted if he had any fight left in him. Jean had thought the bruises on Zane's hands would never fade. They had, eventually, but the festering wound in Zane's mind couldn't. "Not Grayson, because Grayson killed himself. Who could have seen that coming?"

"Who would have?" Jean sent back.

Zane had to hear the accusation in it, but instead of

addressing that he said, "Heard he came to visit you at the end. One last bite for the road, hm?" Zane laughed again, and Jean realized too late he was holding his throat. Zane bit his own knuckles until they bled. "Took the fast lane straight to hell. Must be getting crowded there, Johnny. We're all dying. All of us except you, when you're the one who should've kicked it first. Why are you still here?"

"Because I keep my promises."

"Except you didn't, and you got exactly what you deserved," Zane said. It was so uncalled-for Jean took a step back away from him. Zane sucked blood from his knuckles and spat it to one side. "Exactly what you wanted, even. I remember. I was there. I heard you begging for it, you disgusting wh—"

A flash of color warned Jean they were no longer alone. In the same breath Jean registered *Coach*, Rhemann decked Zane hard enough to throw him. He looked ten feet tall as he towered over Zane's crumpled body, radiating a rage he'd never once turned on his own players. Zane came to his feet snarling and ready to fight, but the second he realized who'd hit him he ground to a halt. Once a Raven, always a Raven; Zane was not a student anymore, but there was nothing he could do to a coach. For the first time Jean wondered if they would ever learn to stand their ground.

Rhemann gave him a moment to square up. When Zane only stepped back and averted his glare, he said, "Get out of my locker room, and don't you ever come back to my stadium. Do you understand?"

"Sure," Zane said, with a last sideways glance at Jean. "Nothing of value here anyway."

Rhemann pointed back the way he'd come, and Zane stalked past him without another word. Rhemann didn't turn to watch him go but put his phone to his ear. "Reacher is on his way back to the inner court," he said as soon as someone picked up on the other end of the line.

"Make sure he's escorted out of the park and urged out of town. Call whoever you need to, but get it done. I don't want to see his face around here ever again."

Rhemann hung up and turned toward him, and Jean quickly dropped his stare to the floor. He wasn't sure how much Rhemann had heard. Voices carried when the locker room was empty, and neither Raven had been quiet in their anger. Jean didn't have the right to ask, but maybe that was for the best. He didn't trust his voice to hold steady.

Rhemann put out a hand like he expected Jean to make a break for it. "Jean, look at me."

Jean dragged his stare to the collar of Rhemann's shirt; that was as far as his gaze could go. He worked his jaw on apologies he couldn't voice, but Rhemann didn't have time to fuss at him for getting in a fight. The sudden cacophony of rowdy voices said the Trojans were on their way into the locker room at last.

Rhemann caught hold of Jean's arm and said, "With me," before leading him down the hall. Somehow they made it to the coaches' hall without running into Jean's teammates, and Rhemann sat Jean in the chair opposite his desk.

"Give me two minutes," Rhemann said. "Do not leave this room."

Jean finally managed a, "Yes, Coach."

Rhemann closed the door behind him when he left. Jean stared down at his hands and tried his best not to think. Rhemann could have been gone two minutes or two hours. Time meant nothing as Jean fought for a center he couldn't find. The silence when Rhemann opened the door again was eerie, but Jean didn't care enough to ask where the Trojans had gone.

Rhemann had an armload of medical supplies with him, including some fresh ice packs. Jean hooked his jersey over his shoulders so Rhemann could strap one to

342

his chest with fresh gauze. As Rhemann was finishing up, he started with a careful, "Listen, Jean."

He was interrupted by a brisk knock on the door. The visitor didn't wait for a summons before stepping into the room. Jean catalogued the stranger from a great distance: dark hair, darker eyes, maybe early fifties. He didn't have the badging that would have marked him as press, but he didn't look like a coach. He was dressed like an uptight professor who'd gotten lost on the way to his classroom.

"Oh, sorry," the man said. "Saw your team back on the court, so I thought it was safe."

Rhemann waved off the apology. "Adi, this is Jean."

"Really!" Adi said, turning on Jean with renewed interest. "*The* Jean Moreau? I've heard a lot about you."

"Hasn't everyone?" Jean asked without thinking.

It wasn't at all funny, but it started an awful, hiccupping laugh out of him. He wanted to peel his face off. He wanted to dig this acidic heat out of his chest before it melted his bones away. He held onto the edge of the chair between his knees and squeezed until his fingers ached.

coward washout traitor sellout reject whore

He'd thrown the Ravens' furious letters away, but now he was getting mail from strangers who'd never even met him but who still wanted to blame him for the Ravens' downfall. He thought of Hannah Bailey's sly comments, of the irritated strangers at the mall this summer, of the paparazzi hounding him and Jeremy on the walk to campus. He thought of Hinch's rude comments on the court and Zane saying he should have been the first to die.

I do not care what they think of me, he thought, with a desperation that felt terrifyingly endless. *I don't. I can't. It only matters that I play.*

"I'm going to be a minute," Rhemann said. "Don't wait for me."

"Sure," was the uncertain response. "Take your time."

343

The stranger let himself out again, but Rhemann didn't move until the latch caught behind him. Silence settled in the room once more, heavy enough to smother him. Jean focused on the sound of his own heartbeat so he wouldn't go mad.

At length Rhemann pulled another ice pack off his desk and crouched to get a look at Jean's battered face. Jean refused to return his heavy stare, but he couldn't hide a flinch when Rhemann said, "Reacher had no right to say such cruel things to you."

He'd heard enough, then. The only appropriate response would be a "Yes, Coach," but what crawled out of Jean was a ragged, "Didn't he, Coach?"

Rhemann would beat Jean within an inch of his life for shoving the ice pack away so rudely, but that was for the best. If Jean was unconscious, he wouldn't have to think about any of this. But Rhemann only set the ice pack aside and sat back on his heel. He considered Jean with an unwavering gaze and said, "Talk to me."

"I did ask for it," Jean said. Rhemann needed to know that about him before he wasted his time getting offended on Jean's behalf. "They—" *hated me they all hated me* "—asked me if I liked it, and I—" *was so afraid* "—said yes. I wasn't allowed to say no." That last part wasn't meant to be said aloud, but it was out before he could catch it. Jean pressed unsteady fingers to his lips and shoved until he tasted blood. "I didn't—" *want it I hated it I hated them* "—know what else to do."

Riko was cruel, but no fool, and he'd ensured only the male backliners were present when he offered Jean up on a silver platter. For three days, the Ravens had been largely oblivious to Jean's plight. Then Ellison ratted him out to the locker room unprompted, declaring himself the best Jean had been with so far. Jean couldn't save himself without undermining Riko, so he'd panicked and agreed. The damage was done: the too-young freshman sleeping his way down the line had no remorse or intentions of stopping.

Grayson smelled blood in the water, and he couldn't resist taking a bite. He'd set out to hurt Jean as badly as he could that fourth night, then dragged a hand through Jean's tears and said, *"You like this too, right? Ask me for more."* Jean would have said anything to make him stop, and he'd begged until he finally lost his voice. None of it had earned him any mercy; it had only fueled Grayson's hunger. Jean had kept Zane up half the night afterward, crying so hard into his pillow he nearly threw up. And now Zane dared look him in the eye and say—

Except he wasn't wrong, was he? Three years had changed nothing. Jean had held out as long as he could, but it wasn't long enough. With his arm pushed near to dislocating and him in so much pain he could barely think, he'd still given Grayson whatever he demanded. He'd known it wouldn't save him, but he'd been so desperate for a reprieve he had to try. Jean wanted to tear his skin off everywhere Grayson had touched him, but Rhemann's low voice distracted him before he could get a good grip.

"Listen to me. It doesn't matter what you said. You were just a kid trying to survive as best you could. No one can blame you for that."

"But they do," Jean said. "They always will. And they've made sure everyone else will, too."

I don't care. It doesn't matter. Then why did he want to scream until his throat bled?

The pit in his stomach was the same he got when Riko shoved him down the stairs: a split-second of freefall before pain set in. Jean scrambled back from that edge as fast as he could go, trying to put as much distance between himself and Rhemann as he could: "I'm sorry, Coach. I have no right to complain. I crossed a line, and I got what I—" But it caught in his throat with an audible choke, and Jean bit his tongue as hard as he could.

345

"Deserved?" Rhemann finished, in a tone Jean never wanted to hear from him again.

"Yes, Coach," Jean said.

It was the wrong thing to say. Rhemann's hands were a sudden unyielding weight on his shoulders. Jean braced for a blow, but Rhemann only said, "Repeat after me: I didn't deserve what they did to me."

Rhemann didn't know what he was asking; he didn't know what this would cost. Panic chewed a line from Jean's gut to his heart. He couldn't refuse a coach's direct order, but he could beg: "Please don't make me, Coach."

"I need you to say it and mean it, Jean," Rhemann said. "Please."

Please was so uncalled-for Jean could only stare at him, heart hammering louder than his thoughts. He could feel every chain straining, waiting for the words that would rend them powerless at last. He was afraid to open his mouth again lest he get sick, but at length managed a hesitant, "I didn't deserve—" *heavy hands, heavier racquets, dark rooms, darker blood, teeth and knives and drowning, I'm drowning, I'm drowning* "—what they did to me."

A warning lurch in his chest had him clapping a quick hand over his mouth. He swallowed hard against the fire that wanted to devour him whole. It didn't work; there was a knot in his throat that was impossible to breathe around. He swallowed again, trying to dislodge it, and nearly gagged. Jean hit himself instead, slamming his free fist into the fresh bruises blooming on his cheekbone, and Rhemann caught his wrist in a careful grip.

"Don't," he said, but Jean barely heard him over his own heartbeat.

He was all at once aware that his hand was the only thing keeping him together; the lava that eaten through his chest and soul was now hard enough to crack, and it would surely pull him apart if he gave it an inch. Jean

346

wrenched free of Rhemann so he could clap his second hand atop the first. He dug in so hard he thought he'd break his own nose, eyes closed tight so he couldn't see Rhemann's expression.

Careful hands settled on his shoulders, not to shake him or strike him, but to hold him still as Rhemann said, "We never should have let him get that close to you. We should have protected you better. I'm sorry that we didn't."

"I'm sorry," he said, as if it was at all appropriate for a coach to apologize to one of his players. It was so unexpected and so unwarranted Jean forgot how to breathe, and the fleeting, traitorous thought that followed tore his heart wide open: *he is not the one who should apologize to me.* The gall of it was nearly as frightening as the truth of it, and Jean couldn't hold on tight enough to muffle a choked sob.

Don't, Jean thought, desperate. *Endure it. Please—*

"Jean." Rhemann gave his shoulders a fierce squeeze. "You're safe. I've got you. Let go."

Jean crumpled in on himself with an awful sound, and the weight of Rhemann's arms around him wasn't enough to keep him from shattering.

CHAPTER EIGHTEEN
Jean

Jean woke in an unfamiliar room in an unfamiliar bed. He stared up at a pale ceiling, fuzzily trying to put the previous night together. It came in fractured moments: the sick heat of grief too-long buried, the steadying weight of strong arms, the bitter tang of pills to help calm him down when Jean couldn't pull himself together again. Brake lights and streetlights and a rickety car that was decades past its prime; Jean couldn't remember getting out of the car again, but he knew in a heartbeat where he was.

The horror of it sent him stumbling out of bed in a panic, but the sheets tangled around his ankle and nearly dragged him to his knees. He caught at the wall for balance, heart an unrelenting jackhammer in his temples. It took him a few seconds to fight himself free. Jean wasn't sure whether to make the bed or strip it: surely Rhemann would want to clean the sheets before anyone else slept here, but leaving it in such disarray seemed unspeakably rude. At last Jean set it to rights with quick efficiency, though it took his unsteady hands a few tries to get the corners crisp.

They'd put him to bed in his jersey and shorts, but his shoes were just inside the bedroom door. Jean tucked them under his arm, eased open the bedroom door, and peered into the hallway. Across from him was an open doorway leading to a bathroom; nearly every other door he could see was closed. Jean weighed his options before ducking across the hall. Whatever Rhemann gave him last night left his throat unbearably dry, so he sucked down a few handfuls of water from the sink when he was through with his business. His face was a battered mess between

348

Hinch's punches and Zane's violence, and a line of bruises circled his throat from Zane's rough fingers. Jean tore his gaze from the mirror and left the room.

The voice echoing down the hall was female, but the closer Jean got to the stairs the more reassuring he found it. He'd heard the weekend morning news often enough at home to recognize the anchor's easy twang. Jean took five steps down to the main floor, surveyed the empty living room with a cautious look, and crossed over to the next open doorway.

The dining room and kitchen were connected as one long room. A small table with two chairs was at one end, and a chattering TV was mounted to the corner nearest it. Rhemann was on one of the bar stools at the low wall that helped set the kitchen apart. He had a newspaper open in front of him as he worked through a mug of coffee. The stranger from last night—Adi, Jean remembered—was washing dishes by hand at the sink, but he went still when he spotted Jean.

"James," he said.

Rhemann glanced up and followed Adi's stare to Jean. The sight of his wayward backliner hovering just out of the doorway had him pushing his coffee and newspaper aside, and he turned on the stool to give Jean his undivided attention. "Good morning. Were you able to get any sleep?"

"Yes, Coach," Jean said. "I'm sorry, Coach."

"You have nothing to be sorry for," Rhemann said, as if Jean hadn't ruined opening night by having an ugly breakdown in his office. Maybe something showed on Jean's face, because Rhemann heaved a weary sigh and turned back to his coffee. "Do you understand now, Adi?"

"Don't bully him," Adi complained. To Jean he said, "Good morning! Adijan Bregović, at your service. You can call me Adi. And you're Jean." He smiled, but it was weak. "Speaking of apologies, I'm sorry for what I said

349

last night. I didn't know at the time it was such a loaded statement. It's just that James spent all summer talking about you," he said, waggling his elbow in Rhemann's direction as he washed and dried his hands. "Moreau this, Moreau that, I was starting to think you were the second coming of Christ."

Jean had no idea how to address any of that, so he started with, "Are you a coach?"

"God no, no no no. I know nothing about sports." At the look Rhemann sent him, Adi made a dramatic gesture. "Okay, I've picked up a bit about Exy, *of course*, but most everything else is happily beyond me. Are you hungry? Sure you are," he said before Jean could deny it. He collected three plates from a nearby cabinet and put them out side-by-side near the stove. "You have excellent timing. Come, come, there's enough burek for all, I was just letting it cool a bit."

"Eat," Rhemann said. "It'll do you good."

Jean obediently crossed the room to accept a plate, and he studied the rolled-up chunk of bread Adi had given him. He wanted to ask what the nutritional breakdown was, but he had to trust that Rhemann would not lead him astray. Adi served Rhemann at the counter before dishing his own breakfast up, and he motioned for Jean to precede him to the table. He set his plate down opposite Jean but didn't sit yet. It took him two trips to get everything settled: one to hand out little cups of yogurt to everyone and another to bring Jean some black coffee.

"We have cream," Adi said as Jean hid his shoes under the table.

"No," Jean said, and remembered to add, "Thank you."

"Eat up," he said, dropping into his chair at last. "Eat, drink, and be merry."

Despite his chipper words, breakfast was an unpleasant affair. The news overhead couldn't make a dent in the heavy silence that settled in the kitchen.

Rhemann finished eating first, and he cleared his dishes away with easy efficiency. "I'll let Jeremy know you're awake," he said, looking across the room at Jean. "It's about twenty minutes from your place to mine, so make yourself at home in the meantime. I'll be out back if you need me."

"Your hat's hanging in the laundry room," Adi called as Rhemann left. Jean looked from the doorway to Adi and back again, refusing to contemplate such impossible thoughts but unable to fully relinquish them. Adi drained his coffee before sitting back to study Jean. "Don't take his attitude personally. I know he's worried sick about you; he's just under the impression you don't feel safe with him, so he doesn't want to be underfoot."

Jean said nothing, but he didn't have to. Adi saw the last answer he wanted on Jean's face, and his expression went grave. "Oh, but he wasn't lying, was he? He would never, ever hurt you. I need to know that you know that."

But he could, Jean thought, remembering how easily Rhemann had knocked Zane off his feet last night. Close behind that were stranger memories: Rhemann's bone-deep weariness every time Jean skirted his gaze or tried to apologize for his Raven conditioning, agitated fingernails picking at a whistle when Jean offered contrition, and careful hands on his shoulders like he thought Jean might break under an indelicate touch. Jean fought back every easy deflection in favor of a disconcerting truth:

"I know," he said, avoiding Adi's searching gaze.

"You sure?" Adi asked, and Jean forced a nod. Adi waited to see if anything else was forthcoming, then motioned to Jean's empty plate. "Good, yes? I made Baba teach me before I left home. Difficult mornings deserve comforting food."

"Yes," Jean said. He'd never considered beef a breakfast meat, but it came together well enough. He tacked on a belated, "Thank you."

"Tour of the place?" Adi asked as he collected his
dishes. Before Jean could answer, Adi's pager went off.
Adi checked the number and whistled through his teeth.
"Trust work to ruin the moment—looks like I've got to
make a couple calls. Please make yourself at home.
There's plenty of coffee left, and the bathroom's just up
the stairs if you need it. Good here? Good. Sorry, sorry."
He sailed away, already rummaging through his pockets
for his phone.

Jean sat alone for a few minutes more, but at last he
collected his shoes and went on a slow tour. The entirety
of Laila's house could probably fit into the first floor with
room to spare. It was comfortably cluttered, with wide,
arched doorways that helped each room breathe. The TV
in the living room was half-again as large as Cat's, but it
was the bookshelves that caught his eye. Every other shelf
was devoid of books in favor of framed photographs. Jean
spotted Lisinski in a few, and this one had to be
Rhemann's family: the three men standing shoulder-to-
shoulder with him looked too much like him to not be
siblings or first cousins.

More than half of the pictures were of just Adi and
Rhemann. Jean lingered longest over a photo of the two
men on a boat at sea. They were noticeably younger here,
without any visible gray in Rhemann's hair. Adi was
holding up a tiny fish with unabashed pride while
Rhemann laughed at his side. The photograph cut off near
their waists, but Jean was sure that was a thumb showing
around the flowing hem of Adi's unbuttoned shirt. Maybe
Rhemann was holding onto a railing that was just out of
sight, but—

The sound of footsteps on a hardwood floor had him
hastily returning the picture to its spot, but whichever man
was on the move didn't approach him. A door closed in
the distance, sending the house to silence once more, and

352

Jean retreated from the shelves with too many questions eating away at him.

The first office he passed had to be Rhemann's, considering the place was wall-to-wall Exy articles and team photos. Jean knew better than to trespass but continued onward, first past a closed door through which he could hear Adi's voice and then passing a laundry room with its own cabinetry and sink.

Eventually he found himself at the back door. The door was propped open, leaving just the screen door closed, and he peered out at a yard that was three times the size of Laila's narrow one. Rhemann was on his knees in a garden bed, carefully prying carrots free of the dirt. Seeing him like this was bewildering; Jean had foolishly believed Rhemann ceased to exist outside of Exy. It was a ridiculous thought, seeing how he'd spent part of spring trapped with Wymack, but Jean honestly couldn't imagine coaches having personal lives.

"Lend a hand?" Rhemann asked, pushing the brim of a floppy hat out of his eyes.

Jean had been caught. He toed into his shoes, let himself out, and took the stone path toward Rhemann. Rhemann showed him with a few careful tugs how to get the carrots free of the dirt, and he left Jean to finish the row while he went to inspect the next set of vegetables. Jean added his prizes one at a time to the half-filled bucket Rhemann left behind. Having something to do helped settle him. It was a defined task with expected results, and although it wasn't Exy, it helped restore the hierarchy between them.

Rhemann returned with a few cucumbers, but he was slow to leave again. He studied Jean for a minute while Jean worked, then finally said, "Tell me how I can help you." Jean slowly went still but refused to return his stare. Rhemann only gave him a few moments to come up with a response before continuing with, "I know you aren't comfortable with me, and I know you don't trust me enough to confide in me, but I need to know you're safe. I need to know that you're okay. Do you understand?"

"I'm okay, Coach."

"Jean." There was more regret in his name than exasperation. "Is there nothing I can do?"

Jean thought about Rhemann delaying an interview as long as he could and barring USC's gates when the press followed the Trojans to class. He thought of Rhemann cleaning Grayson's bloody bites himself and the careful way he'd strapped ice to Jean's bruised ribs last night. He'd gotten Jean out of sight before the Trojans could see him, knowing Jean's control was in tatters, and brought him here so he could recover away from their smothering concern.

Jean didn't know how to handle or process these undeserved kindnesses; in no universe could he ask for more than what he'd already gotten. It was already unbearable—a coach was supposed to take, not give.

Aren't they? he wondered, thinking of Wymack's steadying presence this spring. It was enough to make his stomach ache. Were Rhemann and Wymack the exception to the rule, or were the Ravens' coaches the wicked anomalies?

Rhemann was still waiting for a response. "No, Coach," would only disappoint the man, and "You've done more than you should have, Coach," sounded horrifically ungrateful. Jean couldn't come up with a safe middle ground, so he stared at the dirt under his nails and said nothing.

Rhemann had no choice but to give up on him. With a weary sigh he changed topics and walked Jean through the layout of his vegetable patch. The garden was Adi's idea, supposedly, and Rhemann had pushed back against it for years. He'd killed every single houseplant he ever brought home; why should he be trusted with a bigger project? But

354

he'd eventually tried anyway, over and over and over until he finally figured it out. There were still setbacks, but Rhemann saw more successes than failures these days. The coach surveyed his crops with quiet pride, and Jean studied the greenery with new interest.

He'd never once considered growing anything, but as he turned a tomato between his fingers Jean wondered if there was enough room in the tiny backyard at home to try. Would it be too much trouble and effort in the long run, or would it be satisfying to tend something from seed to plate? Idly he wondered if peaches grew on vines or trees. He almost asked, but he didn't know how Rhemann would react to his ignorance.

The back door creaked open then, and Jeremy stepped out onto the path to consider them. He hadn't brought his crutch with him; perhaps he hadn't been lying that last night's coddling was mere precaution. The tense set to Jeremy's mouth looked more like worry than pain as he studied Jean's face. Jean let him look his fill, offering no greetings or reassurances, and finally Jeremy remembered his manners.

"Good morning, Coach. How's my pumpkin coming along?"

"Haven't killed it yet, but I've still got a few weeks." Rhemann clapped dirt from his hands before turning back to Jean. He held the bucket of vegetables out in offering and said, "These are for you. Keep the bucket if you can figure out a use for it and toss it if you can't. I swear we've got at least ten of them around here somewhere, so I don't need it back."

Jean hesitated before taking hold of it. "Thank you, Coach."

"Go on, now," Rhemann said as he got to his feet.

Jean stood and dusted his knees off one-handed. Rhemann walked the two of them to the side gate so he could unlock it for them, but he didn't follow them through. He motioned to Jeremy and said, "Be careful if you stop by the stadium for his things. Security should be on high alert, but I'd rather not leave anything to chance." He waited for Jeremy's serious nod before glancing over at Jean and adding, "Keep an eye on each other, and let us know if you need anything."

"Yes, Coach," was the chorused response, and Jeremy led Jean away.

A narrow path took them to the front of the house. An unfamiliar car was side-by-side with Jean's at the head of the driveway, and Rhemann's creaky ride was parked behind them. There wasn't really room for Jeremy's car, but he'd done his best to fit. It meant most of his trunk was poking out into the road, but there didn't seem to be much traffic around here. Sprawling houses and sculpted trees lined both sides of the quiet street.

Jeremy preceded him to the passenger door, but instead of opening it he turned to study Jean. Inevitably his gaze dropped to the bruises circling Jean's neck, and Jeremy's face fell.

"I knew it was a bad idea," Jeremy admitted, so quiet Jean could barely hear him despite how close they were standing. "You've never really talked about Zane, but the careful way you avoided bringing him up made me suspect he was a problem. I didn't trust him, and I didn't want you to leave with him, but I didn't think I had any right to refuse you. Then Lucas practically pulled Coach off his feet saying Zane was trying to kill you, and I—" Jeremy couldn't finish it.

Technically Zane wanted to kill Lucas, but Jean couldn't get into that. He knew what assumptions Jeremy would make about Grayson and Zane if Jean put that target on Lucas's back, and he didn't have the strength to deal with it right now: no stomach for the ugly truth, and no interest in a lie that would erase Zane's sins. It was easier to focus on the rest of it: that Lucas had gone running for help after he escaped. Jean hadn't stopped to wonder how Rhemann made it to them so quickly.

"He wasn't. This was a fight eight months overdue." It did nothing to take the guilt out of Jeremy's stare, so Jean added, "It is good he came. I needed to see him one last time."

He was surprised that he meant it, but there were tender scars where there'd been open wounds before. It was a curious development; he would have expected Zane's viciousness to leave him more broken, not less. Maybe it had less to do with Zane's aggression and more to do with Rhemann lancing the poison from his shattered heart afterward. The bone-deep tension he'd carried for too many months had finally snapped free of him, leaving him empty and tired.

"Good," Jeremy echoed, soft and disbelieving. He reached for Jean's neck but stopped a hairsbreadth from touching the mottled skin there. "Enough is enough. If you're not comfortable speaking out against him, at least let me make a statement on your behalf."

"There is nothing to say."

"We can't just ignore this."

"Says the man who refused to care about his own bruises," Jean said, voice sharp.

"Jesus, Jean. It's not the same. Faser—" Jeremy winced as he realized his misstep. Jean committed the man's name to memory even as Jeremy tried to distract him: "Zane was obviously trying to hurt you, and you won't hold him accountable. You deserve better than that."

That word again; Jean wanted to claw it from Jeremy's tongue. He grabbed Jeremy's chin to force his head up. "Fuck what I deserve. What about what I want?"

A bold demand—and unbearably thoughtless. This wasn't at all what Jean meant, but he felt his mistake as soon as Jeremy's startled stare locked with his. The ghost of Riko's knife at his throat had him snatching his hand

357

back, and Jean retreated to a safer distance. Jeremy stepped back in turn, but he had nowhere to go. He leaned against his car instead and studied Jean's face with a steady, unwavering gaze. Jean refused to meet it but counted heartbeats until the danger passed.

At last Jeremy said, "What do you want, then? Tell me, because I don't know how else to help you. They're coming after you at home, at school, at the court—I can't watch them do this to you all year. It isn't fair or right. I need you to feel safe with us."

"Most of the time I do," Jean said, and meant it. "You promised you wouldn't look away, so I will let you look. But let him walk away, captain, and let me lock the door behind him. He will not be back. He came here for a truth, not a number. There is nothing else he can take from me."

Jeremy said nothing for an age, then offered only a defeated, "You're sure?"

"Yes," Jean said immediately.

"I don't like this," Jeremy said.

"This is your prerogative."

Jeremy dropped his gaze, conceding the fight. Jean let him go, and Jeremy pulled open the passenger door for him before starting away. Jean put the bucket of vegetables on the floor between his feet, and he buckled as Jeremy climbed in on the driver's side.

There was no chance they'd make it home in silence, but Jeremy held out until they were on the interstate. Then he rummaged one-handed in his cup holder and offered Jean a coin.

"Nickel for your thoughts?"

Jean wasn't sure what his thoughts were, but maybe there just wasn't space enough in his head to untangle them. He took the coin and rolled it between his fingers while he stared out the window. "I didn't like the Bobcats," he said. He felt Jeremy's eyes on him as he started in the least expected spot, but his captain held his tongue and forced his attention back to the road in front of them. "I should have, yes? They play the way I was trained. The right way," he added, knowing it risked an interruption from Jeremy.

Jeremy didn't take the bait, and Jean worked through his prickly thoughts in peace. All summer he'd fought an uphill battle, trying in vain to drag the Trojans off their high horse and grumbling discontent about the restraint they demanded of him. He'd argued for them to see sense and sort out their priorities, and they'd gleefully refused him at every turn.

They'd been brilliant last night, as he'd known they would be—they were Big Three, after all, and the stars of Kevin's dreary world—but it wasn't their performance that rattled him. It was the jarring contrast between the Bobcats and Trojans, emphasized by Zane's unapologetic heartlessness afterward. What a sharp reminder of how far he'd come from a hideous normal.

"I don't want you to be like Zane," Jean said, slow as he tried piecing it together. "I don't want Coach to be like the master. I don't want to teach Tanner contrition when he continuously fails my drills or to break my racquet over Cat's back if I think she should have performed better. I don't ever want to go back to how things were. Maybe you are fools, and I am the biggest fool for indulging you, but better to be reckless fools than Ravens."

He held the nickel out toward Jeremy. "We will do it your way, and we will win anyway."

At last Jeremy smiled, and it almost looked real. He reached blindly for the coin, and Jean pressed it into his palm so Jeremy could keep his eyes on the road. Jeremy gave his fingers a quick squeeze and said, "With you on our side, how can we lose?"

He was going for warmth, Jean knew, but his tone fell a bit short. Still upset over letting Zane get away with this, Jean assumed, and he cast about for an appropriate

359

distraction. What he stumbled over was an ill-advised, "Coach is—" that he couldn't finish. It was unforgivably bold to make such a presumptuous statement about a coach. He settled for a vague and uncertain, "Coach and Adi."

Jeremy finished it for him: "Are partners, yeah. They've been together something like twenty-seven years. Maybe twenty-eight, now. But they're pretty lowkey about it. Don't know what people will say about a gay man running a college sports team. Locker room, impressionable athletes, all that prejudiced nonsense. Officially Adi is Coach's best friend from college. Two bachelors living the dream in LA, or something.

"I'm not even sure how many Trojans have figured it out, to be honest. Adi generally avoids the stadium outside of championships, and Coach doesn't bring him up in mixed company. I met him my freshman year, after…" He trailed off, knowing Jean could guess the circumstances without his help. Jeremy gave him a moment to take it in before cautiously asking, "Does that make you more afraid of Coach or less?"

Jean settled for an honest, "I don't know."

On one side was Riko's scathing, *"I will bleed this out of him,"* Kevin's weary, *"They were supposed to be a warning, Jean,"* and a thousand judgmental slurs hurled his way with devastating accuracy. On the other was Neil's blasé, *"I'm sure he knows,"* when Jean warned him to hide Andrew from Ichirou, the Trojans' casual acceptance of their floozy line, and a partnership that somehow survived twenty-eight years in this heartless world.

Jean picked at his knuckles as he considered the vast distance between these realities. It was a waste of time to wonder, he knew. He was Moriyama property; there were lines he could not cross no matter what.

"I would trust him with my life," Jeremy said, "but I

360

haven't had to face the things you have, so I won't try to convince you. I know you need to get there on your own."

The silence that settled between them wasn't comfortable, but it was calm, and Jean chased his thoughts in exhausting circles. In the end he only found peace by counting: *A cool evening breeze. Rainbows. Open roads. Friends. Fireworks.* After a beat he added a tentative, *Coach,* but that was so repulsive he had to reject it. Tetsuji Moriyama was also a coach, and Jean refused to associate Rhemann and Wymack with that violent nightmare.

He'd run into this same problem when trying to account for his teammates, but there was no easy solution this time. Jean turned it this way and that in increasing frustration until a stray memory brought him up short. *"My kids,"* Wymack had called the Foxes, and Rhemann had said the same this summer: *"You're one of my kids now."*

Fathers? Jean thought, but that was so horrifically inappropriate he reached for the door handle.

"Hey," Jeremy said, startled by the crack of Jean's knuckles against the door. "Are you all right?"

"Yes," Jean lied as he stared out the window. He tried to bully his thoughts into submission, but they refused to let go and move on to other suggestions. For a moment he considered asking Renee for ideas, but he swiftly rejected the idea. This one was too vulnerable to share; he would have to sort it out on his own. But miles later he'd still come up with nothing else.

Maybe, he thought. After all, they never had to know. And it wasn't like the word came ingrained with sentimentality. Hervé Moreau had seen to that.

Jean gingerly counted it out again, ending with *Fathers.*

It still put a nervous twist in his chest, but Jean would learn to live with it.

Familiar streets distracted him from uncomfortable

thoughts a minute later, and soon enough Jeremy pulled up behind Laila's car. Two men in suits were standing at the bottom of the stairs. Jean recognized only one face, but the uniforms were familiar: it was the same company who'd provided Laila with security when the press were showing up at the house.

"Her uncle's men," Jean said. "Precaution or reaction?"

Jeremy grimaced an apology at him. "Ingrid was still at the bench when Lucas came running for Coach, so she heard that Zane had gone after you. After Coach White kicked her out of the stadium without an explanation, her colleagues stopped by last night demanding proof of life. They wouldn't back off until security got here. I think we've only got them for three or four days this time, but hopefully that's enough."

"How much longer will her uncle tolerate me disrupting her life?" Jean asked.

"You make Laila happy, and that makes him happy," Jeremy said. "Don't worry."

Jean collected his vegetables on the way out of the car, feigned not to hear his name being called by reporters down the street, and followed Jeremy up the stairs. He wasn't sure if Cat and Laila heard the yelling or just recognized the familiar rumble of Jeremy's engine, but they were waiting in the hall in their pajamas when Jeremy and Jean made it through the front door. The grief that twisted Laila's face when she got a good look at his new bruises was quickly stamped out, but Cat crossed the hall in record time.

"When are they going to stop?" she demanded, sharp with anger. "Jean—"

"It doesn't matter."

"It does matter," Cat insisted. "He really hurt you."

Jean put the bucket up between them before she could feel the swollen line of his throat. Cat obediently took it,

362

but her stare didn't waver. Jean snapped his fingers in the air between them until she dragged her gaze up to meet his. "I am actively working to forget he exists. Do not undermine my attempts." The stubborn look on her face said she wasn't swayed, so Jean said, "We are not discussing it further. Take it up with Jeremy if you do not like it."

Cat turned a disbelieving look on Jeremy, who shook his head. "It's his call, Cat."

Cat's sour expression said they were going to have words later, but she was smart enough to bite her tongue now. Jean tapped the bucket to distract her from Jeremy and said, "Gifts from Coach."

She dutifully inspected his vegetables. "Oh, he's getting better at this," she said, with forced enthusiasm. Jean didn't care that it was an act; if she kept it up long enough, she'd trick herself into a better mood. "Nice. I'll get them washed and put away."

"Coffee?" Laila asked. "We started a fresh pot when Jeremy went to get you."

"Coffee," Jean agreed, and the four of them moved to the kitchen.

Cat pointed at the island on her way through the door. Her laptop was set up there with a colorful browser open. Jean sat to investigate while Jeremy poured coffee for them both. Cat was on an Exy news site—rather, the photography-adjacent section of it that archived every shot captured from last night's NCAA matches nationwide. She'd already filtered it to display only the photographs from the Trojan-Bobcat match, and the page of thumbnails went on and on. Jean clicked through them as Cat set to work scrubbing vegetables at the sink.

The series started with the Trojans' arrival for warm-ups. Here and there were sets that were practically slideshows; the photographer had hoped a worthy moment coming and was determined to capture the best shot of it.

Most such sets centered around scoring chances, but a ridiculous amount centered around Jean: going through warmups before the match, interacting with his teammates on the sidelines, and then on the court itself. Jean tabbed through those as quickly as he could, uninterested in seeing himself through a stranger's prying eyes.

Laila sat at his side and motioned, and Jean relinquished control to her. She clicked into the next tab. The article covering the game was pulled up there. Bold lettering across the top read: **USC DEFEATS WHITE RIDGE IN HOME OPENER; GOLDEN RAVEN SOARS IN DEBUT**. The photograph directly beneath it was of the Trojans' celebration at the final bell, but halfway down the page was a shot of Jean launching off Lander's shoulder.

"'Soars', indeed," Laila said. "I couldn't believe you did that."

"Springboard off Lander?" Cat guessed over her shoulder. "Look at his face!"

Jean hadn't seen it last night, too intent on reaching the ball first, but Lander looked deeply offended to be treated as a prop. It didn't make Jean's ribs hurt any less, but it afforded him a bit of annoyed satisfaction. He pressed careful fingers to his jersey, testing the ache that a night of rest hadn't cured, and said, "Asshole."

"They are a team of charmers," was Laila's dry response.

"At least we got them out of the way early," Cat pointed out.

Laila scrolled to find the paragraph she wanted and read: "If not for the Ravens' vocal campaign against him this spring and the unmistakable number on his face, anyone watching this match would be hard-pressed to remember Jean Moreau is a transfer from Edgar Allan. He looks as at home on the Gold Court as he ever did at Evermore, matching and supplementing the Trojans'

364

infamous good-natured playstyle with unexpected ease."

"Not unexpected," Cat said, belligerent. "People just don't listen."

Laila studied Jean for a moment before saying, "You were stellar, you know. And I mean both on and off the court." She went to a third tab, where she'd opened one of the photographs on its own page: Cat tucked into Jean's side, with Jean's mouth at her temple. Without context it looked almost peaceful, but Jean remembered what they'd been talking about at the time. He was annoyed someone had captured the moment and put it up for anyone to see.

He glanced away from it, but Laila wasn't finished: "The Ravens put in so much time trying to paint you as an ill-behaved problem child, but now everyone can see who you really are. Anyone could call your interview a scripted attempt to sweeten your image, but everything people saw last night was genuine." She clicked through a few more tabs, lingering only a few seconds on each one so he could see they were additional writeups on the game from other sources. "Overall tone is thoughtful and positive."

"I do not," Jean started, but his *care what people think of me* evaporated on his tongue. Last night proved that the six months of aggressive and antagonistic attention had gotten to him whether he wanted it to or not. He downed the rest of his coffee in one go and said instead, "I don't want to read my mail anymore. Throw it all away if you get to it before I do." He didn't bother to specify Kevin as an exception, knowing they'd check the senders for familiar names before tossing his letters into the trash.

"Gladly," Laila said. "I'll buy a shredder today."

Silence descended in the kitchen, but it couldn't last. Jeremy gently nudged him and asked, "Are you going to your appointment today, or would you rather get it rescheduled?"

Jean glanced at the clock and saw it was a quarter after nine. He'd missed last week's session because of the

365

banquet. He would rather never go back, but he had promises to keep. "I have to go, but I need to shower first." The thought of getting wet when he knew what was coming for him in an hour left his stomach in shreds, but he'd gone to bed gross from a game and knew he was a mess. "I will be quick."

"You always are," Jeremy said, holding out a hand for Jean's mug.

Jean turned it over and left the room. In the short time it took him to wash up and get dressed for the day, pictures from this morning's return home were posted online. He saw them pulled up on Cat's laptop when he checked the kitchen for his friends. The morning sun was kinder to his bruises than the harsh light of Rhemann's bathroom, but the ones around his throat were clearly left by fingers. Jean didn't care to read any speculation about his encounter with Zane, so he turned his back on the kitchen and tried the living room next.

Cat was brushing Laila's hair as Laila tapped away on her phone, and Jeremy had a foot on the coffee table as he checked his ankle. Jeremy smiled at Jean's arrival and got to his feet. His LSAT guides were on the table with his French book, but after a brief hesitation Jeremy only grabbed the latter before leading Jean to the front door.

Jean watched him take his keys off the hook before saying, "I want to sell the car."

"Sure," Jeremy agreed.

Cat's frantic, "Wait!" almost drowned out Laila's indignant squawk. The thump of furniture getting knocked aside made Jean think Cat vaulted Laila to get out of the room faster. She caught at the living room doorframe to stop her skid into the hall and reached for him. "I mean, yes! Yes, you should. Let me take you when you do it. My uncle would buy it off you in a heartbeat. It's a collectible to the right people, and all, so between that and me vouching for you, you'd make bank on it. Five figures

366

easy."

"You don't believe that," Jean said skeptically.

"I know I'm right," Cat promised. She motioned frantically toward him, like she thought he'd walk away before she got through her spiel, and said, "But Jean, you could even trade it in for a motorcycle of your own and still have plenty leftover. You don't have to, obviously, you can use this starter one indefinitely, but wouldn't it be nice to have something that's just yours?"

She made it sound easy. Maybe it really was. Jean hesitated before saying, "I'll think about it."

The guards saw them off with serious faces, but Jean didn't hear any more cries for his attention. Maybe the reporters were satisfied with the shots they'd gotten already, or the guards ejected them when they tried to come closer for a statement. Either way, Jeremy got them on the road north without any further setbacks. Jean watched the city slide past his window and tried not to think about what was coming.

Jeremy gave him peace until he parked, and then he said, "I spoke to Renee Walker last night." It was unexpected enough that Jean could only stare at him. Jeremy studied him with an inscrutable expression before explaining, "She couldn't get ahold of you, so she had Kevin call me. She'd heard the rumors that Reacher attacked you at the court and needed to know you were okay. I told her Coach was looking after you and that you'd talk to her today. Is that all right?"

"Yes," Jean said. "I will need to pick up my phone."

"We'll get it on the way home," Jeremy promised.

They were early for his appointment, but the minutes passed easily enough. At last Jean was shown to the back, and he closed the office door behind himself. He took his seat when his doctor motioned to it, and the man sat back in his chair to consider Jean. A slow gaze tracked the new bruises staining his face and neck.

"Do we need to talk about this?" he asked.

"Home game last night," Jean said.

The doctor's stare lingered on his throat, but he decided not to push. "I'm glad you came back. I wasn't sure you would."

There was no point lying. "I didn't want to, but I—" The easy excuses fell apart; they were still true, but they rang hollow in the moment. It was Rhemann's voice in his head, Rhemann's and his friends' and Neil's, drowning out his miserable thoughts and excuses with unrelenting force. Jean squeezed his hands until his fingers went numb and willed himself to believe the words as he slowly spoke them into existence: "I deserve to get better."

"You do," the doctor said, with an easy and unhesitating compassion that would somehow keep Jean sane during this horrible session, "and you will."

"One week at a time," Jeremy had promised him.

Jean drew in a slow breath and nodded. "Okay."

CHAPTER NINETEEN
Jeremy

Monday morning practice was as tense and miserable as Jeremy knew it would be, and that was despite him spending all of Saturday and Sunday arguing with his teammates via text. This was the second time Jean had been attacked at the Gold Court by a former teammate, and the Trojans were justifiably riled up about it. That Zane had put his hands on Jean and gone home again with no repercussions whatsoever was unforgivable; that Ingrid's story made it sound like a two-sided rivalry was worse.

Jeremy understood his teammates' anger, and his own hurt was a lingering weight in his heart, but he'd promised to follow Jean's lead. He didn't have to like it or agree with it; within a few days it was obvious Jean knew what he was doing. He'd been taking slow and careful steps away from the Ravens all summer, but for him to finally and emphatically reject everything they stood for was a tremendous leap toward healing at last.

This was the most settled Jeremy had ever seen him, though it took time to pinpoint the change: Jean was finally treating the Trojans like his team instead of the team he'd been assigned to. It was a tiny but critical shift in his outlook and demeanor. Jeremy wouldn't ever forgive Zane, but for now he would let sleeping dogs lie.

It helped that the press had bigger fish to fry this week. Due to Rogeson's death, the Ravens had been excused from the southern fall banquet on Saturday. Their first public appearance of the season was now their upcoming match against the Foxes. Both Edgar Allan and Palmetto State had campus events all week to hype up their respective student bodies, and Wymack invited the press to his locker room on Tuesday afternoon.

Because of practice, Jeremy had to wait until he was back home before he could watch the video, but Jean's private lessons delayed his friends almost as long. Jeremy messaged Laila when he was home and settled at his laptop, and she let him know when they'd gathered around Cat's computer. It wasn't as fun as being there with them, but it made him feel a little closer as he finally hit Play.

The Foxes' freshmen went first, and Jeremy listened with no little exhaustion as they wrote the Ravens off as overhyped has-beens. It was a bold stance to take, seeing how long the Ravens had been dominant and how little of NCAA Exy these kids had experienced so far. The upperclassmen were only marginally better, but Jeremy would have been surprised by civility. The Foxes had been kicked around for too many years, the butt of a thousand cruel jokes, and had learned years ago to bite back any chance they got.

They were called up in pairs, and it was inevitable that Kevin and Neil would be thrown together for their bit. Kevin couldn't be rude with a camera in his face, but Jeremy could read between the lines: Kevin had no interest in the rematch whatsoever. Edgar Allan was a shattered ghost of its former self. Without the perfect Court or Coach Moriyama on the line, the team had no challenge or value to him anymore. Kevin gamely did his best to keep Neil out of the conversation, not trusting his vice-captain to speak, but the interviewer was persistent.

"What about you?" the man asked as he stuck his microphone in Neil's face a third time. "Are you looking forward to the match?"

"Sure," Neil said. "If they bother to show up this week."

After a few awkward moments, the reporter joked, "That's it? Last year you had such strong opinions about the Ravens."

"Most were about their coach and Riko, but those two aren't a problem anymore." Neil shrugged indifference. The way he was jostled made Jeremy think Kevin kicked him where the camera couldn't see it. Neil returned Kevin's withering look with an unimpressed stare and only said, "If you'd ever be honest when people ask you about them, I wouldn't have to be."

"Says the least honest man I know," Kevin said.

"They don't deserve kindness from me after everything they've put us through," Neil insisted. "I hope they lose every game this season, and I'll say it as many times as someone asks me. They don't belong on the court until everyone Coach Moriyama trained has been cleared out of there. Edgar Allan should have farmed them out to other schools and dismantled the entire program, if you ask me."

"He didn't ask you," Kevin said. "Stay on topic."

"The topic was the Ravens," was Neil's unrepentant response.

"Speaking of misplaced Ravens, I assume you watched USC's match last Friday," the reporter said, tipping his microphone back toward Kevin. It worked like a charm: Kevin forgot all about his contentious teammate in favor of Trojan gossip. "Setting aside how the night supposedly ended, what a brilliant start for your favorite team."

"Supposedly," Jeremy echoed, and got the same indignant message from Cat a few seconds later.

"A little unfortunate for me," the reporter admitted with a laugh. "My coworkers and I had an informal bet that Moreau would get in at least one brawl. I thought for sure we would see the Trojans' first red card."

Maybe he expected Kevin to agree with him, but Kevin affected confusion. "The USC Trojans don't fight on the court. It's their most controversial and well-known

371

statistic. I'm sure you know that."

"Yes, but—" The reporter floundered for a moment. "It being Moreau's first game with such restrictions, I would have expected him to fall back on old habits. Impressive that he didn't," he added when it was obvious Kevin was not going to help him out. "A fantastic debut all around, wouldn't you say?"

"Sure," Neil said, with a smile that had Jeremy leaning away from his computer. "Glad to see his ribs healed up without any lingering consequences for anyone involved." He grimaced when Kevin kicked him again. Kevin's face looked carved from stone as he stared down at his short teammate, but he didn't have to say anything. Neil let it go with an easy, "Anyway, we're over our time and need to get back to the court."

"You mentioned Moreau's ribs?" the interviewer pressed.

"Renee and Andrew are last, right?" Neil asked as he stood.

Pin-pon, Jeremy's phone went, and Jeremy read Laila's, "Forever an instigator."

Jeremy started typing out a response, but the interviewer tried a last ditch, "Kevin, would you care to explain that comment?" and Kevin went still.

Jeremy set his phone aside to watch the way Kevin and Neil stared each other down. That Kevin gave ground first was unexpected, but at last Kevin tilted his left hand where he could see his scars. He rubbed idly at the pale skin for a few moments, then flicked a steady look at the off-screen interviewer.

"With all due respect, there is no point," he said. "You will never take anyone's word over theirs, so you are best off asking the Ravens for the truth. But good luck: they do not know how to tell it unless one has been fed to them." He motioned for Neil to get a move on. This time Neil went without argument, starting for the door without

372

another look at the interviewer. Kevin turned after him with, "Thank you for your time. We will send you the next pair."

Jeremy belatedly remembered his phone. "Scale of one to ten, how angry is Jean?"

"And I quote, 'Rancid menace'," Laila answered a few seconds later. Before Jeremy could worry, she sent a few more texts: "He left the room as soon as Kevin sicced the reporter on the Ravens. Cat went after him. Going to pause here until they get back, though I'm not sure Jean will watch the rest. What about you?"

Jeremy glanced at his screen. Andrew Minyard and Renee Walker were now settled in front of the camera, Renee with a small smile and Andrew looking bored into the distance. Jeremy paused the clip to study the Foxes' goalkeepers. Andrew was technically the greater threat on the court, but Jeremy's gaze lingered on Renee. Before Friday's short phone call, his only interaction with her was the handshake at last year's semifinals, but he knew she was important to Jean. They texted on a regular basis, and Kevin had recognized her cross on sight when he saw Jean wearing it.

She looked sweet enough, but Jeremy knew what sort of people Coach Wymack recruited for his line. More than that he remembered Jean saying Renee was the one who'd taken him from Edgar Allan after Riko beat Jean within an inch of his life. Jeremy wasn't sure how literally he meant it, but he finally hit play to hear her answers.

She existed in jarring opposition to her teammates, reflecting on the upcoming match with caution and a gentle concern for the Ravens' questionable wellbeing. Since Andrew refused to say a word, no matter how often the interviewer tried to include him, she was forced to handle the entire bit with unflagging patience.

"One last thing, before you go," the reporter said, "though I'm not sure you can help me with it. Neil mentioned a rumor we haven't heard yet, that Jean might have sustained additional injuries last spring that weren't reported. Perhaps he's said the same to you?" Renee's smile faded, and she studied the man with serene calm. The reporter allowed her a few seconds to respond before trying, "We're just trying to sort out where this gossip might be stemming from."

Renee chose her side with an easy, "Insider knowledge. Jean spent time with us before moving to California, but that is as much as I can tell you. Even if it wasn't inappropriate for me to discuss Jean's injuries without his consent, we promised President Andritch our discretion on the matter." Jeremy didn't hear what Andrew said, but Renee laughed. He tried replaying the part twice with the volume turned up, but Andrew's muttered interjection was for Renee's ears only. Jeremy gave up and let it play.

Renee smiled at the reporter, but this time it didn't reach her eyes. "I'm sorry, but our hands are tied. You will have to ask Edgar Allan for the rest of the story."

"They are notoriously hard to get a comment from," the reporter said dryly.

"Sometimes they are," she agreed. "Perhaps you are trying the wrong Ravens."

It was obvious he wouldn't get better out of her, so he wrapped it up with quick thanks and sent the pair on their way. The last few minutes of the video cut back to the studio, where two men dissected the Foxes' answers. Jeremy didn't need to listen to the wrap up, so he closed the video and pushed his laptop to the back corner of his desk.

A few minutes later he picked his phone up and started a new message to Laila: "She's pretty, right?" He studied it for a moment, thumb hovering the button that would send it, and erased the last bit. A second later he deleted the rest. Cat had already weighed in on Renee's favorable looks, and it was irrelevant either way. Saying such a thing unprompted would only get Laila thinking, and Jeremy didn't want her asking questions when he genuinely didn't mean anything by it in the first place.

He was saved by a knock, and he looked over to see William in his bedroom doorway. Jeremy checked the time and said, "Late for you to be working, isn't it?"

"Just wrapping up a few items before I call it a night."

William followed Jeremy's beckon into the room and offered a manila envelope. "This is the preliminary list of French instructors who speak with the Marseille accent. The most experienced is overseas and arranges lessons over… Skype?" William leaned forward to check his notes over Jeremy's shoulder. "The one in San Francisco has eight years of experience and is also willing to teach you over the phone.

"The last has no teaching experience but is both local and a native speaker, if you prefer a more informal setting face-to-face. I've attached copies of their profiles and, for the certified instructors, select reviews from other students. If none of them are to your satisfaction I will continue the search."

"No, this is great, thank you," Jeremy said, lingering over the last. "Chances of Mom challenging the charges when she sees Leslie's spreadsheet?"

William gave it some thought before saying, "Middling. For obvious reasons she would prefer you study Latin again." He answered Jeremy's grimace with a wan smile that was quick to fade. William studied him with such a serious look Jeremy felt eight years old again. He realized too late he was fidgeting with the folder and forced himself to stillness. "French has its uses and appeal of course, but this is very specific dialect. It is public knowledge your newest teammate hails from Marseille. You know your mother does not approve of him."

"She doesn't even know him. She's been taken in by a

smear campaign."

"You deny his criminal affiliations, then," William said.

"No," Jeremy admitted, "but why is he responsible for his parents' crimes? He's been dealt a rotten hand in life, but he's made it this far because he refuses to give up. Every single day he puts in the work to get better and be better, and no one seems to care because healing journeys don't sell as many newspapers."

The bland look on William's face said he was pitching his argument to the wrong person; William himself had no strong opinion on Jean either way. Jeremy subsided with a quiet sigh and said, "Did you know he barely knew English when he enrolled at Edgar Allan? Sounds like it was such a last-minute decision he had no time to really prepare. But they wouldn't let him speak French because no one could understand it. I just thought that…" He gestured helplessly at the folder. "I want to show him we're as committed to him as he is to us."

William folded his arms across his chest as he thought it over. "Mathilda will find out you are studying French, and she will guess what inspired you, but she needn't know the finer points. I can make a strong enough case in your favor to stay her hand, perhaps: a new interest in international law or immigration studies, with intent to branch into additional languages down the line as your career requires."

It was a bit weak, but Jeremy knew it would work. Nan had hired William over twenty years ago at the recommendation of her personal assistant, and he'd been with the family ever since. Mathilda was his employer now that Nan was gone, but she trusted and respected William more than she did most of her supposed friends. The unguarded fondness that slipped out of her sometimes when she spoke with him was warmer than anything she directed toward her own children.

It was a sour thought to have when William was trying so hard to help him, so Jeremy stamped it down as quickly as he could. "I don't want to make you choose sides."

Maybe some of that bitterness showed, because William treated him to a long look. At length all he said was, "If you still have to ask whose side I am on, you have not been paying enough attention." Jeremy was forced to look away, jaw working on a grief he didn't dare acknowledge or voice. William stepped back, giving him space to breathe. "If there is nothing else, I will retire for the night."

"Nothing else, thank you," Jeremy said, tugging his folder closer so he wouldn't have to face the man. "Get some rest for once."

He waited until he heard William's footsteps on the stairs before spreading out the profiles William compiled for him. The first and second were the obvious better choices, but Jeremy couldn't deny the appeal of less-structured classes in person. Fitting them into his messy schedule would be a headache, but his mother's approval might be the tipping point. She'd excuse a late arrival home from practice if she knew he was meeting with a tutor.

It was early to get his hopes up, but Jeremy pushed his homework aside in drafting a letter of introduction. He'd hope for the best and adjust to the worst; it was all he knew to do when it came to family.

-

It took reporters only a few hours to decipher what Renee might have meant by "the wrong Ravens", and the ensuing forty-eight hours were chaotic and angry. Edgar Allan had ensured their current lineup was untouchable, and the Ravens' classmates would happily close ranks to protect their fallen stars, but there were years' worth of graduates scattered around the United States and abroad who had fewer safeguards in place.

Jeremy ought to be impressed with Renee's gentle scheming, but he watched each disastrous and short-lived run-in with a growing sense of dread. It was glaringly obvious that the Ravens had serious issues, even so many years out from Evermore. It wasn't just the widespread reluctance to speak to the press, or how soundly they refused to speak about Coach Moriyama and the Nest. Half of the Ravens who'd graduated and signed to professional teams were already on their way out of the league. The average Raven career seemed to last only five years.

Looking at them one or two at a time, the sustained injuries and chronic pain were simply unfortunate, but parading so many uncooperative Ravens in front of a camera back-to-back made it glaringly obvious. Years of sixteen-hour days, with so many few days to rest, coupled with their hideous concept of contrition, had shattered these players on a bone-deep level. Jeremy wondered why it took anyone this long to notice—then wondered if people simply didn't care. While they could still play, the Ravens burned bright and ferocious, and there were always so many players desperate to replace them when they sputtered to ash.

Jeremy feared for Jean's long-term health, but he feared for Kevin's more. That evening he messaged Kevin an unprompted, "You have to stop night practices."

When Kevin didn't answer, Jeremy tried calling. It took six tries before Kevin finally answered, and Kevin had absolutely no interest in Jeremy's warnings or concern. He'd said earlier this summer that he practiced with Neil and Andrew, but Jeremy didn't have their numbers. Jeremy had a feeling Andrew would be a dead end, which left only one other choice. Jean was hesitant to share Neil's contact information with him, even after Jeremy explained himself, but Jean could only refuse him so long. Jeremy wasn't entirely surprised that Neil didn't answer, but at least he'd tried. He set aside his phone with a weary sigh and turned back to his homework in a dour mood.

At least the morning brought an effective distraction, as the Trojans had an away game against Utah. It was eleven hours to Salt Lake City without accounting for a lunch break, and the Utes were a time zone ahead. The Trojans had to be on Utah's campus at least an hour before a six-thirty serve, which meant leaving Los Angeles no later than a quarter to four in the morning. When Jeremy's alarm went off at three o'clock on Friday, only three hours after he'd finished his homework, he nearly bludgeoned it with his pillow.

Since the Foxes had agitated the Ravens this week and Laila's security detail was released back to other sites, Jeremy drove his friends over to the stadium and parked his car there for the day. Lisinski was asleep on the strikers' bench, never mind that Tony and Bobby were making a serious racket getting the Trojans' gear ready for the trip. Jeremy flagged a few of the freshmen down to roll the stick racks out to the parking lot as each was finished. Jimenez split everyone else up onto their rows in the locker room so he could take roll easier. Whichever line was fully present first got to board first. Unsurprisingly the goalkeepers won, as there were only four to account for, and the five dealers were close behind them.

The charter bus came with a team of two drivers who would switch out halfway through and who fortunately looked significantly more awake than the athletes filing onboard. There were fourteen rows of seats, though the first four rows were reserved. Each coach got a pair of seats, and the row ahead of Rhemann and Lisinski was reserved for the drivers. Tony, Bobby, and Angie had the row right behind them, and the Trojans were free to spread out as they liked in the rest.

379

With only forty open seats and twenty-nine bodies, it was inevitable that some of them had to share. The usual suspects piled in together, but Jeremy hesitated when he spotted Tanner standing beside Lucas's seat. Lucas and Haoyu had been inseparable their freshman year, but Travis's arrival last year meant someone had to be the odd man out. Lucas had drifted to the outskirts and sat alone ever since. He wouldn't agree to Tanner's intrusion—except he did after only a brief argument against it. Maybe he was just too tired to fight.

"All set?" Rhemann asked at his back.

"Set," Jeremy agreed as he dropped into his seat.

Rhemann slipped past him to finish his headcount. He did it twice: once on his way to the rear, then on his way back, and he gave the driver an okay to get on the road. Jeremy closed his eyes as the bus pulled away from the stadium, and he was asleep before they even turned onto the 10.

-

The Trojans made good time, pulling into Salt Lake City just before five. It was earlier than the Utes perhaps wanted to host them, but since the Fox and Raven game started at seven eastern, USC was more than happy to stick to their locker room. Warmups and a game of their own would keep the Trojans from watching all of it, but Jeremy might catch most of the first half. He was off the bus right behind the coaches and had the locker room TVs on as soon as he could find them. Two were already set to the right station. Jeremy turned the third off rather than mess with it and stood silent and still as the starting lineups were called to the court.

Despite the Foxes' bold words on Tuesday, Wymack was taking no chances. His freshmen were sidelined tonight, and he filled the court with his strongest players: Kevin and Neil on offense, captain Danielle Wilds as starting dealer, and backliners Matthew Boyd and Aaron

Minyard in the rear. Andrew Minyard was the last on, and he propped his racquet to his shoulder as he nonchalantly took his spot in goal.

Jeremy was distantly aware of the Trojans filling in the space around him. The only one who mattered right now was Jean, who was staring at the TV with a tense look on his face. Jeremy could only imagine what was going through his head. He'd rejected the Ravens' way of doing things, but his relationship with the violent team was a complicated mess that would likely take years to untangle. Jeremy knew he'd watched their championship games, but for most of that time he'd still been a Raven in hiding. Now they were strangers to him, an obstacle Kevin and Neil needed to crush.

He almost asked, but Jean beat him to speaking with a flat, "She is not captain."

"Wilds?" Cat asked.

"Lane," Laila guessed. To Jean she asked, "Unqualified?"

"It doesn't matter how talented she is," Jean said. "The master would have never approved—"

Jean cut himself off a heartbeat too late. Jeremy was slow to realize his misstep, but then Pat demanded, "The *what?*" in a tone that promised a reckoning. Jeremy flicked a quick look from him to Jean, who was now standing ramrod straight as he stared at the TV. His lips were bloodless where he was shoving them hard into his teeth.

If it was just Pat around, Jeremy could probably convince him to back down, but by now at least half of the team had gathered to watch the game. The locker room was a sea of bewildered and baffled faces.

"I misheard you," Xavier said, looking from Jean to Jeremy. The lack of surprise on Jeremy's face did nothing to improve his mood, and Xavier swung a dark gaze back to Jean. For a few moments the only sound in the locker

381

room was the noise of the game now underway on the screen, and then Xavier asked, "You want to explain that to us?"

The look on Jean's face said he very much did not, but Jean didn't have it in him to refuse a vice-captain's direct questions. Cat took one look at him and swooped in with the best and worst distraction she could think of: "You think that's creepy, wait until you hear Kevin say it."

"*Catalina*." That horrified protest was from Jean.

"Nah," Derek started, but the rest was forgotten when the announcers started yelling.

Jeremy glanced back at the TV and saw Neil half-crumpled on the court floor. Lane swung at him with her racquet, and Neil managed to kick her leg out from under her just in time. She fell on him as she went down, jamming her racquet sideways across his throat with every intention of breaking his neck. Neil scrabbled at it with his gloved hands, but he couldn't seem to get an edge on her. Whatever blow first knocked him down had taken most of the fight out of him.

Referees pulled the doors open, but the Foxes were faster and closer—and so were the Ravens. Kevin was only two steps toward Neil when Dawson threw his racquet aside and jumped him. Kevin wasn't expecting the sudden weight and was dragged to his knees. He got some breathing room with a fierce elbow to Dawson's helmet, and somehow he managed to wriggle around so he was facing the Raven backliner.

It was a vicious fight, but Kevin had more at stake: his injury was healed, but the lingering fear of damaging his hand again was evident in how often he tilted his left side away from Dawson. Dawson had no such restrictions and was keen to press the advantage. He managed to slam the back of Kevin's head down against the court floor, and then Wilds barreled out of nowhere to throw him off to one side. Kevin didn't stick around to help her but scrambled to his feet and ran for Neil.

The referees reached Neil first, and it took two of them to haul Lane off him. Neil didn't try to get up but rolled weakly onto his side and tucked into an agonized ball. Jean put both hands flat to the TV screen, muttering in jagged French. Cat dragged him back some so she could see what was going on past him, but Jean didn't seem to notice.

The camera swung briefly to the Home court, where the Ravens' coaches were trying their level best to pry their angry strikers off of Boyd and Aaron Minyard. Andrew took longer to spot until Jeremy realized he was with Wymack. Jeremy didn't see his racquet anywhere; maybe it'd gotten lost in whatever scuffle left him so visibly unsteady on his feet. Wymack had a hand on his jersey, either to slow him down or hold him up, and Andrew was practically dragging him across the court toward Kevin and Neil. He held one arm tight to his side as he moved, and the limp way his hand dangled by his hip chilled Jeremy's blood.

The crowd and announcers had sunk to horrified silence as the line brawl escalated. Jeremy heard Lane's strident voice echoing off the walls but couldn't make out anything she said. Andrew caught up with her right as she broke free of the referees, and he didn't even hesitate. She was halfway to Neil when Andrew got her in a one-armed chokehold and dragged her to the ground.

Both players were immediately buried beneath Wymack and the referees. Jeremy jerked his numb stare back to Kevin, who was on his knees at Neil's side. The Foxes' team nurse was hunched over Neil as she checked on him, and the tension in her expression was not at all reassuring.

An unfamiliar man dressed head-to-toe in black crossed the court to crouch at Kevin's side, and Jean's reaction was immediate and visceral. He launched at the

TV again, slamming both hands against it to throw it into the wall behind it. This time Jeremy caught hold of him to yank him back, and the white fury on Jean's face set his heart tripping.

"Who is that?" Jeremy asked.

Jean didn't have to say anything; Rhemann recognized the other man on sight and spoke up from his spot on the outskirts: "The Ravens' head nurse, Josiah Smalls." Jeremy glanced his way in time to see the sidelong look Rhemann sent Jean. Rhemann said nothing else, and Jean didn't volunteer a better explanation.

Wilds and Dawson were still trying to fight each other despite the officials bodily separating them. Boyd caught up with them and somehow managed to pry Wilds loose. One referee followed close behind them, pointing toward the court door, but Boyd dragged his captain straight to Kevin and Neil. Abby Winfield was still trying and failing to get a satisfactory response from Neil. Aaron Minyard hovered nearby for a minute before prying his own helmet off and spitting blood off to one side. He gave Kevin's thigh a light kick before starting for the court door, and a few moments later Kevin got up and followed.

Security finally entered the court, sensing more bodies were needed to restore order. One by one the Foxes were forced off the court, until the only two left were Neil and Andrew. At last Wymack emerged from the dogpile with Andrew in a chokehold of his own, and he held fast until the referees hauled a limp Lane toward the Away court door. Smalls followed them at an unhurried pace, and only when the last Raven was gone did Wymack drop Andrew beside Neil. Jeremy realized too late the announcers were speaking. He wondered when they'd started; nothing they said had penetrated his hazy shock.

Maybe if he was listening, the abrupt jump to a replay wouldn't have startled him as much, but suddenly he was treated to every view of the brawl in quick succession. It had started with the Ravens' strikers just thirty seconds into the half. Both Winter and Williams charged the goal, one presumably to score from just outside the line and the other on hand for a rebound, but Winter didn't wait for his partner to take a shot. He swung his racquet like a baseball bat at Andrew's chest the moment Andrew turned away from him.

Jeremy assumed one of the backliners yelled a panicked warning, because somehow Andrew turned his stick just in time to eat the blow. The impact was still enough to throw him into his goal, and he teetered when he hit the wall. That he lost his balance probably saved his life—Williams took a swing at his head, but Andrew wasn't where he'd been a moment ago. The racquet glanced off Andrew's helmet and hit his shoulder hard enough to drive him to his knees. Andrew's twin and Boyd were on the strikers a heartbeat later, fists flying. The Ravens' dealer rushed in to help, but Boyd had no problems taking on a second body. Wilds took one step that way before turning and running for Kevin instead.

Neil was out near half-court still from serve, but he started for Andrew as soon as the fight started. A second of distraction was all Lane needed, and she aimed for his side with a vicious swing. He was faster than she was expecting, and she only managed to clip him. The force behind her blow was still enough to send him stumbling. He fell hard, one gloved hand on his side and the other trying in vain to keep his face from hitting the floor. Jeremy had seen the fight from there, but knowing how it started and how quickly it escalated made the whole thing worse. At his side, Jean had both hands clasped over his own ribcage in horror.

The cameras returned to a live feed after Wilds tackled Dawson to the floor. Someone had finally gotten Neil to his feet, and Andrew was somehow keeping him there. Winfield and Wymack bracketed the two as they finally

385

limped toward the door. A camera in the inner court had a better shot of their faces as they reached the door, and the tight look on Neil's face was all pain. Only the Foxes' freshmen were still at the bench; the rest of the Foxes were presumably in the locker room. Winfield would have her hands full trying to put them back together again on her own.

A three-man crew entered the court to clean up the blood. The distant echo of an amplified voice was the stadium's announcer, but Jeremy couldn't understand a word. A few moments later the cameras cut to Rossi on the sidelines where he was surrounded by security and referees. He wore the look of a man who knew his career was over. It didn't make Jeremy feel any better to know he'd had nothing to do with this, and he couldn't spare energy yet to pity him. Rossi had had all summer to realize the Ravens weren't ready.

"It's a good thing Josten's so short," Cody said, with an attempt at humor that fell flat. "If he was any taller, Lane's racquet would've caught him right in the kidneys. Looked to me like his armor caught most of her swing."

"Armor didn't save Jean," Lucas said. "It won't have saved Josten, not entirely."

Jeremy was lost until he remembered how adamantly Jean attributed his grievous injuries to a rough scrimmage. Cat and Laila were the only other two here who knew who'd really cracked Jean's ribs last spring. Jeremy imagined Riko taking a swing at Jean the way Jasmine Lane swung at Neil, and it pulled his chest so tight he thought he'd tear something.

"Getting word from tonight's officials," one of the sportscasters said, and the broadcast moved to where she and her colleague were sitting at a desk. She was scribbling notes as she wrote, but she used her free hand to track her progress down the page as she read aloud. "The game has been postponed, but no date and time has been determined yet. The following penalties have been assessed for tonight's misconduct. For the Foxes: yellow cards to backliners Matthew Boyd and Aaron Minyard. Red card to captain Danielle Wilds. Red card and a five-game suspension to goalkeeper Andrew Minyard. For the Ravens: red cards to the entire starting lineup."

She started down the list of Raven names, but Jeremy barely heard her over the new chaos in the locker room.

"A suspension?" Sebastian echoed. "You can't be serious."

"Excessive force," Shawn said, watching the TV with a morose look. "You can't choke someone out without repercussions."

"He could have broken her neck taking her down like that," Shane added. "He should have let the referees handle it and focused on his teammate."

"She started it!" Dillon said, flailing in disbelief. "Why wasn't she suspended? Why weren't the ones that went after Minyard? Why only him?"

"When have the Ravens ever been held accountable?" Laila asked.

"Have faith," Rhemann said, with steadying calm. "Tonight's officials will likely escalate the matter to the ERC, and Coach Moriyama is no longer in their ranks to protect his team." He glanced at Jean at that, but Jean didn't seem to hear him over the TV. Rhemann didn't press the matter but checked the time on his watch and looked to Jeremy. "We're a bit early to head in, but standing around here speculating isn't going to solve anything. Take them on some laps. Slow and easy; it's been a long day."

Jeremy opened his mouth to protest and thought better of it. "Yes, Coach."

"Moreau, stay a moment," Rhemann said as Jeremy motioned for the Trojans to follow him to the changing room.

The TV was showing replays again as Jeremy turned away. It didn't matter how many laps he ran with his team; every time he blinked, he saw Neil broken and still on the court floor.

CHAPTER TWENTY
Jeremy

The Utes were a raucous team that hadn't been a real threat in years, which provided a rare and golden opportunity for the Trojans' third line. That lineup was predominantly sophomores who'd been benched all last year, with a few upperclassmen mixed in to provide support as needed. Jeremy was excited to see what they could do—or he had been, until the Ravens' horrific violence ruined his mood.

Normally Nabil would be promoted to starting lineup for such a match, but with Ramadan underway he would be fasting until October. He could still practice and play, but he felt more comfortable and effective as backup. Ananya would start, and Nabil would come in for Timothy as needed in second half. Jeremy was off the lineup entirely, as was Jean. Jeremy wasn't sure if it was a blessing or a curse: he wasn't sure he could give a game his full attention, but he had nothing solid to distract him from the Foxes.

On the Trojans' third lap, the Utes' captain Micky Telsey and vice-captain Bruno Winslow were waiting at the Home bench. Jeremy assumed the Utes' assistants flagged them down, so he and Xavier peeled off to pay their respects.

Telsey skipped a greeting to say, "You saw the Ravens' match?"

"Yeah," Jeremy said, trading easy handshakes with the two. "Hoping we get some updates before the match starts."

"It doesn't make sense," Telsey said. "People were rooting for them, you know? Don't get me wrong, it was

389

super satisfying to watch them get humbled last spring, but their crash and burn this summer's been kind of scary. I really thought they were going to get it together before the season started."

"How could they?" Winslow asked. "People have been making a spectacle of their tragedies this summer. This whole thing is on the Foxes," he added. When Xavier frowned at him, he insisted, "You saw their interviews same as I did, I bet. They were looking for a fight; they can't cry the victim when one found them."

"Talk shit, get hit," Telsey agreed.

"The Foxes' antagonism is understandable," Xavier said. "The Ravens started this fight when Kevin transferred. Their fans did, anyway, and Edgar Allan only once called them to order. Arson?" he asked when the Utes looked unimpressed. He counted it off on his fingers. "Defacing Palmetto's campus and stadium? Police raids? Remind me how many cars got destroyed at the athletes' dorm last spring."

Telsey waved him off. "The Ravens aren't liable for what their fans do. Put the blame on the Ravens' administration and their crazy followers, not on them. It's not their fault their talent and popularity put them front and center of all this madness. I don't blame you when USC and UCLA tear each other's campuses up over your football rivalries, do I?"

That accusation was leveled at Jeremy, who weighed his options as carefully as he could. "Being a victim doesn't automatically absolve someone of their wrongdoings," he said at last. "I can regret what they're going through now, but I am not required to forgive them for what they've done to people I care about. I genuinely hope they get the help they need, and I hope it happens as far from the court as possible. Josten was right: none of them are ready to be back yet. It isn't fair to them or anyone they're up against."

"That's bold," Telsey said, and added an unkind, "and self-serving, since they've always stood between you and the crown. It's in your best interests if they're taken out of the running."

"All due respect, we've always been less concerned with who we play than how we play," Jeremy said. Telsey didn't look convinced, but it was such a secondary argument Jeremy saw no need to push it. Instead he asked, "Split the court for drills?" The Utes only numbered eighteen, which meant it'd be crowded but doable to have both teams out at once. "If someone can come by and unlock the door on our side, we'll take the Away court."

Winslow motioned to Jeremy. "True story Reacher tried to kill Moreau last week? I saw the pictures." He mimed choking himself one-handed and searched Jeremy's expression for the truth. "Long way to go to kill a guy who's supposedly so innocent, don't you think?"

"Thank you for your concern," Jeremy said.

When it was obvious they were getting nothing else, Telsey sighed and gestured. "Yeah, we'll have someone get the door for you. See you for the coin toss."

Xavier waited until they were half the court away from the Utes before saying, "I think I hate him."

It was unexpected enough Jeremy almost tripped over his own feet. "Telsey?"

"Coach Moriyama," Xavier said. The hard tug at the corner of his mouth said he was fighting a scowl. The stadium was empty this far out from serve, but after three years with the Trojans Xavier was used to schooling his expression in public. "He shouldn't have up and disappeared like that. The intrigue behind that abrupt exit makes it impossible for anyone to let him go and move on. The Ravens are still his darling proteges, the wounded ideal everyone should aspire to. No one can think critically about them; everyone's keeping a light on for a man who's not coming home.

391

"But speaking of the Ravens." Xavier caught hold of Jeremy's arm and dragged him to a stop. "Who the hell is 'the master', Jeremy? Someone with rank, someone with the final say on who could or couldn't captain that team, I know, but tell me I'm not connecting the dots right." Xavier searched Jeremy's face for answers, but Jeremy's grim expression did nothing to reassure him. Xavier let go of him like he'd been burned. "You aren't serious."

"The more I learn about Edgar Allan, the more creeped out I get," Jeremy admitted.

"You think?" Xavier rubbed away a sudden chill and stared up at the stands. He tended his angry thoughts in silence for a minute, then jabbed a finger into Jeremy's chest and said, "Jean's got no real filter when he's pressed. Make him say that on TV. It'll get a conversation going, I guarantee it."

"No," Jeremy said, and insisted, "No," when Xavier only frowned at him. Jeremy grasped for something to say to deter him, but the best he could offer was the truth: "Xavier, he's scared of Edgar Allan." It wiped that annoyed look off Xavier's face immediately, and Jeremy pressed his advantage with, "He doesn't want to challenge them. I don't have to like it, and I won't stop encouraging him to stand his ground, but I'm not going to force him into a confrontation he's not ready to have. He's learning how to trust us. I can't betray him."

Xavier grimaced but didn't argue, and they set off toward the Away benches once more. They were nearly to the locker room when Xavier said, "If Coach Moriyama was up to some shady nonsense there, Edgar Allan was covering for him. Walker practically said it, didn't she?" He frowned as he thought, then said, "Palmetto State promised President Andritch discretion."

"Clever, wasn't it?" Jeremy asked. "She confirmed Jean's injuries were worse than reported and that Edgar Allan's board knew about it without outright accusing

392

anyone of anything."

"The Foxes are sharper than they let on," Xavier agreed. Mention of the Foxes had them picking up the pace. Xavier got the door for them and said, "Maybe Coach will have heard something by now?"

But Rhemann shook his head as soon as Jeremy made eye contact, so Jeremy had no choice but to put the team from mind. His Trojans needed him present and focused. If he couldn't be an anchor for them, what good was he? He put everything he had into warmups and drills, and Xavier and Cody were quick to follow his lead. The three did their level best to keep the Trojans occupied and distracted until first serve. Only when the crowd was chanting a final countdown did Jeremy let his attention fracture again, and he looked for Rhemann.

Rhemann had spent most of the last hour on his phone, fielding calls and texts from colleagues who'd seen the Ravens' ambush and wanted to hash it out. Surely somewhere in there was a real update from Palmetto State. Jeremy glanced toward Jean, who was sitting blank-faced and silent on the Away bench like he didn't know a game was happening in front of him. He dug around for something reassuring to say and came back emptyhanded; Jean wasn't the type to take comfort in hollow promises.

A worthy distraction came when Rhemann made his first set of subs: Lucas, Min, and Ananya went in for Ashton, Sebastian, and Jesus. Jeremy went to them as they filed off the court. They looked tired and stressed, uncertain how to feel about their performance, but Jeremy was happy to praise the parts they'd done well. Most of the rest would sort itself out, as their weakest spots were due to inexperience and age. He was proud of them, and watching their giddiness return in the wake of his easy compliments and encouragement helped chase the lingering grief from his thoughts.

Thirty minutes into first half, Rhemann got a call

serious enough he collected his coaches to his side afterward. The four stepped out of earshot of the bench to talk. From here Jeremy could only see Lisinski's face, and the look that crossed it pulled his stomach into a tight knot. Jimenez's hands moved in emphatic, angry gestures as he made his opinion known. Rhemann shook his head through most of it, but even from here Jeremy could see the tense set to his shoulders. Finally he dismissed his colleagues, but White and Lisinski moved together toward the court wall. Jimenez remained, but his heavy stare settled on the back of Jean's head.

Rhemann called for him, and Jean went to them immediately. Whatever Rhemann said to him, it landed like a physical blow: Jean lurched back from him, one gloved hand locked on the front of his own jersey. Rhemann tipped his head toward Jimenez, who motioned for Jean to follow, and the two men started for the locker room. Rhemann watched them go, expression serious, and noticed Jeremy watching him only after they'd disappeared. He finally joined his team at the benches, but all he had to say was,

"We don't have news from Palmetto State yet," Rhemann said. "Let's focus up."

It was and wasn't reassuring; if it wasn't the Foxes' injuries that drove Jean from sight, this development had to do with the Ravens. That was worrisome, but not as personal, so Jeremy forced his attention back to the game. At last the buzzer sounded to release both teams to the locker room. White and Lisinski ran interference for the reporters who approached for a halftime interview, urging them to keep their distance from the team. That was unusual enough that Jeremy picked up the pace, and he managed to pass half a dozen teammates in his hurry to reach the locker room.

Jean was nowhere to be seen, but Rhemann's lingering look warned Jeremy not to hunt him down. Tony and

394

Bobby were quick to pass out drinks while the Trojans stretched. Rhemann waited until they'd stepped aside before moving toward the center of the room.

"We have a lot we need to cover, and only so much time," he said, checking his watch. "This is not where I would prefer to start, but I don't want it to be the last thing you hear before we return to the court for second half."

He swept the room with a look as his Trojans went still to hear him better. "The ERC reviewed the match between Palmetto State and Edgar Allan. After speaking to all involved parties, they've made a ruling: Coach Rossi is stepping down effective immediately, and the Ravens have been suspended for the remainder of the season."

The silence that followed was deafening, and then Jeremy managed a startled, "What?"

Rhemann held his stare and said again, "They're disqualified."

The locker room erupted in pandemonium. Suddenly everyone was shouting, but Jeremy couldn't understand anything anyone was saying. He could only stare at Rhemann in disbelief until Laila caught hold of him. She shook him until he looked at her, and the chaos came into too-sharp focus. Across the room Derek pumped his fists in triumph and yelled, "No Ravens in finals! Let's fucking go!"

The younger Trojans teetered between nervous excitement and alarm, but the upperclassmen had a hungry look in their eyes. They'd spent four and five years coming up short at the finish line, but how could they possibly lose now? While Jeremy would've preferred to defeat Edgar Allan fair and square, he'd take victory in any form. He wanted to win so badly he felt ill.

Cat plastered herself against his side. "It's down to us and Penn State. *Maybe* the—" Here she faltered as reality set in, and she motioned to Rhemann. "Any news from the Foxes?"

"No official statements have been made," he said, and that was sobering enough to quiet his team down at last.

It wasn't an outright no. Jeremy wondered if that meant he'd heard something from Wymack off the record. He honestly wasn't sure how often the two coaches spoke, since the Foxes and Trojans had only crossed paths the first time last year. He knew Rhemann had great respect for Wymack and the way he'd crafted his unorthodox team, and Rhemann had never hesitated to throw his weight behind Palmetto State when the ERC seemed poised to strike the small team down, but they had an entire continent between them. It was still possible, he supposed; such setbacks hadn't stopped him and Kevin from forming an unlikely friendship.

"All right," Rhemann said. "Now that we're all on the same page, let's trust Coach Wymack to handle his team and the ERC to do what they can for Edgar Allan. We've still got half of a match left to get through, so let's get our heads back in the game."

They had about twelve minutes left of break, enough time to acknowledge the solid efforts of the starting lineup and prep the second-half crew with tips and insights. Jean slipped into the room with only a few minutes left and immediately took up a spot at Jeremy's side. There was still more tension in him than Jeremy wanted to see, but Jeremy couldn't blame him for being uptight. Jeremy wanted to ask how he was holding up and if he'd spoken to Renee or Neil, but he didn't want to distract his teammates this close to serve.

He managed to bite his tongue until the half was underway, and then he asked, "Have you heard from the Foxes?"

"I called Renee," Jean admitted. His eyes tracked the ball as it was thrown this way and that, but Jeremy could tell in a glance he wasn't paying attention to the match. Jean's thoughts were with Renee still and whatever news she'd had to share. Jeremy wondered if Jean would make him ask, but then Jean dug his fingers into his side as hard as he could. Jeremy knew what he was going to say before Jean said it: "Jasmine fractured two of Neil's ribs. The angle of her blow and his padding saved the rest."

It was what he'd feared, and Jeremy couldn't stop a quiet, "Jesus." That took Neil off the lineup for the rest of fall semester; he'd be lucky if he made it back in time for the last one or two matches before winter break. It was a minor blessing that the Foxes had recruited more strikers, but they were both unseasoned freshmen. If either was half as clever or talented as Neil, the Foxes still had a fighting chance, but it was a miserable way to start the season.

Better than a fatal overdose, Jeremy thought, and asked, "Kevin?"

"Bruised and angry," Jean said.

There were still too many shadows on his face. Jeremy mentally went down the lineup and asked, "Andrew?"

Jean's hand slid up to his shoulder, finding the spot where Williams' racquet made contact. "Fractured clavicle. Winfield hasn't determined yet if it needs surgery; she is seeking a second opinion." Jean's mouth pulled tight in displeasure. "Renee will tell me as soon as a decision is made."

That Jean seemed equally invested in Andrew's recovery as he was Neil's was unexpected, but Jeremy couldn't be heartened by it right now. He couldn't think of any teammates over the years who'd broken their collarbones, but he imagined it would sideline Andrew for at least a few months. Renee was reliable enough, and they had a freshman to fall back on if she needed relief, but the Ravens had put the Foxes on a hard back foot. Jeremy wasn't sure they could pull off two miracle years in a row.

"He's lucky," Jeremy said, turning an unseeing gaze

397

toward the court. "It looked like Williams was aiming for his head."

"He was," Jean said without hesitation. "Ravens understand that missteps and mistakes must be punished. Andrew broke Riko's arm at finals, setting in motion the events that led to his death. Brayden and Cameron wanted to even the scales." He tipped his hand this way and that before leveling it out. "A life for a life."

"Cam's an asshole," Cody said, moving up on Jean's other side.

"Yes," Jean agreed.

"Say the word and I'll fight him over Christmas break," Cody said. "I wasn't going to go home for it, but I'll make an exception."

Jean waved that off. "I hate him more than he hates me." At the look Cody sent him, Jean shrugged and said, "He was irrationally rude to Thea at every opportunity."

"What'd he have against Muldani?" Jeremy asked.

"She's black," Cody said. When Jean muttered a correction, they gestured and said, "Yeah, but you can't see any of her father in her." Cody counted years on their fingers and said, "Oh, I guess you would've overlapped with her for a year. Have we finally discovered a Raven you got along with?"

"Kevin," Jean said.

"I'm hoping there were more than two," Jeremy admitted.

"Finn," Jean said, as the buzzer sounded on a Trojan goal. Jeremy thumped on the wall in approval and encouragement, but his focus was on Jean as he added, "Sergio, most of the time. Brayden. Colleen. Zane."

The last was so quiet Jeremy almost missed it. At the sharp look Jeremy sent him, Jean dug his hand into his own chest. For a moment the grief on his face was endless, but Jean schooled it a heartbeat later. That Jean could scrounge up so much emotion for a man who'd practically left fingerprints on his throat was unbearable. How Jean's kind heart had survived a place like Evermore, Jeremy wasn't sure. It was bruised and bleeding, but it wasn't broken. Jeremy wasn't sure if that ache in his chest was pride or grief. Whatever it was, it was hard to breathe around.

Perhaps Cody felt the same, because they seemed content to let the conversation die there. The three turned their attention back to the match at last, though only Cody and Jeremy reacted to the Trojans' solid plays and scoring attempts.

The relief Jeremy felt at the final bell was intense enough to be shameful; he'd followed the game on a surface level when his team deserved his undivided attention. He'd have to rewatch this match over the weekend so he could give proper feedback next week. For now it was enough that they'd won seven to six, and he let himself be buoyed by his teammates' excitement as they washed up and changed out for the ride home.

As soon as he was on the bus, he fired off a string of text messages to Kevin. At his side Jean messaged Renee again, but they put Provo behind them without an update. A few miles later Laila's phone started ringing. She rummaged through every pocket on her backpack twice before Cat pushed her headphones up and said, "Back pocket, babe." By then Laila had missed the call, but as she leaned into Cat to dig her phone free, it started up again.

"I'm here," she said in greeting. "No, we're on our way back from Salt Lake City. I'm not sure, we just left campus maybe an hour ago. What's all that noise?" She briefly tipped her phone away from her ear with a wince and asked, "Can't you move somewhere quieter? It's so loud. Yes, yes, I'm looking," she said, leaning past Cat to stare out the window. "Give me a moment, I don't see any signs."

Jeremy reached across the aisle to nudge her and said, "Just south of Provo."

"Jeremy says we've passed Provo," Laila said, with a quick nod to him. "I didn't look at the route, but yes, I assume we're on I-15. Wait, I can barely hear you," she said, pressing one hand flat over her ear. At her side Cat peeled her headphones off entirely to stare at her, worried. Laila hunched forward in her seat like that could somehow help her hear better. "Tell me what's going on. Why does it matter where I am?"

She was quiet for about thirty seconds, and then she silenced the entire bus with a shrill, "What do you mean, *it's on fire*? No! What do you mean? But—" She went quiet and still to listen. With the rest of the Trojans deadly silent, Jeremy finally heard the tinny and distant sound of sirens. Jeremy glanced up as Rhemann appeared in the aisle just in front of their seats, expression grave, but he was quick to return his full attention to Laila. "How bad is it? No, tell me now. I want—" She cut herself off again to listen.

She was quiet so long Jeremy feared she'd gone into shock, but at last she offered a hoarse, "I'll call you back," and hung up.

She sat silent for another twenty seconds, still leaning forward over her knees with her forehead pressed to the seatback in front of her. Jeremy was dimly aware of the floozies hovering in the aisle and Cat's hands resting oh-so-gently on Laila's shoulders; he couldn't look away from Laila's downturned face or the curls that hid her expression to look at any of them.

Laila barely got a hand up in time to smother a sob. Cat grabbed her in a fierce embrace, cradling Laila's head to her shoulder. "Babe," she tried. "Laila, what's going on?"

Laila didn't answer, but Jeremy didn't expect her to. Laila hated losing control with an audience, preferring to lick her wounds in private. Jeremy had known her for three years before she finally trusted him with her hurts; showing Cat her vulnerability was still an ongoing struggle despite how much Laila loved her. He didn't know if Cat could reach her now, so he had to try.

Jeremy crouched in the aisle so he could reach her easier. She had a death grip on her phone still, so he caught hold of her knee and gave it a careful squeeze. "Hey," he said, keeping his tone as even as he could. "Laila, tell me what happened."

Her hand was trembling when she let go of her face. She caught hold of Cat's arm in a white-knuckled grip but turned her too-wet gaze on Jeremy. He watched her jaw work, watched her swallow her grief and horror with obvious effort. Her voice was still a touch too frail when she said, "They've burned the house down. *Our* house."

He heard the words, but he couldn't digest them. All he could do was stare blankly at her and wait for something that made sense. Laila's expression fractured, but she maintained desperate control as she looked up at Rhemann. "Coach, please leave me in Cedar City. My uncle says there's a regional airport there. He'll send his jet to collect me if you're willing, and he'll fax your office any paperwork you need to relinquish me from your care."

"Wait one," Rhemann said, and went up front to confer with the drivers.

Cat finally found her voice. "Burned it down," she echoed, in a tone Jeremy had never heard from her before. "You aren't serious. The house? What do you mean they burned the house down? Babe. Laila."

Laila briefly pressed her knuckles to her chin, fighting for a calm she could barely find. "Security has footage of three men throwing something through the living room window seconds before the alarms went off. I don't—" Laila sucked in a slow breath and tried again. "The firefighters are still working, so Gary can't go in, but he

401

says it's going to be a total loss. It's been burning too long."

Rhemann returned to say, "We can detour at Cedar City, but we're still about three hours out. I'm not sure how many seats you'll have available, but I assume all of you will be getting off." He glanced at Cat, then looked over Jeremy's head at Jean. "Do you need or want one of us to go with you?" He gestured toward himself to indicate the coaches.

"Gary will pick us up at the airport in LA," Laila said as she called her uncle back. "We don't need you."

It was a rude way to refuse, but considering the circumstances Rhemann didn't take offense at her poor wording. He waited in silence while Laila hashed out the details. Flight time to Cedar City was about as long as the drive south from their current location, so Laila could get off the bus and onto the plane almost immediately. It would get her to Los Angeles at least three hours ahead of the Trojans: way too late to save her home, but significantly better than sitting helpless on a bus with so many witnesses to fret over her. Her uncle's jet could fit six, and the glance Laila flicked Jeremy said she expected him on it with her.

"Thank you, Coach," Laila said when she hung up at last.

"Let me know if we can help," Rhemann said, and retreated to give her space.

Cat was still staring at Laila like she didn't know her, and her quiet, "All of it?" broke Jeremy's heart. "It's all gone?"

Laila dragged Cat into a short, fierce hug, then motioned for Jeremy to give her space. "I'll get us some answers, one way or another," she said, getting up when Jeremy returned to his seat. She moved toward the front of the bus, phone at her ear. It felt an eternity before her call connected, and Jeremy knew she'd called her mother when her strident demands came out in Arabic. Cat stared after the stiff line of her back, looking forlorn, but Cody leaned over the seatback to wrap their arms around Cat's shoulders.

Jeremy turned an anxious look on Jean, guilt stricken over how delayed his sympathy was. "I'm so sorry," he said. Jean had come to Los Angeles with a single carryon and two shirts to his name. It'd taken him months to finally fill in the space Cat and Laila gave him, and he'd only recently started adding quiet personal touches to his areas. Jeremy thought of his postcard from Kevin, the wristband from July's fireworks, and the sand dollar he'd picked up along the way. It made him ill, and his voice caught on his pained, "Jean, I—"

"The ERC announced it," Jean said, voice dull and stare distant. He clarified a moment later with, "Their decision to eliminate the Ravens. I saw the segment during break." Before he rejoined the team, Jeremy guessed, but he wasn't sure where Jean was going with this. Jean didn't make him ask but said, "This is my fault."

"Don't say that." Jeremy caught Jean's wrist when Jean didn't look at him and insisted, "You had nothing to do with this."

"Feigning ignorance serves no one," Jean said, with a sharp bite to his words. "When the Ravens are insulted, their devotees lash out on their behalf. You saw it last year with Neil and the Foxes, and the year before when Kevin left. Do not pretend you do not know what is happening here. The Ravens have been ruined, and someone must take the blame. I will always—" Jean couldn't finish it. His teeth clicked as he clenched his jaw tight.

Xavier had listed examples of Raven riots for Telsey just a few hours ago. *Arson on campus*, he'd said, and Jeremy was cold all over. He wouldn't deny that Laila's house was deliberately targeted, but he refused to let Jean suffocate under that weight. He tightened his grip and

403

said, "Look at me. Look at me, Jean, because I need to know you're listening." He waited until Jean met his gaze before saying, "If this was retaliatory, that's still on the people who chose to cross the line. It is not your fault. It never will be."

"You don't believe that."

"Maybe they did it to hurt you," Jeremy allowed, "but that doesn't mean you're responsible. You had nothing to do with the ERC's ruling. You're a victim as much as Cat and Laila are, so don't take on a burden that isn't yours. It won't help any of you. Do you understand?"

"Sometimes Jeremy is smarter than he looks," Xavier said where he was leaning against their seatback. "Listen to him, Jean, and don't go down that road."

"It's an unhelpful spiral," Min added. "They adore you and so will gladly reassure you of your innocence until you believe them, but your unasked-for guilt is a distraction from their loss and grief. They don't deserve that extra stress right now."

Xavier nodded. "The best thing you can do right now is accept that some people are assholes and that it is outside of your control. Mourn what you've lost without carrying more than you should."

Framing it as a shared burden on Cat and Laila was probably the most effective part of their argument. A frown tugged at the corner of Jean's mouth as he thought it through, but it never fully formed, and at last Jean glanced past Jeremy at Cat. Cody had moved into Laila's open seat, but Cat was on her phone now as she spoke in an agitated blend of Spanish and English. Laila had gone quiet a few rows up, but she was sending out quick texts as she paced back and forth in the aisle. The back of the bus was still eerily quiet. No one knew what to say, and they all knew better than to crowd Laila's space when she was in a mood.

Jeremy did a quick mental tally of what few things of

his might have gotten lost. His backpack was in his car at the stadium, so he at least didn't have to replace his textbooks for the semester. His LSAT books were a happy loss, and he'd only had a dozen-odd outfits tucked away in Jean's closet.

He was going room by room when Jean said, "I am sorry about your dog."

A bit of cardboard was a silly thing to grieve when these three had lost everything, but the reminder put a sharp twist in his chest. Barkbark was one of Cat's first gifts to him, an attempt to get closer when she realized his and Laila's friendship was a package deal. Jeremy knew he wasn't a real dog, but… Jeremy rubbed at the ache and said, "Are you? I thought you hated him." He meant it to come out a lighthearted tease, but it fell a little flat. The sideways look Jean sent him said he heard it.

"You didn't," Jean said, like that was all that mattered.

Laila finally returned. Cody dragged Laila into a short, fierce hug before stepping out of her way. Jeremy wasn't surprised Laila didn't return it, and the look on Cody's face said they knew better than to take it personally. They moved wordlessly back to their own row, and Laila settled beside Cat once more. Cat hurriedly ended her call and turned in her seat to face Laila. The headlights splashing through the window had her damp cheeks glistening, but her voice was remarkably steady when she said, "Anything?"

"Get some sleep if you can," Laila said, gently pulling Cat toward her and offering herself as a pillow. "It's going to be a very long night."

Jeremy would be surprised if anyone up front managed to rest. The hours to Cedar City were as miserable as they were endless, but finally the driver took the last turn for the airport. Laila tugged at Jeremy's sleeve in a silent demand for him to come along as she carried her bag to the front of the bus. Cat was close behind her, so Jeremy urged Jean ahead of him before following. They were quick to disembark, but he hung back for a moment to face his coaches.

"Thank you," he said. "I'll let you know when we're on board and when we've touched down in LA."

"Be careful," Rhemann said. "Take care of each other."

The bus pulled away as soon as Jeremy was clear of it, and Jeremy jogged to meet his friends at the door. Twenty minutes later they were taxiing down the runway in plush seats that faced each other. Laila waited until they'd reached altitude before pulling a notebook from her bag. She flipped to the back where she knew she'd find enough blank pages to work with, and she stared down at it with a morose look on her face.

"Gary said we'll need a list for our insurance claim," she said.

They only got halfway through the living room's contents before Cat finally started crying in earnest, and Laila pushed everything aside in favor of holding onto her. Jeremy quietly tried to take over, but the more he wrote the heavier his heart grew. It felt impossible that that homey space was gone, with its mismatched lamps and tables, the handstitched quilts from Cat's grandmother, and the games they'd laughed around so many nights.

Jeremy finally had to turn the notebook over so he couldn't see the list, and he stared out the window in silence for the remainder of the flight.

CHAPTER TWENTY-ONE
Jean

They didn't make it to Santa Monica Airport until four in the morning. It was too dark out still to get a proper look at the house, but Laila's uncle Gary Dermott knew they needed to see it before they could rest. He picked them up at the airport and took them straight to what was left of their home. There was a bag of flashlights in the backseat with them, so Laila passed them out as Gary put the car in park.

Jean noted first the security team parked outside to deter looting, then the jagged wrongness of the gutted house. The front wall was half-collapsed, and the roof above it had burned away in several spots. The hood of Laila's car was ruined, as were the motorcycles that were always parked between her car and the front of the house. Cat stood over the blackened bikes even as Laila followed Gary through the yawning doorway. Jeremy hesitated, not sure which girl to follow, so Jean motioned him after Laila.

"Guess you have to buy a new bike now," Cat said when Jean moved up alongside her.

Jean knew she was going for lighthearted, but her tone was defeated and empty. Jean weighed every possible response: reassurances that sounded clumsy even to him, guilt he wouldn't voice but couldn't relinquish, and the simplest path of agreeing with her declaration. In the end he went with the least familiar, reaching for her like she'd reached for him time and time again this summer. It was easier than he'd thought it would be to fold his arms around her, and Cat came without resistance. She clung to him, fingers digging in like she could drag some strength

407

out of him. Jean propped his chin on her head and waited for her grip to finally go slack.

"We should head in," she said, so Jean let her step away from him. She took his hand as she started for the door, locking their fingers, and led him inside.

Jean regretted the decision immediately. It looked terrible, and Jean knew it would only look worse in daylight. Each room they visited was a charred mess, their furniture and possessions warped. He and Cat found Laila and Jeremy in the girls' room, with Laila rummaging through a small safe.

"Good?" Cat asked.

"They're all right," Laila said, slamming the door shut again.

Cat surveyed their ruined bedroom with a miserable look. "Jesus, Laila."

Jean let a slow gaze drift over the walls. A few frames still hung, but the pictures inside were gone, and the corkboard where they'd exclusively hung pictures of the two of them on dates was gone entirely. He left them to take it in and moved to the study. The desks had survived only in that they were recognizable as desks. Laila's was in the best shape, but Cat's and Jean's had each lost at least one leg. His blackened laptop was cool to the touch. Jean opened it already knowing what he would see, then set it aside with a quiet sigh.

The desk drawers were full of ash and scattered bits of paper. Kevin's gifts, first ruined beyond recognition by the Ravens themselves, were now truly gone. His gaze went unbidden to where Kevin's newest postcard should be hanging on the wall. Only the thumbtack remained. There was nothing left of Renee's picture, and only ash where his sand dollar and wristband ought to be. For a moment his anger wanted to eat him alive, but the sudden trill of his phone jarred him from his thoughts.

Jean stared down at the caller ID for three rings before

finally answering. "Yes, Coach."

There was a pause, as if Wymack hadn't expected him to answer. "I just saw the news. Are you all right?"

"I am not one of your Foxes," Jean reminded him as he started down the hall. "You do not need to feign concern."

"You sound all right," was the dry response.

Jean said nothing until he reached his bedroom. The destruction awaiting him gave him pause, and he gazed at his ruined closet as he said, "We weren't home. We had a game against Utah last night." He meant to leave it at that, except Wymack's welfare check gnawed at him. Laila's car was parked in the driveway out front, as were the motorcycles. "Did they know we were gone? Did they even care?"

"I don't know," Wymack said, but his grim tone wasn't comforting.

Had the arsonists slowed to check, or was sending a message more important? What if it'd been a home game, and they'd all been asleep when it happened? Laila and Cat's bedroom wasn't far off from the living room where the fire started. This spring Jean had asked Wymack how much it would hurt to be burned alive; now he imagined the fire catching up to his friends and it almost took him to his knees. He knotted his free hand in his shirt, fighting to calm his roiling stomach, and turned away from the closet.

"How can I protect them?" he asked. "The Ravens won't listen to me. They never have. They will only listen to their own."

"We will think of something."

Jean turned his back on the charred beds and saw light bobbing in the hallway. A few moments later his friends stepped into the doorway to survey the room, so Jean said, "I have to go, Coach." He waited for an easy affirmative before hanging up, and Cat tipped her flashlight past Jeremy to light up his chest. Jean put his phone away as he

409

moved to meet his friends and said, "We are on the news. Coach Wymack saw it."

"Oh, I didn't know you were keeping in touch with him," Cat said.

"I am not," Jean said. It was and wasn't true, but the details didn't matter.

Laila looked past Jean at the ruined room. "Gary's willing to take us home with him so we can get some sleep, but I don't want to go so far from campus. I'm thinking we'll stay at the Radisson where we put Kevin and Andrew last month. He can drop us off, and it's an easy trip back here when the sun's up. Thoughts?" She looked from face to face as they nodded. "Then let's get out of here for now. I can't keep breathing this in."

Gary accepted their decision without protest. He checked in with his security team one last time while the Trojans climbed into his car, and he had them over to the hotel just a few minutes later. Check-in was easy enough, and they ended up a floor apart: a king bed for Cat and Laila, and two double beds for Jean and Jeremy. Cat and Laila took the elevator to the fourth floor while Jean and Jeremy walked to the third, and Jeremy let Jean precede him into the room.

"She's probably setting alarms for seven or eight," Jeremy said, with a glance toward the clock on the shared nightstand.

He tapped away at his phone, presumably double checking, and Jean left him to it in favor of getting out of his shoes. They had nothing to change into but the clothes they'd worn on the ride north, as they hadn't planned on needing something to sleep in. Jean was tempted to simply sleep in what he was wearing, but denim made for uncomfortable rest. He stripped down to his underwear and peeled back his blanket.

"Seven," Jeremy said, with a weariness Jean felt in his bones.

Jeremy fiddled with the alarm clock before setting backup alarms on his phone, then kicked out of his shorts and tossed his shirt after it. He was asleep almost as soon as his head hit the pillow, and Jean studied his slack face for only a moment before rolling over.

He was almost asleep when his phone beeped on a message from Renee: "Coach just told us about the fire. Are you okay?"

"Yes. Are you?"

She returned the same easy lie: "Yes."

Jean turned his phone off, stuffed it under his pillow, and willed himself to get what little rest he could.

-

Most of the morning and early afternoon was a series of miserable conversations. First was a call to Jean's psychiatrist, who accepted and rescheduled his appointment to the following morning. Jean had that handled before they left the hotel, and the Trojans went home via Exposition Park so Jeremy could collect his car. They were nearly to the Gold Court when Jeremy finally heard from Kevin, but their worried exchange was almost immediately interrupted by Jeremy's family. Jeremy passed his car keys to Laila so he could deal with the call.

"Hi, Mom," Jeremy said as he climbed into the passenger seat. Jean wasn't sure what she said, but Jeremy's expression shuttered almost immediately. "Yes, I should have called, we just—" He paused to listen before offering up a tired, "I'm sorry. I wasn't trying to embarrass you. We've just been dealing with this since we left Utah. Yes, Utah, the state. We had a game last night."

Jean glanced across the backseat at Cat. Cat didn't need him to ask but curled her lip in scorn and said, "He's only been playing for fourteen years, you can't expect his own mother to know how an Exy season works." Jeremy grimaced at her over his shoulder as he pushed his door open again, but Cat didn't wait for him to get out. She

411

raised her voice and called, "We won, Mrs. Wilshire! It was a great game!"

Jeremy slammed the door behind him and walked away. Laila flicked Cat an irritated look before getting out as well, and Cat subsided with a fierce scowl. Laila waited by the hood of the car for a few moments as Jeremy paced, then sighed so heavily Jean saw her shoulders sag. She moved toward him, snagging his sleeve to haul him to a stop, and gestured between them. From this angle Jean couldn't see her expression, but the tight look that crossed Jeremy's face wasn't promising. Laila was insistent, and finally Jeremy relinquished his phone to her. Laila took over the conversation with Jeremy's mother.

Jean glanced over his shoulder at Cat and said, "A Dermott is better than a Wilshire. Yes?" At the blank look she sent him, he clarified, "Rank. She implied as much when Bryson visited. She said the police would never side with him over her. But his grandfather is a senator. Who is hers?"

"It's not her grandfather," Cat said, "and technically, it's not even her father. He's an FSO—a foreign service officer," she explained when Jean shook his head. "If you square 'em up against each other on their own, then yeah, dear ol' granddad Wilshire is going to win every time, but Laila's dad has much better friends. One in every alphabet," she said, ticking them off on her fingers, "CIA, NSA, DHS…"

She glanced over to make sure Jean was following. "Pretty sure he's the only reason Jeremy's allowed to stay with us over summer breaks. Better to be friends with Hugh Dermott than enemies, and all that. Here we go." She sat back in her seat, and Jean followed her gaze to see Laila dragging Jeremy back to the car. Laila didn't get in until Jeremy was settled, and she turned them toward the ruins of her house without a word.

A no-nonsense representative from the insurance

company stopped by the house only minutes after their arrival to take pictures and statements. Laila turned over the list of items they'd lost in the fire, and he added it to their growing file. They walked the length of the house with him, and from him Jean heard more details of the video.

The arsonists had all been wearing dark hoodies, with the strings pulled tight to hide as much of their faces as possible. They didn't slow to ring the doorbell but went straight for the bay window: first to put a rock through it, then to throw in spare gas cans they'd brought. The third had apparently lit a sopping USC t-shirt on fire before tossing it in to get the blaze going, and they'd taken off as quickly as they'd come. The man flipped back and forth through his notes before finishing with,

"Security company called the fire department as soon as the alarms went off. You're lucky Station 15 is so close; they were able to get over here in under six minutes. But," he said, with a slow look around the house, "there wasn't much that could be done at that point. Looks like there were heavy renovations done when it changed ownership?"

"It had been the landlord's on-site office," Laila confirmed. "My uncle updated it so he could lease it out."

"Doomed you in the doing," the agent commented as he made notes. "Newer materials burn quicker. Not that I blame him for sprucing it up, of course," he was quick to add. "It likely wouldn't have made that much of a difference either way. All right." He scribbled one last note at the bottom of the page before handing out business cards to each of them. "I'll head back to the office and get all of this in the system. We'll coordinate with Mr. Dermott for the repairs, but I'll have someone from my team contact you about having your personal property reimbursed."

"Thank you," Laila said.

"Looks like you've got company," he said, stepping over the crumbled remains of the front wall.

Jean followed his gaze to see the press were back. Security had said they'd been by twice already before the Trojans made it over. The guards were running interference now, keeping the cameras in the street and refusing access to the porch. The insurance agent ignored all calls for comments as he climbed in his car and pulled away from the curb. Laila turned away, muttering under her breath, and surveyed the living room with a steady stare.

"Something has to have survived," she said.

Jean doubted it, but he kept that to himself. They split up to opposite ends of the house: Laila to her bedroom, Cat to the kitchen, Jeremy in the living room, and Jean to his bedroom. For an hour they sifted through the wreckage for any trinkets that were relatively unscathed. Jean pushed the remains of their beds around, checked the gutted dressers, and poked at the charred cloth in the closet. Nothing here was worth salvaging, so he finally turned and left the room.

Laila was on her knees in her bedroom as he passed, face in her hands and shoulders shaking with silent grief. There was no sound from the kitchen where Cat was supposed to be working. Jeremy was sitting in the living room where the coffee table should have been, fighting melted plastic on DVD cases. Why he was wasting his time on such nonsensical things, Jean wasn't sure, but maybe hope was easier to lean on than common sense.

Jean settled at his side and picked up movies one at a time. Most cases were nothing more than misshapen hunks of plastic. The few that were vaguely rectangular still were melted shut. Jean gave one an honest effort before chucking it back to the pile. He watched Jeremy struggle a little longer before taking the case out of his hand. Jeremy reached for another, but Jean caught his wrist to stop him.

"Enough," he said. "They're gone."

"I had all of Nan's movies here," Jeremy said without looking at him. Jean thought of the fond pride in his voice as he showed off the actress's memorabilia and slowly let go of him. Jeremy dropped his hands to his lap and studied the wreckage before him with a distant gaze. After a minute he finally said, "It'd be easy to replace them, I know, but I..." Jeremy trailed off, gave himself a shake, and put on a see-through smile. "It was worth a try, at least."

Jean wordlessly reached for a case.

"No, you're right," Jeremy said, turning toward him. "I'll just—oh?"

Jean followed Jeremy's stare to the doorway. The man standing just inside the living room was almost familiar, but he wasn't one of Laila's security guards. Jean scanned his dark suit and serious expression before noticing the man at his back. This one was easier to recall. Two and a half months ago he'd flicked a to-go box at Neil's head and demanded their cooperation.

Jean dragged his stare back to the first man as the pieces clicked. The last time he'd seen this face, it'd been on a TV screen. Jeremy was saying something at his back, but Jean could barely hear him through the heart pounding in his temples.

"Agent Browning," Jean said, and Jeremy shut up immediately.

"Moreau." Browning picked his way around the wreckage, taking it in with a slow gaze, and stopped just out of arm's reach. "Wilshire."

"He is not a Wilshire," Jean said.

"Uh-huh. Owens, figure out where the other two are," Browning said, and his partner slipped away in search of Cat and Laila. Browning didn't wait for him to return but said to Jean, "I don't care what name he's using; he

415

doesn't need to be here for this conversation. Either he can make himself scarce, or you can come sit and chat in the car with me. Decide which one makes you happier in the next three seconds."

"Jean?" Jeremy asked.

Jean motioned an okay, and Jeremy slowly got to his feet. Owens returned and guided him out of the room when he didn't move fast enough for their liking. Browning came to crouch in the space Jeremy had left. He pushed aside the pile of wrecked DVDs with a bored hand, buying his partner time to force the Trojans further back in the house. Only when the other man returned to the doorway did Browning turn a steady stare on Jean.

When it was obvious he wasn't going to start, Jean said, "I didn't do this."

"Figured that much out," Browning returned, unimpressed. "We've already pulled call logs and the security footage. I know exactly where you were when the fire started, and I already know who started it. The good news is it wasn't an inside job; these morons have no connections to the Moreau or Wesninski businesses." Browning sighed at the look on his face. "I don't know why you look so surprised. Try to remember you're a material witness in the biggest case of my career."

"You've mistaken me for Neil," Jean said.

"This time it was fanatics," Owens said. "Next time it might not be. Our office wants to offer you a spot in Witness Protection. You'd have to leave Los Angeles and start over somewhere else, but in exchange I promise we'll get you to the other side of the trial in two or fewer pieces."

"Leave," Jean echoed. "We are only two games into the season."

"I hate this sport," Browning said to his partner. "Explain to me why they're all like this."

Owens only shrugged. "You've got me, boss. I'm a

Knicks fan."

"I cannot stop playing. I—" Jean caught himself at the last second, but the near-miss had his heart pounding in his temples. These people knew Nathaniel Wesninski and Jean-Yves Moreau; that familiarity had almost led him to admitting promises that were not their business. He swallowed hard and forcibly changed what he was trying to say. "—promised I would see the Trojans to finals. It is important."

"So is not ending up like this." Browning waggled one of the crumpled DVD cases at him. When Jean refused to look at it, Browning tossed it back to the pile. "Can't say we didn't try, but maybe you'll be more valuable as bait." He motioned for Owens to approach. Jean eyed the proffered file warily until Browning said, "Sometime today. My team already translated it into French for you."

Jean accepted the folder and flipped it open. There were stapled packets tucked into each of the two inside pockets. He started with the one on the left. Jean wasn't sure what he was expecting, but a writeup on a nearby apartment was not anywhere near the top of his list. The first page was a snapshot of the floorplan, and each successive page outlined details of the immediate surrounding area. The next packet was the same for a second property. Jean looked from one to the other before turning a blank stare on Browning.

"I don't understand."

"I need you alive for a few more months, and obviously we need a more hands-on approach going forward," Browning said. "It doesn't matter to me which address you choose so long as it is one of these two. My office will offset your rent to match what you were paying here, and we will handle your security from now until the trial pro bono. That's all you see of us; your day-to-day life continues unchanged outside of the route you take to class."

"There is a catch," Jean said. "I do not have the information you want. I've told you everything I know about my parents, and what little I know about his. I have nothing left that is worth this."

Browning's gaze was calm. "I guess we'll see, won't we?"

It felt very much like a trap, but Jean wasn't sure either man would tolerate refusal. "This was not my house. It is not my decision alone."

"Go on, then." Browning got to his feet and waved him toward the door.

Owens followed Jean out of the room and down the hall. His friends were standing against the back wall of his and Jeremy's bedroom, a line of crossed arms and tense expressions. Owens waited in the doorway, like he honestly thought they'd make a break for it if he turned his back, while Jean went to set the folder on the remains of his bed. His friends came up on the other side to see what new problem he'd brought them, and Jean laid it out as succinctly as possible. To their credit, they said nothing until Jean was done.

"I want more details on this supposed security system," Laila said, looking past Jean at the agent. "I refuse to have your cameras and bugs in my apartment. I'd rather find my own place and pay full price than let you spy on my private life."

"Nothing past the front door," he said. When Laila stared him down, he shrugged off her concerns and said, "Miss Dermott, I know who your father is, and I know who Wilshire's grandfather is. We are not trying to start a fight with either of your families when we have so much else on the line. We want only to keep our asset safe and our case intact."

"Until the trial ends," Cat said. "Then what?"

"You'll have the lease and our security detail until the end of the school year even if the trial ends early. After

418

that, two of you will graduate, and the remaining two will have to find a new place anyway. It's a good deal."

"Supposedly," Laila said. "I can't read any of this."

"We would have brought an English copy if we'd known him incapable of making his own decisions," Owens said.

"Rude," Cat muttered.

Jeremy pointed at a word on the page and translated, "Bedroom."

Jean motioned confirmation and summed up the features of both places. Most of it meant little to him, at least until he finally flipped to the last page of the second option and saw a printout of the neighborhood. These street names were familiar; his psychiatrist was only a few blocks away from this apartment.

"I know this place," he said.

Jeremy leaned closer to see. "There's Staples Center," he said, and squinted at the street names. Recognition set in a second later with a surprised, "Oh. Yeah, you're right." He knew better than to elaborate in mixed company but dragged a finger down the road toward campus. Jean was terrible at reading maps and putting them into perspective, as he'd never really used them, but after two trips to his doctor he knew this apartment was three times further away from campus than the house was.

"Can we discuss it?" Laila asked.

"No one's stopping you," Owens said, blithely ignoring the implicit "in private" in her request. The best he did was turn sideways and feign great interest in his watch. Laila leveled a stony look at him before glancing from Cat to Jean.

"What are you thinking, Jean?" she asked.

"I am not sure it is a real choice," Jean admitted. "Their preference would be to take me out of Los Angeles until I've testified." It didn't make sense. This was the kind of protection they should have forced on Neil, seeing how it was his father's empire on trial. Maybe they were leery of crossing Stuart, who was obviously still keeping tabs on his nephew, but Jean meant what he said: he had nothing left of value to give them. It would come back to haunt him later, but for now it offered them a way forward. "I cannot decide this for us, but I will not fight it."

Laila was clever enough to know there'd be a price to pay for the FBI's involvement, but she was also exhausted and defeated, standing in the wreckage of a home she'd lived in for so many years and running on only an hour of broken sleep. She wanted to linger in this dreary place as much as he did. She scrubbed a weary hand over her eyes before tilting the packet toward Cat. "Babe?"

"Yeah," Cat said, barely looking at it. "Yeah, we'll make it work."

"Lofts?" Owens asked, squinting across the room at the papers Laila was brandishing. When she nodded, he did too. "Good. How much longer will you be here?"

Laila's response was quiet. "I'm done here."

"I just need to grab what's in the kitchen," Cat said.

"Then we'll meet you over there," the agent said, and he and Browning left.

Jean listened for a door before remembering there wasn't one. Jeremy sent a last look at the papers in Laila's hands, looking a bit spooked by this newest development. "Are you sure about this?"

"I'm sure we will have to sort it out later, if later isn't too late," Laila said. "My father can get us some answers, or at least some trustworthy guarantees."

Jean followed Cat to the kitchen while Jeremy went out front with Laila. Cat had salvaged a half-dozen glasses and most of their silverware. The terracotta pot from the windowsill, long empty, was tucked into one of the glasses on the end. Jean instinctively looked for the framed photograph of Barkbark von Barkenstein, but its frame sat

420

warped and dark on the sill. Jean knew better than to comment but helped collect the surviving dishes. Both Jeremy and Laila were on their phones, Jeremy tapping away a text message to someone and Laila finishing up a call to her uncle. Laila sent one last look at her house before following Jeremy to his car.

By the time they arrived at the Lofts, the agents had secured keys and all the necessary paperwork for them. That they'd squared it away so quickly made it seem more a foregone conclusion. Either they'd used this building before, or they'd argued an arrangement into place before stopping by Laila's house.

Cat and Laila made the agents wait while they read the contract top to bottom, but Jean signed every spot dotted with a yellow highlighter. If he had to read through these endless paragraphs, they'd be here all day. He trusted the girls to warn him if something looked wrong.

He was turning the last page over when Laila said, "Dog."

Jeremy looked over his shoulder immediately, but Laila was staring at her paperwork still. She put a finger on the relevant paragraph and said, "It's a pet-friendly building. One animal per lease."

"Is it?" Cat asked, flipping to see. "Oh, wow."

"What if—" Laila faltered.

Cat was as gentle as she could be: "Let's revisit the idea after everything's calmed down."

Laila subsided, but she didn't look happy about it. Owens took their papers back to the office when the girls were finally done, and Browning lingered only long enough to hand Jean his business card. To Laila he said, "A maintenance crew will be by this afternoon to install the cameras on your floor. They won't need entry to your apartment, so it doesn't matter if you're home, but try not to draw attention to their work."

"Seattle," Jean said before Laila could answer. "Not

Baltimore?"

Browning glanced from him to his card. "I've been transferred to Washington until the trial. It was where Wesninski was first arrested, after all," he added, "and it means I'm not even a three-hour flight away should I need anything else from you. I will be in touch." Jean wasn't sure whether to take that as a promise or a threat, but Browning wasn't waiting for a response. He caught up to Owens at the front door, and the agents slipped out without a look back.

"I don't trust him," Cat said.

"No," Jean agreed.

Laila's expression said she concurred, but all she said was, "Let's head up."

Their welcome package had their apartment listed as being on the second floor. Laila got the front door unlocked, and they filed one at a time down a narrow entryway. The first door opened into a bathroom, and then the rest of the odd apartment unfolded before them.

The living room, kitchen, and dining area were one giant, shared space, with two bedrooms neighboring each other on the nearer wall. The third bedroom was past the kitchen, with its own private bath attached. Half of the walls were painted, and the other half were exposed brick. The windows gave it a fair bit of light, but it was so empty and open it felt sterile. Jean noted the narrow glass door at the far end of the room that opened onto a square balcony, but he could tell from here the view would be uninspiring.

The four drifted apart as they inspected their new home. Cat opened every kitchen cabinet like she half-expected to see it stocked with goods. Most of the appliances looked newer than what she'd lost, but she seemed more distressed than impressed by the upgrades. Laila ended up by the living room window, silent and grim. Jeremy stuck by Jean's side and said nothing, knowing his opinion on the place was the least important.

"We will have to get some basics," Laila said, in a tone that said she was wearied by the prospect. "Toilet paper, toiletries, something to change into that doesn't smell like a bus…" She plucked at her dirty shirt but made no move to step away from the window. "Thought I saw a sign for a grocery store when we made that last turn. We could start there."

"Divide and conquer after that?" Cat asked, before remembering, "One car."

Jean glanced between them. "I haven't sold mine."

"Absolutely not," Laila said. "I'm not riding around in a Raven car after their fans torched everything I own."

The silence that fell after that flat rejection was heavy, and then Laila pushed away from the window and approached him. She took his hands in hers and stressed, "Thank you, Jean. I know you're trying to help, and I know it's the smart thing to do. I just can't do it, I'm sorry. I'd much rather you stick to the original plan and get it out of your life as soon as you can."

She waited for his nod before backing away from him. "Maybe you and Cat can go by the dealership tomorrow? I know she'll wither away to nothing if she doesn't replace her motorcycle as soon as possible."

"I liked *my* bike," was Cat's quiet protest, but she rallied herself with a bit of forced cheer: "The next one will be even better. Maybe we'll get a matching set." The smile she sent Jean was almost real, but it was her sly comment afterward that made her seem most like herself: "And then you two will go on a celebratory ride with us to help cheer us up, right? I've always wanted a biker bitch."

"I've always wanted to live to seventy," was Laila's dry response. She glanced toward Jeremy and asked, "Are we going to regret this?"

"Only if we survive," Jeremy said.

"You've got a little time to steel yourselves," Cat said, waving off their lack of enthusiasm. "Jean and I need to

423

figure out what kind of ride he's looking for, and then I'll want him to practice with my weight first. Now let's get going, all this talk about the lack of toilet paper is making me need to pee."

They started for the door, with Cat still talking: "Maybe we should invite the floozies over for dinner? I'm sure at least one of them has some spare blankets we can borrow for a few days, and this place is a bit creepy with just us in it."

"Company might be nice," Laila agreed. "Jeremy?"

"I'll text them," Jeremy promised, and looked over at Jean. "Ready?"

"Yes," Jean lied. He sent one last look around the barren space before following Jeremy to the door.

CHAPTER TWENTY-TWO
Jeremy

The floozies had left as many blankets as they could spare, but comforters could only do so much against this painfully hard floor. Jeremy woke up sore in a half-dozen places Sunday morning and grimaced as he pushed himself up. Jean glanced over at the movement before turning his attention back to his phone. There was only one person he'd be texting this early in the day, but he didn't look tense from bad news. Gossip and general updates, then; Jeremy could live with that.

"Good?" he asked, just in case.

"Andrew had surgery last night. No complications, so he will be released this morning." Jean set his phone aside and kicked free of his blankets. The movement was enough to make him wince, and Jeremy didn't miss the sullen edge in his, "Forget the motorcycle. I will sell the car for a bed."

"Assuming Cat's right about its worth, you can afford both."

If she was, Jean would be the only one getting any rest around here. It could be weeks before Laila and Cat saw a payout from their renters' insurance, and longer for Gary's court case against the arsonists to produce any money. Cat's parents would send what they could spare in the meantime, and Laila's would wire money over on Monday, but for now they were all strapped for cash. Yesterday's priorities had been outfitting the bathrooms and kitchen, and then enough shirts and jeans to get them started. Furniture would have to wait.

"Maybe we'll get camping cots," Jeremy suggested as Jean staggered to his feet. Jean made an awful face as he pressed both hands to the small of his back, and the agitated sound he managed had Jeremy rethinking how badly he wanted to get up. The decision was made for him when Jean offered a hand, and Jeremy braced himself before catching hold. Jean hauled him up before folding the blankets into tidy squares.

Stretching did nothing for him, so Jeremy gave up and said, "Coffee?"

"Coffee," was the ready agreement.

Morning light streamed harsh and bright through the living room windows, putting an uncomfortable heat into the air. Curtains were a priority around here, as much for that as to afford some privacy while they changed. The living room windows faced apartments, but Laila and Cat's bedroom window was aimed at a neighboring office building. The girls had to change for bed in the bathrooms last night.

Cat had tried sticking to basics yesterday, focusing on pots and pans over the splendid array of appliances she'd once had access to, but she'd made sure to buy a coffee maker. They had exactly four mugs in the cabinet, so Jean set them out on the counter while Jeremy got the pot started. On any other weekend, there was no chance Cat would stumble out of bed until at least ten, but they had a mile-long list of things to do today, and she needed to come along for part of it.

Jean put together an easy breakfast. Cat joined them only seconds after the coffee maker beeped, scrubbing at her eyes with clumsy fists. Jeremy glanced past her toward the bedroom door, and Cat only shook her head at the silent question in his stare. Even if Laila was awake, she wouldn't be joining them. Jeremy quietly put her mug and the fourth plate away.

There was nowhere to sit, so they propped themselves against the counter to fuel up for the day. Jeremy ceded the first shower to Jean while he cleaned up the mess, and

426

Cat poured what was left of the coffee between their two mugs. She considered the filter a moment as if tempted to start a second pot, then turned a serious stare on him.

"She's not going to let you come back."

It wasn't a question, and they both knew the answer anyway. Jeremy drained his coffee in one go and set to work washing the mug. Cat leaned against his back, winding her arms around him in a slow, fierce hug. Her plaintive protest was muffled where she buried it against his back: "It's not fair. Tell her we'd feel safer if you were here with us." Jeremy didn't have to say anything; Cat's fingers went bruising as she added, "I know she doesn't care, but…"

"It's just for a few weeks," Jeremy promised, with no confidence.

"We need you more than she does. She doesn't deserve you."

"She's my mother, Cat." Cat grumbled something incoherent and held on tight. Jeremy put his mug on the drying rack and draped his arms over hers. They stood in silence until Jeremy heard the bathroom door open. Cat withdrew when Jeremy gave her wrists a gentle tug. As he turned away, he said, "I'll let you know when we're on our way back, okay?"

"Yeah," she agreed, unenthusiastic. "I'll be ready."

Jeremy washed up as quickly as he could, and he and Jean set out. The drive over to Jean's doctor was startlingly quick from this new address, and although Jeremy wouldn't be staying, he parked and followed Jean up to the fifth floor. They sat together in the waiting room until Jean was called back, and then Jeremy got up and left. He collected his car from the parking garage and set off northwest.

The early hour could only mitigate weekend traffic so much, but Jeremy had made this drive enough times he knew he'd be back about the same time Jean finished. The spot directly outside of Jenny Spader's house was taken, but he managed to squeeze in a half-block down. He knew the code for her gate, so he texted her a heads-up before punching it in.

Dr. Spader was waiting in the doorway for him as he headed up the path, hip propped against the frame and arms folded across her chest. Jeremy knew by her expression he wasn't going to wriggle out of this as quickly as he'd hoped, but it was still worth a try. He offered her his most disarming smile, knowing she'd never been fooled by it, and followed her into the foyer. There was room on the rack for his shoes, so he toed out of them and locked the front door behind him.

"Good morning, Jeremy," she said as she led him down the hall to her kitchen. Two glasses of iced tea were across from each other on the counter. One was beside the envelope he'd come for, but he reached for his drink first. Spader collected her own before saying, "Please give my condolences to your friends for their loss."

At the side-eyed look he sent her, she arched a brow and motioned over her shoulder. A small TV was mounted to the end of the counter, currently on but turned down to an indistinct hum. "I do watch the news."

"So does Mom," he said, and swallowed every biting word that wanted to follow that. That she and his mother could watch the same station and come away with entirely different knowledge about what was going on in his life was impossibly cruel, but this wasn't the time or place to get into it. The measuring look Spader sent him said she could guess where his thoughts were spiraling without him voicing it.

Jeremy looked away and asked, "Where's Lily?"

If she pressed him, he'd probably answer her honestly, but this wasn't Jeremy's monthly session. After a brief pause Spader allowed the change in topic and only said, "She's been admitted again. Her father is with her today."

It was the answer he'd feared, so Jeremy offered a quiet, "I'm sorry."

"Thank you."

Little Lily Spader had been in and out of the hospital since her birth; her health was the main reason Spader tried referring all her clients to other therapists two years back. Jeremy was the only one left, in part due to his mother's stubborn interference and mostly because he'd found a workaround that suited them both. Spader still billed his mother for weekly sessions, but she refunded one to Jeremy in cash each month. It was easy side income for her while she cared for her youngest, and it gave Jeremy spending money his parents couldn't track. This was earlier than Jeremy usually collected it, but she had agreed to have it ready for him.

Jeremy drained his tea before tucking the envelope into his back pocket, but his thanks got stuck in his throat when he glanced Spader's way. Kevin was on TV, but for once he was the less important face on the screen. Jeremy banged his elbow on the counter in his hurry to snatch up the remote.

"Sorry," he said, "I'm sorry, can we—?" The rest was forgotten as he got the volume up high enough to hear, and Spader moved so she could watch the news as well.

Kevin was offering a practiced statement regarding his teammates' injuries, but Jeremy didn't hear a word. Theodora Muldani was standing at his side outside the Foxhole Court, racquet slung across her shoulders as she waited for him to be finished. Her pastel makeup was unmistakable, as was the 14 emblazoned on her loose Houston Sirens t-shirt. Jeremy scooted around the island to get a better look at the small screen.

"Someone important," Spader guessed. She'd started following Exy only after he became her patient, but she was loyal to the Trojans first and foremost. She didn't have the time or energy to invest in any professional

429

teams, much less the national Court.

"Maybe," Jeremy said. "A former Raven, but she shouldn't be in South Carolina."

Right on cue, the reporter tilted his microphone toward Muldani and said, "The most unexpected development of the weekend might be your presence here at Palmetto State University. Care to explain what you're doing here?"

"I do not need your permission to travel."

Kevin flicked her a disapproving look, but Thea stared him down until Kevin huffed with displeasure and looked away.

"It's just curious," the reporter said, unflappable in the face of her rudeness. "This soon after the Ravens and Foxes went toe-to-toe, how else can we interpret your visit but as a show of solidarity?"

"With this joke of a team?" Muldani asked. "I would rather slit my throat."

Kevin waved her off. "They've gotten—*idiot*."

The camera spun to see what had caught Kevin's eye. A Maserati had pulled up to the curb nearby. Jeremy understood Kevin's anger when he saw Andrew in the driver's seat, except the man who climbed out on the passenger side was also Andrew. The second had one arm in a sling, which at least cleared up the who's-who of the Minyard twins. One of the back doors opened moments later to reveal Neil. He tested the doorframe as he weighed the best way to get out, then grimaced in pain as he went for it.

Kevin stalked toward them with a curt, "Excuse me."

The camera followed him while the reporter gave a quick, "As you know," rundown of the Foxes' injuries and the estimated timeline for their return. Jeremy was more interested in whatever Kevin was saying, but the Queen knew to keep his voice down. That didn't keep the impatience off his face or out of his sharp gestures as he

430

tried to exile his injured teammates from the stadium.

Kevin turned on Andrew next, who ignored him in favor of raising a pack of cigarettes to his mouth. It was easy work to tip a stick between his lips, but Andrew didn't light it. He bobbed it this way and that for a few moments, then broke it into pieces and cast it aside. Irritation tugged hard at the corner of his mouth, and the deadly look he turned on Kevin was enough to kill the argument. Kevin was obviously still angry with them, but he stepped back so Neil could finally close the car door behind him.

"Context?" Spader asked, taking advantage of the lull.

Jeremy only managed a, "Did you watch—" before Neil hobbled past Kevin and said too-loudly, "Oh, Thea. Welcome back."

The implication she'd been there before had the camera swinging back toward her with dizzying speed, but Muldani only stared Neil down with obvious contempt. She batted away the microphone when it tipped toward her: a grave mistake in retrospect, as it meant the reporter turned his full attention on Neil instead. Neil didn't acknowledge the camera, but he obediently stopped when the reporter said his name.

"Not her first visit to the Foxhole Court," the reporter guessed.

"The court? Unknown." Neil gave a careless shrug he immediately and obviously regretted. He pressed a hand to his injured side and sucked in a slow breath through clenched teeth. "She stopped by last spring. When was that?" Neil asked Andrew, but didn't wait before adding, "April? Jean came down in March, so it had to be after that. I know she visited them both while she was here."

Neil didn't give the reporter room to speak but glanced at Kevin and pointed toward the court. "Coach here? Okay, then we're heading in."

He and Andrew set off. Kevin waited until they

disappeared through the door before turning back on the camera and trying his best to salvage the conversation. "Thea is here because I invited her. I wanted to talk about the Ravens' latest developments with someone who would understand."

"What Ravens?" Muldani demanded, expression dark. It was enough to startle a quiet "Oh," from Jeremy, but Muldani wasn't finished. "A Raven who cannot play is no Raven. These disgraceful creatures do not deserve the uniforms they wear.

"Victory," she stressed, heavy with rage and indignation, and she finally turned on the camera like she could stare through it to her former team. "Supremacy on the court above all else. That is our calling and our purpose, but you have irrevocably destroyed it. You've ruined everything he gave you and stained his legacy beyond repair. He will never forgive you for embarrassing him like this."

Our calling, as if she hadn't graduated years ago. Jeremy took a step back from the TV.

Muldani spat to one side to emphasize the point, then motioned to Kevin. "I have nothing more to say about these cowards. Let's go."

Kevin said nothing for a moment, as if considering what else he could add. All he came up with was a pleasant, "Thank you for checking on us. We appreciate your support and concern."

"This will not end well," Spader said as Kevin and Muldani walked away. The camera followed them, and the reporter was giving a hurried closing statement, but Spader muted the TV and turned a serious look on Jeremy. "You told me what happened to the Ravens after they lost championships. Being shamed by one of their own on the tail-end of a canceled season will have disastrous consequences for them. I hope they have access to the help they need."

432

Jeremy thought of the Ravens' short careers, Reacher's gaunt appearance, and Jean flinching every time Tetsuji Moriyama's name was uttered. "I don't think they ever have. Edgar Allan has never prioritized their longevity or sanity, only their reputation." He clapped a hand over his pocket to try and muffle his phone; the flurry of alerts said at least two teammates and Rhemann had caught the news. "I need to get to Jean and warn him."

"Let me know if I can help," Spader said.

"This helps," Jeremy promised, patting his pocket where he'd put her cash. "Thank you."

She saw him to the door, and Jeremy got back across town as quickly as he could. Staying for the interview had cost him precious time, and Jeremy parked right as Jean's session should be ending. He texted Jean a quick, "On my way up," as he took the stairs at a run. Jean was sitting tense in a chair in the waiting room when Jeremy arrived, and Jeremy smiled apologies as he held the stairwell door. "Sorry, had to step out for a bit to meet someone. We need to talk, but it can wait if you need a moment."

"We have a problem," Jean guessed as he followed Jeremy down.

"We don't," Jeremy promised, but waited until they were at the car to say, "Muldani turned on the Ravens."

Jean froze with his hand on the door handle. "No. No," he said again, sharp and incredulous. "She fought too hard to join the line. She would never turn on his team."

"It is not his team anymore," Jeremy pointed out. "That was her argument. Come on."

He should have texted Cat that they were on the way back, but Jeremy wanted to make sure he and Jean got through this before she joined them. The ride back was too short to hash it all out, but by the time Jeremy parked at the Lofts Jean had stopped arguing in favor of staring at him. Jeremy finally messaged Cat, then turned as best he

433

could in his chair to study Jean's blank face.

"She really came to see you in South Carolina, didn't she?" Jeremy said.

Jean waved that aside. "She came to confront Kevin. She did not know I was there until after she arrived."

"But she saw you," Jeremy pressed. "She knew what they—what *he*—did to you."

Jean glanced away. "Yes." Jeremy thought he would leave it at that, but Jean flexed his hands and felt the line of his knuckles. Jeremy had seen him check his ribs often enough to know Jean was chasing phantom pain. Jean finally explained, but the answer dragged out of him slow as molasses: "But she thought it was someone else. The last time she saw me in such a state, it was. I am not surprised she got it wrong."

Grayson, Jeremy guessed, except Jean wasn't reaching for his throat like he did every time the man came up. It should have been reassuring, but Jeremy only felt sick to his bones. Jean had left Edgar Allan with a string of horrific injuries this spring. Finding out it had happened before, and that neither Riko nor Grayson were to blame, was unbearable. He wanted to demand a name, but he knew Jean would deny him.

"Jean," he started anyway.

Cat pried open the back door with a loud, "Holy shit, boys. Tell me you saw that."

"I did, at Dr. Spader's," Jeremy said. He shifted so he could dig the envelope out of his pocket and offered it to her over his shoulder. "She let me come get this early."

Cat hesitated before tucking it into her purse. "Thank you. I mean it."

Cat obviously wanted to gossip about this new development, but Jeremy didn't know how to get to her uncle's motorcycle dealership. She tried juggling directions and chatter for a few streets before giving up on the latter, and finally Jeremy could pull up to the curb

434

outside the front door. Rhemann had beat them here and was waiting on the sidewalk.

There was no point getting out, so Jeremy wished them a cheerful good luck. "Let me know how it goes!"

Cat leaned between the front seats to kiss his cheek before following Jean out of the car. Rhemann turned the keys over to Jean's waiting hand, pointed to where he'd parked the Raven car, and lingered to exchange a few serious words. He only moved toward Jeremy's car when Cat ushered Jean inside. Jeremy peeled away from the curb as soon as Rhemann was settled in the passenger seat.

"Thank you, Coach," he said. "They could really use a pick-me-up."

"I can imagine," Rhemann said. "I assume they're still at the hotel?"

"No," Jeremy said, dragging it out as he thought. Figuring out how much to say was easy; Rhemann had known about the FBI since the police first cornered Jean at the Gold Court this summer. The coach listened in dead silence as Jeremy explained their visit and the pressure to move into a specific building, and Jeremy finished up with, "They're probably safer now than they've been in months, but I don't like it. Agent Browning said they won't bug the apartment itself, but ..."

Rhemann considered that, then asked, "Any updates from the Dermotts?"

"They're still looking into it, last I heard," Jeremy said. "No news yet."

"And your parents?" Rhemann asked.

Jeremy drummed an agitated beat on his steering wheel as he turned into Rhemann's neighborhood. "I'm not safe with Laila anymore." His mother's decision, and it stuck in his throat like a stone. "I thought about telling Mom the FBI is involved, but I think that would rattle her even more. I'll just keep my head down until she changes

435

her mind. Maybe she'll feel better after my LSAT exam."

Without Jean's car in the driveway, it was easy to pull in behind Rhemann's ancient ride. Jeremy put the car in Park and said, "I'll let you know if anything else exciting happens."

"Let's take a break from excitement for a few weeks," Rhemann said dryly.

"No arguments from me, Coach."

He waited for Rhemann to get inside before finally turning his car toward home. William had the door open for him before Jeremy even reached the porch. As Jeremy moved past him, the butler said, "Your mother is at work until seven. Mr. Wilshire is on a conference call in his office, but he asked to see you when you arrived." He locked the front door behind Jeremy and took his keys. "I will let you know when he is off the phone."

"Great," Jeremy said, with no enthusiasm.

William spoiled the surprise for him: "They are going out of town on Tuesday. Arnold has invited his sons to attend a fundraising gala with him."

Jeremy knew better than to get his hopes up, especially when William looked so serious. They wouldn't take Jeremy with them, but neither could he expect freedom in their absence. They'd called him home knowing they wouldn't be here to keep an eye on him. Testing his obedience, he assumed; it wasn't the first time, and it wouldn't be the last. He swallowed a sigh and said, "I'll be upstairs until then."

"I will start some coffee," William promised.

"What would I do without you?"

He expected William's usual response, but the man only said, "Let us not find out."

Jeremy interpreted that the only way he could: his parents were in a fouler mood than usual. He swallowed every protest that none of this was his fault and took the stairs up to his room two at a time. The bed he dropped onto was heaven after a night on the floor at Laila's new place, but comfort came hand in hand with grief. He didn't want to be here, and he didn't want to be there, either. He wanted the cozy home he'd built with Cat and Laila and Jean.

We'll make a new one, he promised himself, but it was hollow comfort in this arctic space.

He didn't mean to doze off, but William woke him an indeterminate time later with a hand on his shoulder. Jeremy scrubbed the grogginess out of his eyes as he sat up, and William handed him a mug of coffee once he was on his feet. Jeremy buried his thanks against the rim as he preceded William out of the room. He probably could have drained it before he reached Warren's office, but facing his stepfather empty-handed rarely turned out well. He rapped on the doorframe, waited two minutes for Warren to acknowledge his arrival, and let himself in.

There were two chairs on this side of Warren's mahogany desk, but Jeremy knew better than to sit without an invitation. He stood between them instead, holding onto his mug for dear life, and waited for Warren to finish his busy work. The squeaky scratch of Warren's pen was nearly as aggravating as the too-loud second hand of Warren's expensive watch. Jeremy tolerated it as long as he could, then sucked down half of his coffee in a noisy slurp. It worked as intended; his stepfather put his work aside to fix him with an irritated stare.

"You wanted to see me," Jeremy said.

"Your mother and I are flying to Boston tomorrow morning," Warren said. "I trust you will conduct yourself appropriately in our absence."

Jeremy affected surprise. "Implying I can ever meet your standards? That's new."

"I'm only going to say this one time, so listen up, you little faggot." Warren sat back in his chair and folded his hands across his stomach. Jeremy went still as stone to

437

stare at him, coffee forgotten. "The attitude goes, or you do. You are on thin enough ice as it is right now; the next time you fall through I will stand at the edge and watch you drown. Do you understand me?"

"This is my mother's house," Jeremy said. "You can't tell me to leave."

"Call my bluff," Warren invited him. Jeremy opened his mouth, closed it again, and held onto his mug for dear life. Warren gave him another minute to come up with something before saying, "If I get one call or text from anyone that you are acting out, you will regret it. Now get out of my office. I don't want to see you again until dinnertime."

Jeremy did a sharp about-face and left. He was halfway to the stairs when William flagged him down. Jeremy tried to wave him off, not in the mood for conversation, but William stepped neatly into his path and said, "You have visitors out front." Rather than explain, he put out a hand and said, "Mug?"

Jeremy drained the last bit before turning it over, and William got the door for him. The relief that seized his heart when he saw Jean and Cat sitting at the fountain almost took him to his knees. Cat turned at the sound of the door, but Jeremy didn't trust his expression to hold. He looked back at William, buying a few critical seconds, and said, "Thank you. I'll make sure they don't stay long enough for him to notice."

William nodded and eased the door closed, and Jeremy went to join his friends. Cat sprang to her feet to strike a dramatic pose, and Jeremy followed her outstretched arms to the pair of motorcycles parked a few feet away. They appeared to be a matching set, metallic black with silver highlights.

"What do you think?" Cat asked in lieu of hello. "Fancy, right? I'm going to have to get mine painted, though, so I can tell 'em apart better. Jean, show it off!"

438

"He can see it," Jean said, but he was already drifting to the nearer bike.

When he took too long to extoll the virtues of this model, Cat launched into a rapid-fire explanation. What little Jeremy heard went way over his head; he knew nothing about motorcycles, and Jean was more interesting by far. The Frenchman was tracing a slow line from the handlebars to the seat cushion with one gloved hand. The light in his eyes was unfamiliar but enough to kick Jeremy's heart up a beat. *Satisfaction*, Jeremy thought, or perhaps quiet pride. Something a little too hungry to be pleased, like Jean couldn't believe this was truly his.

Jeremy realized too late that Cat had gone quiet. "I'm glad you found something you like. They look very nice."

"They're awesome," she agreed. "Makes you wanna come for a ride with us now, right?"

As unsettling as the prospect was, Jeremy was briefly tempted. "Thanks, but it's not a good night."

Some of the joy went out of her as she glanced past him toward the house. "Figured." Her subdued tone was enough to distract Jean from his contemplation, and he turned a heavy stare on Jeremy. Jeremy kept his eyes on Cat until she sighed and went for her helmet. "We'll be on our way, then. Just wanted to christen them with a good first ride and thought we'd hit you up on the way."

"I'm glad you did," Jeremy said, and Cat swung past him for a fierce hug.

He watched them zip away, stamped down on his regrets, and turned back toward the house.

-

On Monday afternoon, Jasmine Lane took her life.

Jeremy heard the news as he and Jean left their pottery class. Loathe as he was to break the news when Jean still had a lecture to get through, he couldn't let him get blindsided by anyone else. Jeremy texted Shane a quick warning before pulling Jean aside outside of Hoffman, and

439

Jean listened in stony silence as Jeremy relayed the latest tragedy. He tried to brush it aside, deflecting with assurances that he and Lane had hated one another, but Jeremy could read the tension in him when he left to join Shane.

By the time Jeremy got home, Brayden Williams and Cameron Winter were gone.

"I thought they'd be under watch," Cody said when Jeremy called. There was a bite in their voice not unlike Jean's conflicted grief: the cousins despised each other, but Cameron was still family. Cody didn't know what to feel or do about this unexpected tragedy. "You can't tell me Edgar Allan wasn't expecting this. I don't—" Cody stopped and took a deep breath. "Mom's blowing up my phone. I gotta go."

"Be safe," Jeremy stressed. "Call me if you need anything."

"Will do, cap."

Cody wouldn't, not when they had Pat and Ananya to lean on, but it had to be said. Jeremy spent the rest of the evening staring at his textbook without absorbing a single word.

He had to stop keeping up with the news on Tuesday. The papers and stations covering the Ravens' second collapse were good at feigning concern, but there was such a judgmental hunger in their approach Jeremy couldn't stand it. Cat had a stronger stomach for it, and she kept him updated throughout the day with sporadic messages.

At some point almost everyone was to blame for these deaths: Muldani and Kevin, for their heartlessness despite the Ravens' public struggles; Coach Rossi, who'd put a team on the court knowing they weren't ready; Edgar Allan, for not keeping a better eye on their cherished athletes; Coach Moriyama, for abandoning his team so swiftly and thoroughly after their first loss; on and on it went, with increasing heat and speculation. For once, the only name not tossed about so carelessly was Jean's.

Laila texted him Tuesday evening to ask, "Do you think it's over?" When Jeremy took too long to answer, she added, "Those three started the fight. They cost the Ravens their season by injuring Andrew and Neil. If they've absorbed the blame, the rest might be able to move on."

"I don't know," Jeremy finally sent. "I hope so. How is Jean?"

"A little lost," she admitted. "We're keeping an eye on him, but I wish you were here."

Jeremy typed out six different responses before settling on, "I'm sorry." It wasn't what she wanted to hear, he knew, but it was all he had to offer. With a sigh he tossed his phone toward his bed and turned his attention back to his schoolwork. He didn't remember putting his head down, but William woke him with a hand on his shoulder sometime later.

Jeremy smothered a jaw-cracking yawn and peeled his face off his textbook. He sent a fuzzy look around for a clock before blinking up at William. "Mom?" he guessed. Instead of answering, William stepped to one side. Jeremy glanced toward his bedroom doorway and the person standing there. "…Laila?"

"I rode a motorcycle to get here," she said, chucking a sleeping bag and backpack into the nearest corner of his room. Jeremy watched them land, then turned a bewildered stare on his best friend. William moved so Jeremy could get up, but Jeremy stayed put. He wasn't convinced he wasn't dreaming. "I thought I was going to die at least ten times. You are the only person I would do that for, I hope you know that."

"I will prepare some drinks," William said, starting for the door.

"Thank you," Laila said, shifting so he could get by.

441

Jeremy finally got up, and he pulled her into a tight hug when she moved to meet him halfway. "What are you doing here?"

"If the mountain won't go to Mohammed..." She propped her chin on his shoulder and heaved a heavy sigh. "You said your parents won't be back until Sunday, right? We'll duck out Saturday morning with no one the wiser. Just swing us by the apartment tomorrow so we can get some clothes."

"You hate it here," Jeremy reminded her as she wriggled free of him.

"If your family isn't here, I hate the new place more." Laila caught his hand and dragged him after her. "Now come on, Cat is threatening to take Jean on a tour of the second floor. She was saying something about loosening every screw on Bryson's desk and chair."

Despite that threat, Jean and Cat were waiting patiently in the foyer. Cat called a cheery greeting up at him when he appeared on the landing and collected her bags from by her feet. Jean hung back for only a moment before following her up, and Cat caught Jeremy's free hand to kiss his knuckles.

"We're invading," she said. "Resistance is futile."

"No resistance from me," Jeremy promised, and moved so she and Jean could get by. He checked Jean's expression as he passed, looking for tension and grief. He saw neither. Maybe the ride had helped clear his head, or he was suitably distracted by the change in scenery. Jeremy was grateful either way, but he'd want to keep a careful eye on his friend tonight anyway.

It was too early to sort out sleeping arrangements, so the two added their things to Laila's small pile. Cat propped her hands on her hips and spun to consider his room. Her "Sheesh!" was to be expected, and Jeremy could read the disapproval on her face. "I forgot how boring this place is. You *still* have those ugly sheets? One

442

of these days we're going to buy you a set with like…
spaceships or little sasquatches on it, just to see what your
mother says."

"Oh, I can imagine," Jeremy said.

"Unfortunately, so can I."

Jean studied the room with a slow and quiet interest,
lingering longest over the pictures hanging on Jeremy's
walls. Jeremy put away his homework as quickly as he
could while Cat chatted about the ride over. The
exhaustion that had dogged him all day was gone,
scattered to the wind by the warmth his friends brought
with him. They ended up on his bed while he sat opposite
them in his desk chair, and Laila was halfway through a
story about one of her classes when William returned.

Jeremy helped arrange the drinks along the edge of his
desk, then laughed as he accepted a bowl of popcorn.
"You're a lifesaver."

"I will add it to my resume when I next petition
Mathilda for a raise," William said, tucking his tray under
his arm.

Jeremy didn't miss the considering look William
turned on Jean, and he gestured between them. "William,
this is Jean Moreau. Jean, this is William Hunter, my
mother's live-in butler. He's been with our family for
almost twenty-six years now. Longer than any of us kids,"
he added. "I'm not exaggerating when I say he's the
linchpin of this household."

"Imagine how many embarrassing stories he knows,"
Cat said to Jean. "Unfortunately, he's too loyal to be
bribed."

William smiled. "I apologize for not introducing
myself on your previous visit, Mr. Moreau. Please feel
free to make yourself at home and let me know if you
require anything while you are here." To Jeremy he said,
"I will be downstairs until you need me."

"It's late," Jeremy said. "You shouldn't be working. I

443

promise we won't bother you."

William left with a polite good-night, and Jeremy passed the popcorn over to his friends. They'd get butter on his sheets for sure, but Jeremy couldn't care. They were here; that was all that mattered. They stayed up far too late, laughing and flinging fistfuls of popcorn at each other, and only called it a night when Jeremy couldn't stop yawning.

Jeremy ceded his bed to Laila and Cat and stole a sleeping bag so he could stretch out next to Jean on the carpeted floor. He worried Jean's thoughts would catch him with no conversation to distract him, but Jean looked more pensive than distressed as he settled down for the night. Jeremy listened for Laila's breathing to even out and Cat's quiet snores to start before nudging Jean with a careful hand.

"Are you all right?" Jeremy asked.

Jean thought it over for a bit before saying, "I carry some of the blame for this. Yes," he said, when Jeremy started to protest. "I asked Coach Wymack how I could protect you, and Thea was his answer. He only dragged her into this because I asked him to, and she knew exactly how to break them." Jean gestured helplessly before offering a slow and careful, "I am not sorry. Perhaps I should be. But I will choose you every time. You, and Cat, and Laila, every time. I will lose them all if I must."

Cat stirred with a sleepy query. Jean reassured her with an easy dismissal, then rolled onto his other side. Jeremy was left staring at the back of his head, heart pounding so loud Jean had to hear it. His head was an echo chamber, spinning Jean's words out of context on endless repeat. He should say something, but Jeremy was afraid to open his mouth. He wasn't sure what might come out.

At last he managed a weak, "Good night, Jean," as he tugged the sleeping bag up over his head.

It'd be a miracle if he got any sleep tonight, and Jeremy prayed he wouldn't dream.

CHAPTER TWENTY-THREE
Jean

Wednesday morning Cat and Jean rode their motorcycles back across town, since Jeremy was afraid a neighbor would notice how long they were parked out front and report back to his parents. Laila staunchly refused to get on Cat's bike again, so Jeremy gave her a ride in his car and promised to meet them at the Lofts. Traffic was light enough at this ungodly morning hour that Jeremy could almost keep up with them, but Cat and Jean peeled away in the last few miles.

Jean had his clothes half-packed into a plastic bag when Jeremy and Laila finally showed up, but Laila came to his room instead of her own. She propped herself against his doorframe and studied him with a serious look while Jeremy hovered just behind her.

"Tell me about Lyle Holden," Laila said. "Do you know him?"

It was so unexpected Jean could only stare at her. The "do" was at least a little reassuring, as it meant Lyle was still alive. Jean slowly set his bag aside and folded his arms across his chest. "Number thirty-three, left-handed goalkeeper." A young brunette obsessed with spiking his hair despite not having the face for it, he had so much gel in his hair at any given time his helmet crunched when he strapped it on. Jean glanced between Laila and Jeremy as he continued, "He is a sophomore this year. Why?"

"He's been hospitalized," Jeremy said. "He had a nervous breakdown in his first class this morning."

Still alive for now, Jean silently amended. If he'd crashed so publicly that California was already hearing about it, heads were going to roll. Jean slowly reached for his bag and shoved his clothes deeper. He was dimly aware of Jeremy saying his name, but Jean kept his eyes on his work as he said, "No one will be surprised he broke, and no one will mourn his absence from the line. The Ravens despised his stutter."

A vile understatement, but Jean refused to explain further. The Ravens mocked Lyle so mercilessly his freshman year he tried to stop talking altogether, but the coaches thrived on cruelty for cruelty's sake. They'd called on him in team meetings at any given opportunity, then brutally punished him for his inevitable struggle. It reminded Jean of his early days in the Nest, when English was more noise than language. Maybe Sergio also understood, as he'd fought to be Lyle's partner last fall after keeping his distance the year before.

Jean hadn't heard Cat approach, but her subdued, "It's creepy, isn't it?" had Laila looking over her shoulder. Jeremy took advantage of her distraction to squeeze past at last, and Cat burrowed into Laila's side with a troubled look on her face. "Where are the Ravens' parents in all this madness?"

"Ravens do not have families," Jean said.

"They do," Cat insisted. "But fuck, they might as well not."

Jeremy stared at her. "Cat, easy."

Cat gave a sharp jerk of her hand. "Like, yes, they got their kids therapy this summer when they were falling apart, but then they sent them right back to Edgar Allan to try again. Now three more Ravens—four, if you include the freshman last week—are gone, and their parents are dead silent. Sorry," she said, wincing at her word choice. "It's just… How many Ravens have to die before their families finally step up?"

Laila wound an arm around Cat's waist and gave her a slow squeeze. "I imagine," she said slowly, with a glance at Jean for confirmation, "that the Ravens' contracts with

447

Edgar Allan are to blame. A school that can force its players to drop all contact with their families for five straight years must have strict contingencies and countermeasures in place. Either they can't speak out, or they've been well compensated for their discretion. Maybe both. Jean?"

"Perhaps. I did not read the contract." The silence that followed that statement was deep enough to drown in. Jean refused to believe they were surprised, and a hint of impatience bled into his words: "What it said was unimportant. I had no choice but to sign." Property had no right to contest the terms of ownership, but Jean couldn't say that. The best he had was, "I could not go home again."

Cat's expression turned immeasurably sad, but Jeremy found his voice first: "Jean, tell me you at least read the contract we sent you for USC."

"Some of it," Jean admitted. He shrugged indifference in the face of Jeremy's obvious dismay. "It was very long and very boring. All I needed to know was if you included what I asked of you. It does not matter. What matters is that we will be late to practice if you do not hurry up and pack," he added, shaking his bag of clothes in Laila's direction. "I do not want to talk about the Ravens anymore today."

She held her tongue, but he didn't trust the look in her eyes. It was a little too knowing to be curiosity, and a little too prying to be sure, but he didn't want to know what inspired it. It was enough that she turned away without further comment, and that Cat followed her across the apartment. Jean turned an expectant look on Jeremy, who mimed zipping his mouth closed, and sat down on his blanket to wait on the girls.

Despite rejecting the conversation, his thoughts stayed with Evermore. Sergio would know what was going on with Lyle, but Jean didn't know his phone number. For a

448

moment he considered calling Josiah Smalls for it, but the thought was enough to turn his stomach. Eventually Edgar Allan would spin a story for the news, and Cat would relay it to the group. Until then there was nothing Jean could do.

Except when Edgar Allan finally made a statement that afternoon, there was no mention of Lyle's breakdown. Campus president Louis Andritch was more interested in introducing the Ravens' new head coach: Joel Coer, a member of the Ravens' original lineup and the team's first captain. He'd dropped off the face of the planet after a seven-year tenure with the Ohio Thunder. That Edgar Allan had found him again wasn't surprising, but Jean could only imagine what they promised to draw him out of retirement.

Jean's statistics class had ended almost ten minutes ago, but Cody had seen the Coer headline when packing up to leave. Now they were the last two in the classroom, and Cody's laptop was angled so both could read the screen. Cody finished first, of course, but they waited for Jean to sit back before asking, "Thoughts?"

"Undecided," Jean admitted. "He has been away a long time, but he is a Raven. He will know how to guide them."

"Hope so." Cody tugged the laptop closer. "Let me email this to Cat real quick, and then we can go."

Jean had his backpack half-packed when Cody's words sank in. He checked his bag before remembering his laptop was nothing more than a charred hunk of metal. "I need to visit the library before practice."

"Oh? Sure," Cody agreed, finishing up and pushing everything into their bag. "Before or after we eat?"

"I will be quick," Jean promised, and off they went.

He found an open computer near the window and put in his student credentials. There were a dozen-odd unread emails in his inbox from the last few days, notifications

449

from professors and the campus, but Jean ignored all of them. It didn't matter that he didn't know Sergio's phone number. Edgar Allan, like USC, used a very straightforward system when assigning email addresses to its students. Jean remembered his, which meant he knew Sergio's. Jean opened a new message and filled in the TO line before hesitating.

Cody was on their phone, but Jean was still so long they glanced up. "Good?"

"Maybe," Jean said noncommittally.

He hadn't spoken to Sergio since he left Evermore, but Sergio was a Raven, and he'd closed ranks against Jean. He'd sent a letter to Palmetto State with Jean's notebooks, same as the rest of them had. The chances of him answering Jean were slim; the probability of it being a pleasant response was even more unlikely. There was more to lose than gain by reaching out. Jean glanced at the mouse, telling himself to let it go, before typing out a simple, "Lyle?"

He sent it before he could change his mind and logged out.

"Done?" Cody asked. "Great! Let's eat."

"Yes," Jean agreed, and forced his former teammates from mind.

Afternoon practice got out a few minutes early, and Jean followed Cat and Laila to Jeremy's car for the long trek west. The Wilshire family chef had the week off, since Jeremy was the only one home, but Cat was excited to get her hands on his expensive appliances. Jeremy was obviously unaccustomed to hosting people at his place, and the best entertainment he had to offer was a tangled-up yo-yo and a hacky sack. They ended up watching a lot of TV, as the house had five across three floors.

William was up before them the next morning and sent them off with four travel mugs of coffee. Cat sang his praises until Laila kissed her to silence with a grumpy,

"Too early, babe."

Jean and Tanner went from Lyon to the library, where Jean suffered through an uncomfortable, stilted conversation with Dobson. As soon as he hung up on her, he led Tanner over to the computers. Tanner didn't care where they went so long as he could find an open chair, since he had two quizzes to study for. He settled down and immediately got back to work, and Jean logged into the system.

Beneath a few new automated messages from USC was a response from Sergio, time-stamped for three in the morning local time. Jean tapped into it and read the short message in silence: "He's gone. Andritch terminated his contract and sent him home last night." It was followed by a few blank lines, and then, "You look dumb as fuck in red, Moreau. Almost had to gouge my eyes out when I saw you."

Jean scowled and wrote back, "It is hideous, but it is better than wearing black." He pressed Send, started to close out of his inbox, and hesitated when he understood the greater implication. He opened another message and said, "It is too early in the year for the Ravens to watch USC's games."

He sat back and considered the clock. With the Nest closed, the Ravens should be living in real-world time this year, but Jean wasn't sure how Edgar Allan was handling their classes. Did they fire the Ravens' dedicated professors or simply move them to a static, daytime schedule? It wasn't worth asking about when he and Sergio were on such thin ice, so he set to marking his other emails as Read. Halfway down, his inbox refreshed. A new message from Sergio now sat at the top.

"Fuck USC," was the predictable response. "Finn heard Zane visited you and wanted to see how it went down." On its heels, another email: "First time I've ever seen you look afraid of him, JOHNNY."

451

Jean shut down the system immediately.

-

Friday night was a home game against Las Vegas. Shawn resumed his rightful place on starting lineup, so Jean was left on the sidelines after the halftime break. Tanner ended up on one side of him, and Derrick and Derek on the other. The double-Ds were prone to hollering and hooting at every clever move, whereas Tanner saved his loudest cheers for the goals. Jean would surely be deaf by the time they let him on the court, but it helped distract him from the indignation of playing as a sub.

The Trojans took the game nine to four, and Jeremy slammed an energy drink before fighting Friday night traffic across town. His friends' excitement did nothing to hide how long a drive it was, and Jean refused to believe Jeremy could tolerate this endless trek day after day for months. No wonder the man slept every time they let him out of class. He would surely be a ghost by the time championships started.

Either William had a way of tracking Jeremy's location, or he'd been actively listening for the sound of his engine. He opened the door for them before they even reached the porch and offered both a polite greeting and the receiver for the house phone.

"Missed her," Jeremy guessed.

William checked his watch. "By thirty-seven minutes or so."

Mathilda Wilshire had called anywhere from one to three times every evening the Trojans were here, sometimes spacing her calls only a half-hour apart and once letting three hours slide between them. Jeremy managed to get off this call relatively quickly, and he returned the phone to William's waiting hand.

"There is sparkling cider in the fridge," William said, "and I've set a snack tray on the counter. Do you need anything else?"

"I need you to enjoy your evening," Jeremy said. "We're good, I promise."

"Thank you for letting us stay this week," Laila added. "We'll be gone tomorrow."

William smiled. "Thank you for visiting. It is a rare treat to see Jeremy happy."

Jean glanced at Jeremy as William left, but Jeremy was already on his way to the kitchen. Between the four of them it was easy work to get their treats and drinks upstairs, and they sat on his carpeted bedroom floor to dig in. It had been a long day, but no one was in any hurry to sleep. Morning meant going back to that empty apartment and leaving Jeremy alone here, and Laila resisted that eventuality with everything she had.

Exhaustion finally dragged them under around two in the morning, and then Jean woke when William crept into the room. The butler roused Jeremy with a hand on his shoulder, and Jeremy heaved a weary sigh before taking the phone.

"Morning, Mom," he said, voice gravely with sleep. "Yes, I'm still in bed, it's..." Jeremy fumbled for his phone and squinted at its glow. "...not even six here. No real plans, just studying and working out. Xavier was talking about going for a run at the beach, so I might join him. Yeah, okay." Jeremy hung up, looked fit to fall asleep with the phone still in his hand, and groaned as he remembered to return it to William. "Go back to sleep."

"I will set up the coffee," William said instead.

Jean held his tongue until William was gone. "She doesn't trust you."

Jeremy was quiet so long Jean thought he'd gone under. Then: "No, not yet."

"It's been four years." Jean caught the sleeping bag when Jeremy looked ready to burrow under it and held on tight. "If she doesn't know you enough to trust you now, she never will."

453

Jeremy's protest was soft: "You don't know that."

"Jeremy."

"Let's not do this today," Jeremy said. "Okay? Not today."

Jean let go and withdrew with a scowl. He thought his irritation might keep him up a bit longer, but once Jeremy dozed off it was easy enough to drift back under as well. That they were woken up two hours later by another phone call was not as surprising as it should be, but Mathilda only beat their alarms by a few minutes. Jeremy managed to sound alert for this call, and his voice was enough to wake Cat and Laila.

The four shuffled downstairs to find breakfast, and Jeremy practically clung to the coffee maker while it brewed. Jean smothered a yawn behind a heavy hand and silently resolved to reschedule his appointments to a later time slot. Ten had sounded reasonable at the time, but life kept getting in the way. He drank half the coffee Jeremy served him in one go, then pushed his pile of grated cheese toward Cat to add to breakfast.

Packing up was easy, and by a quarter to nine they were out the door. Jeremy dropped Laila and Cat off first, then took Jean over to his doctor. Jean suffered through the entire session before finally bringing up the schedule change, and he was directed to the front desk to hash it out with them. There was no afternoon or evening spot that wouldn't conflict with practices or games, but after some digging the receptionist managed to find a late morning slot on Sundays. Jean wasn't sure how that would work when Jeremy couldn't stay over on the weekend anymore, but he would figure something out.

Jeremy parked at the Lofts but didn't kill his engine. "I wish I could stay and help."

"Then stay," Jean said, knowing he couldn't.

Jeremy only sighed, so Jean let himself out of the car and went inside. As disconcerting as Jeremy's perfect

454

house was, this place was equally offensive. The apartment was as empty now as it'd been last weekend, and Jean could only imagine how quickly Laila's mood tanked when she walked in this morning. Jean had cash from the sale of his car, and Laila and Cat had received some money from their parents, but they'd spent the week hiding at Jeremy's house instead of putting this place together.

"Home?" Cat called as she opened her bedroom door.

"Home," Jean said. "Shower."

He hated showering this close to therapy, but they had too much to do today for him to put it off. He was in and out as quickly as he could go, and he found the girls sitting in the middle of the living room when he was dressed. Cat texted Cody when they finally left the apartment, then again when they reached the dorms. They'd be borrowing Cody's car this weekend, since Laila couldn't replace hers anytime soon. Cody showed them where it was parked before offering Laila the key ring.

"Thank you," Laila said.

"Keep it as long as you need it," Cody said. "We can use Pat's if we need to go anywhere."

"We'll have it back tomorrow," Laila promised.

They were out the rest of the day, to the point they had to pick up both lunch and dinner on the town. Laila drifted from thrift store to box store to the mall and back again, knowing she needed to outfit her new home but desperately craving pieces she could connect to. She had fewer opinions about bedroom sets than she did anything else, so they at least managed to get beds and dressers ordered with a next-week delivery.

Laptops for school were next, and Cat looked for a tower that could handle her games. Jean was quietly horrified by how much these things cost, but equally pleased that he could pay for his own things this time. He'd been reliant on Cat and Laila for everything he needed since his arrival in California. It was nice to take this small burden from them, even if dire circumstances had brought them to this point.

Cat dragged Laila into a bookstore that afternoon, knowing she needed a pleasant distraction after the day's disappointing progress, and waited with Jean at the in-store café until she was done. They lost another hour trying to further rebuild their wardrobes, during which Jean was mostly left to his own devices. Cat and Laila would occasionally wander over from the women's section to check on him, but they couldn't stay long when they also needed to be trying things on. Jean dug for familiar colors and styles, and finally carried his things over to the girls and their cart.

"Starting to think blue is your favorite color," Cat said, inspecting his finds with obvious approval.

"It is not," Jean said.

"It's Jeremy's," Laila said as she draped an armload of hangers over one side.

Jean had figured that out, but he only offered a noncommittal, "Hm."

"I like pink," Cat said. "Laila's is purple. What about you?"

Jean frowned as he thought it over, gaze drifting over the assortment of clothes piled in their shopping cart. At last he settled on the only one that made sense: "Brown." It was not the answer Cat was expecting, judging by her reaction, but Jean didn't waste his time explaining. Brown like the soil in Rhemann's garden, or the sand where the tide washed ashore, or the dirt roads Cat had led him down time and again. Brown like the gaze that sought Jean out in every room, but that last thought wasn't one he could linger on.

"That's a first," Cat finally said, and added an obligatory, "I like it."

"Done here?" Laila asked, looking around like she'd

456

forgotten something.

"Yes," Jean said, so Cat pushed the cart to the front.

After that there was nothing to do but head home. Despite nine hours shopping, they came home with very little of substance. The only furniture Laila approved of were three lamps and two end tables. She arranged those endlessly while Cat got the curtains hung, and then precariously balanced a new TV on the larger table. The four movies she'd picked up went on the ground beside it, and she stacked her books along the wall.

"Shelves tomorrow," Laila promised. "Desks, too. I guess we'll—"

She cut herself off to stare across the apartment. Cat kept working for another minute before realizing something was wrong, and she stepped down off the stool to ask, "What's wrong?"

Jean was closer to the front door than she was, so he'd heard it, too. "A dog is barking."

"Babe," Laila said.

Cat didn't need her to spell it out. She crossed the room to tug Laila into a brief, fierce hug. "It's not a good idea, Laila. We've got classes and practices and games. How could we possibly take care of an animal with our schedules?" She searched Laila's face for understanding and tried, "Who would walk it when we're gone with Away games?"

"A dog sitter," Laila said without hesitation.

Cat wasn't expecting that ready response. "I just— let's just think about it, okay? Make sure we know what we're getting into."

"You think about it," Laila said. "I'm going to bed."

Cat reluctantly let go of her, and Laila firmly closed the bedroom door behind her. Cat rubbed her temples before upending bags of clothes on the living room floor. Jean brought his over to join her, and for a few minutes they worked in silence. Stickers and tags were mercilessly

457

stripped and crumpled, and finally Cat said, "What do you think?"

"It is a mistake," Jean said.

"Probably," Cat agreed. "But they've been talking about it for years, you know? A pup for Jeremy to keep and Laila to cuddle. But her uncle refused to budge no matter how many times she asked him about it."

Jean studied the look on her face and knew how this would end. Cat wanted to be the voice of reason, but she would pry the stars from the sky if Laila asked for them. Jean wrenched his last tag free with more force than it needed.

"It is a mistake, Cat," Jean said again.

She didn't answer, and Jean had the sinking feeling he was going to lose this fight.

-

On Sunday they returned Cody's car and collected Shawn's truck instead. Laila was determined to find more furniture today than she had the day before, but the first few stops frustrated her so badly they stopped for an early lunch at the mall. She sipped her boba tea in sullen silence and stared into the distance while Cat attempted to fill the silence as best she could. At last Laila pointed across the way toward a store and said, "I'm going to check again."

"Yeah, sure." Cat waited until she'd left before scrubbing a weary hand over her face. She hadn't finished her lunch, but Jean didn't think she would. She'd been pushing the last few bites of curry listlessly around her paper plate for almost ten minutes now. The look on her face said she had something to say, but it took her another minute to find the words: "I don't know how to help her."

Jean looked at the half-finished tea Laila left behind. "If she doesn't like this apartment, maybe they will move us to the other."

"Wouldn't solve anything," Cat said. She set her fork aside at last in favor of jabbing her straw into what little

458

was left of her drink. She'd surely bend it against the chunky ice taking up half her cup, but Jean held his tongue. "I told you my family's from the bay area, yeah? Five generations born and raised in the same house. Wherever I go in the world, that's my home. That's my family." She pressed her fingers briefly to her heart.

"Laila doesn't have roots," she said. "She was born overseas, and her dad's career means he's got to move every couple of years. The only reason she came to LA was because she wanted to pursue Exy more seriously. Moved in with Gary at fifteen so she could attend a local high school. And he's a nice enough guy, don't get me wrong, but I think he likes Laila a lot more now that she's grown up and out of his house. Not really the family type. More a landlord than an uncle, yeah?"

Jean nodded to show he was following along. Cat twisted to see if Laila was on her way back before continuing, "I know she had an apartment after high school graduation, but she doesn't really talk about it except to say her neighbors were a problem. Must've been a mess, because Gary overhauled the house that fall and let her move in over Christmas break.

"It was the first place she could truly call home, and they took that from her," she finished, so soft Jean might have imagined it. "They destroyed something she doesn't know how to lose."

A morose silence settled over the table, but Cat couldn't stand it for long. She gave a deafening clap and stacked her garbage onto her plate. "Come on. Let's see if she found something she'll tolerate."

Jean carried Laila's drink so Cat could throw the trash away, and they crossed the hall to the home goods store Laila was wandering. Jean spotted her first, but as he was turning after her, his gaze caught on a nearby row of art. Cat stopped when he did, but Jean handed over the tea and motioned for her to go ahead.

As soon as she left, he turned down the aisle, and he stopped before a green and yellow painting halfway down. He picked it up, put it back, and picked it up again as he weighed Laila's potential reaction. Every piece of art she'd had at the house had been an original work, most of them snatched up from estate sales and thrift stores, and this was obviously a mass-produced reproduction. He couldn't imagine she'd want this, but he wasn't willing to leave it behind. He still hadn't made up his mind when Cat and Laila came looking for him a couple minutes later.

"See anything you like?" Cat asked.

Jean turned the painting toward them, earning a soft, "Oh," from Cat. Laila crossed the aisle in record time with her hands out. Jean passed the frame to her and watched her trace the field of daffodils with a slow fingertip.

Jean held up his hand in case she wanted him to put it back. "It is not the same."

"No," Laila agreed as she hugged it to her chest, "but it's a start."

Cat came over to kiss her, and Jean watched Laila's shoulders slowly relax as she leaned into it. They stood forehead to forehead for a minute after as Laila tended her thoughts, and finally Laila said, "Okay. Let's go back for those shelves."

"You sure?" Cat said. "I didn't think you liked them."

"We'll make it work," Laila said, so Jean went in search of a cart.

They were only out a few more hours, but they made more progress that afternoon than they had the day before. Laila committed herself to filling the apartment with grim determination and made overdue concessions on most of the basic furniture. They came home with boxes of things that needed assembly and spent the early evening swimming in Styrofoam and ripped cardboard. Cat volunteered to take the truck back so she could pick up dinner, and Laila went out to the balcony for some fresh

460

air.

Jean surveyed the room with a slow gaze. It was offensive, still, bare of the personal touches that would make it feel homey, but the daffodil painting on the wall was a silent promise they'd get there eventually. He filled two glasses with water and took them out to where Laila was leaning against the railing. She looked tired but not as defeated as she had these last few days, and she watched strangers go by as she worked her fingers through her hair. Now and then she winced as she snagged on tangles.

"Thank you," she said, giving up in favor of taking her drink from him.

He meant to leave her to her thoughts, but he set his glass by his feet and reached for her. Aware that he might be crossing one too many lines, he slipped his fingers into her dark curls and took over where she'd left off. How often he'd seen Cat and Laila brush each other's hair as a sign of affection; how readily she'd tried to extend that same comfort to him while Andrew's trial was underway. He didn't know what else to offer her that would help her now. Four and a half months later she was still a bit of a mystery, half of Jeremy's whole and a little too smart.

"You weren't born here," he said when she didn't shrug him off.

Laila hummed confirmation into her water. "Capetown. Mom called me a happy accident. They'd been talking about having kids for years but weren't sure it was a good idea considering my father's career. I came along anyway."

Jean could hear the smile in her voice. "But only you."

"No siblings by blood, but Jeremy's my brother in every way that matters," she said, quiet and warm. "I love him more than life itself. I would do anything for him."

Jean's hands slowed as he turned her words inside out. He thought about Lucas and Grayson, Jeremy and Bryson, and Kevin and Riko. He thought of Derrick and Derek's

461

shameless affection and of Tanner following him around like a little duckling of his own. He thought of Kevin calling him brother on Hannah's show, and the sour sting it'd evoked then was a dull and lingering ache now. He thought of Noah and Elodie, and he had to close his eyes against his grief.

"A brother is a complicated thing," he said.

Laila turned her head to say, "You were a brother."

It wasn't a question, but Jean said, "Yes."

He slowly separated her hair into sections. It'd been years since he'd done this for Elodie; he could barely remember how it was supposed to go. He tried and failed and tried again, until he got far enough to understand what he was doing. He worked Laila's hair loose before starting over, and this time he managed to get a loose braid to stay. He had nothing to hold it together at the end, so he pinched the tail between his fingers.

Laila reached up and felt the plait with careful fingers. "Will you tell me about her?"

I can't, he thought. *It's too big; it's too much.* He'd buried her so deep he'd surely fall in if he looked a little too long. But the braid in his hand was a rope back to sunlight and solid ground, so Jean said, "She liked blackberries and sandcastles and ladybugs, but faerie tales most of all." He'd read them so many times he didn't even need the books anymore, but Elodie loved staring wide-eyed at the pictures as he spoke. "She prayed for a dragon to save her."

Laila's tone was gentle, like she thought he'd retreat if she spoke too loudly. "Not a prince?"

"A dragon could tear our house apart to free her and carry her far away." He didn't say, *I wish one had*, but he felt the truth of it in every aching heartbeat.

Laila stayed silent, buying him time to claw his way back from his memories. Only when he let go of her did she say, "We could grow them here, if you want." She

462

half-turned to study his face before realizing he couldn't follow her train of thought, and she nodded toward the open corners of their balcony. "Blackberry bushes, I mean. I don't know anything about gardening, but we could learn."

"Not blackberries," he said, because how could he eat them without thinking of home?

She accepted his rejection with an easy, "Maybe something else, then."

Jean considered that. He had a feeling he knew the answer, but it was worth a try anyway: "Peaches are trees?" Her nod had him grumbling discontent into his water, but he paused long enough to say, "I will think about it."

"Anything you want," Laila promised.

They stood side-by-side at the railing, tending their own thoughts as the world rushed on beneath them. A man went by with two gangly Dalmatians in tow, and Jean didn't miss the way Laila leaned out to watch them as long as she could. He thought of Cat's weakening resolve and Jeremy's tangible grief over Barkbark, and his determination to hold his ground as the bastion of common sense faltered.

"It wouldn't be that big," he said. Laila turned a look of polite confusion on him, and he clarified, "Your would-be dog. It wouldn't be that big."

It wasn't approval or agreement, but it put an unholy light in Laila's eyes. "No."

He was going to regret this, but Jean looked away and said, "Then do as you like."

CHAPTER TWENTY-FOUR
Jean

Laila waited to tell Jeremy until he picked them up the next morning, and Jean understood why as soon as she cornered him in the kitchen. Jean could watch every other reasonable thought evaporate from Jeremy's brain as Laila went over breed restrictions and basic ground rules. Jeremy nodded along to everything she said, but Jean wasn't entirely sure he was listening. He was practically vibrating as he endlessly shifted from one foot to the next.

Laila had researched nearby shelters last night, so she handed Jeremy the address to the nearest and said, "It's open until eleven tonight. Go after practice."

"Yes," Jeremy agreed immediately.

"What'll you tell your parents?" Cat asked.

Jeremy didn't miss a beat. "Group meeting pushed late because of Exy."

That he could lie so easily for a dog and not his day-to-day happiness was more than a little annoying, but Jean was staying out of this. He'd done his part by consenting to the madness; everything else was their problem to sort out. Or so he hoped, but it was impossible to distance himself from this decision once Jeremy was involved. By the end of morning practice all of the Trojans knew Laila and Jeremy were getting a dog, and the floozies were hard at work brainstorming a list of names.

If Jeremy lost focus during afternoon practice, Jean could at least take him to task, but his captain went full-tilt into every single drill and scrimmage. He was out of the shower only two minutes behind Jean, and he paced restless circles around the strikers' bench until Cat and Laila showed up.

Jean assumed they'd go straight to the shelter, but Jeremy parked at the Lofts. On her way out of the car, Laila said, "Take Jean with you."

Jean stared at her. "No. It's your beast, not mine."

Laila leaned over to eye him. "Technically it's Jeremy's."

"Your partner, your problem," Cat chimed in. "The boy can't be trusted. Let him go to a shelter alone and he'll probably come home with a half-dozen puppies. Thank you for your sacrifice, Jean. I said thank you and goodbye," she added, when Jean started to argue again. She gave him a meaningful look and gestured between herself and Laila. "Read the room."

"You don't even have a bed yet," Jean complained.

"I have a face she can—"

Laila hauled her out of the car before she could finish and slammed the door closed. Jean pinched the bridge of his nose until he thought he'd break it and slowly counted to ten. At seven Jeremy jostled him and said, "We're walking from here. Let's go," with such childish glee Jean had to put both girls from mind. He got out of the car like he was marching to his doom and followed Jeremy deeper into the city.

The shelter they were looking for was only a ten-minute trek up the road. The young woman at the front desk had a series of questions for Jeremy that Jean tuned out halfway through. Most of it sounded tediously particular, though he assumed it was all necessary: what type of animal was he looking for, what sort of home was he bringing it to, what kind of time could he devote to its wellbeing, and so on. Jean bit back his uncharitable opinion about this entire decision and let his gaze wander.

There were bird cages in the front two corners. Past the desk was a kennel with a half-dozen clumsy kittens. Jean honestly wasn't sure which side of the room was producing more noise right now. The room stank of air freshener, presumably to cover up the messes such beasts were creating. Jean breathed as shallowly as he could and wondered if he ought to wait outside until Jeremy was done. He glanced Jeremy's way just as the two finally wrapped it up, and Jeremy motioned to him with an uncharacteristic nervousness.

The kennels in the next room seemed to be primarily smaller rodents, and here the smell of bedding and wet little bodies was a little more prevalent. Jean heard the dogs long before they passed the second room of cats, and at last they pushed through a final door. One wall was all kennels, two rows atop one another. The other had filing cabinets and three metal tables for checkups and grooming. The assistant handed off her notes to the young man filling food bowls.

"Apartment with students," she said. "Smaller breed, preferably a few years old so it'll require less hands-on care and is used to being left alone for a few hours. Gender unimportant, usual restrictions otherwise." When he nodded, she turned a perky smile on Jeremy and said, "Christian will recommend the best fits for you based on our current selection and walk you through the rest of the process. I'll be up front if you decide to move forward."

"Thank you," Jeremy said, already distracted by the kennels. She'd barely left the room before he was poking his fingers through the grating of the nearest one. "Hi," he said, in a soft tone Jean didn't recognize. "Hi, how are you? Yeah, I love you too, you're so cute. I'd take you home with me but you're a little big for us, baby girl. Yeah."

Jean glanced from him to the worker, who didn't seem at all unnerved by this silliness from a grown man. Christian was comparing his coworker's notes to his own files, and he wrote a string of numbers across the top of his page. Kennel numbers, Jean realized a moment later, because Christian scooped up his clipboard and offered

466

Jeremy his hand.

"Hi, I'm Christian," he said. "Let's find you your new best friend."

"Jeremy," Jeremy said, accepting his hand.

Christian glanced toward Jean, noticed how far back he was keeping, and beckoned to Jeremy. "We'll start at this end," he said, and Jeremy hurried after him.

Jean went the other direction, hoping the barking would drown out Jeremy's adoring conversations with each of his prospects. His gaze went unbidden to the kennels, with their assortment of beasts in every color and size. One dog was tearing a stuffed toy to shreds, filling the corner of his kennel with piles of cottony fluff. Three fist-sized little pups were sharing space, two barking at each other for no discernible reason while the third tried and failed to scale the grating. Each cage had a card pinned to it with information about the dogs trapped within.

Jean made it to the far corner at last and leaned against the wall to wait. He checked his phone, saw a string of missed messages from Renee and Cody, and decided he didn't have the energy for conversation right now. He put his phone away and looked up to see how far Jeremy had gotten, and in so doing accidentally made eye contact with the dog across from him.

At first glance he thought it was sleeping, it was so still and flat on its side, but its gaze tracked his face with unblinking calm. Jean waited for it to look away, but he bored of the staring match first. Jeremy was in an animated conversation with Christian, so Jean turned back to the dog. It was still watching him, and this time its tail thumped a few times in either warning or approval. It was an uneven mess: its tail and ears were scraggly, but it had short fur everywhere else, black and white most everywhere with brown splotches on its face and legs.

"I don't see the appeal," he told it. Its tail thumped

467

harder, and Jean reluctantly crossed the room to study it better. In French he said, "He has so many distractions already, and not enough time to sleep as it is. You are an unnecessary complication. He ought to wait until graduation."

One ear went ramrod straight, as if the dog could understand him. That was ridiculous and offensive, and Jean poked a finger through the grating to press it flat. "You are fooling no one," he said, as the tail went thump-thump-thump against the bottom of the kennel in earnest. The dog finally half-rolled onto its stomach, and Jean snatched his hand to safety. It watched him for a few moments, then curled in on itself to kick at the ear he'd touched.

"Your foot is dirtier than my hand," Jean said, but it was undeterred. He didn't care and wasn't interested, but his gaze went to the card hanging from the bottom corner. The scrawling handwriting was such a violent turnoff he almost walked away, but Jean put a finger to the first word and fought his way through the description. A six-year-old mutt who'd been given up when the owner moved out-of-state, supposedly.

Jean pressed his fingernail hard against the paper. "Your parents threw you away, too." That was too sour a thought to dwell on, so he flicked the dog a bored look. Did this creature ever blink? Maybe it perfectly timed its own to his and that was why he always missed it. Jean stared it down, refusing to lose to a beast he could easily shove inside his backpack. He lost, but only because the dog pawed at his hand through the grating and startled him into withdrawing.

"Oh, that's Rex," Christian said from a few kennels down. "He's not very friendly."

"Neither am I," Jean said.

"He doesn't bite," Christian hurried to say. "He's just a bit depressed, I think. Last owner gave him up a couple months ago. He wasn't crate trained, so he's not adjusting well to the kennel life, and people seem put off by his age. Everyone wants a cute puppy, right? If he'd perk up a bit more, he'd have a better chance of getting out of here."

He gave a helpless shrug, then turned his full attention back to Jeremy. Jeremy was currently crouched in front of a kennel with both hands hooked on the grate. Jean wasn't sure what dog he was staring at now, but he looked so blissed out Jean couldn't watch him for long.

Jeremy was running out of kennels; he would have to decide soon if one of these animals stood out more than the rest. Jean looked back at Rex, who had his toenails hooked on the grate now. His toe pads were black and warm to the touch, and he let Jean unhook his foot without protest. The most he did was snuffle at the front of his kennel, and Jean grudgingly left his hand where the dog could smell it. Rex sniffed so enthusiastically Jean started to feel unclean, and then a hot and wet dog tongue had him snatching his hand back again.

"Rex, you said?" Jeremy said right at his ear, and Jean nearly jumped out of his skin. The wide-eyed look Jeremy turned on him for that reaction had Jean scowling and looking away. Christian went over Rex's story again with unflagging patience, but Jeremy's stare never wavered. Jean refused to return that look but feigned intense interest in the card on the neighboring cage. At last Jeremy took pity on him and put out a hand for Rex to sniff. "Hi, boy. How are you? Oh, you really do have such sad eyes." To Christian he said, "Can we see him?"

"You're looking right at him," Jean said.

Christian popped the bar out of place and swung the door open. Jeremy offered Rex his hand, waited while the dog snuffled at it, and brought the other up when Rex got bored of the first. "Hi," he said again. "Can I touch you? Can I hold you? Is that okay?" He waited like he thought the beast might answer, then gently hooked his hands around him.

"Oh, oh, oh," he said as he lifted the dog from the cage, and he cradled Rex to his chest like a baby. The dog immediately draped his head on Jeremy's shoulder and let out a world-weary huff. Jeremy closed his eyes at the sound of it and pressed a kiss to the dog's shoulder blades. Thump-thump, went the tail, before Rex tucked it neatly against his legs. Jeremy swayed this way and that for a minute, looking more relaxed and at peace than Jean had seen him in months.

Maybe Jeremy felt his stare, because he asked, "Do you want to hold him?"

"No," Jean said immediately. "Never."

"He doesn't mean that," Jeremy assured Rex, with another kiss to his shoulders. He opened his eyes and turned toward Christian. "He's so sweet, and he looks like he's the right size for our apartment. Does he check the rest of the boxes?"

Christian tapped the top of his page, where Rex's kennel number was the last in line. It was one of two that had a question mark scribbled in above it. "He's housebroken, neutered, and up to date on all his shots," he said. "The only thing we can't guarantee is how he'll react to being left alone in the apartment. Might have some lingering abandonment issues. He doesn't fuss when we leave the room unattended, and we haven't noticed any distress on the overnight security cameras, but it's a strong 'probably okay' and not a promised 'yes' that he can handle it."

Jeremy gave it some serious thought before turning toward Jean. "What do you think?"

"It is not my decision."

"It's your apartment," Jeremy reminded him. "If you want to keep looking we will."

"I do not care," Jean said. That earned another world-weary sigh from Rex. Jean side-eyed him, idly wondering if dogs could understand English, and added, "It is a stupid name. It is not as bad as the last, but it is still unforgivable. He is not a dinosaur."

"We can rename him," Jeremy said, studying Jean's face like the secret to the universe was just out of reach. "It might just take some work and time for him to get used to it, especially if he's six. Here, hold him a sec."

"Put him down. He has four legs to stand on," Jean said, but Jeremy had already closed the short space between them.

Shifting Rex from his chest to Jean's was easy work, and if Jean didn't catch hold, it would be a long drop to a very hard floor. Jeremy ignored his muttered complaints in favor of fixing Jean's grip, and he stepped back only when Rex appeared secure. The dog was oblivious to or unmoved by Jean's disapproval and instead pressed a wet nose to the underside of his chin. Jean tipped his head away, earning a huff before Rex went still.

Jeremy studied the dog a minute longer, then said, "He's asleep."

"He's faking it," Jean said.

"He likes you," Jeremy said, pleased. To Christian he said, "We want him."

"*We* do not," Jean corrected him, but both men ignored him.

Christian flipped his stack of papers to the last sheet so he could give Jeremy a rundown of Rex's health as the shelter understood it. Jean tuned it out, keenly aware of the slow breaths puffing against the side of his throat, more aware of the small chest that rose and fell against his collarbone. Was it normal to feel a dog's ribs like this? Christian had called him depressed; maybe he'd been doing the bare minimum to stay alive. Could dogs even be depressed? Jean knew next to nothing about animals. He almost asked, then decided he didn't need to give the impression he cared. Maybe Renee knew more on the

471

matter, but he didn't think he could get his phone out without waking the beast.

"Great," Jeremy said as Christian finished up. "Sounds great."

"Then let's get you back up front," Christian said. "Audrey will take it from here."

Jean would surely wake the dog up if he moved, but at least then Rex could walk. But Rex didn't stir. The blind trust despite their unfamiliarity was bewildering, almost offensive. Did the creature have no survival instincts whatsoever? Something this small and fragile ought to have a bit more common sense. Jean was sure he'd carried bags of sugar that weighed more. He shifted his grip until his fingers lined up with the dog's rib cage again. Like this he could feel Rex's heartbeat, soft as a hum.

"Oh, Rex?" Audrey said, startled to indiscretion when she saw them. She hurriedly tried to redeem herself with an enthusiastic, "That's fantastic. Did Christian go over his medical records? Good. Then I've just got a couple quick forms here, and there's the matter of the fee."

Jeremy passed over his bank card, and Jean didn't miss the way his smile didn't reach his eyes. "Can I get a receipt for that? Thank you." Maybe Jean was seeing things, because Jeremy set to work on the forms with unabashed enthusiasm. The only thing that tripped him up was their address. He got halfway through the old one before realizing what he was doing, and he crossed it out with a wince.

Audrey checked the form front and back to ensure Jeremy hadn't missed anything, then returned his card with a receipt. Jeremy tucked both into his wallet, and Audrey snagged a reusable bag off a hook under her desk. She emptied its contents one at a time onto the desk in front of them: a simple black leash and matching collar, a tight roll of plastic something or other, and a few sample bags of dog kibble.

"Goodie bag for your new best friend," Audrey said, repacking the food and green plastic. "Obviously you'll want to stop and stock up if you haven't already, but at least this way you don't have to rush. You can take him home and get to know him without having to worry about what he'll eat later today. You can also choose a toy for him," she said, pointing to the shelf lining the wall behind her.

"Shark," Jeremy said immediately, and she jumped to get it. Jeremy tucked it in the bag as Audrey passed it over, and finally Jeremy deigned to take Rex from Jean. He smothered the dog with apologies as he lowered Rex to the ground. The dog gave a full-body, noisy shake when Jeremy snapped the collar in place, but for the first time there was a hint of energy to the tip of his head.

"He knows he's going home," Audrey said when his tail started wagging in earnest. She sounded on the verge of tears, and she crouched to give the dog a few final pets. To Jeremy she added, "Let us know if you need anything at all. Our information is printed on the bag." She pointed to the logo of the gift bag she'd handed over, and then she went to get the door for them. Rex beat Jeremy outside, moving with purpose with his freedom at hand.

"I told you he could walk," Jean said as he followed Jeremy out.

Jeremy was smiling ear-to-ear, completely unbothered by Jean's refusal to play along. "He sure can," was his chipper agreement. "Look at him go! What a good boy. Look, he knows we're talking about him," he said, because Rex had turned to watch them both. Jeremy leaned over to offer enthusiastic scritches and a giddy, "You're a good boy, you really are! Do you want to go home? Yeah? Wait until you meet Laila and Cat. They are going to love you."

He was so deliriously happy that Jean swallowed the rest of his complaints for later.

It took only ten minutes to get here, but twice as long to get back. Jean was sure Rex stopped to sniff every single crack in the sidewalk and dried spot of gum. How the dog managed to piss six times was beyond him, but Jeremy only laughed when Jean insisted, "That cannot be normal." Maybe it was, then, but if this thing tried urinating in the apartment Jean was going to return it to the shelter.

They were nearly home when Jeremy's phone started ringing that awful tone that meant his family was calling. Jeremy didn't look surprised to receive it but passed the leash to Jean so he could answer.

"Hi, Mom. Yes, that was me. Classmate's running late from dinner, so I went off campus for a bit. Wanted to get Laila a housewarming gift for her new apartment." Jeremy glanced at Rex but didn't elaborate. "Yes, it's a one-off. She'll get everything else she needs after her insurance cuts a check. Sorry, yes, you're right, I should have warned Leslie first. Okay. Yes, I'll let you know before I get on the road tonight."

Jean considered returning the leash, but Jeremy was busy squeezing his phone between his hands. Instead he asked, "Leslie?"

"My mother's bookkeeper," Jeremy said. "She oversees the joint account Bryson and I are on, and she gets an alert if I pass a certain dollar threshold on any purchase." Jeremy checked his phone for damage before tucking it away. "I'll still have to submit the receipt for review, and that'll start a whole new conversation, but it's a problem for later."

"Jeremy."

"It's not my money," Jeremy said. "I don't make the rules."

The look on his face said there was more to it, but they were out of time. Jean tucked it aside to fight over later and let them into their apartment building. Rex handled

474

the stairs to the second floor easily enough despite his small size. Jeremy freed him of the leash while Jean got the door, and he gave the pup an encouraging scritch as he straightened.

"There you go," he said as Jean held the door for them. "Welcome home! What do you think of the place?"

By the time Jean locked the door behind them, both girls had emerged from their bedroom. Laila hit her knees so fast Jean thought they'd bruise. "Oh," she said, hands outstretched and entreating. Rex went still as stone to stare at her for a minute, then went to sniff her fingers. "Oh, he's perfect. Hello there. Hello, you're perfect." Laila scooped him up into a hug. "What's his name?"

"It was Rex," Jeremy said.

"Like a T-Rex?" Cat asked.

Jean motioned to her but looked at Jeremy. "I told you."

Jeremy laughed and went to sit at Laila's side. He took one of Rex's paws between two fingers so he could rock it up and down. Rex didn't pull away but pushed his nose to Jeremy's hand in silent protest. "Let's see what the floozies have for us, then."

Jean sat opposite them, and Rex immediately wriggled out of Laila's arms to steal his lap. Jean scowled down at him. "I did not invite you."

Laila should have been offended at being abandoned, but she smiled. "He likes you."

"It was love at first sight," Jeremy said, tapping away at his phone. "He's not crate trained, but he is housebroken and chipped. The shelter got his full medical history from his previous owner, so we're good to go on that front. And we've got this."

He traded his phone for the shark toy, and Rex decided that was more important than Jean. Jeremy waggled it over his head before flinging it across the room, and the dog gave chase with unexpected speed. Jean listened to the rapid clicking of his toenails against the hard floor as Rex gave chase, then hooked a knee to his chest so he no longer had a lap to offer. Louder was the nonstop chirp and chime of his friends' phones as the group chat responded to Jeremy's text.

Name suggestions were quick to flood in, with the three reading them aloud as they arrived. They started off basic and harmless, such as Patches and Fido, before escalating to more ridiculous options like Monsieur Bowwow. The withering look Jean sent them for that had Cat nearly crying with laughter, and Jean valiantly tried to tune the rest of the madness out.

The soft beep of his phone made him worry he'd been looped into the cacophony, but it was Renee checking in. The Foxes' practice had been rough, and they were still fighting hours later. Neil was irritated to be sidelined, and the freshmen's continued disrespect was adding fuel to the fire. The upperclassmen were taking bets on who'd swing first, Neil or someone named Jack. Jean knew it'd be Kevin.

"Get it together," Jean sent back. "The Trojans want to see you in finals."

"We will do our best!" she said, and then, "How are things going there?"

Jean tapped idly at his keys before settling for, "Complicated." Across from him Rex was dangling an inch off the floor, jaws locked on his shark, while Jeremy laughed himself sick. Jean took a picture of them and sent it with the message, "Grief has driven them to madness, but I do not think we can return it."

"He's handsome," Renee returned. Jean had a flat rejection half typed out when she added a cheeky, "The dog is also cute."

Jean stared down at her messages in disbelief, refusing to read into them but unable to interpret it any other way. He erased seven curt responses before settling on, "Tell

Kevin to stay out of it."

Jean could almost hear her "Oh, Jean." After a pause, she sent, "I don't ask Kevin about you. Andrew clocked Jeremy immediately, and three of every five messages you've sent me this past month are about him." It was an obvious exaggeration, but Jean refused to check their messages to prove it. Renee wasn't done but said, "I was curious, but it never felt appropriate to ask."

"There is nothing to ask," Jean sent. "It is against the rules."

"Whose rules?" Renee asked.

Stuart's voice bit at his memory: *"The dead kid?"*

Jean almost chucked his phone across the room. The weight of a body settling on his leg startled him from his gnawing thoughts, and he frowned down at the beast. Rex kept sliding down his thigh, then scrabbling to find his perch again. Cat reached over and clapped Jean's hip until Jean finally sat cross-legged again. He flicked her an unimpressed stare as the dog settled in his lap with a huff.

"Do not encourage him," Jean said.

"He likes you," Cat said, unrepentant. "Don't you, Jabberwocky?"

Jean stared at her in disbelief and only tried, "Jab."

Cat enunciated it this time: "Jabberwocky. From Alice in Wonderland? I used to have the whole poem memorized, but it wouldn't do you good to hear it. It's half-nonsense," she explained before Jean could take offense. "Made-up words and the like. But it's catchy, so it stuck, like an annoying commercial ditty. Maybe the English major remembers it."

Jeremy crouched over the dog and hooked his hands like claws as he said, "Beware the Jabberwock, my son! The jaws that bite, the claws that catch. Something something, snicker-snack. Callooh, callay!" He laughed and gave up with, "That's all I've got, sorry."

The dog was staring wild-eyed up at him for the

unprompted performance, so Jeremy tipped in to plant a kiss on his furry forehead. Jean lurched away from him so quickly he sent Jabberwocky sprawling, and it took Jeremy only a moment to realize what he'd done. He scooped up his frightened pup but kept his eyes on Jean's blank face.

"Sorry," he said, tense with concern. "Sorry, that was—"

Jean pried Jabberwocky from his unresisting hands, needing a barricade between them. Jeremy obediently sat back on his heels to create more space, and Jean forced himself to look at Cat. He barely heard his own voice over his heartbeat: "Say the ridiculous name again. Maybe it will be less stupid on the repeat."

Cat glanced between them but said, "Jabberwocky." She waited for him to echo it, flashed him two thumbs up, and ruined everything by saying, "More precisely: Jabberwocky Moreau."

He'd misheard her. "This thing is not a Moreau."

Jeremy managed a weak smile. "I'd rather not name him Knox or Wilshire."

"Alvarez," Jean said, but Cat waved him off. "Dermott."

"You've been outvoted," Cat said. "Embrace fatherhood."

This was asinine and ill-advised, and they would all regret this when the semester and season burned up all their time, but Jean sighed defeat. Jeremy's shoulders were still a tense line when Jean turned toward him, and his eyes were shadowed with regret and discomfort. Jean didn't know how to fix this, so he held the dog out in peace offering and said, "If he is going to be a Moreau, he will have to learn French."

Jeremy gave a serious nod. "I accept these terms."

Jeremy set Jabberwocky by his shark plush. The dog immediately picked it up and gave it such a vigorous shake he fell over, and Jeremy dissolved to helpless laughter. Jean tucked his knee to his chest again, content to watch while his thoughts went to war. *"Whose rules?"* Renee asked, and Neil's voice answered a carefree, *"The rules have changed."*

Not for me, Jean warned himself, but for one moment, just this moment, he would let himself pretend.

Acknowledgments

All my love to Tashie, Hazel, Elise, and Anna M, who somehow put up with me for another book. I don't know how y'all did it, but thanks for not giving up on me. Jean and I would be chilling at the bottom of Lake Superior without your friendship and patience this past year.

Special thanks to my sister, who found out about a week before the book's release date what the cover art was supposed to be but still managed to produce something spectacular.

Made in the USA
Las Vegas, NV
01 April 2025

20352209R00272